THE ARMS OF GOD

LESLIE K. HAMMOND

ISBN 978-1-64569-458-8 (paperback)
ISBN 978-1-64569-459-5 (digital)

Christian Faith Publishing, Inc.
832 Park Avenue
Meadville, PA 16335
www.christianfaithpublishing.com

Printed in the United States of America

CHAPTER 1

Summer, 1956

Mike Wakefield was fourteen years old the year Stella Clement shot Junior Clement dead. He lay awake in the immense heat of the August night, sweating. The window above his head looked out across the front porch where June bugs thumped against the screen door. The swamp cooler drew in air at the other end of the Wakefield's white wood-frame house, and the open window behind his iron frame headboard was too far for the draft to bring him much relief. Each evening, they would apportion a few gallons of water to the cooler before bedtime, and it had long played out. His father lay sleeping in a frayed recliner in the living room in his overalls with the television displaying only static; a glass of iced tea still sweating on the table next to him. They'd won the television set in a promotion at the Montgomery Ward store in Abilene, and his father had refused his mother's demand to exchange it for money.

Nineteen fifty-six would be the fifth year the cotton wouldn't make, and the worst. The Clear Fork of the Brazos, which passed at the back of their farm, was all but dry in most places and hadn't run free in three years. Ancient pecans in the bottoms were dying or dead. A single one-inch storm in May had given them a hope to get a crop up, but it was the last rain they'd seen and the cotton was withered beyond chance now. His father had grown unnaturally quiet lately, and Mike could see defeat settling in on him. There was talk between him and his mother that they might have to move into

Abilene. They'd been hauling water for the house now for two years, and but for the fact so many in the county were in much the same shape, the bank would have shut them down.

Mike heard her coming before he could see her. The soft grind of gravel on leather out on the road. He rolled over and watched through the headboard as she materialized out of the darkness and opened the gate into the yard, then in astonishment as she crossed the yard and mounted the porch to knock on the front door. Junior and Stella lived a mile and a half from the Wakefield's, and Mike wondered to himself whether she had walked all that way in the middle of the night or broke down somewhere. A thin, severe woman, she was dressed as though for Sunday morning with her handbag across her arm. He saw his father open the screen door, his hair all haywire, with a bewildered concern on his face. By the time he had thrown on his overalls and stepped into the hall, his father was rushing toward his room.

"Go bring the truck around to the front. I'll meet you out there in a minute."

His mother was up now, wrapping a robe around her, and his father quickly whispered a few words to her. She sat Stella down on the divan in the living room, and his father went into the kitchen and got on the telephone.

"She says she's killed Junior," his father said when they turned out onto the road.

*****

Junior's pickup was in the yard in front of the porch when they drove up. They'd seen the mark on the road as they got close where he had driven home on a rim, either too drunk or too lazy to pull over and change the tire, or even too drunk to even know he was driving on a rim. That explained why Stella was walking. They were careful as they approached the house. Stella had told his father she had taken the kids out in the cotton field and laid them down out there between the rows, and she had seemed certain they'd still be there. His father told him to go out and find them and stay with them until he said otherwise.

"I'm stayin' with you for the moment, Daddy."

That made sense. Neither of them knew what they were into. His father nodded, then gathered himself and opened the front door screen. They both stood inside and tried to make sense of the scene before them. Stella was obsessive about keeping her house, and there was no sign of anything unusual. In fact, the house was in perfect order other than Junior Clement lying flat on his back on the dinner table, his hands crossed across his chest. His father walked in to the table and touched his hand to Junior's throat, then turned back to Mike. There was no blood apparent anywhere.

"Go out there and find those kids. She said south of the house about a hunnerd yards. Don't tell 'em what you seen. Just stay with 'em until I holler at you."

Mike knew the Clement kids from church, so he quietly called out to Trace as he walked out into the rows. He was almost on top of them when Trace spoke.

"Daddy's dead, ain't he?"

"I'm afraid so. Did you go up there?"

"No. Momma told us to stay put, so we stayed put. I heard it."

His eyes were adjusted some now, and he could see the other two huddled close to Trace, looking up at him.

"We're supposed to stay here till my daddy calls out. I'm real sorry, Trace."

He sat down in the still-hot dirt with them, and they looked back at the yellow light spilling out of the windows of the house. The little girl whimpered a bit, and Trace pulled her up close. The youngest seemed to be already asleep again. There was no other sound but the constant night sound of the crickets across the field. Before very long, a couple of sets of headlights began making their way down the road toward the house, and his father called out for Trace to come up.

"Set the kids in the pickup there, and you all stay put."

Sheriff Claude Hardwicke and the preacher went into the house and shortly after reemerged onto the porch. Mike watched the three of them talking out of earshot. It was almost an hour before another set of headlights appeared on the road. The three men walked out and stood to meet Fowler Clement as he stepped out into the drive.

5

Fowler Clement was a large man, past sixty now. He had once been very handsome. His face had weathered poorly, he being light complected, and bore several recurring skin cancers that were often raw. He had the ruddy look of an alcoholic, though he wasn't a drinker. Except on Sunday, where he went bareheaded, he always wore a narrow-brimmed, sweat-stained old Stetson hat and had apparently a whole wardrobe's worth of khaki Dickies work clothes. Fowler listened with his jaws clinched in desperate pain, and his iron gray eyes bore in while the sheriff told him what was inside, then stepped around them and advanced toward and into the house. Mike could see him through the screen as he entered the house and stood over Junior's body for the longest time, maybe a half hour, not moving, not crying, just standing and looking down at Junior. Then he turned abruptly and walked back, only once stopping, turning to look at the three kids in the front seat of the pickup, their faces lit by the light from the still-open front door. There he stopped; his face stern, sad, implacable. Then he turned and approached the sheriff, the preacher, and his father, and to each he seemed to give instructions, then turned again, turned abruptly, walked to his pickup, and drove away. Mike's father approached the pickup.

"Take the kids back to the house and put them to bed. Stay up. Don't go to sleep. I don't want you to be conspicuous, but you keep an eye on that woman."

"What are you gonna do?"

"I suppose I'll pull up a chair on the porch and sit here until somebody else relieves me. Ain't like I'm an old hand at this sort of thing. But it don't seem right to run off and leave a body unattended."

*****

There would be no investigation or arrest or trial in the death of Fowler Randolph Clement, Jr. By daylight, everyone in twenty miles knew Junior Clement had come home drunk, as he did most nights. That Stella had decided once and for all she wouldn't be beaten again. That she had taken her children out into the bosom of a withering cotton field and returned to her house to wait for her husband to stumble through the door. How she took a chair and sat it down in front of that door and loaded a shotgun with double-aught buckshot and waited, and when he came in, she deliberately shot him square in the chest dead. How she somehow, against all reason, dragged him through the house and up and onto the dining table and cleaned the body and dressed it and cleaned the front room and the kitchen of blood and burned whatever could not be cleaned, since she would never again have that opportunity. Then cleaned herself and fixed her hair up and dressed as though she were going to church and walked barefoot almost two miles over to the Wakefield's in the pitch black of night, whereupon she put on her hose and shoes and entered again the society of civilized people. How against all imagining she had stolen back her dignity after having apparently lost the last shred of it. How the justice of it was clear to every single human in the community, save one. How Fowler Clement had seen that and knew it immediately and determined it to be so by his own will, that only he would bear the shame and the punishment and not the woman, and least of all the three grandchildren.

And so by morning, the women had mustered out to that house to sit mostly in silence with Stella, and in the afternoon buried Junior in the town cemetery without even a funeral at the church. The preacher had said a few words which might have been recited out of a book, such that Junior himself was effectively and practically acknowledged as the perpetrator of his own demise. Fowler had gone home from Junior's that night, and whatever was said between him and Leticia Clement would never again be repeated out loud, but it had been settled forever, and Leticia's terms were affirmed in time for all to see. She walked with him to the graveside ramrod straight that day, with a look of cold, determined hatred in her face for the few who gathered to see, and when it was over, turned without a word, and Fowler took her alone back to the ranch. There was a bargain struck between them in those first few dark hours when Fowler had gotten home. She would have her outrage and her vengeance, but it would not be visited on the town or Stella or even the children. She would demand no public trial and punishment, though she would never forgive the town or even Fowler, maybe especially Fowler, the affront

7

of excusing the murder. Neither would she ever again be asked to lay eyes on Stella or allow Fowler to acknowledge in her presence even the woman's offspring so long as she lived. Thus, Fowler Clement substituted himself alone as the foil and shield against that outrage, bearing up under it and even honoring it, knowing it was eating out the very soul of the woman he loved more than anything, but honoring it nonetheless, hopeless to do otherwise. If ever there was a man who held a virtue so tight he turned it into a sin, it was Fowler Clement. He would keep his word, and no one doubted it. And so, he and the entire community became complicit that day in a cold-blooded murder, and to their credit, buried any further mention of it along with the body. No one grieved over Junior Clement.

*****

Fowler had gone to work quickly that next morning, waking Judge Reynolds at dawn. He'd had in mind the woman's sister in Carthage would take on the raising of two of the children, but three would be too much for her already-crowded family. Judge Reynolds had the thought of getting Wmearle Franklin to take care of the oldest.

"His girl moved off to Fort Worth, and he's all by himself since Jeannie passed. Fowler, you know there's not a better man alive."

Fowler squinted into the sunrise through the Judge's dining room window. Judge Reynolds was among his oldest friends.

"What are you going to do with the woman, Fowler?"

"Send her back to her people in East Texas. Her father is a capable man. There's something else. Why the kids can't be with her. It wasn't just the beating and the drinking that did it. I'm not educated in such matters, and I haven't had many opportunities to see it, but she's disturbed. There were things going on over there we didn't know about. The preacher did, though. He was in a tight spot over it. I don't think he knew what to do either, between Junior's drinking and her...Bill, it was a mess."

"I'm so sorry, Fowler."

"I know it. I surely am too."

CHAPTER 2

January 1964

The varmints were out. He had seen four sets of eyes glowing in the brush alongside the river road since he turned off the highway. Trace Clement idled the truck along while a porcupine waddled down the middle of the caliche road in the headlights. It was cold, and the dust was hanging layered in the still air like fog in his headlights.

He reached down and threw a rag over the big hole in the floor-board next to the gear shift to keep the cold out. The heat was just starting to catch up in the old pickup when he crossed the iron trellis bridge and turned in to the gate, which wasn't really a gate but rather a spot where the fence simply stopped and two gravel tire tracks ran backwards up the high bank on the other side of the river. About a quarter mile upriver, he turned upward away from the river and into the draw and sped up as he neared the steep spot in the hill, then skidded through the loose rock up onto the top.

Iladio was there, and only Mike. Blas was probably staying home with the wife, what with the baby being close. Nick. Nick was just getting undependable. It would be a girl somewhere he figured, but so far, Mike had no information on it. So it'd just be the three this week. His feet hurt when he stepped out and stomped his boots against the cold. He hadn't thawed out on the short drive out from town. The stars were shining bright in all directions. There'd been dust the night before and then sleet, but by morning, it had blown past. Now the wind had died and clouds had cleared and the cold was settling. He was thinking there would probably be a heavy frost the next morning as he hopped onto Iladio's tailgate next to Mike.

"Fellas."

Mike took a swig from the whiskey bottle and handed it to him. "Smoother'n you'd think it'd be."

Trace drank. He was wary of whiskey, but he liked how it made him feel warm on a night like this. Smooth wasn't something he could ever figure applied to whiskey, never mind how smooth he should expect it to be. Mike always talked like that, trying to sound worldly, as though he were calling upon some deep reservoir of experience in the relative merits of whiskeys. He passed the bottle to Iladio.

"You been on the tractor all day?"

"Just since church let out. Taking Mr. Collier's trailers back from the gin."

"How's he gettin' along?"

"Pretty happy. He seems to think he come out all right."

"Some of 'em didn't."

"Whatta you got going this week, Iladio?"

"Moving cattle on the Windmill Pasture. *Un par de días.*"

"*Como esta la senora Clement?*"

"She never speaks any more. But her eyes are…ah…*vivido. No se tardara mucho.*"

Mike took another swig off the bottle, then set it down and reached behind him for the flashlight. Trace leaned back against the side of the bed and traced the crystalline stars of the Milky Way up and across. Orion was just off the top of the mesquites in the southeast. The lights from town were below them to the north, and coyotes were yapping in the flats. Mrs. Clement was Trace's grandmother. He had neither seen her nor spoken to her in over seven years, she living only six miles up the river in that stone fortress. Iladio and Blas worked on The Clement as people called it, as though it were one thing, people, land, cattle, brand; ninety sections of grass put together by Fowler Clement in the late twenties. Fowler he did see frequently. They never spoke. But for those times when he would see Fowler standing inside Wmearle's shop talking, he tried not to think of his grandparents at all. That had always bugged Mike, so he brought her up just to get a rise out of Trace. He didn't.

Mike tucked the flashlight under his arm and pulled the ragged little spiral notebook from his shirt pocket. "Damn, it is cold out here."

"Why don't you ever bring a coat?"

Mike almost always wore the same thing. Unless it was an absolute blue norther, it was Levis and a western shirt with the oyster snap buttons, a leather belt with some rinky-dink rodeo buckle and a gimme cap.

"Here's what we got. Trace, Miss Ware's got something in her attic. She's too frail to get up in there, and it's keeping her up at night."

"Like what?"

"Probably coons or squirrels. Could just be rats, but she was pretty sure whatever it was, was bigger. Said it sounded like holy rollers having a revival. You'll likely need to do some patching. I'm sure she could use the visit anyhow. Then, let's see, Charlie Hutto's water pump is out. I think he's using the old cistern to get by. See if it's the pump or the foot valve. Somethin' might've chewed up a wire. Charlie can't see anything anymore, so who knows. If the motor's gone out, tell Wmearle, and he'll figure something out."

"What if the well's just gone dry?"

"Don't know. Not likely. Didn't dry up before. If it has, he don't have many options."

"That's a hand-dug well. Might have to get down in there and dig out some if it sanded up."

"On your way back, you can stop off at Lucy Blair's place." Now Mike was ribbing him. Mike had sent Trace out there once, and he had walked up on her watering her flowers without a stitch of clothes on. Hadn't seemed to have bothered her, but Trace was embarrassed by it, and he was wary of going around there. Trace ignored him. Iladio was smiling there in the dark under his straw hat.

"Anyhow, he's got a mill back behind the barn he tore down when he put in the pump. Worse comes to worst, we could put that thing back up if we need to."

"Iladio, I got a hard one for you. You'll need to get Blas and Seferino and maybe some others to help. Irena told Marie down at the salon that Luciano's foot is infected. His whole leg is swelled up. She can't move him, and he's been drinkin' hard. He won't let her get the doctor out there. Just sits in that chair sulking. He'll die if we don't get him to town."

Iladio stomped his boot in the dirt. *De qué estás hablando.*

"Well, he's gotta be three hundred pounds. Y'all are gonna to have to wrastle him down someway and get him in the back of the truck and haul him to town. I'm bett'n once Dr. Kemp sees him, he'll just send you on to the hospital with him. But he'll be a handful."

"Sera pasado mañana."

"Buen hombre."

Iladio had been on the Clement since Trace was little. The Clement didn't call him foreman, but he was the man they all looked to as the leader. Iladio was different than the other Mexicans who worked on the Clement. Trace had always wondered about that. He wore the same clothes, the same taco shell straw hat and the Levi jacket and the pointed boots. But he didn't look the same. He wasn't brown like the others, taller, and could speak English if he wanted to, with almost no accent. Iladio was quiet and serious, and seldom smiled. Despite an almost brooding nature, he gave you the impression you could trust him in a tight situation.

Blas and Nicholas and the others were little guys. Strong and brown and furious workers. But they were happy, playful people who seemed to enjoy their music and their fun. Iladio was none of that. He had a family, they all did, living in a circle of stone houses a half mile upriver from the Clement headquarters. Iladio was a loner, somehow always watching from the periphery of whatever was happening. But when he spoke, there was a bearing about him that lent natural authority to his position among the men. The other hands responded as though whatever he said was received wisdom.

"Trace, you got Wmearle a birthday present yet?"

"No, and no idea either."

"Better get an idea. It's what? Saturday?"

"Georgette was at church this morning."

Mike stopped, then reached for the bottle. Then, absently, "How'd she look?"

"Tired. Pretty as ever, but I think it's been hard." Mike drank then put the flashlight back in the toolbox.

"Let's get out of here before we freeze our peckers off."

Trace sat in the pickup for a bit after Mike and Iladio had dropped off into the draw. There was still-warm coffee in his thermos, and he sipped on it. Mike had first asked him out here three years ago when he turned twelve, and Wmearle got him his truck. Wmearle had fixed that with the judge so he could have an emergency permit. At the time, his legs were barely long enough to push the clutch in, but he had grown a foot and a half since then. In the beginning, the rationale had been to save Wmearle the chore of getting him back and forth from school, but Trace had immediately figured out the mobility gave him an opportunity to earn. He started, as many farm boys do, with a hoe. Before long, he was stomping cotton and feeding and working cattle and shoveling grain and whatever work was to be had as the seasons came and went.

"Come on out. Every Sunday night. Ten o'clock."

At first, he pretended like it was some kind of illicit party or secret society. Finally, he just laid it out. "Listen, it ain't nothin' like that. It's just there's a lot of folks around need stuff done sometimes. They're either old or broke or sick or what have you. I'm at the coffee shop every day, and I pop in at the gin and here and there, and I hear this and that, and somehow me and Iladio just got into the habit of doin' stuff. At first, it was just me and him, but we got outstripped. So we started gettin' Nicholas and later Blas to help out. A lot of folks don't like to ask nobody for help. They flat won't do it, least of all from the church folks. Seems like it doesn't bother 'em as much if it's one of us heathens. They all got their reasons. Some don't like owing anybody. Some are just proud, or they just don't have the wherewithal to figure out what needs doing. We just fell into doing it, and then we decided to meet the same time every week to get calibrated, so we'd know who was going where and when and who was doin' what. Only one absolute rule. Keep your mouth shut about what you do and who for. People's private problems is just their own.

13

Anyhow, you seem like you'd be a good addition since you got wheels and seem to be handy. You in or out?"

The town below would be quiet. It was always quiet. Like most small towns in West Texas, it had seemed forever to be drying up. It was not as though there had been some kind of calamity; the town was not struggling because of anything that happened. Rather, it was struggling, as it always had, because nothing ever did. There was no mill or factory or mine or oil field that created a reason for its existence. A single orange blinking light swung at the only paved intersection in the town, the rest of the streets being caliche. There was a scattering of houses here and there, many of them on wheels, but there had never been a town square or the edifice of any building that suggested real prosperity. Those that had been, now stood dilapidated, in ruins. Once, there had been a bank, and a gin, and even a newspaper, but they had all failed in their time, leaving only the few businesses necessary to give convenience to the town for their groceries and fuel and to service the ranchers and farmers and roughnecks. Then there were the churches, a Church of Christ, a Baptist, and a Methodist, all within two blocks of one another. It was a place with no particular character, other than that of practicality. From the high bluff over the river, he could see the orange light blinking across from the station, and the red one above it on top of the water tower.

The moon was well above the trees when he turned back onto the river road, and by the time he pulled up in front of the trailer, there was a silver light settling, and shadows were stretching across the ground. Wmearle didn't stir when he stepped into the trailer. Trace was long accustomed to his snoring and the rank smell of the trailer. He had been with Wmearle for seven years now, living in opposite ends of the small trailer behind the service station and catty-cornered from Wmearle's shop. W. E. Franklin Tool & Machine had been taking over the block for over twenty years now, and except for the main shop in the middle of the block, the remainder was littered with the rusting pieces and parts of every manner of equipment. He had always been indifferent to the mess in his yard, but inside the shop, he was very particular about how things were laid out. Wmearle Franklin was a giant man. Not so much in the frame, he was just a little over six feet, but in his thickness. He was broad and round, but not fat; his hair always misshapen on account of the safety goggles or being under a welding hood off and on all day. It was not gray so much as steel-colored, and bent like some outraged wire wheel.

Trace slipped into his room, closed the door, and draped his Levis across the pile of junk accumulating in the corner. He pulled the blankets up over him and closed his eyes on the moon rising into the slatted window of his room and started his prayers. Wmearle… Lydia…Mike…Iladio…Blas…Nicholas.

When his eyes opened again, it was still dark. The moon was no longer shining into his window. It would be just before six. He woke, as he did every morning, to the sound of Lydia sweeping the pavement around the station before opening. Wmearle had been long up and would already be cooking as he could see the kitchen light seeping in under the door. He would have been sitting at the table for an hour now, drinking coffee and reading his Bible. Trace grabbed the Levis off the pile and slipped them on, then shoved his feet into his boots and grabbed a clean shirt off the hanger.

"Grab ya a cup."

Trace poured his coffee.

"Got ya a headache?"

Trace smiled and slid into the seat across from Wmearle. They sat in silence for a long while, sipping their coffee. Then Trace said, "Just a swig or two was all it was."

"Biscuits is about done. Reach in there and get 'em out."

Trace grabbed the welding glove hanging from a string next to the oven door, reached in and put the biscuits on the table along with a stick of butter.

"Where you at this morning?"

"Joshua. Amazin' thing that."

They buttered their biscuits and spooned out the cane syrup onto their plates.

"Tell it to me," Trace said.

He watched Wmearle navigating the process with his immense hands. They would never again be clean. The sweet smell of the gel hand cleaner he used every day before leaving the shop formed part of the smell of the trailer, but the hands would only get so clean. The Bible lay next to Wmearle's plate, and he carefully turned the pages with his little finger; it being the only one left that didn't have Steene's syrup on it.

"Remember how God told Moses he wasn't going to get to go into the Promised Land? Well, he held to it, but he let Moses go up on top of Mount Nebo and at least look over in there. Then Moses died. God told Joshua to get everybody lined out and ready to go, and the priests took the ark and…see, the Jordan River was on the rise. I seen a picture of it one time. It's about like the Clear Fork. Maybe a little bigger." Wmearle paused for a bit. "Bet it surely don't taste as bad. Anyhow, it was on the rise, just like the Clear Fork does, so he told Joshua to go get the priests to carry the ark out in the middle of it. When they did, the river stopped running. Piled right up and spread out across the country. Then they got everybody to take all their stuff and walk across while the priests stood there with the ark. It don't say how long it took 'em, but I bet it was a long time. I heard the preacher say one time it was a couple of million people went across, so that'd have to take all day long at least. Anyhow, when they got across, they sent twelve men down in there to get a rock out of the bottom of the river and take it with 'em to pile up and make a monument. Then the priests walked out with the ark, and the river turned back loose again. And that was that. Hell of a thing." He shook his head and turned back to his biscuits.

"They didn't have a party or anything?"

"Didn't mention it."

"You'd think they would, after forty years."

"What you got going today?"

"I'm headed out to feed now. After school, I gotta go out to Miss Ware's and check on something. I ought not be too late gettin' in."

"Sometime this week, you gotta drive over to the courthouse and see the judge. He stopped by the shop Friday to tell me he's got something you need to sign for to get your permit renewed, or else you'll be outta business."

"Came all the way over here for that?"

"That and some other stuff that's none a your business." He leaned down to continue reading.

They finished their coffee and biscuits in silence, and Trace took the plates up and washed them and poured Wmearle another cup, then put on his jacket and hat and rubbed Wmearle on top of the head on his way out the door.

*****

Trace stepped out into the cold morning air and walked around the side of the station into the light under the canopy. He went inside to see Lydia behind the little desk flipping through the worn paper file box full of gas tickets. She was white-haired and wrinkled and incredibly thin; her skin blotched with freckles. She seemed ancient to Trace. Kids at school would laugh about how she would sit with her legs crossed smoking a cigarette, and she was so skinny both feet would be flat on the floor. But Lydia was a dynamo, and she moved quickly around the station and seemed to be constantly in motion, although other than her obsession with keeping the pavement swept and maintaining the ticket box, there didn't seem to be much to keep her occupied. Everybody pumped their own gas, and Lydia always farmed out the flats. She never smiled. At least, Trace had figured out not a regular smile. It was more of a look of amazement or concern he had learned to take as the same as a smile. Trace figured she was ashamed of her teeth. She wore a set of reading glasses on a string around her neck, and she placed them on her nose to look at a bundle of gas tickets.

"Cuttin' somebody off, Lydia?"

"Might be you," she said without looking up.

"Nope. I'm paid up. Got my money from the gin last week."

"I've done told you not to go gettin' in that cash register. Next time you want to pay, you give it to me, and I'll put it in the register."

"You was busy, and nobody seen me do it. I got my tickets out of the box too." She sat back and glared at him.

"There's other people's business in there besides yours. You want them looking at how much you're owin'?"

Lydia lived on the outskirts of town with her husband, Cactus. If he had a real name that was different, Trace had never heard of it. Cactus had long ago ceased to do anything of any consequence. Long ago, he had worn his body out roughnecking, and then one day, he stopped. He had little of interest to say to anyone, so he hardly ever spoke. His days were spent moving from the breakfast table with Lydia to the bench in front of the feedstore to the domino parlor out behind and then back again to his recliner. Cactus was a source of endless amusement on account of the way he moved about. Trace would watch him, his steps impossibly slow, such that there was an expectation that at any moment, he would finally come to a complete stop. His motion was so slow and deliberate that often a full inch and a half of ash would curl downward from the end of the cigarette hanging from his lips without breaking off.

Trace walked around the desk smiling and warmed himself over the butane stove. Lydia had a point about the ticket box. He did for a fact know how much everybody owed and who was slow to pay. There were a handful of old classroom chairs circled around the stove for later when a string of regulars would come in and smoke and tell tales and drink coffee.

He reached up onto the shelf behind her and got a can of snuff and some peanuts, then grabbed the little ticket book from the table and wrote out the charge and signed it. She took the ticket and flipped the cards over to *C* and stuck the ticket in.

"You off to feed?"

"Mmm. Hmm."

"When you start dippin'? Wmearle'll tear you a new one."

"Ain't for me," he said, walking out the door. "You be nice to everbody today."

In a minute, he was heading out of town in the old Ford and holding his hands down under the dash to warm them. The eastern sky showed no light as he turned into the Hearndon place and on past the house to the caliche hill behind the barn. Alvin Hearndon worked for the pipeline company and was always gone way before Trace got to the farm each morning. He backed the truck into the pit dug up into the side of the hill and began forking the silage into the bed. He liked the smell of the stuff, and it reminded him of the whiskey he'd had the night before, only it smelled sweeter. Once loaded, he drove down the narrow, broomweed-choked lane through the mesquite pasture until he saw the feed troughs in the headlights. He had no more backed up to the trough than the black shapes began loping through the trees toward him, red eyeballs glowing from the tail lights. He liked this: the cows all around him blowing smoke in the cold and bellowing and shoving to get in place. When he had finished unloading, he grabbed the sack of bone meal and stepped off the tailgate into the trough and shook out a few gallons on top of the silage, then hopped back into the bed and over the rail. There would be three such trips before he pulled out and headed back into town for school. The eastern sky showed only a little light when he pulled into the schoolyard parking lot.

*****

He walked into the foyer of Judge William Reynolds's office and took his hat off. The judge's clerk, Louise, looked up from her typing and smiled.

"Hello there, young man. You've grown a bunch since you were in here last. Somebody's feeding you well."

"Yes, ma'am."

"Let me see if he's busy." She slipped behind the tall oak door to the judge's office.

"He'll see you now. Go on in."

Judge Reynolds was a small, elegant, silver-haired man. His appearance had only one variable: in April, he put the silver belly hat on the rack and replaced it with the short-brim Panama. In October, he would do the reverse. Aside from that, he always wore a white starched shirt, black suspenders and dress pants, and a small dark-blue bow tie. He looked over his silver wire-rim spectacles and rose to meet Trace as he stepped around the desk to shake hands. The judge's office had a large arched window looking out over the courthouse square. The side walls were floor-to-ceiling bookshelves, and like the rest of the courthouse, smelled of pine cleaner and cigar smoke, though the cigar smell advanced as you got closer to the judge's quarters.

"How've you been, Trace?"

"Doin' well, sir, yourself?"

"I have no complaints. Sit yourself down."

The judge sat down and turned to the library table behind his desk and flipped through a stack of papers in a wooden tray. When he located the document, he passed it over to Trace.

"I need to get your signature on this in order to extend your emergency driving permit."

Trace stared at the page for a long while. "Affidavit Of Fact... I Fowler Randolph Clement III..."

Judge Reynolds watched Trace for a minute or so.

"Is there something there you find objectionable?"

"No, sir. I wouldn't call it that. I never use the name. Everybody calls me Trace, and it's the name I use and sign with. I'm just not used to seeing it written out like that."

Judge Reynolds settled back in his chair, and his face softened a bit. He looked at Trace for a long while then opened the top drawer of the desk and drew out a cigar.

"Let me crack this window a bit. Louise has an insufficient appreciation for cigar smoke."

He opened a little bone handle pocket knife and carefully cut the end off the cigar and placed it in the crystal ashtray. The judge had used this little maneuver for years whenever he needed to stop and think a bit in the middle of a conversation. When he'd lit the cigar and taken a few puffs, he turned his stare back to Trace.

"Trace, do you see the title of the document?"

Trace nodded. "Yessir."

"It is an affidavit of fact. Your name is Fowler Randolph Clement III. That is a fact. Is it not?"

"Yessir."

"It is: a legal and practical fact. Now, whether you are aware of it or not, there are a great many things about your current"—he paused and drew on the cigar—"disposition that are anything but legal. They are just plain old practical. Do you understand?"

"Yessir, I suppose."

The judge leaned back and looked up high into the bookshelves. "Do you know what we do here?"

"I think so."

"This place is all about the last resort. It's why we build a grand building in the middle of the square, so everybody can look up here and see there *is* a last resort. In here, you have all these books, the accumulated wisdom of centuries worth of judgments at the place of last resort. All this is for whenever people's dealings with one another can't be managed within normal reason and compassion and humanity and sense. Right outside that window, walking around the square, are people working and dealing with each other and marrying and buying and selling and what have you with nary a judge or sheriff anywhere to be seen to oversee their doings. They manage on the basis of humanity and respect and common sense. There's a hell of a lot more wisdom in that than you'll find on these bookshelves."

"Yessir, I reckon." Trace was looking up at all the leather-bound volumes.

The judge saw him looking and sat back deeply in his chair and swiveled around slightly to look out the window. "I have alas, Philosophy, Medicine, and Jurisprudence too, and to my cost Theology with ardent labor studied through. Yet, here I stand with all my lore, poor fool, no wiser than before."

"Faust."

The judge raised his eyebrows. "You're telling me you've read Goethe?"

"Yessir. They got it in the library at school."

"Well, I wouldn't question you, but I expect you might be the only one that ever did read it, let alone remember the words. You read a lot?"

"Ever'thing in the library, not that that's much. Lot of 'em twice."

"Good for you. I mean that." He tilted his head and shook it.

"Your...disposition, if we can call it that, is precisely the kind of practical wisdom I'm talking about. You are the beneficiary of that, and by all accounts, it's worked out pretty good so far. But here's the important part. You are also the beneficiary of something else, and the time is coming when you'll have to face up to it. Do you understand?"

"I'm not sure I do."

"The name son. It's not going away. You go by Trace. The Mexicans on the Clement started that when you were a baby. *Tres.* Three."

"Judge, I don't have nothin' to do with those people."

"I know you don't." He tapped the cigar on the edge of the ashtray and sucked it back to life, turning the chair sideways to look out onto the square.

"There are more things in heaven and earth than are dreamt of in your philosophy."

"Sir?"

"I'm sorry. It's been a slow day. I guess I've been daydreaming. Wmearle is looking after you, okay?"

"Yessir."

"Grades okay?"

"Yessir. Schoolwork's always come easy for me. What do you mean about my philosophy?"

"I mean, sometimes things aren't the way they seem. In fact, they almost never are, and we usually can't tell how they really are till they're a long way behind us. I mean to tell you to keep your mind open about how people are and about who you are. It'll serve you well to do so."

Trace signed the document and got up to head out the door, and the judge told him to leave it with Louise on the way out. As he went out, he leaned back in through the door. "*Hamlet.* Act I."

The Judge laughed. "Hmmph, there I thought it was something Snoopy said."

He walked out onto the courthouse square into the bright cool winter sun, then crossed the street towards the department store. He had seen Wmearle pull his billfold out the day before and it was near falling apart, so that solved his birthday dilemma. While he looked through the glass counter at the billfolds, he thought how funny it would be to get Wmearle a necktie for his birthday. So he got it too.

CHAPTER 3

February 1964

Trace had told Wmearle to be ready, and when he got back, he found Wmearle slicking his hair back, reeking of aftershave lotion. They would drive the thirty miles to the motel out on the interstate and celebrate Wmearle's birthday. The waitress took their orders and left them looking out over the patio where the swimming pool was glowing blue. Trace reached into his jacket pocket and brought out the box with the new billfold.

"How about that. Mine's bout to fall apart on me. Much appreciated."

When Trace produced the box with the necktie in it, he had the thought it would be funny; that they'd have a good laugh over it. Wmearle had never worn a tie as long as Trace had known him, and Trace thought it obvious he would look flatly ridiculous in one; hence, the joke. When Wmearle opened the box and acted as though it were the most precious thing he had ever been given, his heart sank, a profound sense of shame sweeping over him. He sat in the restaurant booth looking at this huge man wrapping the tie around his neck with the broad smile on his face. He was thinking about his "disposition," as Judge Reynolds had called it. The shame coming over him from that night when he was eight years old, being orphaned in a moment by his mother's defiance, and that "disposition" being formalized in the glow of the porchlight beyond which his father lay murdered. Not especially ashamed at what she had done, Trace had always figured his daddy had it coming, but the notion that he was a creature who had a disposition, a special dispensation: an artificial arrangement agreed upon by a preacher and a sheriff and the old man and later affirmed by Judge Reynolds and by everyone in the whole community, and he the walking embodiment of the deal that was struck, because he lived openly in the community according to that arrangement. He didn't hold it against anyone. No one ever brought up what happened. But everyone knew. And here, this good man who had never batted an eye over taking him in and becoming more a brother than a father to him, and he had bought that tie to make a joke of him. Wmearle caught the distant expression on his face.

"Whatsa matter?"

"Nothin'. I just had something cross my mind."

"About what the judge said to you the other day?"

"Mmmhmm."

Over the years, there had been a few instances where Trace's family and his status as a ward of the court would pop up. Wmearle was pretty deft at leaving it alone. He would be there to listen if Trace wanted to talk about it. So far, he never had. So Wmearle just nodded and continued fiddling with his tie.

"Wmearle, I wanna thank you."

"What for?"

"For taking me in. Givin' me a place to live. You didn't have to do that."

Wmearle stopped fiddling with his tie and had a quizzical smile on his face. "Well. You're welcome. I suppose." He smiled real big and leaned across the table. "Who'd I have to eat my biscuits with if you wad'n around?"

"I'm serious. I appreciate it. I ain't never told you that, so I'm telling you."

"Well, all right then." Wmearle sat back in the booth and looked at him for a moment or two.

"It ain't like you're a burden or anything, Trace. I'm thankful ever day that you come to live with me. When I say who'd I have to eat my biscuits with, that ain't no small thing. Starts the day off good. Keeps you thinking you're part of the world instead of just yourself."

He smiled big again. "And, I got this nice new tie and billfold out of the deal!"

The waitress approached with two glasses of sweet tea and put them on the table, along with a small saucer with little butter cups on it.

"What were you doing out at Miss Ware's place?"

Trace broke into a smile and chuckled.

"That was quite a thing. Mike told me she was having a problem with something in her attic, so I went out there to see what I could do."

Trace went on with the story. Maggie Ware's family had been one of the first to settle in the county after the T&P railroad came through to the south. Most of the family had been wiped out long ago in an epidemic, leaving Maggie and her younger sister Sarah, alone. Neither of them had ever married, and they lived in the same unpainted two-room house together until Sarah had passed in '58. The two of them had supported themselves by running a small herd of black cattle and leasing the cultivated land on their place. They'd gotten a couple of wells on the place in the forties, and the royalties solved any money troubles they had. Maggie kept an old-fashioned swept yard, outlined against the mesquite pasture by a string of white limestone rocks. Inside the boundary, the yard was only the swept red-clay dirt with a stone pathway from the caliche drive to the front porch. Maggie kept a black shepherd-collie dog on a screened back porch. Whenever any visitor would enter the single front room of her house, the dog would begin a process of running the length of the back porch and flinging itself against the back door. He never barked, but as he ran toward the door, a low growling sound would build until he leapt and crashed against the door, very nearly at the top. The front room was arranged around a large cast-iron stove in the middle, with an iron bedstead against one end of the room and a dinner table at the other. The kitchen formed the back end of the house and opened onto screened porches on both sides.

Maggie was a hard, weathered-looking woman, but she was a kind soul, and Trace knew her well from church. She met him at the end of the drive when he pulled up after school.

"Mr. Clement. What brings you out this way?"

"I heard you've had a problem with something running around up in your attic."

"Ha. You bet! Somethin' has moved in up there. Law it sounds like a stampede goin' on all night long. I can't get up in there to even see what it is. 'Fraid I'd break my neck."

They walked up onto the front porch. "You have a scuttle hole or something?"

"It's on the back porch." Trace stopped.

"No. The other back porch. Go around the side that way, and I'll meet you there."

Maggie had a freezer on the porch, and Trace climbed up onto it and opened the scuttle-hole latch. He had brought a flashlight and stuck it in his pants and hoisted himself up. The attic space was tight over the kitchen part of the house but opened up a bit over the front room. He couldn't see much with the light from the scuttle hole blinding him, so he lowered the door back down to let his eyes adjust. Then he could hear them, all around him. He reached behind for the flashlight and turned it on to see what looked like seven or eight sets of eyeballs, but they were in constant motion around him, the eyes too wide set for rats and too narrow for coons and making what sounded like a cat barking. Just then, one of them ran right up his backside and began clawing into his scalp.

Trace woke up sitting against the wall of the screened porch with Maggie on her knees over him. She had a wet dishrag she was holding against his head.

"Whoowee, I thought you was dead."

"What happened?"

"Well, you come outta there in a little too big a hurry, I think. You fell out of there and landed on your head. You're bleeding a little, but I don't think it'll need stichin'. But you got a big bump. What was it?"

"I'm not sure. I ain't ever seen anything like 'em before. They got a tail like a coon, but they ain't coons. They're little bitty and fast as the dickens."

"Oh, those are ringtails! My Lord. I haven't seen one of those since I was little. They're a terror!"

*****

Wmearle was having a good laugh at his expense.

"What did you do?"

"Once I gathered myself back up a little, I went out and found a bunch of old rabbit wire and fashioned me a big trap with a wire trap door on it. I tacked it to the ceiling of the porch and had Maggie pull it up snug with a string when I went back up the scuttle hole. This time, I left the scuttle hole door open, and I just went up in there amongst 'em and started chasin' 'em around with a broom. Sooner or later, they all went right for the daylight and fell right through the trap door. I's proud of Maggie though. She held on to that string until I got 'em all with eight of those ringtails barking at her through the wire. That sound they make will unnerve you. I still got the heebie-jeebies from bein' up there in the dark with 'em screamin' at me."

Wmearle was enjoying this, and his big belly laughing was filling up the restaurant.

"Wha'd you do with 'em?"

"I took 'em down the river road and let 'em out at the bridge. Ain't no houses anywhere nearby. I thought oncest or twice about just throwing the trap in the river and drownin' 'em. Anyhow, I turned 'em out."

"Swanny. You're lucky they didn't eat you alive."

"Liketa did!"

The waitress returned with the steaks and baked potatoes and fried onion rings, and they dug in. Trace paid for the dinner and put a tip under the butter saucer. Wmearle made a halfhearted try to chip in.

"Did you rob a bank I ain't heard about?"

"I been stealin' outta the collection plate. It's my grand scheme to get rich."

"Well, you can repent in the mornin'."

CHAPTER 4

Fowler sat in his pickup perched on the high-side bluff overlooking the Clear Fork. It would be another half hour before sunrise, but he could see the dust rising out of the mesquite flats where the hands were moving cattle a mile or so across. They'd met earlier as they did every morning in the Big House for breakfast where they'd make a plan for the day. From his vantage point, he could see for miles up and across the Clear Fork valley, and everything he could see, he owned. He couldn't ride anymore on account of the pain in his hip. Sciatica, or arthritis, he didn't know for sure, but it had cured him riding. He had tried to work through it and found if he did mount up, the pain would go away after a while as he loosened up. But it would be worse the next day, and for the next week, he would be stuck in his chair. So he had given it up. Fowler had never been a natural horseman, but he was a natural hand, and the Mexicans who worked the ranch respected him in that way.

This was where he did his thinking. It was the one place where he could take in both the silence and beauty of it and have some sense of the scale of his life. To look at him, there was a grim, determined feature to his face. But it was not true to his nature. He was, in all material respects, a hopeful man, and in spite of everything that had happened, his thoughts were out in front of him.

The pastures were in better shape now, but the winter had been dry, and he needed rain. The drought in the fifties had been hard on the land, and he had all but emptied the ranch of cattle by the end. The deal he'd made with Iladio's father in Muzquiz to move the herd down into the high country of northern Mexico had worked out well. He was able to rebuild faster than most and had left half of the original herd down there in a partnership with David Ramos. The Texas herd now was almost back to normal numbers, and they were moving the cows up into a series of small pastures on the high ground. They'd begin calving in a week or two, and it helped to get them concentrated.

He could see down into the bare mesquite pastures that rose steadily away from the river to the north. The bottoms held a hazy lightness that faded as the elevation increased. There were ancient mesquites in the bottoms, some that grew to be two feet in diameter, and when the sun peaked above the horizon behind him, the haze caught the light, and the broad bottom country was suddenly gilded before him. There was a dew, and the mesquites were all wet with it. The whole of the country glistened. He wondered to himself where the moisture came from with the ground so dry.

The cattle were bunching up now, such that the dust cloud was growing more prominent on the horizon. When the hands came in view in the higher pastures, he started his pickup and backed away from the bluff, then eased back south across a flat mesquite plateau called the Buffalo Pasture. All the pastures had names that had materialized in one way or another out of experiences over time. The Buffalo Pasture, named not because of any buffalo, they had at one time been everywhere here, but because the hands had come across a skeleton of what had probably been a buffalo hunter. It had been found under an algerita bush where a rusted Sharps rifle lay next to the blackened, almost petrified remains of heavy leather clothes mostly gnawed away over the years by field mice.

He accelerated slightly, then floated the transmission out of gear and rolled to a stop and killed the engine and rolled down the window. The cool of the morning suspired in the windless silence, with only a quail call and a small rustling in the grass. A skunk meandering through stopped when it got into the road and raised its tail briefly when it saw the truck before moving on. Juanita would be bathing Let back at the house by now, and if she heard his pickup pull up, she would get upset. So he would wait. Now in his mind, it was a different morning—hot, summer—the land browning as it did every July. He had asked Let to come down before he left at graduation, and it was her first morning on the ranch, still before sunrise. Everything had changed at once. He was nervous. She was proper, a society girl, daughter of a judge, Eastern and refined in her manners, and as far as he knew, had never been horse-back. So he was nervous as they rode down and crossed the river, then topped the bluff into the open mesquite pasture and out and on into the summer dawn. Then she had suddenly yelled and slapped the horse on the rump and took off like a banshee with him long in her dust. He sat in the pickup and sucked in a quick breath and held it as he felt again the moment when he had first marveled at the beauty of it, her auburn hair floating straight out behind her, how she'd had no fear at all, the untamed fearless and absolute beauty of it. It was not as though he had fallen in love in a moment, but as though he had suddenly always been in love with her, that he had never not been and would never not be. When he caught up to her already at a stop looking out over the bluff into the wide river bottoms, she turned, and he saw her eyes were a greenish blue, and his spirit was given over forever. He asked her to marry him as soon as he got air in his lungs. She said only "Yes," turned the horse on its back feet and flew off again, and by the time he had caught up with her at the barn, he had wondered if any of it had actually happened.

Fowler stepped out of the pickup and leaned, stretching into the pain running down his leg. He had grown stiff from sitting too long. There was a strong scent of prickly ash on the air, and he walked a few yards into the pasture to loosen up and found where several branches on the bush had been broken and were mud-smeared. A sow had nested up under there. He relieved himself in the grass then eased back into the seat of the pickup and poured a cup of coffee out of his Thermos. A light southwest breeze had picked up, and the wintergrass was green under the bare mesquites. He was no longer a restless man, but deliberate and patient. David was dying of cancer, and he needed to get down there and see him before it was too late. He tried to focus on Let and whether she was getting close herself. He didn't want to leave her, but he never could size that up rationally. Whenever he tried to think about it, his mind resisted and wandered to other places and times. He might lose Iladio when David passed; he knew that was possible. Iladio might go back to work the ranch at

Musquiz with his brother, so he would be short a good man here. He needed to get some bulls bought, and he had heard from the hospital in Rusk that The Woman—that's how his mind formed his thought of her—The Woman, had gotten much worse and that what little threads of attachment she had to reality were fading fast. He needed to talk to her people. He shook his head and let loose an audible growl and pulled his mind back to Let.

The stroke had been over a year ago now. The morning it happened, he had gone up after his morning breakfast with the hands to drink coffee with her. They had for a long time come to a form of peace about the boy and The Woman and what happened to Junior. The latent outrage had dulled over time, and though she had given no quarter to it, she had been affected when first they got news the little one had died in a measles outbreak. Then the other, the girl, had been killed along with The Woman's sister in a car wreck. So she knew the boy was alone in the world. Whether it softened her mind against the boy, Fowler couldn't tell as she never spoke about any of it. But she had softened toward Fowler, at least, and they'd found a way of going about each other that had gotten easier.

She was talking while she ate that morning about some social thing in Fort Worth they'd be going to, when she held up and sighed and sat back in her chair, her face confused, angry, paralyzed. He'd gotten her into the bed and called Dr. Kemp out and then got her to the hospital in Abilene, but that was the last time she ever spoke.

Juanita would have had time to finish bathing her by now. There had been a change. Before, Let had a focus in her eyes, and Juanita could sense what pleased her and what didn't, and they formed a kind of communication. But there had been a change. While her eyes were still focused and followed whoever came into the room, Juanita said she didn't understand anymore, that something had been lost.

Fowler jumped suddenly, started the pickup, and sped down the dirt lane across the pasture. The lane circled back around to the river, and he plowed downward across the concrete low water crossing and past the house and headed into town to see Wmearle.

*****

31

Wmearle punched the button to shut down the lathe and lifted the visor on his head and turned to find Fowler standing in the open door of the shop watching him. He had long ago figured out the contradiction in the way Fowler looked and the way he was. He stood there, tall in his khaki work clothes and that stained Stetson pulled down low over his eyes. While he was a big man, it was the bearing in his face and eyes that would unsettle most people. His eyes were a light-gray colored, and he wore a stern, Wmearle had come to see it as sad, expression that gave a stranger the impression of a man prepared to fight, desperately, at any moment. Wmearle knew better. Fowler was a gentleman, and when he spoke, his words belied the expression on his face. He was an educated man and spoke with a mannered kindness, an even effeminate formality. Wmearle didn't think of him as defeated; the jury was still out on that, but he knew he himself had become a part of a battle Fowler was fighting to regain some shred of what he had lost.

"How are you today, Wmearle?"

"Well, sir." He laid the visor on a worktable and walked forward and extended his hand.

"I wonder if we could visit for a little bit if you're not too busy?"

Wmearle opened up a couple of folding chairs, and they sat together in the open garage doorway. He would start, as he always did, by asking on about Wmearle and how he was doing. It had taken Wmearle a long time to get around to believing it was more than some kind of genteel mannerism. But he was certain now Fowler had a genuine concern, maybe out of appreciation, maybe just out of plain decency, he didn't know. But Fowler always started off the same before getting around to whatever he needed to know about Trace.

"What's the young man been up to?"

"Same as usual. He's a go-getter. He works too much, out feeding ever morning early. Saving his own money. Bought me a necktie for my birthday. He's a turk sometimes, but he's a sweet kid. You know he's in with that Wakefield kid in that do-gooder society of theirs. Damdest thing that. So he's here, there, and yon ever day on some errand or another."

Fowler smiled a bit. The thing with Mike Wakefield had worried him some when he first got onto it. He didn't know the kid very well and had his concerns about whether Trace had gotten into some bad company. But then he found out Iladio was in on it too, and so he had told Wmearle to sit back and watch. It was strange the way they'd just set themselves up in that kind of business on their own merit, but as far as he and Wmearle could tell, it was all genuine. Fowler was quietly proud of the whole bunch of them.

"I received some news that I wanted to talk with you about. I got a call from a Dr. Winters. He's the physician at the state hospital in Rusk who is responsible for Trace's mother. She is not doing well."

Wmearle frowned.

"He has only seen his mother the once since she went away, when you took him down there?"

"Yessir. About a year after she first left. I called her daddy, and he set it up. Trace was just eight or nine then. I'm pretty sure he never even knew it was a hospital. It looked like a park. They brung her out under the trees and sat her on a park bench and left. So I don't think he knew then how it was. He knows now. He's smart that way. It was a worrisome thing though. She was skittish. Nervous. Like she had ants in her pants. It turned out okay, I suppose. They never talked about what happened at all. Nothing at all really, just small talk. But Trace hardly talked all the way home."

"Has he ever asked you about her since then?"

"Not a single word. I think he knows she's touched."

"Why do you think that?"

"I figure otherwise he would ask. But what happened? What happened before that? He was old enough to see she wasn't right. If he didn't know, I expect he'd have asked something. He's free with me about most everything."

"May be. May be."

"You say she's not doing well. What do you mean by that?"

"Dr. Winters says it's a psychotic break. I am no better educated on such things than you are, Wmearle, but it means she's completely lost her hold on herself. He said she'll start to deteriorate rapidly and probably not survive long, even if she doesn't do herself harm. They can't help her. Therein lies the predicament."

"What predicament?"

"We need to decide whether to talk to Trace about this. Is he better off knowing or not knowing? Would it be proper to take him back down there to see her in her condition and know, or not know? My guess is, it would be a mighty hard thing for him, or anybody, to see."

"Would you want to know, if you was him?"

"I don't know. I think I would want to know what is true in this world. I think the Lord has His reasons."

"You want me to talk to him?"

"You know I can't."

Wmearle understood. It was a boundary line Fowler wouldn't cross. It was a point of irritation to Wmearle. On the one hand, the whole arrangement was an abomination, but there was no point in pursuing that line of reasoning. Too much done that couldn't be undone. But Fowler bent on keeping a promise that shouldn't have ever had to be made in the first place was hard to fathom.

"Where's this all heading, Mr. Clement?"

Fowler stared at him as though out of some impenetrable misery.

"Wmearle, there's none of us that deserves salvation. The best we can hope for is to get it anyway."

*****

Fowler turned through the two stone columns and rattled across the cattle guard toward the house. Juanita was coming down the stairs with the linens when he stepped in off the porch and put his hat on the rack. The stairs were a challenge for him as each step irritated the throbbing nerve in his leg. When he entered her room, Let was sitting up, braced by pillows Juanita had arranged around her. Her eyes followed him as he pulled the chair beside the bed and sat down. He took her hand and held it for the longest time and looked into her blue-green eyes and wondered if she was looking into his.

CHAPTER 5

Trace was first to arrive at the meeting place. Iladio and Blas were together, each in their straw hats and denim jackets, and Mike trailing right behind them. It had been a warm, clear, windless day, and the night air was cooling quickly as it did in late February. Mike wheeled his truck around and backed up to them, then hopped out and put the tailgate down.

"La ehorabuena, Blas."

Mike slapped Blas on the shoulder, and Blas cracked a wide smile, then pulled a photograph out of his shirt pocket. Mike hopped backward onto the tailgate and shined his flashlight on the picture.

"Damn. *Ese nino esta enorme.*" Blas smiled even bigger.

"You Mescans have the hairiest babies I ever seen."

He passed the picture and the flashlight to Trace.

"Congratulations, Blas. How's Marina?"

"She's okay. Happy."

Mike kept carrying on, picking at him. "You sure he's yours? That's a huge baby for a little guy like you."

Blas couldn't be got at. He was a proud fellow and got the compliment.

"Estoy feliz por ti." Blas nodded.

"What's his name?" asked Trace.

"Maximo."

Trace handed the flashlight back to Mike and the picture to Blas.

"Well, he looks like a Maximo. I'll say that. Anyways, I ain't got a single thing on my list tonight except one. I found out why we hadn't seen Nicholas. He got picked up by the Border Patrol. They sent him all the way to Saltillo before they dropped him off."

"Nicholas ain't wet, is he?" Trace asked.

Iladio and Blas shrugged.

"I never thought so. He's been here as long as I ever knew. I thought he was born here. Prob'ly didn't matter. He was up in the panhandle somewhere on an errand for Clement and got caught up in a sweep of some kind. They got a couple a busloads of 'em."

"How's he gonna get back?"

"Well, that's the deal. We gotta go down there and get him. He said he can hitch a ride to the border. Iladio, can you get away?"

"No puedo."

"I don't even need to ask you, do I?" Blas was still smiling.

"So it looks like me. You want to go Trace?"

"Go where exactly?"

"He said he could meet us in Acuna."

Blas and Iladio exchanged glances, and Mike picked it up quick.

"No. No. Hell no! Ain't gonna be any of that." Blas and Iladio were not sure.

"You think I want to explain to Wmearle Franklin how Trace wound up in Boys Town?"

That was more believable. That would not be a conversation anybody would want to have.

"We could head out Saturday morning and get there in plenty of time to eat and get started back."

"I gotta feed early, but yeah, I guess."

"Clear it with Wmearle."

"Iladio, how is Luciano getting along? I heard y'all had a bit of a rodeo."

"They took the leg. Diabetico."

"Damn. I's afraid of that."

Mike reached behind him and produced the bottle and some solo cups and spread them around and poured each a drink. *"Larga Vida Maximo!"*

*****

It was an hour before dark when the guard on the Mexican side of the International Bridge looked up from his newspaper and waved them by. Nicholas had given Mike the instructions about where to go.

"He said bear left off the bridge and take the first right and go six blocks."

"You ever been here before?"

"No. Been to Piedras Negras several times. Looks about the same as there as I remember."

"So I gather the place has a reputation."

"Overblown, I bet. I mean Boys Town is for real, but I bet you for ever ten stories you hear, maybe one of 'em came close to actually happening. I expect if somebody comes down here looking for trouble, they're likely to find it. But people like to tell tall tales. Everbody I ever knew when I've gone over has always been sweet people."

Mike pulled over and parked on the street. Two little boys ran up and had cartons of Juicy Fruit and Spearmint gum to sell. Trace gave them some change and bought a couple of packs.

"Place we're looking for is La Macarena. Blas said it was a good eatin' place."

"Wmearle give you a lecture?"

"You might call it that. I tell ya, overblown or not, you mention you're going to Acuna, and people get suspicious in a hurry. Boil it down, it was more like a mortal threat than a lecture on morals."

"He knows I ain't gonna do anything like that."

"Better'n you have made the mistake."

"Where is it, do you think?"

"Enough about that. You want to go get you a souvenir or something?"

They browsed through a couple of the shops along the street, each smelling of Mexican leather. Trace bought some hard candy and a sack of saladitos and stuffed them in his jacket. They got directions to La Macarena and headed across the street. The restaurant was dark in the front near the bar, but there was an open courtyard with tables, so they crossed into the light and sat down. The restaurant was empty, but the servers were busy, so they figured the place must get busy later. A group of policemen came in and took a big circular table in the front room. The waiter who approached the table wore a white outfit with a small black bow tie.

"Buenos tardes. Que de gustaria?"

"You have Coors?"

"Si."

"I'll have a Coors. Trace, Coke okay with you?" Trace nodded.

The waiter left, and Mike looked over Trace's head at the policemen sitting in the front room. They were passing beers around off the waiter's tray and talking loudly over each other. One was looking at them.

"What time is Nick supposed to be here?"

"He just said before dark sometime. He said not to wait on him if we wanted to eat."

The waiter brought the drinks and placed them on little cardboard coasters.

"Te gustaria ordenar?"

"No, I think we'll wait a bit. We're meeting a friend of ours. His name is Nicholas Nieto. Has he stopped by here?"

"No lo creo. Vere." The waiter disappeared.

"Bet you ten that guy speaks perfect English."

"I saw you talking to Georgette at church."

Mike dropped his head as though he were looking at Trace over some nonexistent reading glasses.

"I'm not sayin' anything. Just that I noticed. Don't get sideways."

Mike swigged his beer and glanced again over Trace's shoulder. The policeman was still looking at him.

"She's had a hard time of it. Asshole dropped her like a hot potato in Arizona. She had to call her daddy just to get enough money to get back home. Broke her up pretty bad."

Mike and Georgette Holloway had been a pair for most of their high school years, and Mike had been certain he would be marrying her as soon as they graduated. But Georgette had gone off to the Stamford Rodeo the July before their senior year, and in one night, she fell for a traveling rodeo cowboy and took off with him. Her daddy had gotten the Texas Rangers after them, but by the time they got on the trail, they were almost to Calgary for the Stampede. She had called her mother from there and told them she was never coming back. Mike had tanked after that, and Trace knew it was a sensitive subject with him.

"So how you gonna play it?"

"Son, you go right in for it, don't you?" He sipped his beer.

"I love her. Always will. But it don't matter if it ain't a two-way street. Both end up miserable. I ain't foreclosing on nothing. We'll see."

"This Coke tastes funny."

"There's a policeman been staring at us. He's comin' over here."

The policeman was young, about Mike's age. He had a crew cut and filled out his uniform. He looked to be a stout character. Mike nodded as he approached the table.

"*Buenos tardes.*"

"What are you gentlemen in town for?"

"We're here to meet a friend. He's supposed to meet us here."

"What is your friend's name?"

"Nicholas Nieto."

"Please come with me. We have a man by that name in custody."

*****

Trace and Mike sat on the steel beds staring at the white tile walls of the cell. They had been driven up to a hilltop fortress that was the town jail, and once inside the courtyard, they had been moved directly into a line of cells and the door slammed shut. The policeman had not given them any reason. In fact, he hadn't spoken another word. The cell was filthy and smelled of urine and vomit and bleach.

"I'm a dead man," Mike moaned.

"Surely it ain't that serious."

"I mean Wmearle."

"What do you reckon this is about?"

"No idea. I heard all my life about idiots windin' up in a jail in Acuna. Now here we are."

There was a single bare lightbulb hanging from the ceiling of the cell, and it was blindingly bright. The sounds they heard elsewhere in the jail were unintelligible. Trace sucked on a saladito and offered one to Mike. After a while, they just sat in silence and stared at the white tile walls of the cell. They lost touch with time, but within a couple of hours, they heard footsteps approaching. A jail officer opened the door and a small silver-haired gentleman entered. He wore a dark-blue tailored pinstripe suit with a blue tie. His age was hard to guess, but he was very old, and the ebony walking stick with a carved silver handle added to the effect. He had a very close-cropped silver moustache and appeared to be well-manicured. Still, the dark bronze skin had seams rather than wrinkles, and his eyes were almost black. He was clearly a hard man, and he could just as well be wearing a bandolier in a picture with Villa.

"Gentlemen, could you please follow me." It was not a question, so they rose and followed him back out into the courtyard, which was now flooded with an orange light. Concertina wire sparkled around the top of the courtyard walls. It was dark now and cool, and they had lost any awareness about how much time had passed. The elderly man walked them to a black Lincoln parked in the courtyard, and a driver opened the door. He got in behind them, and the driver pulled out through the arched opening to the jail and headed back into town. The Lincoln came to a stop and parked across the street from where Mike's pickup was parked.

"Oh shit. Look! They're stealing my tires!"

"You're mistaken," said the old man, holding up his hand. "They're putting them back on."

Mike and Trace were thoroughly confused.

"I'm afraid there has been an unfortunate misunderstanding. The officer that placed you under arrest was acting on information relating to a young woman who was badly harmed last night in La Zona Rosa. Apparently, you matched the description given by witnesses of the man who harmed her, and the officer was planning to hold you until a proper identification could be made. The officer was entirely justified in detaining you, however mistaken he may have been. I hope you will understand."

The man's English was near perfect, with only a slight lyrical accent.

"Who are you?" Trace asked.

"My name is Alejandro Vega."

Mike and Trace continued to stare with quizzical looks on their faces.

"I don't understand," said Mike.

"Let's get out and take a stroll. Don't worry, you'll have no more difficulties with the authorities."

They each got out of the car, and sure enough, the boys across the street were kicking the hubcaps back on the pickup and scurrying away. The street was busy now, and Mike looked at his watch, and it said eleven o'clock. They could tell as they walked down the street that all eyes were on them. The store clerks were stepping out of the souvenir shops to watch, and the little groups of boys peddling chewing gum stopped and grew silent as they passed. Before long, they stopped in front of La Macarena, and Trace turned and noticed that the Lincoln had been following them up the street.

"I received a call from an old friend who you may know, David Ramos. David called and told me who you are and about your trouble and asked if I could be of assistance. Since I have some influence with the authorities, I was only too happy to help. My understanding is that your friend is inside waiting on you."

"Mr. Vega, I still don't understand. I don't know David Ramos. But I do appreciate your help. I thank you for helping us out."

"It has been my pleasure. I can only tell you that David Ramos knows you." And with that, he turned, and the driver popped out of the Lincoln to open his door. He entered and was gone.

Nicholas was standing at the bar in La Macarena when they entered. They hugged him and slapped him on the back, and Trace said, "Let's get out of here. I want to get across that bridge."

*****

They had no trouble at the U.S. checkpoint on the other side of the river. They gassed up in Del Rio, and before long, they were in empty country headed through the night toward Sonora. For a long time, they were silent, as though they were holding their breath waiting for the next bad thing to happen. Mike was the first to speak.

"What the hell? What just happened? Who was that guy? Nicholas, what was that all about?"

"Que quieres decir."

"Who was that Vega fellow?" Mike asked

"Ah. Sindicato. Padrino. Angel de la muerte."

"Who is David Ramos?"

"Que es el padre de Iladio. En Muzquiz."

"How did you know to call him? I never even heard of him."

"Yo no he llamado Ramos."

"Doesn't make any sense."

"Who did you call?" Trace asked. He already knew the answer.

"El jefe."

Mike carried on and on for a while. He was wound up. By the time they pulled into San Angelo, he had played out and found a roadside park to try to catch some sleep. After a while, they gave up, and Nicholas got in the driver's seat. Trace had put it together what had happened. As with all things having to do with Fowler Clement, he would have preferred to keep it to himself.

"That was damned strange. You ain't said two words."

"Prob'ly you won't need to tell Wmearle. I bet he don't know about any of this. Just get him upset. I'll tell him when it's right."

"What was going on with that old man? Walking down the street like that."

"It was a statement. He wanted everybody to see. So nobody'd mess with us."

"What's the matter with you?"

"Man, ain't said so much as a word to me in seven years, and I spend no more'n three hours in a Mexican jail, and he reaches all the way down there in Mexico like God hisself, and just like that, some old gangster kingpin snatches us out of there, and here we are like none of it ever happened. Yeah. I'd say that was pretty damned strange."

CHAPTER 6

April 1964

"A dead man is the life of a fence."

Trace liked working with Shorty and Herbert. The two spent most of their hours in the domino shed behind the feedstore. It puzzled Trace as to why Hearndon, or for that matter anybody, would hire them, as they didn't really do any work. He wondered if in fact they actually were hired. For all he knew, they just showed up out of boredom and, thus, never had any intention of getting sore. But it didn't bother him. The old coots were entertaining. Shorty was a wiry bald man with a leathery complexion. He was spry for his age. Herbert was the opposite. Pudgy and pale and arthritic, he didn't seem capable of what work he did do. Though on occasion, Herbert would surprise you with how quick he could move when he was inspired. Both were sharp as tacks though.

"That there's some wisdom now, son. You know, Shorty would have been a college professor if it hadn't been for his pecker being so little. It's so little, they disqualified him. Why they call him Shorty."

Shorty handed Trace a section of pipe and fed the loops of barbed wire down into the T-shaped ditch.

"Run that through the loop and stomp it down in the bottom there."

Trace had figured out the idea, although he had never put in a brace before. He'd already dug the holes and put in the big cedar posts. Shorty had shown him how to bevel the top of the posts to let the rainwater drain off rather than seeping into the grain. Said it would make the posts last twice as long. Shorty put a length of galvanized pipe through the wire and started twisting it.

"Let's fill it in and start tamping. Dang if it ain't gonna come a storm."

Trace was down in the ditch and could barely see above the grass and brush, but when he looked up, the sky had turned dark gray in the west. Shorty continued twisting the wire, and Herbert was doing the same thing on the other side of the bracepost. Trace could see how it was locking the brace together. He got the ditch filled in and continued tamping on the dirt with a heavy iron rod. Shorty threw another loop of barbed wire around the post and tied off the twisting pipe. The three of them were hurrying now as the sky was growing dark quickly.

"You gotta watch Herbert. He seems to have altogether too much information about how big people's peckers are, if you get my meaning."

Wmearle had told Trace the story of the two men. They had served together in World War II in some kind of intelligence outfit. Both of them had been near forty years old when they went in. After the war they'd lost track of each other, and both had lost their wives. Shorty's had passed away, and Herbert's had run off on him. They'd met up and moved to West Texas and started playing dominoes for a living when they weren't off on some fishing expedition, which was often. Wmearle said both of them were absolute heroes, but you'd never know it being around them. It was a constant back and forth of insults, mostly about their manliness. Trace had a hard time featuring either of them as war heroes or spies, but he took Wmearle's word for it.

"That ain't gonna move on you."

"Don't the wire rust out before long?"

"Sooner or later. By the time it does, though, the fence will have settled in like concrete. It ain't gonna give."

Herbert was throwing tools and wire and whatnot into the truck. "We better get a move on, or we'll get blown away."

With that, he and Shorty got in their truck and spun off through the pasture. Trace stood in the dead air watching the cloud. There was a low brown dust cloud moving out of the base of it. The darkness that was falling had changed over to a yellowish green light. Trace had heard many times this meant there'd be hail in a cloud. He was stepping into the pickup when the first breeze hit his face with rain smell.

He didn't make it back to town. The wind hit first with a cloud of dirt. The mesquite trees with the fragile green leaves of spring were bending almost horizontal along the fencerow, and he was having a hard time keeping the truck between the ditches. Trace pulled off the road and into a wide yard. The Church of Christ preacher and his wife lived there. Trace exchanged pleasantries with them every Sunday, but other than the day he was baptized, he had never entertained a real conversation with the man. Then, of course, there was that night…

There was an empty shed behind the house, and he pulled under it just in time to see the shed lift off in front of him and go over the top of the pickup and shatter in the wind. There was a blinding sideways rain now, but he could see behind the house, the door to a cellar had lifted up, and a hand was motioning him to come and get in. The rain was stinging him in the face, and he felt like he was running at a forty-five-degree pitch when he got to the door and ducked in. The preacher drew down on a lever that locked the door in place, and they both stepped down into the underground room. The man's wife had a kerosene lantern lit, and they sat down on wooden benches along opposite sides of the little shelter. Trace was soaked and out of breath.

"I'm sure glad you heard me drive up."

"Ha, I didn't hear you. I heard the sound of the shed crashing and looked out to see what happened, and there you were."

"Well, howdy. I'm glad you did or I never would've seen you."

"Good to meet you. I'm Donis Weaver. This is my wife, Mae. You live in town, I guess."

Trace was confused. He had shaken hands with the man virtually every Sunday his whole life. Maybe he didn't recognize him being drenched, or for that matter, with a hat on, he thought.

"Yessir. I been out building fence for the Hearndons down the road. I was trying to get back when it hit. You know me. I'm Trace Clement."

Weaver had been the minister in their congregation since before Trace was born. Trace had always felt he was detached, and wondered often if he seemed detached to everyone else, or if it was just him. He was the same man he had seen standing with Mike's daddy and Sheriff Hardwicke and Fowler the night Junior was killed. He often wondered about him the way he wondered about most everyone; that is, does he remember only that when he sees me? Is that past? Or maybe he was simply in some kind of fog, a thinker. Trace never could figure him. Then he thought. Maybe he doesn't think about me at all. Maybe he doesn't even remember.

"Donis, you know Trace. Comes to church with Wmearle."

"Yes. Yes, of course. I'm sorry." He was scared. That's what it was. Scared of the storm.

The preacher was distracted and turned his head up toward the hole in the top of the cellar that ran up to a vent pipe. The sounds coming down the ventilation pipe changed abruptly. What had been a steady roar from the wind and rain suddenly sounded like grain falling out of an elevator. The three of them stared upward at the vent, wondering what was happening. It took Trace a minute or two to remember that he hated cellars. His eyes started darting around the nooks and crannies of the little room for snakes. Weaver saw him and picked up on his worry.

"I wouldn't worry about snakes or critters in here. Mae puts out mothballs and Comet. Rattlesnakes hate Comet."

"Never heard a that. Wonder what that is? Doesn't sound like rain or hail, either one."

Before long, the wind and the deafening sound from the vent pipe subsided, and they rose and opened the door. When they emerged from the ground, they found what looked like a foot of snow covering the ground. Trace reached down and scooped up a handful.

"It's little bitty hail."

The hail had been thrown into a huge drift across the back of the frame house. Above the line of the haildrift, the house had been sandblasted of paint, and Trace's pickup sat very nearly sideways from where he had left it. They each turned in circles to look out across the pastures surrounding the house where the driven hail had piled up, not behind as in a snowstorm, but in front of bushes and fences. At a glance, it looked as though a winter blizzard had passed, but the landscape was bathed in that strange greenish yellow light that was absorbed into and radiated out of the luminescent pearl-like hailstones. Above them and to the east, the cloud was almost black, and an unearthly constant roar boomed across the land.

"That's not thunder. That's the sound of hail crashing against itself up in that cloud. There's a horrible wind up in there. Come inside if you want to." Weaver headed toward the porch.

The house had inexplicably stayed put on its foundation, but inside, they found that the water had been driven through the siding of the frame house, especially around the ceiling where it had been forced up under the eaves. The wallpaper on the western side of the house was draped across the furniture and across the floor, and there was water on the board floors.

Trace suddenly remembered Shorty and Herbert. They had only been a couple of minutes ahead of him coming out of the pasture.

"Mr. Weaver. Ma'am. I just thought of something, and I need to get on down the road to check on it. Are you gonna be okay?"

"Yes, of course. It's all over with now. We've seen this bad and worse many a time. We'll be fine."

Trace moved toward the front door.

"Drop in on me if you're in the neighborhood sometime. I'd like to chat with you when things are a bit more peaceful."

"Yessir. Will do. Thanks for the shelter."

Trace spun for a bit in the slush before he got moving and slid out of the drive past the wreckage of the shed and onto the county road. It was a mile down the road when he saw Herbert's truck sitting out in a thicket of mesquite, all snapped just above the ground, the yellow insides of the shattered branches at odds with the rain-blacked bark. The fresh new leaves had been stripped from the mesquites, and Trace shook his head wondering what kind of wind would snap them like that. Herbert's truck was several yards out in the pasture lodged against the stump of one larger tree, the top of which was gone, and the haildrift was up the other side to the window level. The truck was plastered with wet dead grass. He hopped out quickly and picked through the mess of barbed wire that had been a fence on the other side of the ditch and made his way toward the truck. Just then, he heard them laughing hysterically inside the cab. Trace waded into the haildrift to the side window and brushed the ice away. He scared Shorty, who stopped his laughing abruptly and leaned away from the window as though he were under some kind of attack.

"Ha, you caught me off guard there, son," he said, rolling down the window. "I never expected you there just then. What in the hell are you doing wading around in all that?"

Trace had nothing to say. They looked to be having a good time.

"Shorty, don't be a asshole. Boy come to rescue us. Unless you're a mind to spend the night out here, you might show some appreciation. Ain't that right, Trace?"

"It's too far for the chain. I'll unspool some wire loops and see if I can drag you out. It's pretty slick."

"See there. Don't let him interrupt you or anything, Shorty. He's just going to tromp around out there in all that ice and corruption while you sit in here on your ass in the dry makin' up lies."

*****

When Trace got back to the trailer, Wmearle had already pulled it back upright with a gin-pole truck and was underneath jacking it back up to level. Trace jumped in and helped him finish the job. The insides were a mess. The trailer had been blown over almost on its side to where it rested against a light pole. Everything in the kitchen was out on the floor.

Wmearle heaved himself up from under the trailer. "Let's call thisun good and go in to the café and eat. We'll clean it up tomorrow."

When they'd finished eating, Trace told Wmearle about the preacher and how he had gotten in out of the storm and how he had found Shorty and Herbert.

"Those two were past the age of fighting when they signed on in the war. I don't know what kind of particular skills or background they had that caught somebody's attention, but they were in there in Europe a long time before the invasion started. They weren't soldiers, I don't think, but I'll tell you this, they were deadly people, and they ain't either one of 'em has any fear left in 'em…of anything, dyin' or otherwise. I expect both of 'em spent so much time expecting to get killed, they never thought about having so much life after it was all over with, so they never knew how to live again like a normal person. Anyhow, whatever it was they did, they got that fear of dyin' business out of their system for good. I expect getting tossed around in that storm struck them as funny as hell."

CHAPTER 7

Wmearle eased into a parking place in front of the long whitewashed stone fortress of the state hospital in Rusk. The hospital had originally been a state penitentiary, primarily for Negro prisoners. In truth, it had been a business, and not a very good one. Somebody had thought to make a lot of money in the pig iron business using prison laborers. The whole thing had been a big failure, and it had been converted into an asylum in 1910. It still looked like a prison, and there was a section that remained as a high-security facility for the criminally insane. They sat in the pickup looking at the building with its barred windows and chain-link screened balconies. It was the bleakest place they had ever seen.

The trip had been quiet. Wmearle had told Trace about the news from Rusk over breakfast one morning. He had offered it as a choice. Wmearle felt wholly out of his depth whenever it came to the family issues with Trace. Over the years, he had avoided it, and Trace had apparently segregated in his mind the pre and the post of his life. In seven years, he had never mentioned his brother and sister, even when they had traveled to Carthage for two funerals in the space of a year. Trace had been stoic. Wmearle wondered at the time if all the emotion had been scalded out of him. He was an enigma. The boy seemed happy and attached and gregarious, but it was as though he had aged into a man all at once and had only adults for friends. He got along all right at school, but he didn't run with the kids or play on any of the sports teams, and as soon as he got that pickup under him, he had moved on to the affairs of men. It was pretty clear that the kids in school were fine with that arrangement. What was in his mind about what happened with Junior and his mother and whatever had gone on in the years before that, he had never once mentioned, saving that one moment when Judge Reynolds had delivered him to Wmearle after Junior's burial, and he had turned and demanded to know how the two younger ones would be cared for. Judge Reynolds had answered every question, and finally, Trace had stopped, seemingly satisfied, and only said, "All right then."

He had been the same over this. He left that morning to feed as he always did, without responding to what Wmearle told him. Two days later, when he came in from building fence with Shorty and Herbert, he ate and washed the dishes, and before he headed for his room in the end of the trailer, he said, "We better go out there and see her."

The doctor had been direct with Wmearle about Stella. He wanted no misunderstanding about what the boy would find when they got there, so Wmearle had tried his best to lay it out for Trace while they made their way down through the piney woods toward Rusk.

"He used the word *anxiety* a lot. He said it kept getting worse and worse where she would get anxious, and it would kind of run away with her. They gave her medicine for it, but it just kept getting worse to where she got to where she didn't get over it. Son, she was hurting herself. He told me after a while she didn't know where she was at and retreated back in her own mind. It was like she kept building up in her mind whatever was making her anxious, but she got where she never said whatever it was, just started getting wound up again. He said she's in a sorry state."

"Sorry state how?"

"She got where she was just kind of froze up. They had to dope her up to get her to relax. I mean to relax her muscles. She'd get where she was all tightened up in a knot. He said she finally got that way and stayed that way all the time. He said she's got where her brain ain't functioning proper anymore, and she's declining other ways, like her body is starting to stop working right. Son, she ain't ever goin' to get better. He said she won't live too much longer. He said you need to prepare yourself 'cause she's a sad sight to see."

"Is she awake?"

"He said she don't hardly ever go to sleep unless they just dope her up to where they're worried it'll cause her to have a heart attack and die. So I expect, yeah, she might be awake. He said she talks sometimes, but when she does, she talks real fast, and it don't make any sense what she says, like it's all just spilling out of her random-like. The doctor is scared about you going in there 'cause you're young, and he don't know you, and he's afraid it will be hard on you. He said to tell you they got her in a bed, and she's tied down."

"Tied down?"

"He said they had to tie her up certain ways to keep her from drawing up and tying herself in a knot. He said it's painful, like her muscles are straining all the time, so they gotta bind her up. He wanted me to tell you that, so you weren't thinking they were bein' mean to her."

Wmearle watched Trace sitting there, staring at the white stone building. He hadn't seen it before until now how Trace had the same expression in his eyes as Fowler, the same set to his jaw as out of some reservoir of abject determination.

"All right then. We better go on in."

It was wet. The moisture in the air was thick, and there were smells that neither were used to. Pine smell, weeds. They'd seen some dogwoods blooming under the woods on the way, and it seemed like springtime was well advanced here. The pine scent gave way to a severe antiseptic alcohol smell when they walked into the small waiting room. A black man in a white orderly's outfit asked their names and picked up the telephone. A small balding man in a suit soon appeared and introduced himself as Dr. Winters.

"Mr. Franklin has shared with you your mother's condition?"

"Yes."

"I'm sorry. I regret that we haven't been able to do more for her."

He led them down a wide hallway with shiny floors. They could hear moaning sounds from various directions up and down the long hallway.

"What are those things on her hands?"

Stella's hands were wrapped in gauze bandages. Large plastic curlers were tied inside, and her wrists were wrapped in towels that were, in turn, wrapped with strapping that was tied to the bed. She had very little hair, and what there was was short and matted in sweat. Her skin was pale, translucent, the small blood vessels visible right below the surface. She wore a clinched, focused expression as though she were sorting through a thousand frustrations, her eyes focused on some indefinite point of space. Her jaw flexed, apparently toothless, as her mouth and cheeks protruded unnaturally.

Trace could see the outlines of how he remembered her. She had always been thin, though not frail. He had ceased classifying the things he remembered of them as good memories and bad memories. In his private thoughts, he had gotten to where he thought he understood them both. There had, at least back then, been the thought that she had driven him to drink with her compulsions and her impossible dreams of some plantation-like wealth. Then conversely, that he had driven her to the edge of insanity with his drunken rampages. And he could remember it all. It seemed as though he could remember in such detail that it were as though he could watch a movie and play it back with smells and sounds and weather and time. Junior had been like a boy at times. He played with them and worked puzzles and bought Trace a .22 when he got to the first grade and taught him to shoot it. He was a boy in business too, and had thrown away his birthright in a final horrible fight with Fowler and then proceeded to trade on the very name he had repudiated to start farming cotton until he'd lost even that with the bankers and speculators and had bankrupted himself and gone back to Fowler to bail him out, and Leticia had written the check herself against Fowler, and he had then begun the whole process again to bankrupt himself yet again a second time, and he knew it, and he knew that he would be back up at the ranch again to beg them, and so he started drinking to dull the dread of it. And her, who cherished her dignity above all else, bankrupted along with him, and having to go every Sunday to that church with everyone knowing it, and then, even knowing how Fowler had bailed them out of it, trying to hold on to the manners and the behaviors of the righteous, and him not even letting her repair that by becoming an alcoholic for everyone to see and wasting away the money Leticia had given them.

And so she would take the children's clothes and scrub them until they were bare, and keep scrubbing them long after they were clean until her fingers would bleed, as though there were some latent stain that resisted everything. And the final insult when Junior started beating her, and that being an even worse insult to that precious dignity, and so she would repair the broken furniture and order dishes to replace the broken ones through the catalog rather than driving into the hardware store where people would know, and still Junior kept coming because he knew, as well as he knew he would be back out to that ranch to get Leticia to bail him back out, that Stella's dignity would never be assuaged or even satisfied. And Trace watching it all, and even seven years old, old enough to see where it would end. He did not see them anymore as good or bad or Junior and Stella, but as a single thing, indivisible, relieved of the him and her and good and bad, and all of it mixed together and impossible to overcome. And so he traced the outlines of her forehead and remembered that he hadn't stopped loving either her or Junior either one. He brushed his hand gently across her forehead.

"The muscles in her hands are involuntarily flexed. We put those curlers there to keep her fingers from digging into the flesh of her hands. They have holes in them so some air can circulate through. We can tell it is very painful for her. Therapists would try for a long time to work her fingers to loosen up the muscles, but it would just cause her unnecessary pain. The padding around those plastic curlers keeps her from cutting off the circulation in her skin. Infection is of great danger to her now."

Trace leaned over the bed and tried to put himself in her line of vision. There may have been some slight change in her focus or expression, but it was merely as though her mind had moved to a different room in a different house. Trace waited a long while, but there was no more change. He stood back from the bed and closed his eyes for several seconds.

"Doctor, I thank you for taking care of her the way you have. It's much appreciated."

With that, he turned and walked past Wmearle and out the door and through the waiting room, put his hat back on, and stepped out onto the sidewalk into the hazy bright spring air. When Wmearle caught up to him, he saw that his legs were trembling.

CHAPTER 8

May 1964

Donis Weaver was out in his driveway when Trace pulled in. He had the beginnings of a frame for a new shed laid out on the caliche driveway. Trace stepped out of the pickup and surveyed the work. Weaver was apparently not a man handy with carpentry. He laid down his pencil and square and pushed his glasses back up his nose.

"Young man! You have excellent timing."

"How's that?"

"You are a perfect excuse for me to quit and go in and get a glass of tea. Will you have a glass with me?"

"You bet. My partners didn't show up for work today. What we had planned is not a one-man job. So I quit too."

Weaver told Trace to take a seat on the porch and poked his head in the screen door.

Trace sat down in a painted wicker chair, and Weaver took a spot on the porch swing. He wore a floppy straw hat that he had sweated through. He took it off and laid it beside him. His hair was stringy and matted, and his face was red.

"Mae's making us a glass. She'll bring it out. Now, I owe you an apology. I didn't recognize you the other day when you came in out of the storm."

"That's all right. It was pretty wild there for a little bit."

"I get rattled in a bad storm. We came down here from Oklahoma in 1948. Lived in Woodward. Our house there got blown away. That one was a tornado, though. Lost pretty much everything. Anyhow, I was a little excited the other day. In fact, I was scared to death. I'm sorry."

"Could you use a hand with the shed?"

"Ha. I suppose I could. I'm useless as can be with things like that. But no. No thanks. I need to do it myself. Good for me to get out and use my hands a bit. I get stiff from sitting at my desk all day."

"You work on your sermons?"

"Oh no. Well, I do. But that doesn't take much time for me anymore. Used to spend all week on one, but I guess I'm not exactly plowing any new ground nowadays. I have a hobby of sorts. I've been making a study of the Indians that lived in this part of the world. Sanaco, Ka Tum Seh, Buffalo Hump, Parker, Satanta. People like that. It's a hobby. Me and Mae will go visit places sometimes where things happened. I've always found it interesting."

"I heard of Buffalo Hump. They had a picture of him in a schoolbook."

"Parker was the interesting one. Ever heard of him?"

"No."

"He was the son of a kidnapped white woman and a chief named Peta Nocona, as far as the Comanche had chiefs anyway. They had smaller bands, and Nocona was the head of the band. Quanah Parker was his son. Some say Quanah watched Peta get killed by Sul Ross up on the Pease River. Quanah disputed that. Anyhow, he got away and escaped back up into the Comancheria, which is what the territory we're in now used to be. Goes all the way to Santa Fe and up into Colorado. Back in those days, Comancheria was about as dangerous a place as a man could find himself in. Quanah became the leader of his own band when he grew up. In all my studying about the natives, he is the singular character that fascinates me."

Mae brought two glasses of sweet tea and handed them out.

"You get to talking about Indians with Donis, you'll be here all night."

"Thank you, ma'am."

"Why him?"

Weaver leaned back and drifted his eyes across the mesquite flats. There was the very slightest hint of green resprouting in the mesquite brush.

"It was the change. The adaptation. You have to understand first what he was. He was a wild free man. Maybe wilder and freer than we can conceptualize. Fierce. He ranged over a territory that was as big as Texas itself. All the Comanche were astonishing horse-people. They would raid far into South Texas and escape far up into the panhandle. And they would ride for days and days on end, covering vast distances. They would raid and steal horses and kidnap people, and they would murder and torture as well, brutality the likes of which we can't feature. But they were brutalized too. It was a clash of peoples across all this wide country, and they were hard, hard people, both the whites and the Comanche. They knew every square inch of the country. You can try, but you can't really understand them, what it was like to be out in it, a part of, this kind of land, the thorns and the storms, and the cold and the hot, and drought and floods, sandstorms, blizzards, and bugs, and them always out in it, always adapting to it and prevailing over it. Knowing no better and not wanting to know any different. They lived, loved, killed, had a whole way of being. If you had found yourself sitting right where you are back then and you saw him, you were as good as dead. He would have been an absolutely terrifying thing to behold. He was a big man. Lean. Strong. His face black with war paint. And he was the toughest and the smartest of all of them. He outwitted the best of them, the most dangerous and determined men the United States could throw at him. He just took his whole band—men, women and children, horses, all their worldly belongings—and he led them up and down that caprock over and over and out onto the Llano and back again, and how they did it, no one will ever really know, but he outfoxed them, escaped capture and wore them down. The Comanche were the kings of this part of the world for a couple of hundred years, but all of them were eventually rounded up except him and his band. Quanah was the last of them to capitulate and go onto the reservation."

"So he did get captured?"

"No. He never did. He was out in that country west of Snyder, Gail, I think, or thereabouts, anyway back out on that caprock country. Nobody was after him at the time. He went out by himself alone and thought for several days about it and sent word that he was going to the reservation."

"He gave up."

"I'm not sure if it *was* giving up. To him anyway. That was what was unique about him. The adaptation. You and me might think about it being a fight over land or culture or some existential or moral battle. I don't think he would have seen it that way. To him, it was never about the land or the culture, and least of all about power. You have to imagine the life, the way he lived out in this place. There was no time their existence was not threatened, white man or not. He adapted all the time to whatever came. He exploited the possibilities that were before him without recourse to some demand of his heritage. White people were probably just the next thing to come at him, providing opportunities and danger and threat, but opportunity still, and he adapted to what was, as though what was before had no claim on him. Can you imagine being that free, that wild, so as to be able to see it that way, so unburdened by what was past?"

"But he went on the reservation?"

"He did, but not like the others. He was successful there. Built a house. Became a successful rancher, even wealthy by some accounts. Hobnobbed with presidents and famous people. Traveled to the big cities and came back. I can't even imagine it. How he acclimated himself to a life so completely foreign to him and not only survived, it wasn't a matter of perseverance, he prospered, he flourished. Enough that he did a good bit to take care of the Comanche people that were on the reservation. I don't know of another character in human history that thrived the way he did in two diametrically opposite patterns of life."

"You say his mother was a white woman?"

"Ah. So perhaps because he had the white blood in him, it wasn't so hard for him? Is that what you mean? Maybe, but I don't think so. He was Comanche through and through. Is there power in blood?

Maybe. Maybe way down deep in a soul, the abilities of one race and the abilities of another matter. I don't know."

He sipped his tea, and they were silent for a long while. Thinking on it. Yellowjackets were starting a nest in a corner of the porch ceiling.

"You know, life always flourishes on the margins, the edge of one thing where it becomes another. You'll find more game at the edge of the brush than you will either in the thick of it or out on the open prairie. Whether it's birds or fish or animals, they find a spot where they can dart in and out of one thing and into the other. They live on the edge of things and exploit two alternatives. If the white blood had anything to do with Quanah, maybe it was that, that it made his ability to adapt that much sharper. Anyhow, I often think about those days he spent alone out there on the caprock, looking out so far across the vast land. What kind of things would a man like him think about? What did he desire?

I understand you went out to see your mother last week. I'm mighty sorry. I expect that was trying."

"How'd you know about that? Wmearle?"

"No. Your grandfather told me about it."

"Figures."

"Yes. I've strayed into something that's personal. Sorry."

"It don't matter. I know he checks up on me. I see him talking to Wmearle sometimes. It ain't no surprise to me."

"He's a complicated man."

"Wouldn't know. I ain't exchanged two words with him since before Daddy got killed. It ain't like I know him."

Weaver sipped his tea and watched a hawk cruising low over the pasture.

"Anyhow, yes. She's in sorry shape. I don't expect she's long for the world. I don't even know if she knows anything. Ain't nothing can be done."

"I'd venture to say that's not exactly true."

"You hadn't seen her."

"That's not what I mean exactly. I know. Her course may be decided. But yours isn't. What you do matters. It matters for you."

"I cain't see it. What's done is done."

"You know better than that, or I've been neglecting my preaching. You can pray about it. You can love her. None of that might change her, but it can still change you. That matters."

"That's true enough."

"You don't hold it against her, what she did?"

"Ain't no point. Cain't undo it."

"What about him? Your daddy, I mean."

"Same, I guess. It don't do no good to stew on it. He did what he did, and she did what she did. It was a long time ago anyhow."

"You're a better man than me. I'd be mad as hell at both of them. I'd be mad as hell at Fowler and Leticia Clement, and I'd be mad as hell at the whole world."

"Like I said. It don't do no good. They're gone. I cain't change any of it."

"Fowler and Leticia aren't gone."

"May as well be, for all it matters to me. They ain't got nothing to do with me."

"But you just said he checks up on you. That it didn't surprise you."

"It don't. But that…what he does is his own business."

Weaver was stymied. The boy in front of him had the identical gray eyes and the determined set to his jaw. He was unweathered and unbent by time and labor and regret, but it was as though Fowler himself were sitting in the chair, as in fact Fowler *had* done many times. She was there too, in his face, the cheekbones, something, and Leticia too. His face was like an old European tapestry with the whole tragic story laid out before him to see all at one time, but the characters still ongoing and unfulfilled because Trace wasn't done yet. Still undefeated, as Fowler was undefeated, still coming, still fighting to see it made right.

He remembered him that night in the front yard standing in the glow of the light spilling out of the screen door beyond which Junior lay prostrate on the dinner table. Fowler had walked out of the light of the doorway and stood and pointed at Claude Hardwicke and said, "I want no prosecution of this woman. She was justified." He had then turned to look at Weaver. "Did you know? Did you know she was this bad?" And he'd lied to him… "No." And then to George Wakefield… "Can you care for the children tonight?" And with that, he had walked away as though he were walking down into his own grave.

And he remembered her that next morning, sitting in the front room of the house with the other ladies in perfect silence. He had visited hundreds of new widows in his years as a minister, but never a murderess. Even as he climbed the steps onto the front porch, he had no idea what words he would say to her. And so he had merely sat down and placed his hand on her forearm. She had been rigid, with an almost imperceptible tremor, and ignoring him, began to pick at a loose button thread on her skirt. As though amongst all the calamity that she had wrought, all the shame and the grasping to recover that precious, hopeless glimmer of dignity, there remained only this last small thread to thwart her undertaking. She became more and more animated and finally reached over to the table by the couch and retrieved her handbag and produced a small set of clippers and clipped the errant thread and carefully placed the small length of thread inside a pocket of her change purse, as though even that could not be completely absolved and disposed of, then began smoothing over the top of the button where this latest affront had been cauterized. And he had thought then that she was broken, that her mind had failed.

And the boy now before him, the physical manifestation of that tapestry—ambivalent, diffident even behind his facade. He remembered him too with the same light of the doorway illuminating the three small tragic faces in the seat of that pickup, and Trace alone among the three in understanding what had happened, and him stoic, alert, and seeming older than the seven years.

"It is, and what you do is yours. I'm not saying any different."

"Well, what then?"

"You're right. At least as far as the past goes. We can't change it. But that is the burden of being human, that we have a memory that is part of our present. You think a coyote or a hawk that gets its dinner stolen by another animal resents it? Gets angry about it? He doesn't. He just starts looking for dinner again."

"You think Quanah was like that? Just like a animal? That he never remembered all the things white people did chasing him all over creation and all the brutality they inflicted on him, and that's why he just turned around one day and changed?"

"No. Nothing of the sort. In fact, quite the opposite. He couldn't have ever forgotten. He might not even have known it was forgiveness, but it was the genius of it that he somehow took all that, all of what he was and had been and what had happened to him and what he had done, and made out of the materials of that, a new life. It was no less a part of him, and I don't think he denied it to himself, but he moved forward nonetheless."

"Well then, he had to forgive them, or else he couldn't have stood to be around them."

"Forgiving is not forgetting. Forgive and forget shouldn't have ever even been combined together at the same time at all, because you can't forgive if you forget, not really. To forgive you have to see the same thing in another person that you have in yourself, to suffer for it even. Because that line between right and wrong cuts straight through the middle of everybody, you included, and you can't forgive another human being without knowing that. You figure out how to see that and accept it, and then if you hold something against somebody else, you find out you can't do that without holding it against yourself. You might try to bury that, but you can't do it."

The light was failing, and several barn swallows were dipping in under the porch to spit their mud onto the beginnings of a new nest.

"But what if it ain't up to you? What if he just saw there wasn't no other way?"

"A lot of people *are* weak. Of that, there's no doubt. People can get beaten down to where they can't get up, and so they do capitulate, give up. But he never was that. That never was an option with him anymore than it is for you, or for that matter, Fowler Clement."

"No. I know *he* ain't weak. I know that. I remember him some. From before. But I cain't make things go back to where they were, and he sure don't seem to want to."

"I imagine he does seem strong from where you stand. And he is. As strong a man as I ever knew. But that doesn't mean he doesn't have his own battles, his own torments."

"Like I said, I wouldn't know nothin' about that."

"Surely you do. It's not only him you've never spoken to. How do you know it's even what he wants? How do you presume to know that he's given up?"

"It'll be eight years in August. I expect that's plenty of time for both of 'em to've made up their minds."

Weaver swung gently back and forth and drank his tea. It was turning into a pleasant evening. He thought it was unusual that the boy seemed comfortable, perhaps even more comfortable than himself, with silence that didn't need to be filled. They sat for a long while watching the swallows and listening to the first evening coyote calls.

"Time's an odd thing. Some things, it spreads out, diffuses, the memory fades, a person gets new perspectives. Other things amplify. They sharpen with each passing day."

"If you're building a fence, things set. Like concrete sets up."

"Ha, you're right about that. I suppose there's one other option for you to consider. Some things have a finite duration, and then they're done."

Trace leaned back in the chair. The moisture from his glass had seeped into his jeans, and the ice was near melted. It was almost dark.

"I think you should let me and some of my buddies come over here and build that shed for you."

"I appreciate that. But I'm going to try to do it myself. It'll be good for me."

"I oughtta run. Wmearle will wonder what happened to me. Can you thank Mrs. Weaver for the tea?"

"Certainly. Enjoyed the visit. Come again."

Trace eased out of the drive and turned his headlamps on. Weaver could see in the light that his windshield looked like a spiderweb from the hailstorm.

He sat in the dark, easing the swing back and forth, listening to the dove calling in the trees and thought about Leticia. He had gone out there earlier that very morning to see her. Fowler had given him instructions about when to go and to take his cues from Juanita. He was nervous, as he usually was when he visited her, and so he paced back and forth in the big hallway until Juanita came down and nodded and directed him up to her room. Leticia's eyes followed him as he crossed the room, the faint smell of waste and disinfectant and the air freshener still in the air and her propped up with her hair done up as best it could be. He would sit and read a devotional passage to her and some scripture and say a prayer, and when he opened his eyes, hers were still there, unblinking, penetrating. He would excuse himself and walk down the stairs past the library where Fowler's chair sat angled toward the stone fireplace. He could see Fowler's Bible on the table next to the chair and a blanket draped over one arm. Fowler had slept there.

CHAPTER 9

August 1926

Fowler stepped off the train onto a dusty platform. The heat was oppressive, so much so that he felt shivers momentarily. The station was busy. Mule teams, oilfield trucks, and the occasional car were moving in all directions. A lot was happening, and Monahans didn't resemble the empty place he remembered. He knew no one.

He had been nearly cash broke in the early summer of 1926 and had stayed in New Haven to work through the summer. The call from Bill Reynolds in late July had changed everything. Oscar Yates had brought a well in on what Fowler's father had called his "savings account."

Fowler turned and could see Reynolds working his way down the platform through the various crates and belongings of the workers fogging into the latest discovery. Reynolds was Fowler's age, but where he had been out of law school for two years now and was building a legal practice in the oilfield, Fowler was still two years from finishing his degree. Reynolds had helped in the sale of the trucking company Fowler had started when he was sixteen with a team of mules. Walker Clement had moved his family from strike to strike as a physician employed by the majors, treating the oilfield hands with the amputations and venereal outbreaks and fevers that would spring up out of the filth of the tent cities. Fowler had loved it, the wildness and the expectation and the sheer creation that the strikes provoked. He had soured on the promotors and speculators, but as a child, the roughnecks and the laborers had been his heroes and his teachers. As they moved across Texas with each successive strike, he had started, at first driving wagons, then owning them. In time, he added to his teams, then later his fleets. Walker had extracted a promise from Fowler that he would be educated, and six years later, Fowler had capitulated to that promise and sold out, heading east for college.

"You're looking fine, Fowler. Fine. A little skinnier than when I saw you last."

"Good seeing you, Bill. You're looking dapper."

"Think I look like a promotor?" He smiled broadly.

"Maybe a little bit."

That was an old joke between them. Fowler detested the promoters who had followed the Texas oil fields. He had defined them one time for Reynolds as a person who looks rich but drives and wears everything he owns.

Fowler took the short-brimmed Stetson in his hand and wiped his forehead with a handkerchief.

"Where we headed?"

"Odessa. I've got two rooms at the hotel. I'll bet you're pooped."

"I am that. If we're going to Odessa, why didn't you just pick me up there?"

"Long story. I'll tell it to you on the way."

Fowler heaved his satchel into the bed of Reynold's Model T Roadster and hopped in. Once they got going, he put his hat in his lap and held his head out the window into the wind, cooling the sweat in his hair.

"This have something to do with Mooney?"

"You're quick."

"He's turned into quite the gangster since you left. He's got gambling and whorehouses and dope peddling going on in every field in four counties. Been bringing liquor up from Mexico. Operating now out of a tent over at the camp at Wink. He's got a bunch of thugs on the payroll now, and they've gotten to be a pretty dangerous bunch. He hasn't forgotten the spat you two had. In fact, he's got a man sitting in the lobby at the hotel that's just there to keep an eye out. Same at the train station in Odessa. Hence, the extra drive."

"Looking for me?"

"Oh no, no, not just for you. Just for general snooping. If they see a mark, they report in. But if they see you, Mooney will know about it pretty quick. You shamed him when you gave him that beating, Fowler. And a lot of people saw you do it. He hasn't gotten over it. He knows you're coming though. Probably somebody listening when we were on the telephone. We'll go in the back door, and he won't be the wiser. How long are you going to be around?"

"I don't have time to linger. I'll need to get over to San Angelo and check in on the folks. So not more than a day or so. Then I need to head back east. Now, fill me in."

"Fowler, your daddy gave you some pretty fine advice sticking your money into that land. I know he never featured anything like this, nor you either, but it sure turned out to be a wise move. You've done a thousand times better with that property than you'd have done in a lifetime running your old outfit. The property is checkerboarded every which way now. They're all trading and swapping. The big boys can't keep up with it, so they're buying and farming it out to the independents, and they're farming it out to the drillers. Yates even took himself out today. Marland, Pure, Texon, Magnolia... It's chopped up into fifty different pieces now, and everybody is drilling. The ladies at the courthouse must be pulling their hair out. You've got an account at the bank in Midland with ten dollars in it, and I have three parties set up to talk to tomorrow. It'll be sold before noon. You still set on keeping half?"

"Yes. Who are we talking to?"

"It'll be Humble, Roxana, that's Shell...Dutch money, and Gulf. I kept it to three as you specified."

"They're not going to be bothered by all the trading and swapping going on on the lease?"

"No, they'll be cleaning all that up in due time. They'll buy it all back before it's all said and done."

"What's your gut on the value?"

"I expect you'll get three, for half."

Reynolds had been waiting for that part. He wanted to see the expression on Fowler's face when he heard it. He had not been practicing for very long, but it was always interesting to him to see how the smell of fortune acted on a man, and Fowler Clement was still young.

"And the surface?"

"I'd let it go with it. It'll be worthless anyway. The place is going to be row-cropped within a year. They'll pay you something, but it won't matter."

He hadn't even flinched. Those soft gray eyes had a calm about them. Reynolds had the impression Fowler had only half of his consciousness involved in the conversation, the other engaged elsewhere.

"Something else on your mind?"

"You wouldn't happen to know the whereabouts of that Ranger? Captain. Operates out of Fort Stockton or Alpine. I can't recall his name."

"He's around. He'll gather up a crew and clean things out from time to time. He gives Mooney hell with the liquor coming up from Ojinaga and La Linda, but it hasn't really slowed him up. They're hauling it up on mules. He lost three men down between Marathon and La Linda a year back. They were going to ambush the Mexicans and got themselves ambushed instead. Out in the middle of nowhere. What does he have to do with anything?"

"I'm not walking in anybody's back door."

*****

Fowler strode straight toward the man sitting in the hotel lobby.
"I'm Fowler Clement. Tell Mooney I'm checking in."

Reynolds handed him the key and watched the man put his newspaper aside, get up and walk out the front door. When they reached the landing at the top of the stairs, Fowler slowed as they approached the door to Reynold's room.

"So I suppose my circumspection was lost on you?"

"Mooney's a thug, Bill. There's no point in trying to hide from him. I think I'll head on to San Angelo now if it's all right. I'll be back

69

before daylight. Can you lend me the use of the Ford?" Reynolds nodded. "Keep one eye open tonight. I don't want you getting caught in the crossfire."

"Aren't you going to want to drive out there and even see the place?"

Fowler paused with a quizzical expression on his face, then chuckled, then broke out in a deep laugh.

Reynolds understood. Fowler had only seen the land the one time, the day before they closed on it two years ago. Based on his father's advice, the property had been no more than a place for Fowler to park his money safely while he would be away. They had never anticipated that the strike a hundred miles to the east would walk itself upward and westward into that arid wasteland. But it had. The inexorable momentum of the Permian Basin boom was about to make Fowler an extremely wealthy man, and he would have become so almost without any attachment to the land itself.

"I've seen the oil patch."

*****

The lights were still on when Fowler pulled into the lane and passed through the pecan orchard that flanked the Concho River. Walker Clement was sitting on the porch just as he had been when Fowler had left for New Haven two years back. He stepped out onto the gravel and quietly mounted the porch, then held his finger to his lips as he passed Walker, and slowly opened the screen door. Walker smiled as he heard the outburst from the kitchen. Shortly, Fowler stepped back out onto the porch and sat down opposite Walker. The heat was lifting, and the night sounds from the river were drifting through the trees. Lightning bugs were flitting about in the twilight.

"How are you, Dad?"

"Look around. I'd say I'm about as good as a man can be right now."

"It's a peaceful spot. Doesn't seem like we're in town. Mother's looking good."

"We're both glad to be out of the camps. If anything, it's still hard for us to get to sleep at night with all the peace and quiet, except for the frogs chirping. The church is going to have a big picnic there by the river Saturday. She's already starting on her pies."

"I noticed she's gone into the pickle business."

"Good Lord, yes. The cucumbers won't stop making, so she keeps canning. We'll be pickle rich the rest of our lives. I don't know if the house will ever smell right again. You didn't call ahead. What's got you all the way back here right before school starts back?"

"Business. A lot has happened, and I haven't had..." Fowler stopped. Walker had a peeve against saying you didn't have time to do this or that. In his way of seeing things, everybody had all the time they needed but were in conflict with their chosen priorities. "I wanted to tell you about what's happened with the property out at Monahans. I leased it out last fall. They spudded the first well back in February. Dad, it came in a good one. Bill Reynolds has been running the show for me, and right now, the whole place is completely covered up with rigs. I'm going to make a deal with somebody tomorrow to sell half the minerals."

"I imagine you're talking about a sizeable amount of money."

Fowler sat back in his chair and balanced his hat on the porch rail.

"I never expected to be where I am. At least not right now. This all happened pretty fast. Yessir, it's a sizeable amount. In fact, it's a fortune."

Walker frowned.

"I'm going back. I'll finish out. I just needed to come in and get this deal done."

"Son, I know that. Ha, I never would have guessed that I'd worry more about you keeping your promises than I do that you won't keep them. Every now and then people do change their minds. Sometimes I wonder if you've got your honor confused with plain old stubbornness." He smiled. "If this means what I assume it means, then I'm not sure what two more years of college is going to matter to you."

"I know. But it's not that entirely. I truly don't know what I'll do next. This all caught me off guard. I need some time to think about it, and I can do that just fine in New Haven. But I did promise you."

They sat for a long time listening to the frogs and whip-poor-wills. There was an ever-so-slight damp rising out of the river bottom, and the mosquitos were beginning to thicken.

"What will you do with the money? You know what I've told you about these bankers."

"I expect I'll do the same with this as I did last time. I'll get Bill to looking for some options."

"Well, these are unsteady times. I expect you can't go wrong with that. At least, if everything else goes to hell, you'll have a place to grow pickles!"

"And what about you? You're not settling into a life of leisure, are you?"

"More leisurely. I've set up here in town. It's not very exciting, but I've had enough excitement. It's good to have a permanent roof over our heads. I still get calls in the middle of the night, but it's more often a baby coming than anything else."

"Well, now for the bad news. I've got to head back tonight. I can't stay. Bill's got me set up with some oil people first thing in the morning."

"You better get in there then and visit with your mother. Talk her into cuttin' one of those pies, and I'll be in there to help you with it."

An hour later, Fowler grabbed his hat and hugged his mother.

"I'll walk you out," said Walker.

They stepped out of the porchlight and into the soft moonlight filtering through the pecans. Fowler stepped into the Roadster and shut the door behind him.

"Son, how long has it been since you slept?"

"Too long. I got a nap on the train this morning before it got hot. I'll be all right."

"Who was that you rang on the telephone?"

"Don't worry about it, Dad. I'm just getting out ahead of some trouble in Odessa. I don't think it'll be anything."

"Don't go to sleep. I love you, son."

*****

It was almost five o'clock when Fowler parked the Roadster in front of the hotel in Odessa and walked into the lobby. He glanced at the row of leather chairs against the lobby wall. There was no one there. The young clerk behind the counter lifted the countertop, ducked under it, and hurried across the lobby toward Fowler.

"Are you Mr. Clement?"

"I am."

"There was some trouble earlier. Mr. Reynolds told me to tell you he is at the clinic. It's up the street two blocks."

Fowler didn't have to ask what kind of trouble. He hurried out and started up the sidewalk. Then, seeing the dark streets mostly deserted, thought better and went back and took Reynolds's Ford.

The clinic was the only storefront on the block with the lights still on. He walked in and smelled the strong antiseptic odor of a hospital. The nurse behind the desk had a small reading lamp and a book spread in front of her.

"William Reynolds?"

"Who are you?"

"I'm Fowler Clement. He's my friend."

"I'll walk you."

Bill Reynolds had been beaten badly. There was a large bandage over his left eye. The two black eyes were the result of a broken nose. There was a wrapping around his chest that suggested there were broken ribs.

"You told me to sleep with one eye open. I failed."

Fowler had death itself in his eyes.

"Don't get worked up. I'm fine. There's nothing done here that won't heal over."

"Bill, I'm sorry. I never guessed Mooney would move that fast. Was it him or his boys?"

"I couldn't honestly tell you. When I woke up, they were in the room with me, and it was dark. I think three, but I was out

73

cold before I knew what was happening. I doubt it would have been Mooney himself. They were probably just mad because you weren't there yourself. If it hadn't been me, they'd have gotten you, and they might not have gone as easy on you. See what I mean by circumspect?"

"You're right. I never meant to get you into this."

"Get me up."

"Why?"

"We've got to get ready for the meeting. It might take a while to get me presentable."

Fowler tried to push him back down.

"Listen, you were right too. We're going to walk down the street to the bank in the morning in broad daylight with Mooney's thugs watching and do the deal."

Reynolds had been correct. By the time he got dressed, he had sweated out a new starched shirt from the strain. Still, he looked horrible when they walked into the meeting with the oil people the next morning, and Fowler was astonished that he could proceed through the three hours of negotiations as though he weren't in pain.

When the oil people left, Reynolds passed the draft across the table.

"Ponder that for a moment, Fowler."

Fowler stared at the draft. Reynolds saw the same calm in his eyes he had seen the day before, apparently unchanged by three and a half million dollars.

"Let's get you out of here. Can you handle the ride to San Angelo?"

"Why would I do that?"

"You need some time to heal up, and I want you out of Mooney Thornton's reach."

*****

Fowler stepped out of the Ford into the hot desert scrub. It had been dark for an hour, and the temperature was still over a hundred degrees. His face was windburnt from almost twelve hours of driving.

The Ranger was sitting in the door of his truck smoking a cigarette. He could see the camp tents at Wink glowing along the horizon two miles distant. The man appeared to be unarmed and without any badge or other indication he was a Texas Ranger.

"So it'll just be me and you?"

"If we go about it right, that's all we'll need," said the Ranger.

Fowler jumped in his roadster. The flat bed held saddles and tack, a half dozen ammunition boxes, and a large wooden crate. When they reached the edge of the camp, the Ranger pulled up and turned to Fowler.

"Thornton will have men around, but they're not ready, and they're not as mean as they think they are. He's got a pretty good-size tent set up right in the middle of the camp. There'll be a couple outside, and I'll take care of them. I'm going to slide straight up to the front door. When we stop, you just hop out and go to cuttin' those cords." He handed him a large combat-style knife. "This'll cut through 'em fast. Don't cut yourself, it's sharp. I'll take care of anybody outside that tent. So if you see somebody, just keep cuttin' fast as you can. Don't get distracted."

"Then?"

The Ranger pointed to two heavy wooden clubs under the seat. "Once you get that tent collapsed, just go to conkin' ever head you see raise up. It won't take long."

*****

It was over as fast as the Ranger had said it would be. When they pulled the collapsed tent back, there were eight unconscious men lying on the floor. Of them, Fowler was only certain that he'd hit two. The Ranger went back to the Roadster and opened the wooden crate. Fowler gawked at the arsenal—a Thompson submachinegun, a Winchester rifle, several pump shotguns and Colt automatics, some dynamite and a large bundle of wire snares. The Ranger took the snares and began cinching up the feet and hands of the unconscious men. He worked fast, and Mooney was the last. A crowd began gathering in the long open area that was used as a road. The Ranger took the Thompson out of the box and handed a pump shotgun to Fowler.

"Ain't nobody gonna bother us. I just want to keep some distance while we get him loaded, and this is good advertising."

"You're not going to take them in?"

"No. Leave 'em. The camp will probably take care of 'em. He's the trouble. He'll do."

They heaved Mooney Thornton into the bed of the Roadster. The Ranger stowed the weapons, and they both hopped into the cab and started out of the camp. When they stopped next to Reynolds's truck, no more than twenty minutes had elapsed. The Ranger stayed put as Fowler walked past the headlights and around to his side.

"Am I going to need to stay around and testify?"

"Son, I've investigated too many cut throats, a lot of 'em women from his whorehouses that were used up, and he was tired of feedin'. There ain't gonna be any testifyin'."

With that, he drove off into the darkness.

*****

When Fowler stepped off the train in New Haven, Connecticut, he had three and a half million dollars on deposit at the bank in Midland, and Bill Reynolds was engaged to find land. Fowler's only specification was "Find me some place with water on it…and no oil."

CHAPTER 10

June 1964

Trace stumbled out the door of the truck in front of the trailer. It was almost five in the morning, and he was dead dog tired. He could hear the new window unit that Wmearle had installed humming from the back of the trailer. The wheat harvest was peaking, and he had taken up working at the elevator unloading trucks. They had been cutting until well after midnight every night for a week, as late as they could up to the point when the moisture would get too high in the air, then there'd be a few more hours waiting in the long line up and down the highway in front of the elevator to unload. It was dry though, tonight, and they would keep cutting all night long. The Co-op manager had sent him home when the night man told him he had been at it for forty straight hours. It was good money though, on account of those long hours, but there would only be about another week of it, and he could rest up a bit. He was tired, but somehow, he didn't feel like sleeping, and Wmearle was keeping that window unit going full blast ever since he bought it. The trailer was like an icebox if he left his bedroom door open and like an oven if he closed it. He was sleeping every night under a pile of quilts the same as he did in wintertime. He smiled thinking how at least he couldn't hear Wmearle snoring as bad over the sound of the air conditioner. He walked around the side of the dark station and sat down on the bench next to the Coke box. He was caked in wheat dust. The light at the main intersection down the street was blinking orange. It didn't have a red-green stoplight, as there was seldom enough cross traffic to need it. A hot south-west wind had come up, causing the blinking light to sway. Across the street, a long-faded sign hanging from the wall of a long-vacant building was swinging in the breeze. Trace closed his eyes and pondered for a long while how the sound of it moaning in the wind was exactly the same as the sound of a pumpjack. But it only seemed to work if you closed your eyes. Wmearle had told him over and over again about how bacon frying was like that. It sounded just the same as rain falling outside if you closed your eyes and listened. His mind drifted. They had read a strange Ray Bradbury story in English class a month back called "Night Meeting" where time was fluid and indefinite, an impossible meeting in the night of a Martian and a human from different times, as though there was some kind of cosmic time warp, and only they were privy to it. He closed his eyes and imagined Quanah Parker riding out of the darkness and into the orange blinking light, some wild, raw-boned painted horse underneath him. Only Quanah couldn't see the orange blinking light or the station or the water tower, but only the emptiness of a mesquite pasture, and Trace couldn't see the buffalo herds blanketing the horizon. What would he say? How would they talk at all? That hadn't been a problem for the Martian and the human, so he figured if some kind of cosmic time warp could solve the communication problem for them, maybe it could for him and Quanah Parker too. So he imagined him talking in English, and Quanah Parker talking in Comanche, and somehow they could understand each other anyway. Still, what would he say to this man out of a different time, this man of unimaginable wildness and strength, glorying in his freedom and savagery? He imagined telling him to "Keep running. Keep fighting." Warning him that everything was going away. "It's all going to change. Hold on, as long as you can."

And he imagined Quanah Parker understanding, hearing his words from on top of that wild painted mustang and looking down, not with sadness or even horror, but attentive still, with his bright, steady eyes juxtaposed against dark bronze skin that stretched across those high sharp cheekbones and him sitting atop that wild unsaddled horse stomping its feet and rolling its eyes at him. But when it came to imagining what Quanah would say back, what the Comanche words would sound like, he couldn't do it, couldn't create the words. And he imagined Quanah turning the horse on its back feet and drifting back away without so much as a look over his shoulder, fading away into the night that was ninety years ago and him sitting there on the service station bench like Tomas Gomez wondering after the Martian left, if it had all been a dream. And he, back in his own time listening to the faded sign moaning in the wind, thought about how all of what he knew would pass and become the same as Quanah's world, a figment of some storyteller not even born yet. How Wmearle, and Lydia and Mike and Iladio and Blas and Nicholas, and then even how the judge and the old man and the preacher would pass on and not be in the world anymore, and what it would be like if it were only him left. And he watched the sign swaying in the wind, its meaning faded from memory, and he thought how the sign had never not been there in his recollection, but that he had never seen the words when they weren't faded beyond recognition. He never wondered before what kind of business had been in the dilapidated old stone building whose roof had long since collapsed. What did those people do? Who were they, and what happened to them? And he thought about Wmearle snoring in the trailer around back with his new window unit on full blast, cold enough to blow smoke in your sleep here in June, and back at her house, Lydia would be getting up and about by now and moving in her ancient way with that stooped and furious determination. He thought about his friends, one by one and where they were, sleeping in the darkness of their own places in the world and how they too would fade away into the night and out of memory. And he wanted to warn them that everything was going away. From his own moment in a kind of time warp of his own imagining, he saw it all as though he were looking at them through some sorcerer's pool, and he wanted to warn them: "Keep running, keep fighting, or else it's all going to go away."

He stomped his foot, for no other reason than to feel it, to jerk himself back into his own time and out of the time seen through the sorcerer's pool. And he watched the wheat dust puff out of his jeans, and even that was blown away in the wind as soon as he saw it.

He stepped into the trailer and felt the cold blast of air in his face and in his clothes, dust- caked and soggy from sweat. He could hear Wmearle's snoring above the whirring of the window unit. He stood there in silence, thinking about how much he loved Wmearle and Lydia and the others, then walked into his room, fell into bed, and pulled the quilts over him and was asleep. He didn't even take his boots off.

*****

The boom was deafening, even inside the trailer with the window unit running. Trace was standing up in an instant, bewildered, blind for a moment owing to his eyelids being stuck together from the wheat dust corruption. His heart was pounding, and he didn't know why. Then he was running through the door of Wmearle's shop. There had been a blast of some kind. The trailer, mounted with some gigantic piece of oil field machinery, was tilted at an unnatural angle, Wmearle's feet sticking out from under it. Trace flattened himself on the shop floor and wiggled under the side of the trailer. Wmearle was face up, breathing heavy, the veins in his neck and face bulging.

"Get outta here. This thing is gonna tip over."

"I'm gonna get a jack under it. You hold tight."

Trace shimmied back out from under the trailer and shot his eyes around the shop. He found the big hydraulic jack he was looking for and fished around frantically for some pieces of heavy steel plate in Wmearle's waste pile. When he turned back, Lydia was bending down to look under the tilting trailer.

"Get out of there! Go! Now! Go and get my truck and back it up as close as you can between the door and the trailer. And stay back."

"Oh Lord." She ran out the narrow space into the light.

"I'm gonna try to git this off of you now."

"I told you to git outta here. Now go on. You're gonna kill yourself. Find some help."

Trace looked to where the broken axle was sitting across Wmearle's legs, just below his belt buckle. The space between the axle and the concrete was impossibly thin. Wmearle was crushed.

"I don't think you got time for that. You're mashed bad."

It was a tight fit. He turned over on his back and fishtailed himself up under the trailer and slowly pulled the jack around by his side. Once he got it upright under the frame, he positioned a piece of heavy plate steel between the jack and the frame and began pumping the handle. When the jack was tight against the frame, he moved up and next to Wmearle's head, their faces inches apart.

"Okay. This is going to either hurt like hell or you're just gonna pass out. We're gonna get you outta here and to the hospital. You're gonna be okay. You ready?"

Wmearle dropped his hand down and patted Trace on the head.

The trailer moved. Before long, he could see light between Wmearle's jeans and the axle. He wouldn't remember the rest of it, how he and Lydia dragged three hundred pounds of unconscious Wmearle out and up into the bed of his pickup and drove the forty miles into Abilene and up to the hospital door. He had passed out himself once they got Wmearle onto the gurney and into the emergency room. When he woke up, he was lying on an emergency room bed in an empty room. He got up, shook the cobwebs out of his head, and walked out into the corridor. Lydia was sitting alone in a row of chairs.

"Where is he?"

"They wheeled him out of here and up to surgery."

"He's alive?"

"I reckon. But they ain't said nothin'. You ain't been out but a few minutes. That doctor ran in there and looked at him, and they just wheeled him out."

Trace sat down and put his head in his hands. Everything was spinning, and he was suddenly aware that he was barefoot.

"How'd my boots get off?"

Lydia looked at him, thinking it was an odd question.

"I's so tired last night, I thought about takin' my boots off and just fell into bed with 'em on. He musta come in sometime after and took my boots off, and I never even knew it."

"You done a good thing. The best that coulda been done. And I mean by anybody. We just gotta wait now."

*****

There was a steady progression of visitors through the day, but there was little information to share. Word had spread about the accident, so there were a lot of pats on the back from people Trace scarcely knew. Lydia had asked to borrow his truck to go back and close up the station, but Trace had no intention of going anywhere, so he wasn't conscious of being afoot. It was midnight when Wmearle came out of surgery and into what they called critical care. A doctor approached and asked Trace if he was the next of kin, and Trace nodded. He thought to himself that the doctor didn't appear to be much older than him.

"Mr. Franklin is hurt very badly. He's got a crushed pelvis and a lot of damage to his hip joints. The dangerous thing was the collapsed arteries going to his legs. I understand you are the one responsible for getting him out and down here." Trace nodded. "There's a chance he may get to keep his legs, but whether he'll be able to walk or how well, well there's no way to know. Crush injuries are very difficult to overcome. It's very fortunate that you were able to get him out of there as fast as you did. If you hadn't, I'm not sure he would be with us now. But he's got a long recovery ahead of him, and we've got to keep a close eye on him for a while to come. He'll be sedated for at least a day or two."

Trace hadn't processed anything the doctor had told him. All of his focus was on words that would tell him only whether Wmearle was alive or dead, and when the doctor walked away up the corridor, he was satisfied that he was at least alive.

When he walked into the room, he was staggered by Wmearle's appearance. The hulking body of the man was covered in a white plaster cast from his thighs to his ribs. The part of him above the cast was swollen beyond recognition, and his normally pale white skin was a dark-red color, all the way up to his head. The wire-wheel-colored hair was twisted in every direction, and rubber tubes hung all over his body. Trace pulled a chair up close to the bed and tried talking to him but got no response. So he bowed his head and started to pray, but he didn't get very far before he started sobbing uncontrollably. He kept trying, but somehow in his mind, he couldn't focus on what he was praying about. His mind would wander to things that had no bearing on the moment, and he would pull himself back in and try again. He did this over and over until sometime in the night he was asleep.

When morning came, Lydia woke him and handed him a Thermos. Trace noticed that his boots were next to his chair.

"How'd those come to be here?"

"Mike. He was up here during the night. I told him you were barefoot, so he went out to the trailer and got 'em before he come in. He came by the station on his way home and said you were asleep, and he didn't want to wake you."

Trace pulled the boots on.

Lydia stepped around the bed and looked Wmearle over.

"My Lord."

Trace could tell she was nervous, probably more from being motionless than anything, but being helpless and out of her familiar boundaries was hard, he could tell. Lydia was a person of habit, and she was out of it.

"The doctor said he would be asleep for a day or two. There ain't no reason to hang around here, Lydia. We'll be okay."

"There's somebody come and left some food for you at the nurse's station. You oughta eat. You ain't had nothin' for goin' on two days."

That hadn't occurred to him. But now that she mentioned it, he was as hungry as he had ever felt.

"I'll go get it. I'll walk you out."

"I left your truck in the parking lot outside."

"I got no need for it. I'm not going anywhere for a while. Besides, how are you gonna get back?"

Lydia had a strange look move across her face, and he could tell she was searching for what to say.

"Fowler's up the hall a ways. I'll catch a ride back with him."

That's when it hit Trace. Ever since he had come home the night before, he'd been in some kind of whirlwind, whether of his own imaginings or the horror of the accident, but still, a whirlwind in his mind, as though he was still peering into the abyss of that same sorcerer's pool. And suddenly, he snapped back into his own time. Someone had brought food. Strangers had said kind things in the corridor. Mike had brought his boots. And now Fowler, and he suddenly became aware that something had congealed in the community, and that people had lurched into gear. He knew they did that, that thing where people rise up and suddenly, desperately, thrash about, trying to help when there's nothing that can be helped. Still, he had never felt it before. He had never sensed being in the center of it before.

The elevator door opened, and he stepped out with Lydia into the broad reception room of the hospital entrance. Judge Reynolds was standing by the door waiting to get in. Trace told Lydia good-bye and stepped back into the elevator with the judge. As the door closed, his eyes met Fowler's, staring at him under the brim of that same sweat-stained Stetson from across the room, that same implacable grave stare. The old man simply tipped his head once, turned and opened the door, and walked out with Lydia.

Trace punched the button on the elevator door to head back to Wmearle's room. Judge Reynolds reached across him and punched the sixth-floor button. As the door opened on Trace's floor, the judge reached out and put his hand on his shoulder.

"If you don't mind, I'd like to chat with you for a minute. Come go with me. I know a quiet place."

Trace stepped off the elevator and walked around the corner with him. Judge Reynolds opened the door into a stairwell leading up and out onto the rooftop. "I've been up here many a time. People have a lot of important moments in this hospital. A lot of unforgettable conversations have taken place up here."

The morning air was still relatively cool. The hot southwest wind hadn't come up yet. Trace wondered whether the judge was going to be making some kind of religious appeal. There was a park bench on the gravel rooftop with a sand-filled cigarette can next to it. Judge Reynolds sat down and fished a cigar out of his shirt pocket.

"How are you feeling, son?"

"I'm all right."

"I mean it as a serious question. You've been through a hell of a thing. I understand you've also been working like your hair was on fire. Any normal fellow would be more than a little sideways in your situation. So I'll ask again. How are you feeling?"

Trace thought for a moment or two and said, "Truth is, I don't even know."

"Good answer. That's an honest answer." He cupped a match in his hands and lit the cigar.

"There's not a thing in the world wrong with being off-center in a situation like this. All I need to tell you is you're not by yourself here. You have...I'd say against all odds...you have a family that's with you in this. Between Lydia and that Wakefield boy and your compadres in that benevolent society of yours, and Fowler and Weaver and a lot more, it's as much a family as anyone's."

"What's Fowler got to do with anything?"

"Son, this is not the time I imagined having to talk with you about that, and I don't like it. I know Wmearle Franklin means the world to you. You wouldn't be human if it didn't make you miserable to see him hurting like he is. It's not my intention to be cruel here, though it might sound like it, but you need to pull your head out of your ass."

"Come again?"

The judge sat back and looked out across the town and the hills in the distance to the south. It was a clear day, and the limestone around the top of Castle Peak was shining in the morning sun twenty miles away.

"What is it you think you know about Fowler Clement?"

"I told you before. I know I ain't got nothin' to do with him, and he ain't got nothin' to do with me."

"What if I told you that's not true? What if I told you there's not an hour of any day that you're not on his mind?"

"I'd say that doesn't make a damned bit of sense is what I'd say."

He laughed. He could see the blood coming up in the boy.

"Okay. Okay." He sighed heavily.

"Fowler was a dynamo when he was a young man. A fierce worker. I knew him back in the oil field days out west of here. I wasn't a judge then, just an oil field lawyer. He was the most focused, driven man I ever knew. When he and Let married, fresh out of college, he changed. It seemed like overnight. He moved out there on that ranch and didn't hardly come off it. They lived in a barn for a year while he built that house, and then your daddy came along, and I never saw a man more settled and happy than him. We were always friends, and me and my wife spent many a Sunday afternoon out there by the river with him and Let watching your daddy and my kids playing. I was always trying to persuade him to get into politics. He could have. But he was never interested in that. It's hard to say how the trouble seeped into their life. But it did. Let loved your daddy so much, it was almost…unhealthy. People will always say that somebody is spoiled, but it was more than that. It was like somehow that love just burned a little too hot. She got so protective of him that it got between her and Fowler, and Junior got lost. I suppose he and Fowler both did. He and your daddy fought like cats and dogs every time Fowler tried to reel him in. That happens sometimes with folks, but usually, time passes and people settle into some kind of livable arrangement, and things cool down. I'm not saying Fowler didn't love your daddy. He did. But he and Let loved him differently. What happened with your mother and daddy broke Let right in two. I don't think anybody can imagine how impossibly shattered she was. And she had no recourse. She probably knew somewhere in her mind that your momma wasn't right, but can you see how she just shut everything down? She had nowhere to go. There was no squaring what had been put to her. Fowler stood there like some kind of god and told her there would be no vengeance against your momma, and she just broke. Fowler was right to do it. How he summoned the courage to face up to that, I can't imagine, but that didn't mean he didn't suffer for it. He was suffering himself in his own way, and I bet he could see just as well what standing there and doing what he did, what needed to be done, would mean. He's never told me directly, but I know it as surely as we're sitting here that she made him promise. She wanted to build a wall and seal out everything that happened. Just close it off, cauterize it, forever. She just didn't have the capacity to accept it and grieve the way most people will. So she made him promise for as long as they lived…it's why he doesn't, won't, talk to you. He promised. He gave her his solemn word. And he loves her more than me or you can imagine, and she made him choose. I don't know how he does it, but can you see that for almost eight years the man has been walking a tightrope? He doesn't blame you for anything. He made a promise to her that no man should ever have to give in order to do the right thing at that moment, in that circumstance, and now he's living with that promise the very best he knows how. I never knew a man with such will. But what he can do, and what he can think and feel are two different things. There's none of this that's right. I know that. But people's hearts can break. That's just a fact. Your grandmother's heart got broken and can't be fixed."

"Why are you telling me this? How does any of it make any difference? It is the way it is."

"Son, just consider his predicament. Consider what it means to completely love somebody and then have them fall apart on you, present you with an impossible choice. I thought like a lot of people over the years that he was simply the most stubborn man there ever was. But you know a man long enough, and you get to where you can see him in a different light. It's fidelity, pure and simple. Faithful to the idea that him and her have to be one and the same, good or bad, and no matter how bad. That's an extraordinary thing in this world, to stay faithful to your love at such cost. You rarely even see it. You gotta ask yourself how much the idea of love matters. I think, more than anything. It's the only damned thing that does matter in this world. Son, it's what got Wmearle out from under that trailer. It's what got you out of that jail in Acuna. It's what had people you don't even know poking their head in that hospital room all night long last night while you were sleeping."

He stood up and thumped the ashes off the end of the cigar and mashed it down into the sand.

"I'm telling you this because I know none of this is right and can't be made right. You're a man before you're supposed to be, and I'm not alone in admiring the way you've grown up, but I want to ask you to just forgive it all. It's the only way any of us have any hope. Just consider it."

*****

Trace slowed when he came to the gravel drive that ran back behind the station, then passed on and through town and up the river road. Lydia had persuaded him earlier that he needed to go home after three days at the hospital.

"Okay. Trace, it ain't about you needin' rest. I was bein' nice. I'll just say it plain. You need a bath. You stink!"

That had embarrassed him. He knew he probably didn't look too presentable, but he hadn't cared about that. Smelling bad was another matter. So he had left, and it had felt good to get out on the road with the wind in his hair. It was sunset when he pulled into town, and that peculiar golden light was all over everything that only comes at daylight and right when the sun goes down. The sight of the trailer had hit him hard. He had never thought about how a place could be alive or dead before, but when he saw it this time, it came clear to him that it was desolate. The trailer had always been alive when it had Wmearle in it. Without him there, it lost its soul and was just a shabby trailer. He suddenly felt afraid, and it came back to him what he had imagined sitting on the bench in front of the station in the middle of the night. Seeing the trailer empty and soulless, he could see it happening already, everything going away, everything changing. His heart popped up in his throat for a moment. So he drove on out of town and turned off onto the gravel road that headed upriver.

The cabin sat on a low bluff inside a small horseshoe bend in the river. The opposite bank was the high side, and the banks rose sharply and sloped up over a hundred feet, with ledgerock outcroppings rimming the little natural amphitheater. The cabin was protected and sat in a grove of pecan trees overlooking a broad gravel bar in the river. He lit a kerosene lamp and took it outside and started a fire in a rock pit in front of the porch. There were canned beans and peaches in the cupboard, so he opened them and sat the can of beans on a rock next to the fire, then got a pot of coffee going. The stars were out before long, and he was finishing off the peaches when he heard the rocks rattle high in the bluff across the river. When the horse stepped down into the river and clattered out onto the gravel bar, he could see Iladio's taco shell straw hat.

Iladio dismounted and dropped the reins on the ground. He walked into the firelight and patted Trace on the shoulder on his way into the cabin. When he came back, he had a can of Bugler tobacco and squatted down on his heels and started rolling a cigarette. He handed Trace the first one and started in on one of his own. Trace didn't usually smoke, but there were some times when it was agreeable to him, so he dropped a twig over into the fire and lit it then held it up and lit his cigarette, then passed the twig over to Iladio.

They sat smoking in silence, drinking coffee. He could smell the sweat from the horse, its wet legs shining in the firelight.

"What brings you down here?"

"I saw the light and came to check."

Trace liked the way the Mexicans talked. The accent seemed to add some quality of gentleness, and maybe fatalism, to normal words. There it was. This was Clement land, though Trace had never considered the cabin as being owned by anyone before. Wmearle would bring him down in here and spend a weekend running drop lines up and down the river or using it as a hunting cabin after Thanksgiving. He had been here many times, but it had never until this moment mattered to him that Fowler owned the place, or for that matter that anyone did or could. He pondered why it hadn't. It seemed to him a place of such peace and isolation and beauty that it wouldn't be subject to such a thing as ownership. The boundary for The Clement was clear for anyone to see from the way the fences were all built the same way: two massive cedar corner posts and a cattle guard framing the river road two miles back toward town. So he knew, he just had never thought of the river or the cabin or the bend as being owned, as though The Clement and everything that went along with it were abstract and apart from the actual dirt and rock and river. He listened as coyotes came out of their dens up and down the river and erupted in those brief raucous howls, then went silent.

"Hell, he even owns the coyotes."

"Que?" Iladio cupped the cigarette and peered over his knuckles at Trace. He was worried about him.

"Nothin'."

"Wmearle?"

"Bad. Looks like he'll live. Prob'ly won't be able to walk. He's all swoll' up."

Iladio whistled lightly through his teeth. After a while, he tossed the dregs from his cup and took the Bugler can back inside. He patted Trace on the shoulder again as he passed, then turned and faced Trace in the firelight. "He's tough. You're tough. It'll be okay." He turned and mounted up and rode out into the darkness the way he came in.

Trace went into the cabin and found a bar of soap next to the sink, then walked down the hill and out onto the gravel bar and began stripping off his clothes. He waded naked out into the dark waters named centuries earlier by some desperate and long forgotten Spanish explorer: Los Brazos de Dios, the arms of God.

CHAPTER 11

November 1964

"I think I'm gonna buy some cows."

"What give you an idea like that?"

Wmearle was in his recliner. There had been quite a homecoming party when he finally got home. It was late fall, and Trace had made Wmearle hold off on throwing a party for his sixteenth birthday at the rest home in favor of doing it when he got home. So they'd set up a pit in front of the trailer and cooked all day, so people could drop in and say hello to Wmearle and eat some barbecue.

Trace and Mike and the boys had worked the trailer over during the months he was rehabilitating. It had become clear that Wmearle would never walk again, so everywhere they could imagine that he might need to get out of the wheelchair and into bed or his recliner or the toilet, they had installed reinforced trapeze bars hanging from the ceiling. A new door was cut out of the front of the trailer; the old one not having been wide enough for the chair. Then they had built an elaborate ramp going back and forth across the front of the trailer. The most dramatic change was in the shop. Trace had done some clever matchmaking in getting Wmearle to warm up to the idea of taking on a partner and convincing Mike to give up his freelance ways, farming and cowboying as a day laborer. It would take some careful adjustments from both of them to work together since both had only worked as a one-man show. Mike, of course, knew comparatively little about machinery, so there would be a lot of sparks flying between them with Wmearle trying to teach him from his wheelchair. But Wmearle's pain was receding, and he was getting accustomed to his new situation.

"Bernerd Wilson is in the rest home over in Stamford now. His daughter is looking after him. I seen her out at their old place the other day and stopped in. She's looking for somebody to take it over. I expect it'd run twenty or thirty momma cows."

"And you got the money saved up, I bet."

"I think I do. I'm going over to the auction Friday and check things out. You got any objection to me workin' a deal with Bernerd?"

"Heavens no. It's your money and your time. You mind gettin' me a sodi outta the fridge?"

*****

Trace was out of school before noon. His afternoon classes were in the ag barn, and he had told the ag teacher what he was up to. The Ranchers and Farmers Livestock Auction in Abilene was a busy place on Mondays and Fridays. He hadn't told Wmearle, but he had already been over there three times before, watching the cattle move through the ring, trying to get a bead on how everything worked. He made his way down into the stadium seats and sat down in the last open seat on the row. Cigar smoke was hanging in a hazy blue cloud across the stands. The men up and down the rows were for the most part either professional order buyers or farmers. He was pretty sure he was the most ignorant man in the room.

The old man sitting next to him was not bidding on calves, but mother cows. Trace struck up a conversation with him and found out he was from out near the Double Mountain and was buying what he called replacement cows. While they were talking, the gate opened, and a single black mother cow ran into the ring. The old man leaned forward and spit tobacco juice into a spittoon, then leaned Trace's way.

"Now son, see that'n there? What you think about her? Reckon I oughta buy 'er?"

Trace was on the spot. He had been around cows for years, feeding and moving them from place to place, but the truth was he really hadn't paid much attention to them in any kind of serious way. A cow had always just been a cow. So he studied this one for a few seconds before answering.

"You bet."

"Why do you say that?"

Now he was really on the spot and wasn't too keen on displaying how ignorant he was.

"Well, she seems to be healthy and fat. She's shiny, so I wouldn't think she'd be sick or anything. She don't seem to have any problem moving around, so her bones must be in good shape. And she don't seem old."

"I think I'm gonna pass on her. I think she's a counterfeit."

"A what?"

"A counterfeit. She ain't what she seems. See, I'm buyin' cows to replace the ones I fed for nine months without getting a calf out of 'em. They didn't breed back. If I feed one for nine months and don't get a calf out of her, I get rid of 'em. You're right. She is fat and shiny. She looks great. But I'll bet you a cup a coffee she looks great because she didn't raise a calf. Somebody's been feedin' her for most of a year, and she didn't pay off. See, a cow that's raised a calf won't have that shiny hair. It'll be dull. She'll look a little wore-out, a little skinny 'cause she's put all her energy into puttin' out a calf, and that takes a lot out of 'em. That one there's been livin' rent free off some feller. You gotta be careful around these old auction barns. Remember, there's always somebody that's sellin' their own mistakes, and you don't wanna be the one to buy 'em."

That was a sobering thought. While he appreciated the information, he was all of a sudden less confident about what he was getting into and didn't want to do something stupid. As he had the previous times he'd come to the auction barn, he started daydreaming about his soon-to-be cattle empire, and his daydreaming tended to move from one thing to the next. He was busy building barns when a gigantic black bull ran into the ring and exploded into the pipe fence. The animal was crazy and stunned from having hit the solid steel pipe wall. It turned, slobbering and wild-eyed and tried to leap over the rail into the stands, perching, suspended for a moment before tumbling back into the ring on its back. The ring boys had long since crawled up and over the top, and they immediately opened the back gate through which the bull disappeared.

"He'll be baloney tomorrah." The old man smiled. "Ain't nobody gonna take a maniac like that home with 'em."

*****

Trace met Shorty and Herbert at dawn the next morning. They wouldn't work during the heat of the summer, but once the weather had broken in September, they had restarted the fencing operation. Alvin Hearndon was not in a big hurry, so he let them go at their own pace. Trace figured they had maybe another week or two before they'd be saying it was too cold to work, so he was anxious to finish up.

"So what changed your mind?"

"Well, I been keeping up with the market. Mr. Burk writes the prices on the blackboard in the ag barn ever mornin'. I figured they're way off, so now would be a good time to buy in. I been goin' up to the auction barn to get a feel for it, but...I don't know. There's lots more to it than I thought."

"That's for damned sure. That's almost always the way it is with things. Ever'thing from girls to politics to cows. Except Shorty. With him, there's always less to it than you think."

"Unless you're talkin' about actually gettin' off your ass and doin' something, in which case, Herbert is altogether out of his depth. He sometimes gets confused about whether he actually did something or just talked about it. His philosophy has yet to dig a posthole."

"Says Mr. Dead Man is the Life of a Fence."

"I think, therefore the fence got built."

"When's the last time you talked to Alvin?"

"Not lately."

"You oughta track him down. He's gettin' transferred up to Borger, and I think he's gonna pack up the family and take them with him. He may be willin' to strike you a deal on the cattle. I'm bettin' he'll be sellin' out the whole kit and caboodle. Prob'ly lease you the place if you think you can handle it. Save you from havin' to deal with those sharpshooters down at the sale barn."

Alvin Hearndon was home when Trace drove up that evening. Trace had a spiral notebook in his hand that he'd bought at the grocery store. On the cover was a picture of a beach and two footprints in the sand and the words *Hang Ten*, the meaning of which remained a mystery to him. When he left later that evening, he had several pages of notes written down, and he'd struck a deal to lease the Hearndon farm and buy the cattle, contingent on whether he could get the bank to back the deal.

*****

The bank was decorated for Thanksgiving. There was an island in the middle of the lobby for filling out deposit slips, and someone had placed a giant papier mâché turkey up there. The walls around one side of the lobby were decorated with Crayola turkey pictures from the elementary school. Trace had combed his hair and put on his good boots and had his Hang Ten notebook in his hand with his plan written out in it. He approached the receptionist in front of a series of glass offices along one wall of the bank.

"I need to see Mr. Compton. I'm Trace Clement."

"That's him back in the corner there. He's got somebody in there with him right now, but if you'll sit down, I'll tell him you're here when he gets finished."

Trace sat down in a small waiting area next to the gigantic stainless steel vault door. He had always been fascinated by the vault, but whenever he looked inside, he saw only the lockboxes. He had a vague memory that must have been from when he was only three or four years old. He was with Fowler who had business to do at the bank with Ford Compton. The ladies at the teller window had been entrusted with his care while Fowler and Compton were talking, and he was roaming around the back of the bank with one of the tellers in tow. He was little, but he was old enough to know there was money about, so he was looking for it. When he went into the vault, there were large canvas bags full of coin stacked behind stainless steel bars. When he looked up, Fowler was towering over him.

"You know what's in those bags? Pennies and nickels and dimes and quarters. Ford, come in here."

Mr. Compton stepped in through the vault door.

"I tell you what. Mr. Compton here is going to open that door there. I'll make you a deal. You can have all the money you can carry out of here. But you gotta carry it out by yourself. How about that?"

All these years later, he could still feel the frustration. He had scarcely been able to budge those canvas sacks of coin. There lay untold wealth free for the taking, and try as he might, he couldn't lift one of those bags. Fowler had given him a silver dollar on the way out of the bank to console him, and he felt better after they visited the drugstore for an ice cream, but he never forgot the frustration.

Ford Compton had aged, and fattened, since that time. As he approached, he stuck out his hand, and they shook. Trace would see him back in that corner office whenever he made his deposits at the bank, but he had never borrowed money before, so they had no occasion to talk. Compton knew him, though. Trace sat down, and Compton walked behind the giant glass-topped desk and leaned back in his chair.

"How's Wmearle getting on?"

"He's home now. Getting used to things. He's healing up pretty good, but you know he can't walk anymore, so he's grouchy about that. He's back doing some work though, so that's making him feel better."

"Hell of a thing that was. I'm glad to hear he's gonna be all right. I know he means a lot to you."

"Yessir."

"How old are you now, Trace?"

"I turned sixteen a couple of months back."

"Whew, time passes. I remember you in here trying to rob the bank one time when you were little. I'm not giving you another chance like that!"

"I know it. Still bothers me that I didn't get rich that day."

"How can I help you today?"

Trace flopped his Hang Ten notebook out and started laying out the plan. He had his budgets written out on pages he got from the FFA manual in ag class and described the Hearndon and Wilson farms and what kind of cattle Hearndon had and how many. When he was finished, he looked at Compton and said, "I need to borrow twenty thousand dollars."

"Okay."

That caught him off guard. Compton hadn't hesitated.

"That's it? You don't have any questions?" His mind was suddenly flooded with suspicion. He could almost smell Fowler being involved. Compton caught the frown. He leaned forward toward the desk, but didn't speak for a long time.

"This is the first time you've ever borrowed money, isn't it?"

"Yessir."

"All right. Let's suppose you came in here with a shaky deal. You're sixteen years old. You want twenty thousand dollars, and I don't know you from Adam. I'd probably be real nice, but I'd never think twice about sayin' no. Or I'd start asking you about who could cosign the note. I'd offer you less money in any case. But that's not what's going on here.

You got a decent plan there. I can see you done your homework. I know all about the cattle 'cause I already carry the note on 'em for Alvin. I know you're the one takes care of 'em already. You have four thousand dollars of your own money that I've seen you accumulate over the last four or five years on your own initiative. Which by the way, in thirty years of banking, I never heard of a sixteen-year-old kid saving up four thousand dollars out of his own hard work before, and I would'na believed it if I had'n seen you coming in here depositing checks from virtually everbody in the county at one time or another. So I do know who you are. I know your reputation. I know I'm not going to ask you for a cosigner for reasons we don't need to get into. And I know Wmearle will keep an eye on you. That make sense?"

"I guess so. Now what?"

"Here's something else for you to keep in the back of your mind. The note is secured by the cattle. It comes due in one year. At the end of a year, you either pay the note, or we renew it for another year, or we come get your cattle. If you don't pay, we repossess the cattle. But there's more than that. If the price of cattle drops, say down to fifteen cents or something, your note isn't secure anymore because the collateral will be worth less than what you owe. That's when a bank gets nervous. If that happens, we might want to get you to sell out rather than renew the note. That's how a man loses all his money. So let me suggest you do this. Borrow a couple of thousand more than you need. You'll have to pay interest on it, so that's bad. Just set it in your bank account and let it be. If the market should go against you and the note comes up for renewal, you'll have a little extra cash to pay the note down, and that'll make a tight renewal go down better."

"No. I think I'll stick with the plan. I'll still be working, so I can save up some more between now and then. Twenty thousand will do it."

Compton typed out the note on a large white envelope with a payment schedule on the back and walked around the desk and sat down to explain it. Trace left the bank with a twenty-thousand-dollar deposit slip.

When he drove up to the trailer, Judge Reynolds was sitting in a lawn chair in the gravel driveway talking to Wmearle. They didn't seem happy.

"Son, I have some hard news. Your momma passed this morning."

CHAPTER 12

The house sat back off the road in a circular clearing surrounded by towering pine forest. He had gassed up in the little town out on the highway before pulling onto the narrow oil-sand road that led down through the piney woods into the low country along the Angelina River. The house was neither as large nor as grand as he had remembered it. In fact, it was rather small and simple, clad in white-painted shiplap. A small porch extended out from the front that was framed by two fluted columns. In his memory, the columns had seemed no different than the entry to a courthouse or bank, but they now appeared far from imposing. The drive leading from the road to the house was lined with cars and pickup trucks, and there were men standing in the yard below the porch, smoking. He parked the truck on the edge of the road next to the front gate. The drive had taken most of the day, and when he killed the engine and the sound of the forest settled in on him, it was as though he had stepped out from a busy city street into a cathedral. Some bird called out from far away, and he stood, listening to the echo, then started his walk up the drive.

Wmearle hadn't liked him making the trip by himself, and they had argued, but Mike was busy with the shop, and he knew Iladio or Blas or Nicholas would be miserable among all the strangers. Lydia had filled a milk crate with enough food to last him a couple of weeks. Before he left, Wmearle had Lydia bring a road map from the station and lined out a route that would take him south of Dallas and Fort Worth to avoid the city freeways.

The men standing in the yard looked mainly like working men, many in their overalls and oiled brogans. But there were a couple that reminded him of his grandfather and uncles from the one time that Junior and Stella had taken the family to visit. Those wore khakis and starched white shirts and suspenders and the straw Panamas. They would be the bosses.

He ignored the stares of the men in the yard, mounted the steps, and opened the screen door into the central hallway that passed through the house to the back porch. He removed his hat and walked toward the steel-colored coffin sitting closed against the hallway wall. A framed photograph of Stella that appeared to be from her wedding was perched on the top among some fresh flowers. When he had passed the open arched doorways to his left and right, he sensed that the house was full of people. The conversation had stopped as he passed, and the house grew quiet. He looked at the bridal portrait and tried to remember Stella when she had looked that way. It wasn't age, or the way her insanity had ravaged her body that didn't line up. In the portrait, she looked as though she was in control. There was a confidence in her expression that he had never seen before. And she was beautiful. He was wondering how far back the problem had gone if he never remembered her when it wasn't there, the worry, the cease-less battle against some unseen thing. Looking at the portrait, he felt an odd relief. There had been a good time, when whatever it was that had got hold of her hadn't yet. He never knew until right then that such a time had even been. And so he felt relieved, and unexpectedly, happy. He suddenly sensed a floral perfume smell and turned to find his grandmother standing at his elbow.

"They told me a tall cowboy had come in. I knew who that would be."

She had piercing blue eyes and looked him over good from head to toe. She had an oblique expression, and he was unsure as to whether he was entirely welcome or not. It had been over ten years since he had seen her, and she had aged a great deal. Her hair was almost completely gray and she had…settled. He thought to himself that it was probably just that he had gotten tall; he was looking down at her now, but it was more than that. She had been a robust woman, athletic even. But now, she was softer and seemed delicate. Her body seemed compressed, smaller in every dimension.

"Walk back here with me, so we can visit a bit."

She led him toward the back of the house and out onto a wide screened-in porch. On one end, there was a room that had been closed in with glass windows. Inside, there were a couple of wicker chairs and an assortment of potted plants and flowers. A soft rain began falling outside, and the men from the yard hurried around to the back where they rolled back the large barn door and stepped into the dark space beyond and resumed their smoking and talking.

"I sit in here if it's not too hot outside and do my sewing." She stepped back from the porch and leaned through the back door. "Sudie, could you get us both a glass of lemonade?"

"I've been visiting so much, I'm about to lose my voice. Ever'body's gonna want to meet you, so I thought I'd give you a minute to catch your breath before you start gettin' interduced around."

A large black woman in a white dress stepped in and placed the lemonade on a table between the chairs. Trace thanked her, but she turned quickly and was gone. Trace could see one or two of the men in the barn looking in their direction.

"That one out there with the hat smoking the cigar is your uncle Jules. The one with the suspenders. Everybody calls him Julie."

"I remember him. Took me fishin'."

She sipped her lemonade and looked at him with that same enigmatic expression for a long while without talking.

"Your granddaddy is over at the rest home in Alto."

Without intending to, Trace immediately looked up at her with a question in his face, and she seemed to just as quickly understand the question he was forming.

"No. A few weeks ago, he got turned around when he got up in the night to go to the bathroom and fell. He broke his hip. So he's over there mending. I couldn't take care of him here."

"I told them not to open the casket. But if you need to, you can. It's just, she don't look like herself."

"No, ma'am. It ain't necessary. I figured why." He swigged his lemonade.

101

"Mr. Franklin called and told me you were comin'. You prob'ly outta give him a call and let him know you got here."

"Yes, ma'am. I will."

"Most of these people will be gone soon as we eat dinner. Julie'll stay around for a while, but then it'll just be me and you and Sudie. Sudie will sit up with your momma. I've got a room for you to spend the night, so when everbody leaves, go pull your pickup truck up here to the house. Then we can visit some more. Tomorrow, we'll git up, and you can have some breakfast early. The service is gonna be over at the cemetery at Pollak. It's a pretty spot. All our family is in there."

"Seems like ever'thing is pretty here."

"You're not used to all this green, are you?"

"No, ma'am."

"Well, if you're up to it, let me trot you around to everbody. Maybe by the time we get through in here, it'll stop showerin', and I'll take you out there and let Julie interduce you to the men."

"All right."

One by one, she led him through the house introducing him to cousins, neighbors, aunts, and far more distant relatives, each with a detailed narration on the nature of his connection. Over and over again, he responded, "Yes, ma'am, no, ma'am, thank you, ma'am, good to meet you, ma'am." He remembered none of them of course, but he was pleased with his performance. The whole group seemed to be happily functioning in an unnaturally pleasant display of manners. When they'd reached the kitchen, Trace stopped, expecting his grandmother to formally introduce him to Sudie, but she didn't, so he simply nodded and thanked her again for the lemonade.

"Julie, you remember Trace. I'm gonna get back in the house before it starts down again. Interduce him around to everbody."

She hurried back across the yard and disappeared into the house.

"By God, you've grown a bunch. You wad'n more than a polly-wog when I seen you last."

He was talking with the cigar still in his mouth. Judging by how adept he was at it, Trace was of the opinion that it was probably a permanent fixture.

"Lemme interduce you to these men. Most of 'em work at the mill for your granddaddy and me. Some of 'ems cousins and relatives too."

They stepped back into the dark opening of the barn door, and Trace could see that not much of anything had been done in there in a long time. There was a dank smell of creosote and cigar smoke in the air. And so the process started again, although there were fewer men, and Trace's response was condensed to a simple *Howdy* for each of them. As he shook their hands, he could tell they were all men of hard labor, with each of them at different stages of being ground down by it. Their grips were strong and calloused. He felt immediately at ease among them. He had a sense, however, nagging his thinking, that he was being paid some kind of unearned respect. But he allowed that it was probably the simple respect men paid to the newly bereaved.

"You come down here all by yourself, didn't you? Momma told me. Said Mr. Franklin was frettin' over it. I met him one time. I think y'all come out to see your momma. Good fella."

"He couldn't come. He had a accident a while back, and he's laid up."

"Sorry to hear that. Catch me up on yourself. I bet it's been ten years since I seen you. I bet you're a football player."

"Nossir. Never got into that kind of thing."

"Whattaya occupy yourself with, sides girls?"

"Workin' mostly. I been savin' up for some time now to get started with some cattle. Just did a deal before I come out here to take on a couple a places and stock 'em. Be gettin' goin' with it when I get back."

Julie had a quizzical look on his face as though that didn't calibrate. He took the stub of the cigar out of his mouth and thumped it off into the wet grass, then pulled another out of his shirt pocket and stripped the cellophane wrapper off. He stuck it in the side of his mouth without lighting it.

"Innerstin'. Let's go in yonder and get a bite to eat. I seen Sudie walk out there on the porch. That means come eat."

He had never seen a spread before like the one on his grand-mother's dining room table. Sudie may have been cooking, but it was clear, food was getting dropped off by everybody in the country. No one person could have cooked that much. He got in line behind Uncle Julie and filled his plate. Julie motioned to follow him, so they made their way through the crowded dining room and across the hallway, past the casket, and into a small living room. The room was modestly furnished except for a large oak rolltop desk against the back wall. Above it was a dramatic portrait of a Confederate general with bunting draped across the top of the frame.

"Who's that?"

"Nathan Bedford Forrest."

That meant nothing to Trace.

"One of our relations?" Julie laughed.

"No. He's just a old Confederate general. One of your grand-daddy's heroes. Some of these old ones still have funny ideas about things."

Trace took a spot on a piano bench, and the conversation in the room died off for a bit as the men all suddenly had their mouths full. Before long, the conversation picked back up among the men, and he could pick out bits and pieces of talk about Johnson, and who killed Kennedy, and communists and pine beetles, and whether somebody had decided to shoot does this year or not. He pondered how the conversation was different. People back home would talk about Johnson and Kennedy and hippies and communists and cotton and cattle and screwworms. So there was some overlap.

Sudie was making her way through the room taking up dishes. Julie had been the only one to speak to her as she passed through.

"Mighty fine Sudie. Hey, you wanna run down and see the mill before it gets dark?"

*****

Trace settled into the seat of Julie's new Buick. The cigar smell was overpowering. He had never been in an automobile that fancy, and he was mesmerized by the chrome and the dials. The whole experience was changing his viewpoint about pickups. Julie was moving down the oil-sand road at a speed that Trace would never have attempted in his pickup, and he could hardly feel the bumps in the road. Julie took off the Panama and set it on the seat between them.

"So you're a cattleman. And you're doin' this on your own initiative? I mean you ain't got any partners or backers or such?"

"Nope. It's just me. I got lucky with a man I been doin' work for that's packin' up and moving. I bought him out."

"Well, that's damned impressive. I suppose I figured you were in it with Mr. Clement or something."

"Nope. Just me."

Trace could tell he was wanting to pester him for more information about that, so he shut up and let it lie. Julie looked at him in the rearview mirror a time or two, but didn't press it. They barreled down the highway for a mile or two, and then veered off onto another oil top road. This one Julie slowed down for. It was bumpy and rutted from heavy truck traffic. They pulled into the yard at the saw mill. Trace had expected there to be more to it.

"Your granddaddy had big plans for this business. He started here with just this one mill. Before long, he took on a partner, and they built seven or eight other ones. Had a good thing goin'. That all fell apart. Now he's back with just this original one."

Trace could hear the awful banging sound of logs being moved around on the equipment inside. It sounded like the place would rattle apart.

"What happened?"

"Partner absconded with the money. Run completely off. Left the old man holding the bag, so he had to sell 'em all to square it up with the bank. Had a payroll to make, and no money to make it with. So he had to get it from the bank. They made him sell out."

"What's that thing?" Trace pointed at a huge conical black structure.

"That's called a wigwam burner. They burn the leftover sawdust in it. Keeps the embers from flying up in the air and catching the whole world on fire."

"So you're running it for him until he gets better."

Julie frowned. "I don't know what's gonna happen. There ain't much money in it now for little mills like this. He's not in good health. I mean other than his hip. He's got all kinds of problems besides that. Just kind of wore hisself out. 'Sides, this ain't my job. I run the bank over at Alto."

"Oh, didn't know that."

"Momma wants me to keep it running as long as Daddy's alive. We'll see. If you don't mind me sayin' so, you seem to be handlin' Stella passin' okay."

"I went to Rusk back in the spring to see her. So I seen it comin'. I was glad when I heard she passed. Don't nobody need to be that way."

"That's a fact. It weighed on Momma and Daddy. Sure it did you too. You ain't worried about what'll happen now."

"No. I'm just relieved she ain't sufferin'."

Julie peeled out of the yard and headed back to the house. Trace thought about asking him if he could drive the Buick, but decided not to.

*****

It was dark when they pulled up to the driveway. Julie let Trace out to get his pickup, and they drove up together at the house. The two remaining visitors were saying their goodbyes, and Sudie was moving the leftover food into the kitchen. Trace walked out onto the back porch and listened to the sound of the forest. He could hear Julie in the dining room talking to his grandmother.

"The people from Loudon's will be here at nine, so the pallbearers will all be here for that, and they'll take her to Pollok. I'll see you then. Goodnight, Momma."

"Night, sweetie."

A quiet settled into the house when Julie drove off. Sudie was still making noises in the kitchen, but the sounds from the woods seemed to Trace to be swelling.

"Peaceful, ain't it."

"Yes, ma'am."

"This time of year, I'll make my bed out here sometimes, till the nights get too cool. You sit down. I'll pull up a chair." She reached into the kitchen and got a chair from under the table. "Let's just sit out here and feel the night."

Every now and then, there would be short spits of rain, and there was a steady drip from the metal rooftop onto the grass. They sat for a long time in silence. Sudie had apparently finished her work and had taken up her spot on a chair in the hallway, presiding alone over some ancient tradition.

"Are you happy?"

"Yes, ma'am. I expect I am."

"I think I told you a lie. I didn't mean to. But I did. I told you your grandpa was mending. I don't think he's ever comin' home. I don't know why I told you that. I'm sorry."

"That's okay. Ain't nothin' wrong with bein' hopeful about a thing."

She watched him in the dim, reflected light from the hallway.

"It's funny. In this light, I can see you better than I could in broad daylight. I can make out her and your daddy and both of your grandpas in your face just now. You got 'em all right there in your face just now, like you're some kind of shape-shifter." She laughed.

"I'm sorry. I'm bein' morbid. I suppose you get your liberties when you have a child layin' there in the hallway like that. But I ought not impose that on you."

"It's okay. I ain't takin' offense."

"No. It's just whenever somebody, anybody, passes, you start thinkin' about whether you done 'em right. Was there somethin' else I coulda done for her? I don't know why I keep thinkin' that. Over and over again."

"There wad'n nothin' you coulda done that you didn't do. Me neither."

"It gives me a peace sittin' here with you."

"Me too."

*****

As she led him to a room at the end of the house, he remembered that he had forgotten to call Wmearle, so he went back to the kitchen and made the call. She told him goodnight and went into her room and shut the door behind her. When he finished, he returned to the bedroom and closed the door and undressed and crawled up into a high bed with a feather mattress. He pulled the quilts up under his chin. The window by the bedside was open, and the cool of the night drifted in and over him, and the slow drip of rain off the tin roof gave meter to the randomness of the forest nightsounds. The smell of the woods was on the air, and he heard a hound baying somewhere far in the distance. He pondered how he could feel such peace in the strange bed in the house of people he scarcely knew, so far from his own bed and his own friends. He thought of Sudie and her vigil out in the hallway and Stella and the look in her face in the bridal portrait that he had never seen before. He fell into a profound and happy sleep.

*****

He woke to the sound of a rooster crowing. There was only the slightest hint of light in the clearing outside. He could hear Sudie in the kitchen. Once he had dressed, he made his way to a bathroom that appeared to be a recent add-on to the house. When he stepped into the kitchen, Sudie pointed toward a small table where a single place was set.

"My grandmother not up yet?"

"Law yes. She done gone."

"Gone? Where to?"

"She up early ever mornin. Goes to Alto to feed yoah granddaddy his breakfast. Says she been doin' it for fifty years, she ain' gonna stop now. She be back directly."

"How long you worked for her?"

"I work for you Uncle Julie. I's just here to help for a little while. She don't wont no help usually. Eat yo breakfast."

Breakfast looked familiar. Biscuits and cane molasses. Only Sudie had fried a piece of ham, and the biscuits were homemade. He and Wmearle were used to the six-cent canned variety.

"How you wont yo eggs?"

"Scrambled is okay."

It was getting light outside, and he could see the forest wall through a light fog. The grass was glistening wet. He could see that above the fog, the sky had cleared blue. When he finished, he put on his hat and walked out into the backyard and into the barn. There were some large circular saw blades against the wall, and in one bay, there were a few large sacks of onions hanging from the rafters. Behind the barn, a metal gate opened onto a few acres of open-grass pasture. He leaned over the cold wet gate and watched a group of egrets stepping silently through the fog and grass. He remembered the place. There had been a white mare. He had nagged Junior into letting him ride her. Julie had assured Stella that she was just an old jughead and would not be dangerous. There being no saddle, Julie put him on and told him to grab a handful of mane with one hand and the reins in the other. That had worked for a while, but some-how, he had spooked her and lost his grip. He remembered bouncing back and back and finally off the backside of the horse as she loped away. He had fallen against a metal feed trough and sliced a gash in his head, and blood was everywhere. Everyone had piled into the car and carried him into town to get it stitched up. He remembered there had been tension in the car. Stella had been mad as hell. Julie had tried to make jokes, but she was having none of it. The doctor had painted that cut with mercurochrome. He could still feel it sting.

When he walked back to the house, he could see her car parked under a small shed next to the house. He walked into the house and sat down in the hallway in the chair Sudie had occupied all during the night. He could hear them talking in the kitchen. "You go on now. You been up all night long. The ladies from church will take care of the meal at the cemetery. Head on home."

She stepped into the hallway and asked Trace if he could drive Sudie home. "If you don't, she'll walk the whole five miles. She won't let me drive her."

When he returned, the funeral home people were there with the hearse, and six men were bringing the casket out the front door wearing little white flowers on their shirts. They were the same men from the mill. It occurred to him then that, of course, it would be. She had no friends on earth. Julie would have picked them to do it. He wondered then if there would even be anyone at the cemetery. But there were enough. Probably on the strength of the grandmother's standing alone, there were enough. The preacher had been awful, speaking bleakly about hell and salvation and the mystery of when we get taken. He obviously had never known Stella and had little to tell about her. His grandmother seemed to point her head dutifully toward the preacher, but Trace could tell she was elsewhere. They sat under a large arbor near the front of the cemetery and listened for half an hour while the man tried to scare them into salvation. Afterward, he had repeated the same *Yes, ma'ams and thank you, ma'ams* as the day before, and they had marched out of the graveyard and up to the church where yet another spread of food was laid out. When the meal was over, people began to filter out and away, leaving only Trace and his grandmother and Julie leaning on the hood of his Buick talking to a couple of men. She approached him and waved him to follow her back down toward the cemetery where a group of black men were placing the wreaths on the freshly covered grave.

"How do we go about gettin' a stone put up?"

"Oh, that's taken care of. Your granddaddy's big on that. He taken care of that with the funeral home a long time ago. Ours too, on the assumption he would go first."

"Well, you were right. This is a pretty spot. Everthing was real nice."

"Personally, I coulda done without the fire-and-brimstone lecture. I don't know why they gotta do that. I suppose you'll be headed back pretty quick." She walked back to the arbor and sat down on the front pew.

"Yes, ma'am. I prob'ly need to get back to school."

"I been thinkin' for years about what you and me would talk about if I ever got the chance again. I expect I'm addled or something. None of it is comin' to me now." She leaned back into the pew and looked out across the glorious fall day. "I always wanted to tell you, you got a place here if you need it. Once we met Mr. Franklin, we never did worry too much about you after that. At first, I was fit to be tied over what Fowler Clement did. I cussed the man for a long time, but later I come to see the logic of it, or maybe I just got tired of bein' mad, I don't know. Waddn't his fault what happened. You and him don't get along I understand?"

"I would'n say that. We just gone separate ways is all."

"I seen you all of four times your whole life. What a thing that is for a grandmother to say. I wonder still how all of this ever came to be."

"I want to thank you for lookin' out for her all these years."

"Well, she would a been proud of you. I'll say that." She got up and grabbed him by the hand to leave. Then she stopped all of a sudden and turned, facing him, looking him square in the eyes. "No, we never do say the real thing the way it is. I'm gonna say this the way it is for once in my life. I ain't never gonna see you again. I's about to say if you ever come by here again and such and such. It ain't gonna be that way. You're goin' back to your life, and that'll be that. You ain't never comin back, and you don't need to. Here's what I wont you to know. Just those few times, when you was born, and I got to hold you, when your momma and daddy came to visit and you busted your head, that's all it took. We loved you even without knowin' you or seein' you all these years, and still do. I'm proud as punch at how you grown up. You go on and live your life and don't look back at all that foul stuff that happened. You go and be whoever you're gonna be and just know wherever you are, me and your granddaddy loved you. That's all you gotta know about us. Now come go back to the house with me. Sudie fixed you some food to take with you."

Julie drove them back to the house, and she brought out a bucketful of food wrapped in tinfoil for him to take, then hurried back inside without a word. She returned with the bridal portrait and handed it to him.

"This'll be the way I'll remember Stella forever. This is the way she is now." She turned and closed the screen door behind her.

CHAPTER 13

December 1964

Trace backed up the steps pulling Wmearle's wheelchair. Donis Weaver held the door open and shook hands with Wmearle as they passed into the little foyer, then picked up a box of rock salt, and went back out again and shook it along the sidewalk in front of the church. The norther had hit right after daylight, and ice was starting to accumulate.

Wmearle wheeled himself down the aisle toward the middle of the sanctuary and parked next to the pew on the right side and set his brakes. Trace sat down just as the song leader motioned for everyone to stand up and started up "All Hail the Power of Jesus Name," so he bounced right back up. The congregation didn't pay a song leader, so they rotated around among a few different men who could carry a tune. Today, it was the man who worked as a car salesman in Abilene. He could be depended on to start every service with a song that would get everyone's energies elevated. The little concrete-block building could only hold about a hundred, and the Sunday morning services were filling the sanctuary to capacity. There were discussions going on about whether or not a new building should be built and what to do with this one. Trace looked over to his left. Mike was there again, with Georgette, sitting near the back and against the opposite wall. He felt bad that he found it so funny to see Mike in such a pathetic spot. He was doing what he had to do, but Trace had always admired Mike as a rebel, albeit a good rebel. He would be wearing the same oyster-button western shirt tucked into the same blue jeans. But every Sunday, he was clean-shaven, and his hair was slicked down, and he looked ridiculous, defeated. There was no doubt about where that was headed, but you had to hand it to them. They were going to go slow and out in the open, and it wouldn't be a scandal when they finally hooked up. Georgette's folks were probably relieved.

The song leader motioned for everyone to sit down, and Weaver got up to make announcements. The senior citizens wouldn't be eating at the church on Tuesday on account of it was expected to be icy. He needed volunteers to carry meals to some of the shut-ins. He asked everyone to continue to remember Trace and his family in their prayers owing to the passing of his mother last week in east Texas. Luciano was back in the hospital in Abilene and wasn't doing well. Weaver looked up and asked the congregation if anyone knew Luciano's last name. When no one spoke up, Trace called it out, "Lara."

"If anybody is going over there, please stop by and visit them. Luciano…Lara."

When Trace glanced around, Mike was already looking at him and rolled his eyes back. Trace figured there must have been some drama to that that he had missed while he was in east Texas.

The song leader got back up and began "Father Hear the Prayer We Offer." So the prayer would be next. Trace was already drifting in his mind, back and forth, from getting some hay out for his cattle and whether he would need to bust ice and for how long, then about his grandmother and whether she was right about whether he would ever see her again and how she would be grieving. Fowler wasn't there in his usual place nearer to the front, which was suspicious since Trace couldn't remember him missing before. Trace would watch him sometimes and try to make out if he was really singing or just mouthing the words. The song leaders tended to drown out everybody else. So it wasn't that you couldn't hear him. You couldn't really hear anyone. He would be there with his songbook open and at least giving the appearance of singing, but somehow Trace found it hard to imagine the voice of Fowler Clement singing the hymns.

Wmearle, on the other hand, he could hear. He sang every word and never ever hit a single note right. The song leader stood back up after the prayer and began "Nearer, Still Nearer, Close to Thy Heart." Trace knew without looking that two men would be stepping back into the foyer to get out the communion trays. He thought about that hound barking in the distance of the drizzly night as he lay in the bed of his grandmother's house. There was peace and sadness and a sense that all of time there had passed on into oblivion, and Julie speeding away in his Buick leaving him to say the final prayer over it all. The song leader gave out the number for the invitation song and went and sat down with his wife. Donis Weaver stepped up behind the pulpit and opened up his Bible.

"A few months back, a man asked me: 'Why did God have to send Jesus to die on the cross?' I told him that it was for our salvation and started explaining how he took on the sins of mankind, so that we could have eternal life. The fellow interrupted me. 'No, I understand that. But that's not the answer to the question. You answered what the purpose for it was, what the effect of it was. I'm asking why he had to come into the world in the person of Jesus in order to accomplish that.' I tried again, but every time I tried, I found myself just repeating the same things using different words, but still, I was just describing what happened, why it mattered. My friend got impatient with me. 'Let me put it this way. God is omnipotent, omniscient, omnipresent. We learned all those omnis in Sunday school. He could have accomplished those things you say in any manner of ways. He could have just waved his hand, and it would have been so. So why that way?'

"I confess. I may have been misanswering his question because I wasn't sure I had the answer. We sing a song that asks the same question, and answers it:

> *Why did my Savior come to earth*
> *And to the humble go?*
> *Why did He choose a lowly birth?*
> *Because he loved me so!*
> *Why did He drink the bitter cup*

Of sorrow, pain and woe?
Why on the cross be lifted up?
Because He loved me so!

"Put a better way, I didn't know how to prove my answer. To say 'because he loves me so' seems inadequate. But on reflection, I think it's not. John opens his gospel thus: 'In the beginning was the Word, and the Word was with God, and the Word was God. The same was in the beginning with God. All things were made by him; and without him was not any thing made that was made. In him was life; and the life was the light of men. And the light shineth in the darkness; and the darkness comprehended it not.'

"And later, 'For God so loved the world that he gave his only begotten Son, that whosoever believeth in him should not perish, but have everlasting life.'

"So we have here a glimpse at the immensity of his undertaking, the eternal nature of God. The *omnis*, as my friend called them, have a way of packaging up an idea, a definition into a word, that gives us the impression that we've got a grip on it. We don't. Those things we can say, but we have to admit that the thing itself is beyond our imagining. To know…everything…is something that can't be comprehended.

"I've had this on my mind, I guess, on account of the time of year. We celebrated Thanksgiving first, now Christmas is coming up on us. So we have our minds on good things, the blessings of life, and we have cause to be thankful for what we have, and that God has given us hope in the person of Jesus. Christmas is coming, and we'll tell the Christmas story. *Immanuel. God with us.* But my friend's question still lingers because it gets to the root of it all. 'Why did he have to? That way?' Of course, unless you subscribe to some idea that he himself is not in possession of free will, you have to answer honestly… 'He didn't have to'. Yet he did. He did it from the very beginning, and he is doing it even now, and the answer remains, simply, 'Because he loves me so.'"

"'Nay, in all these things we are more than conquerors through him who loved us. For I am persuaded that neither death, nor life, nor angels nor principalities, nor powers, nor things present, nor things to come, nor height, nor depth, nor any creature, shall be able to separate us from the love of God, which is in Christ Jesus our Lord.'

"And as long as you're asking questions along these lines… Why didn't he just create us perfect, so we wouldn't need to be saved at all? Why all the suffering and death and misery? Surely, it has always been in his power to simply 'make it so'? All these leave us humbled. And we are left staring at the ultimate questions of our faith. And the answer always comes back to 'Because He loves me so'.

Weaver sat down abruptly. The song leader got up and hastily told everyone to turn to number 784 and to hold their place for the invitation song. The man was determined to keep all his songs on topic. There were some odd glances going around in the pews as the congregation sang, "Why Did My Savior Come to Earth?" Weaver hadn't spoken for more than five minutes. Was it on account of the ice? Trace had heard there was one of the old members who had been hard on Weaver when he first hired on as the minister. Every Sunday when the congregation filed out through the foyer, Weaver would stand at the door and shake hands and get the names of any new visitors. Each week, the man would complain bitterly that Weaver was not preaching from the Bible, and that anything other than Bible preaching was just wasting time. So Weaver began to count the number of verses he included in his sermons. Each week, he would add another scriptural reference. One week, the man passed through the foyer and shook his hand without complaint, so Weaver planned his next week's sermon with one less scripture. Sure enough, the man complained. So Weaver had his number, which was exactly nine scriptural references. Thereafter, he had always included at least nine, and the man had never complained again. Trace had overheard the story at a picnic and had ever since counted the verses during the sermon on Sunday. Today there had been only three. So something was up, unless it was just getting everybody out of there before the ice got too bad.

Mike met Trace at the back of the church.

"How you doin'? Hard week, I bet."

Trace shrugged. "Not like I didn't see it comin'. She was in a bad way, so this is better. I'm all right."

"I know it. You're always all right. You know everbody was thinkin' about you. Nobody knows what to say, but they all felt real bad for you."

"I know. There ain't nothin' that can be said."

"You missed a conflagration at Lucianos the other night. He's scared they're going to take his other leg. He fought like a son of a bitch."

They both looked around quickly. Mike wasn't adjusted to church life yet and hadn't modulated his language. There were a couple of stern glances from the line of people going out the door.

"How many of you were there?"

"All five of us. Iladio got a rope around him, and we hauled him out of there, recliner and all, but it wasn't pretty. Lord, that guy is stout."

"We meetin' tonight?"

"No, the others will be busy on the ranch. They'll be busy gettin' hay out and bustin' ice for several days, I'm sure. I ain't got anything anyway other than deliverin' food on Tuesday. Besides, nobody's goin' up that hill any time soon."

"Help me get Wmearle down these steps. It looks like it's already slick. In fact, I might need some help getting him up that ramp at the trailer. Can you follow me?"

Georgette had her coat on and had wrapped a wool scarf around her neck, but she was holding back, waiting on Trace and Mike to finish talking. It was as though she didn't want to have a conversation that would put her with Mike. She would sit with him, and ride with him, but she was going slow. She was Mike's girl, so Trace was careful to keep his eyes in check. He shook his head on the way out the foyer. She did look good.

Trace threw the wheelchair in the back of his truck and hopped in. Wmearle was heaving himself back upright on the other side of the cab.

"Wmearle, what'd you think a that sermon?" He slid sideways out onto the highway. "Whoa, solid ice."

"That'us different all right. I was thinkin' he musta wanted everbody outta there quick, or maybe he had some kind of emergency hisself. I mentioned it on the way out the door. Turns out he's just got a bad case of the two step. Been on the toilet all night. Gotta appreciate the commitment there. Packed a whallop in a few minutes there, though. Some of them'll get mad, though, 'cause there waddn't no invitation at the end. There's some that think ever Sunday somebody might need to get baptized. I always thought it was stupid. Like if you forgot to ask them about it, they'd forget they intended to go get baptized today. Wha'd you think?"

"I thought it was pretty good. I'm not sure but what I liked it a lot. Better than the long-winded kind. Short and to-the-point. Then sit down. Pretty deep thoughts too."

*****

Fowler followed the winding road that ran along the bottom of a shallow canyon. He had spent the night in Del Rio and left the pavement just south of Acuna. It was after noon when he pulled into Muzquiz. The road up to David Ramos's ranch would be another forty miles, but it was a hard forty miles, and Fowler figured at least three hours. He dreaded the pain he would be feeling when he got there, and even worse, the way it would feel on the way down.

He had stopped in at the police station and walked into the back office to say hello to the captain. When the man turned in his chair, Fowler sat a bottle of Scotch on the desk, and the captain smiled and walked around the desk toward him. Fowler clapped his hands on the man's shoulders, and they embraced.

"Mi amigo viejo."

"How are you, Sal?"

"Good. Better now!"

Salvador and David both liked good Scotch. David was a man of the world, so Fowler understood that. It was an oddity for Sal though, and unlike David, he had few sources for a good bottle. Still, he had always wondered at these two, in this place, finding a liking for Scotch whiskey.

"I'm not staying long. I just wanted to drop in and thank you for helping with that business up in Acuna."

Sal's face grew serious. "I was happy to help. You know Vega was assassinated?"

"No, but I never knew the man personally." He pondered for a second that Sal used the term *assassinated*, which you usually use in the context of a politician or a judge. Fowler knew of Vega only as a hood, albeit a powerful hood.

"There's a war going on among the families up there. Things are very unsettled. When you go back, go through Piedras Negras and don't stop. I don't know if anything would happen, but you should be careful."

"I appreciate that. I'll be with David for a few days. Perhaps I'll drop in on you for lunch on the way out. If not, you need to come up and visit us some time. You can help me with my Spanish!"

Sal laughed. He knew Fowler spoke perfect Spanish. He also knew that he and David had always had an arrangement whereby they spoke only Spanish to each other when they were on the north side of the river and only English when they were on the south. Fowler had been through some sticky situations with Salvador over the years, most having to do with thugs and bandits who pestered him and David when they were moving cattle across the border. When he pulled out of Muzquiz to the west and began the drive up the canyon, he thought about the odd friendship with Salvador. He liked him and enjoyed having a meal with him, and owed him for more things than he could remember. And so he thought of him as Sal had said—*un viejo amigo*. He chuckled to himself when he thought about it. All of that said, he didn't trust the man as far as he could throw him and had lied to him about staying for several days just to be careful.

He turned north and bounced along the limestone road until it crossed the Sabinas, then headed west again. The road from that point on would become rough as a cobb. David's hacienda sat at the base of the Sierra de Santa Rosa at the mouth of a steep canyon that rose a couple of thousand feet through sheer limestone cliffs. The road dipped down here and there into the bottomland along the Sabinas where cypress trees lined the green pools flowing over the pebble bottoms. He remembered summers where these streams would be full of children swimming, but the cool weather had come down, and David had told him that much of the high country had frosted already.

The road dipped down and led to a concrete low-water crossing and marked the entrance to David's ranch. He was still over two hours from the hacienda.

He mounted the first of a series of low benches that spread outward across the eastern flank of the Sierra, and from that first vantage point, he could see the sweeping curvature of the range that ran down from the north, then turned slowly east. He stepped out of the truck and relieved himself beside a guajillo tree. The air was dead still. There was no sound, other than the occasional clicking of the cooling radiator in his pickup. There was a different smell in the air, probably from the pinon. He could see the grass was in good shape now. There had been times when there had simply been none. He spread his legs wide on the ground and leaned from side to side and front to back to stretch. The doctor had told him this would help, but so far, it hadn't. He climbed back into the cab and started upward.

The house was surrounded by a tall stone wall that encompassed some five acres of landscape. A small freestone stream ran under one section of the wall and spread into a series of small masonry canals that flowed through the grounds and around the house. There was no place within the walls that the soft, constant sound of the water trickling could not be heard. Fowler had always liked that. It seemed peaceful. There was an armed man at the gate, but he smiled and raised his hand when he saw Fowler and detached the heavy chain from one wall and dropped it on the ground for him to drive over. He parked in the large circle drive under a massive live oak whose branches in some places were two feet thick. One bent over and down and went under the ground and then back upward again. When he killed the engine, he could hear the soft babbling of the little canals.

David's home reminded Fowler of the Alamo. Not so much the battle, but the church. The thick limestone walls were cool in the summer and warm in the winter. He opened the heavy wooden door and stepped into a small gallery that opened into a large high-ceilinged central room. He heard a squeal and saw David's granddaughter running toward him from across the room. She laughed and put her arms around him.

"I don't know who you are, but thanks for the hug!"

She bounced back with a surprised look on her face. "Maria Louisa!"

"No, that wouldn't be right. Louisa's a little girl about this high. I know her. Who are you, lady?"

That made her happy. "Come sit down in the courtyard. Abuelo will be down soon." She led him out onto a loggia that surrounded a courtyard on three sides. The back side opened up to a wide view of the canyon and the mountains beyond. "Sit down and let me bring you something to drink."

"I'd take a cup of coffee if you have some made."

She smiled and disappeared back into the house. He sat down and stretched back into the chair and dropped his hat onto the table. There was a large stone fountain trickling in the middle of the courtyard with some kind of flowers growing around it, and there was lavender in the air. He sat, admiring the view of the canyon and watched some kind of black salamander walking around the bottom of the fountain. His leg was throbbing from all the jolts along the road up, but he felt peaceful here.

"My friend!"

Fowler was shocked, and the expression on his face showed it before he could recover. He hopped out of his chair and embraced David and was shocked again. He could feel the shoulder bones through the tweed blazer. He backed away and looked at David and didn't try to hide his concern. His eyes were filling with water.

"No. Don't do that now! Sit. Sit."

"I'm sorry. I don't know what I expected."

"How is the leg, or back, or whatever it is that's ailing you? Iladio told me you won't even mount a horse nowadays."

"It's nothing. It's annoying, but...I know. I'm skinny. I can't keep my pants up!"

He sat back and sighed.

"I told you. I'm going away. It's coming, and that's that. It happens to us all, and it will happen to you sometime. For now, my good friend is here, and I'm happy, and we have time to talk and plan how to take over the world like we always do. So get your dick out of the dirt and smile!"

He was infectious. He had always been that way. There were times when he had tried to use that charm on bandits and bad border cops when Fowler was sure it was going to get him killed, but he had always come out all right. Louisa stepped forward and put the china cup and saucer in front of Fowler, then kissed David on the forehead as she slipped away.

"Mr. Ramos, you are a piece of work."

"That's right! How noble in reason, How infinite in faculty!"

Fowler laughed at that. "Ha! Seenyore, I will never forget the look on the faces of those people when they found out they had their first Mexican Hamlet. God amighty, that was funny."

"I never would quit saying perchance without rolling my *r*s. How many million times he yelled at me...*puh chonce!*"

"You ever been back?"

"New Haven, no. Full of hippies now, I suppose."

"Maria Louisa is beautiful. My, has she grown up."

"She is the light of my life. And she is strong! I finally convinced her to get off to college, but she flies back all the time. She'll be finished in another year. Then I think she'll be back here."

"And Esteban?"

"He's gone."

"Gone?"

"He hired on as an engineer for the Amistad project. I suppose I thought he would do that, and once it was over, he would come back. He's not coming back. He loves the engineering stuff. Flying on a jet all around. He came home last month and told me something had happened on the project, and he left. He went to work in San Francisco, and now he's working on some kind of chemical plant they're going to build in Puerto Rico in a few years."

"And Let?"

"The same. Mostly. Juanita's taking good care of her."

Fowler leaned forward and put his elbows on his knees. He was trying to think how long it had been since he and David had been together. He and Let had met him at a New Year's party in San Antonio the year before the stroke. But they hadn't had any real time together in over five years now other than the annual board meetings for the partnership, but those were always businesslike and cluttered. An overwhelming feeling swept through him that things were slipping away. That life was getting out from under him. He was losing David too soon.

David could see Fowler's mind was spinning. "We're cooking some goats. I told everyone to come up tonight, and we'd eat outside. You remember?"

Fowler smiled. So many nights out under the oaks, in that cool mountain air, listening to those little babbling streams and the singing, with all the hands up at the house, carving cabrito off a spit.

"Just don't ask me to sing!"

"Okay, that was embarrassing. Probably what gave Leticia her stroke!"

Fowler smiled again. Nobody in the world would say such a thing but David.

"You get up to your room. Stretch out and take a nap. We'll stay up late and eat all night, and I'll try to get you to drink Scotch."

CHAPTER 14

School was cancelled on account of the gas curtailment. Trace had chained his tires and started early to get hay out for the cattle. There was a half-inch of ice on the tanks when he got there. He stopped by the edge of the water and opened the hood of the pickup, then took a wrench and unscrewed a spark plug. He kept a hose with an adapter behind the seat of his pickup, and he connected it, started the engine, and began airing up tractor inner tubes. He fastened a couple of concrete building blocks to the inner tubes and chunked one out onto the ice a few feet from the edge. The blocks broke through the ice and settled to the bottom. It was supposed to snow and stay cloudy for another day or two, and the weatherman had said it wouldn't be above freezing for a week. He angled his face up into the wind and felt the specks of ice pecking his face. A low roaring sound was building on the wind, and he tilted his head to the side to pick it up. A B-52 was coming down headed toward Abilene, and the sound grew until it was deafening, but it was just above the cloud base, and he saw only a slight darkening as it passed overhead. It was cold. He figured it must be in the single digits, and he could see the ice already forming around the holes where the blocks had punched through. Once the clouds broke, he hoped the tubes would catch just enough heat to keep a little bit of water clear for the cattle. They were clustering around the pickup when he closed the hood and headed back to the pits to start feeding.

He finished before noon and hopped into the truck to head back to town. He felt his ribs. One of the cows had crowded in on him while he was shaking out a bale of hay and whacked him with a horn. He breathed in deep, and it didn't seem to hurt, so he figured nothing was broken. But it was sore.

He pulled into the gravel drive that sat between Shorty and Herbert's houses. The two of them lived in almost identical houses that they had moved in. They were old Camp Barkley buildings from World War II that were still being sold by surplus dealers. The two houses each had a porch they'd built across the front, and the porches faced each other across the driveway. They were an odd pair. Often, you'd drive up, and they would be sitting on their respective porches talking at each other across the driveway. Trace had a thought he would check in to see if they were frozen up or in need of anything. Both houses were closed up tight, and the old pickup was not in the shed. He saw a note inside the screen door of Shorty's house and hopped out. "Gone Fishing." He looked out across the mesquite pastures. The snow was starting to accumulate on top of the ice. There was a brisk north wind, and everything that moved in it made the ice crackle. He closed his eyes and thought it sounded like a cow moving through brush. Where would somebody go fishing on such a day?

He parked next to the station and went inside. Lydia had the fire cranked up, and there were a couple of the old timers sitting in front of it drinking coffee. Lydia was buried up in the ticket box again with her glasses down on her nose. Lloyd Craig was sitting in a chair cocked back against the oil can rack with his arm draped across the checkerboard. Trace was wary of the man. Nobody seemed to know what he did for a living. Though he looked like a hard old cowboy and wore a dusty black hat, nobody Trace knew of had ever heard of him working anywhere. But it was clear from his hands that he had worked, somewhere, for somebody. What he was known to do was snoop around and trade on oilfield intelligence, sitting in his truck miles away from a rig, watching. Roughnecks would tell tales about finishing up a well, and no sooner had the taillights of the company men cleared the horizon after running a log but Lloyd would come driving up out of nowhere with a bottle of whiskey to find out what the well was going to look like. On more than one occasion, those company men had made a U-turn and tried to get him thrown in jail for trespassing, but it never stuck. He gave the impression that he was crooked through and through. Trace had wondered about that. He had never heard of anyone actually being snookered by him or cheated. He didn't have the law after him. Perhaps it was just how clever he was at checkers, and how he seemed to know he was going to beat you before you even started. When it was plain he had you, he would swivel his eyes up from the board and curl his lip ever so slightly. Trace always had the feeling that in addition to getting beat, he was about to get his throat cut. Still, he always wondered about a man having such a nasty reputation when he had never actually done anything to justify it, and he had never tried to get Trace to put money on a game. For whatever reason, and despite the fact that he seemed dangerous and shifty, he seemed to like the old fellow.

He sat down and played. It didn't take long before the customary glance told him it was over before he even saw it. Craig tried to get him to go again, but Trace hopped up and headed out. "I gotta go fix lunch for me and Wmearle."

Lydia looked up from the tickets. "Mike came by looking for you. Said he would track you down."

*****

Fowler could see the outline of the mountains beneath the curtain of stars. There were probably fifty or sixty people sitting around under the grove of oaks with the glow from the fire under the spits dying out. Someone was playing a guitar, and the children were singing. David had left right after he got up and gave a little speech, then told everyone to eat up and enjoy themselves. Louisa sat with him and wouldn't let him serve himself the whole evening. But he had run out of things to talk about and didn't feel comfortable quizzing her with anything more than small talk, and he'd had about a gallon of lemonade. Finally, he asked about David.

"He gets tired pretty fast. So he goes up and lies down. The medicine takes his energy. And he doesn't sleep much. I'll go check on him."

126

Fowler listened to the water trickling past him in the little stone canal and the music drifting through the trees. It had never been peaceful like this at home. In fact, it had never been peaceful like this here when Let was with him. Suddenly, it struck him that he had never been peaceful at any time. He had probably blamed most of that on Let. Whether before the stroke, or even before Junior died, even maybe as far back as college, from the moment she entered his mind, there was a pressure, an intensity, either of conflict or passion or hate or action or the exuberance of love, and he couldn't remember when he didn't think of all of that as just her. And it hit him that perhaps all of that wasn't her, but him. What if it was just him? What if he was doing it even before her, as though everything had been a race, a destiny that he was acceding to?

In time, the cool of the night began to settle, and he noticed that there were fewer people sitting outside the cast of the firelight. Mothers had begun to gather up the little ones, and the men were congregating in groups to smoke and drink out of mason jars. He shivered slightly. Louisa was walking down out of the house.

"He's up now and feeling better. He told me to tell you he's in the library. Let me take your dishes."

She cleared the plates and left. He had the sense that he didn't want to see David because he knew it would be for the last time. They had been friends for over forty years, and there would always be time, but now there wasn't, and there never would be again, and he knew all of a sudden that David had always anchored his world as a separate pole, and that he could dip into and out of David's world whenever he needed to. Had he been as good a friend to David as David had been to him? Could he be still? He looked out across the jagged line of the mountains and the brilliant lights above them and felt as though they were both already gone, him and Let.

David was bent over poking the fire when Fowler walked in. He reached up and grabbed the stone mantelpiece and struggled to pull himself upright, then walked to his desk and poured two glasses of Scotch. He had a broad smile when he held one out to Fowler, but when Fowler took it, the smile faded.

127

"I'll have to pour another. I assumed both of these would wind up being for me."

Fowler took the drink and collapsed down into one of the two chairs facing each other in front of the fire. The library must have held thousands of volumes, and the shelves reached from the stone floor to the high ceilings on three of the walls. He sat the drink on the arm of the chair, crossed his legs, and tossed his hat over his boot.

David sat down carefully and sipped his Scotch.

"I'm sorry I couldn't enjoy the cookout with you. It comes and goes, this thing."

"It was good. Got to visit with Louisa some. Sweet girl. Reminds me of her grandmother."

"Me too. God has been good to me, and to you. We need to remember that. You need to remember that. Right now, you look like your dog got run over."

"Sorry. Can't help it. Turns out I'm not ready. Maybe I wasn't ever going to be ready. I'm gonna miss you. There's nothing to be done. You're sure of that?"

"Yes. I was in Houston, and they're the best. It's done."

"How can I help?"

"Iladio will come home. He and Louisa will inherit everything. Esteban has chosen a different way, and he knows this. He also knows he's out. I know it will be a hardship to lose Iladio and Juanita, but they will be needed on the ranch, and their children need to grow up here. I want Louisa and Iladio close together from here on out."

"They're growing up fast. He already uses them a lot. They're good hands and good students."

"Iladio never was. And he will not be capable of taking over in the end. Louisa has it. She will become Patrón. He will understand this, and it will work. It's not that he's not a good man. I know he is, and I love him. But he cannot be Patrón. He's always been a man of the soil and the animals, and he refused to educate himself, so it will be Maria Louisa. He knows it. My people in Mexico City will manage most of it until she is ready. That shouldn't be much longer. With your blessing, she will run Grupo Elsinore."

Fowler nodded.

"You are Louisa's godfather. I need you to *be* her godfather. She will need you."

"Did Esteban's thing at Amistad have anything to do with Vega getting killed."

"Ah, you talked to the comandante! Yes, indirectly. He's out of it now, but yes, he got mixed up in things that were beneath him. I'm being careful, but I think he's clear of it. You know, my father grew up with Vega. He was always wary of him. The man could be deadly. I paid him myself rather than go to war with him."

Fowler sipped his drink and cut his eyes toward the fire.

"How is the boy?"

Fowler flinched. "He's fine. Better than fine. Acts like he's thirty instead of sixteen. The man that looks after him almost got killed in an accident. He saved the man's life. I don't know how or why, but so far, he doesn't seem to've let any of it get to him. The woman passed last week, and he went out there all by himself to her funeral."

David stared at him, and the firelight danced in the whiskey when he swirled it in the glass. They had argued before about what Fowler had done. He had argued that is. Fowler had simply listened. He marveled at the absolute stubbornness.

"Old friend. I won't try to dig up our old arguments. But I can see it's hard for you. And what's up with the whiskey?"

"I never said I didn't like the stuff. I just decided I wasn't going to drink. Got a lot easier after Junior."

"But you'll drink with me now?"

"Seems like a long time ago. Seems like we're at the end of things, and what mattered then doesn't matter now."

"I hope, for you, that when the time comes, he will come around. I hope the things you've done will still matter then."

Fowler took his eyes off the fire and bored a hole in David, the steel gray catching the firelight.

"If I can't keep my word to the one person in the world that matters more than any other… I did give her my word, dammit. She had to have it. I did it. Who am I if I break it?"

David was silent. His face was drawn and pale. They sat in silence for a long while, sipping the Scotch.

"Fowler, I'm done. You aren't done. I always thought you were just stubborn. I'm sorry. I see now. Perhaps, time is your friend, even though it's my enemy. Let us pray that it is so."

"I will look after Maria Louisa."

"*Dios mio!* Please don't give me your word on it."

It took a while for Fowler to start laughing at that. David was shameless with his humor. He bounded out of his chair and refilled their glasses, and they talked deep into the night, and when they had finished talking over the embers of the dying fire, Fowler could see there was light on the mountains. He held David in his arms and walked out to begin the long drive home, knowing he would never see him again.

He had a pretty good idea when he left the trailer to find Mike about why Mike might be looking for him. Wmearle was snug in the trailer watching Monty Hall, so he hopped in his truck to go find him. Mike was in the feedstore warming himself over the woodstove.

"Musta just missed you out at Hearndons. I seen where you'd already come and gone. Come on. I got something to show you."

Trace turned toward his own truck when they stepped outside. Mike drove fast, and he didn't want to go barreling around the country on this ice and wind up walking home in a blizzard. Mike didn't object and jumped into the passenger side.

"Where to?"

"I don't care. Let's go out to the cabin. We'll build a fire."

He turned up the river road and headed out of town. The roads were snow covered now, but underneath, there was an inch of ice.

"We'll have a pretty good walk getting down there."

"Why?"

"Well, I suppose we don't actually have to walk. What we could do would be slide outta control the half a mile down to the cabin. Maybe. If we didn't go off into the ravine or on into the river or flip, we'd be okay. But assumin' we did all that and didn't get killed, how do you propose we get back up again on this ice? These chains ain't gonna cut it."

"I suppose. That'll be all right. It ain't far."

Both of them had busted their butts by the time they got down the hill into the cabin. Mike put a stack of wood in the fireplace, poured kerosene over it, then flicked a match underneath.

"Prob'ly wadn't the best idea. I wanted to talk private."

Trace went in the kitchen to start a pot of coffee.

"So spill it."

"Lookie here." He fished a ring box out of his pocket and opened it.

"So you brought me down here to tie you up and save you from yourself until we could get a doctor to certify you as a lunatic?"

"Water's froze up." He went out the door onto the back porch and flopped the lid back from the cistern and tossed the bucket in. Out of habit, he scanned the rock ledges inside the cistern in the dim light for snakes, but there were none.

"When you gonna ask her?" He lit the burner and poured a cupful of coffee into the water.

"I don't know. Lookin' for the right time. Prob'ly take her to the show or something. Then ask her afterwards."

"Sure. A show. That'll make it seem special."

Mike was looking for encouragement, and he wasn't getting it.

"Why not? Not the show I mean. I'll figure something better. You don't seem to like the whole idea."

"Sorry. I guess I'm not the best cheerleader for the merits of marital bliss. Lemme start over. You. Are. A. Damned. Fool."

"That's better."

Trace headed back into the kitchen to get the Bugler can out. He returned and sat down on a three-legged stool next to the fireplace. He thought he would buy some time and think for a second before they got too deep in the conversation. Suddenly, he remembered Judge Reynolds and his little routine with the cigar and wondered if he had been doing the same thing. He made a slow and deliberate effort at rolling the cigarette, then offered it to Mike. Mike passed. So he lit up and took a drag.

"Okay, lemme try again. I'm gonna be positive now, like a good friend should be. You're. An. Idiot."

Mike smiled and turned his backside up to the fireplace.

"Good to know I have your complete support. Will you be the best man?"

"Good lord. You ain't even asked her yet. Why don't we see how that goes before we start bakin' the cake. Hang on." He got up and went outside and took a leak off the porch and stood there for a while trying to think about how to slow Mike down. He tried to give Georgette the benefit of a doubt, but he couldn't get over her picking up and hauling off with some cowboy she didn't even know like that. But Mike was smitten. This was going to be bad one way or another.

Mike opened the screen door and stepped out on the porch. "What you doin'?"

"Just watchin' it snow. River's startin' to freeze. Don't see that very often. Pretty ain't it."

The top of the bluff on the other side of the river that encircled the little peninsula was hidden in the snow cloud, and the ledge rock beneath it was topped in white. The wet rock underneath was a deep reddish brown. Ducks came down out of the cloud and splashed into the water.

"That it is."

Trace took the coffeepot off the burner and stuck the end of a wooden spoon in it to settle the grounds and poured them each a cup.

"Okay hoss, I'll tell you. I think you oughtta wait. Let her settle in for a while longer. I remember what you told me when we's down in Acuna. It's gotta be a two-way street. If it ain't, you'll wind up miserable. You have any better information about that now than you did then, or did you just decide to flange it?"

"I think she's comin' around. I know I enjoy bein' with her. If I ask her and she says yes, I guess I'll know for sure."

"Maybe. How's it working out with you and Wmearle?"

"He ain't the most patient soul. I know it's frustratin', but hell, I don't know everthing like he does. He's prob'ly sore at me not bein' down there right now. I ain't used to just goin' to the same place ever day like that. So I don't know."

"Kind of like a ball and chain is what you're sayin'?"

Mike cut his eyes over at Trace.

"It ain't the same."

"It's the same in about a hunnerd different ways, pardner. I grant, there's some ways it ain't too. I'm sure she smells great. But you can run off on Wmearle and he'll figure somethin' out. Marryin' is for permanent."

"Yeah, I get it."

"Well, you know I wont you to be happy. So if you do it, you better back your ears and hang on…for like fifty or sixty years."

"Hey, I heard something. I run into Iladio first thing this morning. He's leavin' to go back to Mexico. Permanent like. Whole family's packin' up."

"Why?"

"Old man is dying. 'Member him? David Ramos? Iladio said he didn't have much time, so he's goin' back to live there. Work on the family place."

"Dang. Why do you reckon Iladio come up here to work for Fowler instead of his own daddy?"

"Never heard him say. I always figured they got crossways. That happens all the time. I heard Ramos is a rich dude, though. Owns like a whole state or something. There's something between him and Clement, though, like they go way back."

"You'd never feature Iladio being a rich man would you?"

"Well, he's fixin' to be."

"You worry any about gettin' drafted? I heard you tell somebody the reason you had'n been was because you're the only son. But that don't get you off."

"No. I ain't worried. I just got one kidney."

"What happened to the other one?"

"It's called dysplasia. I didn't even know I had it until I was a teenager. I got sick, and they put me in the hospital. They said it was a birth defect. I actually got two, but one of 'em is shrunk down to nothin' and don't work. Anyway, it don't cause any problem, but it got me off. They never would let me play football on account of it."

"I never knew that. Thought I had a pretty good bead on all your defects."

"Nah, there's plenty more. Why? You worried you're gonna get drafted?"

"I think about it sometimes."

"You plannin' on goin' to college?"

"Wmearle brought that up the other day. He thinks I ought to. I don't know what for, though."

They sat and finished the coffee. Trace tossed the remnant of the cigarette into the fire. "Here's what you do. Clean up that pigpen of yours and put up a Christmas tree and fix her dinner. You can give her that Cracker Jack ring for a Christmas present. Save you from having to buy her something else. If she, I cain't believe I'm sayin' this, says yes, I'll be the best man. I'll try to look happy about it."

"That ain't a half-bad plan."

*****

He dropped Mike off at the feedstore and circled back to head toward the school. When he got close to the high school gym, he could see the light on in the back basement window. Otherwise, the school grounds were deserted. The snow had stopped, and there was a hard north wind under high gray clouds. The gym doors were open as they always were, but the heat was off, and it was dark and frigid inside. He made his way down through the pitch-black concession lobby and into the gymnasium. A few stray basketballs were lying out on the floor, and he could hear pigeons flapping up in the high windows that circled the roof. He dropped down into the dark stairwell at the back of the gym and knocked on the door to the boiler room but heard no answer. When he cracked the door and poked his head inside, he could see Sammy sitting on his cot. The room was usually stifling hot in the winter whenever the school had the boilers fired up, but they were cold today on account of the curtailment. Sammy was wrapped in quilts and had the little electric heater that Trace had brought him on the floor in front of his cot. He looked up and flashed a big toothless grin at Trace. Sammy had been torn apart somehow in Europe during the war. He had spent years in army hospitals before being turned loose. By the time he returned home, all of

135

his family had either passed or moved on to places unknown. So the community had taken him in and got him the job at the school. At first, they had cleaned up a small house for him to stay in, but before long, they found that he had made himself a place in the boiler room and wasn't going home at night. He had lived in there ever since.

All the schoolchildren were familiar with his scars and the mangled left hand and the big scar that ran across the side of his head and down under his cheekbones. Sammy wasn't bashful about showing them off, and the kids were fascinated by the giant gouges in his back and the faded tattoos on his arms. The damage to his mind was harder to understand. Sammy was handy around the school and had a knack for repairing whatever needed it and seemed to be able to manage it all without much supervision. To talk with him, though, was to talk to a child. Trace walked over and handed him a can of Copenhagen.

"Oh, thanks, Mr. Trace. Is school gonna open tomorrow?"

"Prob'ly not tomorrow. May be a few days, Sammy."

Sammy had a hard time of it in the summers. The football coaches made a point of finding work for him to do, but he would get anxious anyway and would ask everyone he met how many more days before school would start. He didn't engage the kids if he wasn't asked. Somebody had probably warned him about that. He just seemed at ease as long as there were people about and liked working on the periphery of the hubbub.

"You stayin' warm?"

"Oh yeah, heater's nice."

"You got plenty of food and stuff?"

"Umm. Hmm."

Sammy could remember a little bit about the war, but he couldn't make a coherent story out of it. Trace had pestered him a lot when he was younger about what it had been like. Sammy would only point to a scar and say "Monny Casino." If you asked him about Patton, he would smile big and say "Ol' blood and guts." He watched him lower his head and go back to staring at the little space heater.

"I'm gonna run. You sure you don't need nothin'?"

"Copenhagen."

"I just brought you some. It's there in your pocket."

"Oh, okay." He smiled the big toothless smile again and resumed staring at the heater.

*****

The streets were crusted over and popped under his tires as he eased down the street past the elementary school. He passed the little dilapidated frame house down the block from the school and turned back toward the station. He never passed the house without feeling a deep sadness. The baseball field was several blocks away from the elementary school, and in his grade-school days, the kids would make a daily run from the school to the field to play during recess. Trace had his friends then. It was before. It was the time before *it* happened. The boys would have the space of those few blocks to run out ahead of the teacher and find whatever mischief they could get into before she caught up. Most days, they could schedule a whole fight to take place and get it over with before anyone was the wiser. There had been a little girl in that barren frame house with the paint chipping and a yard that had never been mowed or watered, the windows all dusty with closed Venetian blinds. She would stand at the end of the sidewalk in a little thin cotton dress surrounded by the brown dead grass and the goatheads, and whenever the boys passed by, she would try to talk to them. Trace began to hold back and walk over to her. She was incredibly frail. He remembered how her voice was so desperately light, as though she hadn't enough wind to make her words. He could remember that little thin mousy voice saying his name. She had been pale, and the skin under her eyes seemed so painfully thin that they had a bluish color, though not from any bruise. She had seemed only a feather, as though the sunshine itself could pick her up and blow her away, but she would light up when Trace would peel off and walk her way.

She had seemed so excited to see him cross the road to talk to her. She would have been a first grader, second at most. He had been embarrassed, and the boys would yell back at him to catch up, and he didn't really want to be seen talking to some little girl. He wanted to run and outrun and fight and get into trouble if they could find some to get into. But he was inexplicably compelled to stop and immediately knew that it was somehow important to the frail little thing. Often, he would see past the screen door into the dark front room of the house the flare of the light from the end of a cigarette. He couldn't see the man, but he knew he was in there, watching. The boys had said he was crazy. He had fought in Korea and was a psycho. Trace never once saw the man and never put much stock in that kind of talk. And so he always stopped and tried to make small talk with the little whisp of a thing, and somehow he never wondered why the little girl wasn't in school or where the mother was or even what was wrong with her. He had important things to do.

One day, the house was closed. He never saw the girl again. The house simply began the slow process of disintegrating. It was not until years later. *After*, he thought, that he began to worry about her. What happened to her? Did she make it? Did she grow up? And it bothered him that he had never asked about her, never told his mother or a teacher. Had he been the only one who could have saved her? And he would lie in bed at night with Wmearle snoring in the darkness and think of her and wonder why it had never occurred to him to save her then.

The windows in the house had all been broken out now, probably rocks thrown by schoolboys just like him. The roof was sagging across the ridgeline and would soon collapse. There were weeds growing inside the living room. Where had she gone? Whatever had happened to the little feather? He shuddered in the cold, and it occurred to him for the first time in a long time that he had no place to go, and nothing in particular to do.

CHAPTER 16

April 1965

Shorty surveyed the inside of the shed. It was leaning about twenty degrees to the side.

"It's the roof, for one thing. Might be able to straighten her up with a brace across that back wall. Knock that shiplap off the back and turn it around sideways instead of vertical. Surprised it stayed up this long."

Weaver was embarrassed. There hadn't been any kind of storm. Just the normal wind, and it had begun to tilt. Any further, and he figured it was coming down, so he had approached Trace after church and asked him to come take a look. April had come in cold and dreary, but the sun had come out now, and it was warm and pretty outside.

By late afternoon, they had the braces in, and the decking knocked off the roof and were sliding joists up to nail into place. Herbert was tacking the siding on to the back side.

"I never did ask you. What were the two of you doing during Christmas? Sign on your door said you went fishing, and I know that ain't true. Everthing in the country was frozen over."

"A course we did. The hell with all that ice. Herbert. Show him your picture. I guess he gets the credit. It was on his line. Like to killed us both before we finally landed him."

Herbert pulled a picture out of his wallet and handed it to Trace. He and Shorty were standing next to a fish that looked to be about seven feet long.

"What is that?"

"Tarpon. Two hundred pounds."

"Dang. Where is this?"

"Caught him off Trinidad. South part of Cuba. Herbert's got a girlfriend in Cienfuegos. Spent two days gettin' massages over that fish."

"Cuba. You went to Cuba. Either of you two have a TV?"

"Ah, they ain't gonna pester a couple of old farts like us just fishin' and gettin' our suntans."

Trace just looked at them. It looked like a real picture.

"They had this thing down there. You mighta heard about it. Russians. Nuclear missiles. Khrushchev. Whole world liketa got blowed up?"

"Yeah, I heard somethin' about that. Shorty, didn't you tell me about somethin' like that you read in the paper?"

"Don't ring a bell." Shorty kept hammering at the joists.

"Well, I don't know anything about that. Everthing seemed peaceful enough. It was anyway until Shorty got carried away with the Mojitos. All of a sudden, he thinks he's Don Juan. I tell ya, Trace, you wouldn't think it by lookin' at him, but you get a couple of Mojitos in him, he'll steal your girl right out from under your arm."

He knew he was being conned, but which part was true and which part wasn't, was hard to figure. Who didn't know about the missile crisis? Why would they lie about it? He decided they probably just went to Florida and were messing with him. But it didn't look like either one of them had much of a suntan.

*****

The day before, he had counted 92 calves on the ground out of 110 mother cows. He was developing a habit of constantly running through the computations in his head about what they'd bring and when, and whether he would be able to make the cash stretch. But he was pleased with his crop. He enjoyed walking around in the brush looking for the calves. Several times, the momma cows had gotten after him a bit when he got too close. So he was thinking of getting a horse. It would make things faster, that was sure. But a horse was another mouth to feed, so he was running the numbers on that as well when he turned the corner on the river road and saw the motor-cycles lining both sides. There must have been twenty or so with long front forks and flags of various sorts tied here and there. A handful of men were standing in the road. They had long hair and leather vests and rough-out leather pants. They didn't move out of the way when he pulled to a stop, and one of them approached his window.

"Howdy."

"Howdy, he says." The man turned and yelled to the others sarcastically. "Boys. He says Howdy."

The man had a reddish beard and light-blue-colored sunglasses, and when he leaned close to the window, Trace got a whiff of him. It wasn't good.

"You boys need some help?"

"Yes. By God, I think we do need some help."

The man had a sarcastic, menacing look to him. He could see there was a large group of them down by the river, and they had cut the fence and driven a bunch of the motorcycles down near the top bank. There was a big fire going, and they were circled around it hol-lering and carrying on. Cutting the fence was bad business.

"Hop on down out of there and come on down with us. We got a man down there that needs some help."

The man pulled the door open and stepped up close. Trace was frozen and thought about throwing the pickup in reverse and back-ing out as fast as he could, but the man was standing inside the door now, and he wasn't fast enough deciding, and when he glanced into the rearview mirror, he saw there were two of them behind the truck.

"I said hop on down out of there. You're gonna come down here with us and give us some help." The man had a dead serious look on his face.

Trace wheeled around in the seat and popped out onto the cali-che and stood only an inch from the man and met his eyes with the same dead stare. The man backed up enough to let him pass, and the whole bunch surrounded him, so he just stepped out and headed down into the river bottom as though his heart wasn't about to pop out of his chest. It was getting dark, and he was scanning the terrain to figure which way he could take off, but the whole group seemed to be circling in around him.

"Whoah, Major. What is it you brought us?"

"I think he might be a cowboy, Colonel. He said he was here to help us."

A big shirtless man with an enormous black beard and the same squirrely blue sunglasses stepped out of the ring toward Trace. He had colored beads tied into his hair and black leather pants.

"No, I don't think he's a cowboy. More like a butterfly."

He had a dreamy lilting sound to his words. There was laughing around the perimeter of the group. They had a keg of beer sitting inside the handlebars of a big motorcycle, and everyone had a cup in their hands.

"Come sit down over here, little butterfly, and tell us what truth you have heard."

"Come again?"

"If it is help you bring, you must have the truth, for it is only truth that we need. What is your truth?"

"I don't think I have whatever it is your looking for."

"No truth? Either you have truth or you have lies. You cannot have both. A house divided against itself cannot stand. Surely you're not going to come to our party and bring only lies with you?"

"Mister, I don't understand whatever the hell it is you're talkin' about. Why don't you just let me be on my way, and you can go about your party."

"Hell. He speaks of hell. No. You are no cowboy, and you aren't a butterfly either. Perhaps you don't know. That's it, you don't know whether you have truth or lies, so…you are nothing. Sit there. Don't move. You can't move until you are something."

He turned around vacantly and walked into the gloom. Trace had heard about people being high before, but he had never seen it. He figured this was it. The man wasn't drunk, the gibberish was at least coming out clear. He figured him for a druggy. So far, they hadn't laid a hand on him, so his heart rate was slowing down. They seemed intent on drinking beer, and he started calibrating whether that was good or bad. They might be more likely to do something to him, but they'd be slower and clumsier, and it might make it easier for him to outrun them. He had run up and down these riverbanks a million times, and if he could get clear of them just a little bit, he knew they'd never catch him. He hadn't seen any weapons on them other than a few knives hanging from their belts.

When it was dark, the big man they called *Colonel* drifted back into the circle. Now Trace knew. He was clearly on something.

"It is time for the sacraments. Gather 'round. It is only in the sacraments that the little nothing will find whether he is of the truth or of the lie. Is he a cowboy or a butterfly?"

He produced a bottle of cheap wine and a package of saltine crackers and made a slow solemn circle around the fire, handing out a single saltine to each person and giving them a swig at the bottle. Trace was thinking how ridiculous they all were but decided to play along rather than chance provoking them.

When he had finished, several of the group squatted down on the ground and began looking into the fire. The conversation died out as others roamed around in the periphery. A strange music drifted through the air, of a kind Trace had never heard before. It sounded exotic. An hour passed, and no one addressed him again. He thought about just standing up and walking out, and if anyone noticed, he would run for it. The colonel was sitting on the ground staring into space. Suddenly, he had a sensation that was akin to vertigo, as though everything in his vision was tilting sideways in a strobe light. He leaned forward and threw up into the dirt. His heart was racing again, and the strobe-like tilting of his vision began to happen more and more quickly, and each time his vision tilted, the fire in front of him began to grow, and the face of the colonel began to appear out of the fire with only the little blue sunglasses other than the color of fire, and he looked down at the vomit on the ground, and the ground sucked it in and began to swirl and move as though in a current, and his boots began to sink into the dirt, and he felt the fire with the strange little light blue sunglasses in the middle of it begin to burn, and he turned to run, and the darkness and the brush and briar thickets were vibrating in the strobe-like dance, and he ran, but his legs were down in the dirt now up to his knees, and suddenly his legs were free of the dirt, and he was running now in the bottoms faster than he could possibly run, and the fire behind him and the strange music and the little blue sunglasses were receding as though they were being sucked into some black whirlpool.

*****

He woke up in a cold sweat with a fluorescent light fixture above him. His hands were tied with towels to stainless steel rails along the sides of the bed, and he seemed to be covered with bandages here and there.

"Hello!"

A nurse hurried into the room. "Hello there."

"Where am I?"

"You're in the hospital. You're in Abilene. Stay still and let me run down the hall right quick. Your friends are here. I'll be right back."

Lydia was the first to poke her head in, and Wmearle and Mike were right behind her.

"What happened? How'd I get here?"

Wmearle wheeled his chair over to the bed and began untying the towels.

"Git them otheruns off, Mike!"

Mike ran around to the other side and started untying the towels. Lydia leaned over the bed.

"That's better. You look like your old self."

The nurse pushed her way in and took a stethoscope and slid it under the hospital gown. She took her count and said something to Mike on her way out.

"What happened?"

"We ain't entirely sure." Wmearle was up close to the bed now, and he looked sick with worry. "Somebody brought you in here to the emergency room and left without givin' their name or nothin'. You got a bad knot on your head, and you're all scratched up. You remember anything?"

He tried to remember, but the last thing he could be sure of was talking to Shorty and Herbert at the Weaver place. The rest was some kind of strange amalgam of a bad dream that he wouldn't have been able to describe if he tried.

"You got some kind of poisoning or something. It made you kinda crazy there for a while."

He felt of his forehead, and there was indeed a big sore knot right in the middle. He felt feverish and thirsty.

"You're gonna be alright. Just lay there and rest. Lydia, you and Mike clear on outta here and let him get some rest."

*****

Mike came and got them two days later. Trace had no more recollection than he had when he first woke up about what had happened, but he had started to feel strong again once the strange feverish sensation wore off. He and Mike got Wmearle situated, and he could tell the two of them were looking at each other now and again as though they knew something he didn't.

"Come go with me."

Trace climbed into Mike's pickup, and they headed out of town and up the river road. He remembered the spot before he saw it, though the rest was all jumbled. Mike stopped at the place where the fence was cut, and they got out and looked down into the river bottom. There was a tremendous mangled pile of burned motorcycles in a heap where the bonfire had been.

"We think it was Shorty and Herbert. They're gone. Sign on the door at their house says 'Gone Fishing.' There were about twenty of 'em. Motorcycle gang. Somebody seen the fire from town, and they come out here to put it out. All them motorcycles in a big bonfire goin' up in smoke. Ever one of 'em was tied up to trees with barbwire, all out in along here, and I mean like they weren't ever goin' anywhere. Some of 'em were still out cold. They all looked like they'd been beat to an inch of their life. Tire iron or blackjack or something. Somebody did take it to 'em. There was dope ever'where. Ever last one of 'em had it on 'em. The doctor said he thought what you had was LSD. It's big with the hippies. You remember any of it?"

"Maybe. It was weird. I can't exactly explain it. I don't remember taking any pills or smoking anything. I thought I dreamed all of it."

"They found your pickup sittin' right in the middle of the road. Looked all up and down the river for you and even went splashin' around in there thinkin' you musta been drowned. Somebody called the sheriff and told him you were in the emergency room in Abilene. The doctor said it would have been on a sugar cube or a piece of paper you licked or something like that. You were crazier'n hell there for a while. I thought Wmearle was gonna come clean apart."

"What happened to them?"

"Sheriff came and hauled 'em all to the county jail. He said they're a bad bunch. He better keep 'em there too. I never seen anybody so anxious to kill somebody as Wmearle Franklin was when he found out. Man had blood in his eyes."

CHAPTER 17

October 1965

Trace pulled the bridle off the horse and opened the barn door to scoop up a bucket of oats. They had shipped the calves out just before noon. The ag teacher had given him some good advice on that. "Let 'em get up and suck before you load 'em and don't let that driver sit out there and burn diesel to keep his truck warm." Ever pound you save is money in your pocket, and diesel and milk weigh more than you'd think they would. The driver had thought that was ridiculous, but Trace had told him if he wanted to just hand him ten dollars, he would be fine letting him keep the truck warm. Numbers were flying around in his head. All summer, he had been scrounging to keep his head above water. Cattle prices were still sitting at twenty cents, and while he had a draft for almost nine thousand dollars to deposit, he'd had most of a year now to see how the two places could get into his pocket. He had planned all year to pay the note down by at least four thousand, but now he was running through the feed bills in his mind and the medicine and how much he owed Lydia and the fourteen hundred for interest and the rent, and he could see the money evaporating. Even at that, he was looking at four years before he would be out from under Compton.

Still, he was happy. He'd only had one calf die on him, and there had been decent rain, and he had saved back ten of the heifers to put over on the Wilson place. He figured Compton would be happy renewing the note for another year, and he was excited to head into town to settle up with him.

Compton had surprised him when they met at the bank. Rather than paying down his note, why not keep what he was planning to pay and buy another twenty cows in the spring to fill out the Wilson place? So he had paid him just the interest on the loan and was already recalculating his plans when he got up and shook hands and headed out. Compton stopped him just as he was going out the door.

"One other thing. Those cows you sold back in the spring when they didn't calve? Now it's not a big deal, so don't worry about it. I just want you to know how things work. It was fine getting rid of them, made sense and all. You just oughta know that all those cattle are collateral. Technically, you're not supposed to sell 'em without putting the money on the loan. Now I know you bought them replacements, which is all good and proper, but whenever you do that, you need to call me and let me know just to be on the safe side of things."

Trace must have looked alarmed.

"Now I told you not to worry. You're fine. I know you weren't meanin' anything nefarious. Just wanted you to know how things work."

By the time he jumped in his pickup in the parking lot, he was red in the face and regretted jumping so fast to plow the money back into the cattle instead of sticking to his plan. He resolved that would be the last time he would do that. It had been a year, and he hadn't felt the bank at all. Now, all of a sudden, he could feel them, and he didn't like it. It would be cotton-ginning time soon enough, and there would be as much work as he could take on for a couple of months. Now any thoughts about slacking off and just looking after his own stuff were gone. He wanted that money.

*****

He saw her out of the corner of his eye before she went out of sight behind a mesquite fencerow. When he slowed down and backed up to look down the little dirt lane that followed the edge of a half section of cotton, he could see the little beat-up sedan parked at the back of the field a half mile off the highway. It didn't fit. There was nothing out there but cotton fields. So he turned off the road and eased down the lane and pulled up behind the car. Georgette was sitting alone in the driver's seat. He had almost stopped short and turned around thinking that she and Mike might be up to something out there, but it was broad daylight, and Mike had been busy at the shop when Trace got out of school not more than an hour before.

He got out and circled around to the passenger side door and thumped on the window. Either she didn't hear him or was ignoring him, so he opened the door and leaned over to look in.

"Georgette? Everthing all right?"

She seemed to be out in space somewhere. Finally, she sighed real big and turned to face him and gave a halfhearted smile.

"Why wouldn't everthing be all right?"

"Whatta ya doin' out here?"

"I'm not doin' anything. Cain't a person just not do anything?"

"Mind if I sit down and not do anything with you for a second?"

He slid into the front seat and left the door open.

"Well, I guess I don't."

Trace was nervous around Georgette. She was almost three years older, and his misgivings about her and Mike didn't mean she wasn't stunningly beautiful. She had a sadness about her that in some odd way made her even more attractive, but he still thought she was dangerous, and he often found it very uncomfortable to be around her on account of he was bound and determined not to ever be caught staring. So he was always finding a way to look somewhere else, and even that had gotten to be awkward. He sat in the car looking straight out the front windshield at miles of flat empty cotton fields. They sat for a few minutes in complete silence.

"Georgette, there ain't nothin' out there."

"You got that right."

The words were short and sharp. He didn't have the impression she was in any trouble. Maybe just mad about something. He kept his eyes on the windshield and waited a few minutes.

"Is there anything I can help you with?"

"Leticia Clement is your grandmother, id'n she?"

"Yeah… Why?"

He knew Fowler had hired her to look after Leticia and keep house after Iladio and Juanita had gone back to Mexico.

"No reason. I can see some resemblance."

He had no intention of getting into another conversation about all that. It occurred to him that this was really the first time he had ever had what you'd call a conversation with Georgette, and it was turning out to be a pretty weird one.

"It's so sad, the two of them. That big old house. Sometimes, I gotta get away from there. There ain't no place to go, so I just drive out here where there ain't nothin'."

"I heard you and Mike finally settled on a date. April, right?"

"I suppose everbody ends up that way. Sooner or later. One or the other of 'em ends up watchin' the other one die. It don't matter how rich you get or what you do. What's the point of it?"

Trace had no idea how to respond to such talk. A lone C-130 was flying low on the horizon ten or so miles out, and in the stillness, the low-humming sound had just caught up to them.

"You need to perk up. Them's their problems. You oughta be happy."

"So that's a big I-have-no-idea," she said sarcastically.

"Prob'ly not. I ain't the preacher."

"You hear what he said Sunday?"

"Maybe. Refresh my memory."

"He said bein' happy all the time id'n the point. Whether its bein' sad or bein' happy id'n the point. Lovin' is the point. That's all there is."

"I remember. I suppose that's true."

"What if you don't feel it? What if you're just…blank?"

Trace's antennae went up.

"Listen. If you ain't sure about this thing with Mike, you sure as hell better tell him about it. You been stringin' this thing out for most of a year now. He don't deserve to get tooled around."

He was staring straight at her now, but she was focused out into the emptiness.

"Ain't you got somewhere to be?"
He stared at her for a while longer, but she never turned.
"Tell him."
He slammed the door and drove away.

CHAPTER 18

"You wonta go to the football game tonight? Last one at home."

Wmearle had been wheeling himself across the gravel drive from the shop. It was pleasant, and still, and the smell of smoke was in the air across the town from people burning their trash.

"Never knew you had any interest in it."

"Don't. Thought you might."

"I'd just as soon sit out here and listen to it from afar. Kinda tired."

Trace could hear a bunch of noise out in the shop and figured Mike was closing up for the day. He knew it wasn't going well between the two of them.

"What's got you in the dumps? You hadn't said much all week."

"Perplexed. Got a quandary I hadn't been able to figure out."

"Git me a sodi and lay it on me."

Trace hopped up and reached into the cooler on the top step and held the bottle against the top rail of the ramp, then whacked it on the top with his clenched fist to pop the cap off.

"*Gracias.*"

"I run into Georgette. She was sittin' all by herself out in the middle of nowhere. For no reason. I come up on her thinkin' she was in some kind of trouble. But she was just sittin' out there starin' at a empty cotton field."

"Wha'd she say?"

"It was strange. She was just kinda ramblin'. Didn't appreciate me botherin' her neither. So I left."

"Well, first of all. Women. Second, what's the predicament?"

Trace leaned to the side to get a clear view of the shop. Mike was still in there banging around.

"I don't think she wants to marry Mike. Worse yet, I think she might go ahead and do it anyway."

"You and her ain't...?"

"No. Hell no. I just stopped 'cause I saw her car parked out in the middle of the field. Seemed odd." Wmearle blew out a whistle and tilted the Coke back. He looked back at the shop where Mike was pushing the sliding door shut.

"Stay out of it. Stay a damned country mile from it."

"You don't think I oughta warn him?"

"I expect it wouldn't matter. He'd do what he's gonna do anyhow, and then when it all blows up, he'll be even madder at you. This'un you leave alone." He shook his head.

"It'll be bad when it goes haywire. He's been hung up on her since high school. You never told me how you and Jeannie came to be sweethearts."

"Figured it was obvious. She got one look at my physique and fell head over heels in love."

"Prob'ly more like blind love."

"Ya think! I to this day have no idea what she saw in me. I asked her out on a dare with all my buddies watchin', thinkin' we'd all have a big laugh when she slapped me. When she said yes, I got caught off guard. I didn't have any idea she'd ever say yes, so I hadn't considered what we might do. When she asked me where we were goin' to, I just stood there like a goat. Totally discombobulated. Couldn't think of so much as a word to say. She bailed me out. Said we could figure it out later."

"How long was you married?"

"Twenty-two years. She got sick and passed in the space of a year."

"I'm sorry I never knew her."

"You woulda been real little then."

"That's when you bought the trailer, wad'n it?"

"Yeah. I couldn't stand to be in that house anymore after Sylvia moved off."

"Would ya do it over again?"

"Beg your pardon? Well, a course. Sure I would. Why'd you ask such a thing?"

"I'm sorry. That was a stupid question. Somethin' Georgette said bugged me. She was talkin' about Fowler and Leticia. How everbody, no matter what, if somebody gets married, one of 'em ends up watchin' the other one die. So what's the point of it?"

"Girl's got problems, sounds like." He stared down at the Coke bottle. Trace could see the muscles in his face were starting to freeze up on him.

"Wmearle, I'm sorry. I shouldn'a said that."

"Ya know? I'll tell ya the truth. She ain't altogether wrong. Fact is, that's true. Whether she can see the point in it is somethin' else again, and that's her problem. I don't know how to even say it. But you bet I'd do it over. A million times, knowin' ever time how it was gonna end up the same way. A million times if the only part of it I could have would be the worst part. I never thought about it like that before just now, but the best of it and the worst of it and all the plain ole borin' parts in between all end up being the same thing, and I promise ya son if you ever get lucky enough to have it, you better grab it by the balls and not let go."

It was late when he wheeled Wmearle up into the trailer. Lydia had walked over after she closed up the station, and the three of them had sat out under the stars with the lights from the football game illuminating the dust and smoke that lay over the town and talked about everything from Peyton Place to Lyndon Johnson to what to do about all the hippies. He had cranked the window slats open before he lay down, and the cool fall air had seeped into the room. He said his prayers and fell asleep listening to the whip-poorwills and wondering whether Fowler would say the same thing that Wmearle had.

*****

Mike was sitting in the usual place Sunday night. When he wheeled his headlights across them, he saw a new face. Blas and Nicholas were squatting on their heels with their same old taco shell hats and Levi jackets.

"We got a new member of our crew, Trace. This is…lemme get this straight. Enrique Salcedo Guevarra Colön. He's Iladio's cousin, or cousin's brother-in-law or something. He's workin' on the Clement with Blas and Nick. He goes by Tito. Guess he didn't already have enough names."

"Howdy."

Tito held out his hand, and they shook, and he tipped his hat, which Trace took to be overdoing it. He seemed bashful. Mike seemed to be in a good mood. He passed the bottle around. Tito passed, which was notable.

"Nuestra condolencias por el fallecimiento de Señor Ramos."

The three of them crossed themselves.

"Señor Ramos nos hizo un gran favor una vez."

"How's Maximo?" Blas smiled and shrugged. "He's good."

"Nick. I heard the news. When do you go?"

"Dos semanas. Fort Benning. Georgia."

Trace hadn't heard that. It frightened him. He wasn't so disturbed by the war itself. He didn't have much of an idea of what that was all about other than generally horrible and dangerous. The idea that the government could reach down and snatch you out of your life without any choice in the matter bothered him. It seemed contrary to every instinct he had.

"Okay, we need to get out to Henry Laird's place tomorrow. Him and Lucille are both down, and Harriet Odom told me their freezer went out on the back porch. They got a whole freezer full of rotten meat to get thrown out. Gonna stink like the dickens."

Blas was translating to Tito, so evidently he had zero English.

"I think if we all get out there, we can load it in the back of the truck and haul it off without opening it. If it turns out the freezer's fine, and he just popped a fuse or something, we'll have to dump it out and clean it. I personally can't wait. Can everbody make it by six o'clock?"

Mike's flashlight was shining on his little spiral pocketbook, and suddenly Trace caught a glimpse of movement on the ground right in front of him. He yelled and jumped backward and tripped over a rock and slid off the hill upside down. When he recovered and climbed back up, Tito was standing in the middle of the circle, holding a good-sized rattlesnake by the head. Mike had his mouth open, incredulous. "Knothead just reached down and picked him up."

Tito took a few steps out into the dark and flung the snake into the brush.

"Looks like we got us a hand there."

He and Trace both hopped up on the tailgates.

"Sheesh. That'll get your blood pumpin'. Okay, only other thing is Marlene Huey's porch is about to collapse. It'll be a quick fix, but it'll take at least three of us. How about Saturday morning about ten? Trace? Blas? All right."

Mike shined his flashlight everywhere before they hopped down. He and Trace both had the heebie-jeebies. The other three were laughing at them. They got in their pickup together and drove off.

"Georgette said she talked to you. I don't think she likes you very much."

"I just stopped to see if she was all right. Sorry if that was a burden."

"Anything else you need to tell me."

"Nope. Like I always say, she looked good."

CHAPTER 19

December 1965

Wmearle spooned out a blob of the cane syrup over his biscuits. Trace had forgotten to set the can next to the pilot light on the stove, and the cold had caused it to get even thicker than normal.

"What you studyin' on?"

"Good question. I gotta write a paper for Miss Bledsoe about a couple of stories we had to read. Due tomorrow, and I'm drawin' a blank."

"Gimme the short version."

"The first one I liked. It was about this guy up in the Yukon that went out in the dark when it was about seventy-below. He was gonna walk home, and one thing and another happened, and he ended up freezing to death. The other one was crazy. It was about these women that lived together, a mother and daughter, and the daughter was a one-legged philosopher. As in a atheist. It was depressing. They're back and forth, always at each other. Along came this Bible salesman and asked her out on a picnic. Things got to progressing, and he took her up in a old barn, and they started smoochin', and when it got hot and heavy, he asked her if he could see her wooden leg. He just up and swiped her leg and run off with it. Left her there in the barn without a leg and just run off. And that was the end of it."

"This is what you're readin' in school?"

"English class."

"What are you supposed to write about it? Sounds like you got the gist of 'em."

"I'm supposed to write a essay *in which I explore the common themes of the two stories.*"

"Well, now. Professor, I regret to inform you that I'm sorry I asked."

They laughed. "I get the first one. Miss Bledsoe is always havin' us read stuff, and there's meanings and themes and such that I usually don't pick up on until she explains it. Even then, they're sometimes lost on me. The guy in the Yukon was easy. It said it in the very first part of the story. The problem with the man was that he had no imagination. So the whole story you could figure if he had had some imagination, he might imagine what might happen to him, but he didn't, so he froze to death. I don't know what to think about the one that had the one-legged girl."

"Maybe she didn't have any imagination either?"

"I don't know. Take a lot of imagination to figure a Bible sales-man might up and run off with your wooden leg!"

"You like that kind a stuff?"

"Some of it I like, and some of it I don't. I even liked some of the poetry we read, but some of it is was old English. I don't care much for it if I can't pronounce it. Miss Bledsoe's all right, though."

"Why do you say that?"

"Some of 'em ain't ever gonna get it. Roberto or Henry or Donny or some a them. They're lost. She don't embarrass 'em in front of everbody. I see her up there with 'em after school."

"Speakin' of, you thought any more about college? Senior year is gonna be on you before you know it."

"Mike keeps pesterin' me about it. I told him I ain't gonna go to college just to get out of goin' to Vietnam."

Wmearle didn't like where that conversation would lead. He had not talked about it with Fowler or Reynolds, but he figured Trace had a zero-percent chance of getting drafted.

"No, I'm with you there. That ain't a good reason. But there are good reasons. I never had the idea to go, and when the war was over,

I just wanted to get back to Jeannie and go to workin'. But I think you oughta. You got a lot on the ball that most don't."

"And study what? Stories about one-legged philosophers?"

"You got me there. No...maybe... It don't really matter what it would be. Main thing is openin' those eyes a yours to more than just what's in front of you. I think you outta back your ears and just do it. So there. Last you'll hear about it from me."

"I still got time."

*****

The meeting was short. Blas and Tito, but no Mike. Trace quizzed them for any information they had on him, but they were a blank.

"Let's get outta here. There ain't no point in comin' out any more until we hear something. This little enterprise seems to be peterin' out on us."

He had bought everyone a cigar at the truck stop for a Christmas present. He passed them out and shoved the last in his pocket and headed for the truck. He had a bad feeling about Mike inasmuch as he had never missed a Sunday night in three years without passing the word around beforehand. Nobody had seen him in almost a week. He jumped in the pickup and skidded off the hillside and tore down along the river road toward the Wakefield place with a feeling of dread creeping up on him.

The house was dark. Mike's pickup was not under the shed, and the place was deserted. Trace didn't like going there. It reminded him of that night. But the house looked smaller now, as houses from your childhood always do. It was trashy, and junk had begun to accumulate around it, and it needed painting. He remembered walking up into the porchlight of that stifling August night, and how he had found his mother sitting bolt upright on that sofa in her Sunday clothes in that defiant trance. Mike had hurried them back into his bedroom and put all three of them to bed, then taken up a position at the kitchen table that afforded him a view into the living room where he could keep an eye on her as his daddy had instructed, although it had occurred to him that he had no earthly idea what she might be inclined to do, and what he might do about it if she did. But he had stayed put, all night, until his daddy had appeared with the sheriff at dawn.

Trace mounted the steps and opened the front door. It was cold inside, and the rank smell of stale food was in the house. He turned on the light and walked past Mike's recliner and into the kitchen and saw the two plates with the foul-smelling food still on them. Nothing seemed to be in disarray. In fact, the house looked to be in pretty clean shape for Mike. But it was clear he hadn't been there in a week, at least.

When he got to the river road, he paused, and didn't like his options. The only other person who might know what had happened was Georgette, and she was either at her parents' house in town or out at the Clement. He had not been to that house since before *that* night and had no reason to believe he was welcome there. He turned in that direction and quickly determined only to check and see if her car was in the drive. Now he was feeling dread on top of dread. He passed the enormous cedar corners that marked the beginning of the Clement fences and turned out away from the river. The house would be another three miles up and over a range of low hills and back down into the sweeping curve of the Clear Fork. When he topped the hill, he could see the lights from the house and the chimney smoke lying foglike across the flat bottomland pastures. He came again to the river and could see the road disappear over the bank into the blackness where the low water crossing cut through the river, then turned right past the two stone columns that flanked a cattleguard and watched his headlights pan across the grounds. Georgette's little sedan was parked there.

He was frozen with indecision now. He sat with the engine running and argued with himself about what to do. Ultimately, he decided against disturbing things. It had occurred to him that he had no idea what things were really like with Leticia, as he had become pretty adept at tuning out whatever people said about it. The more he thought about it, the idea of knocking on that door at such an hour was impossible, so he backed out of the driveway and headed back the way he'd come. Whatever had happened would have to wait until morning, at least.

*****

He had fed in a hurry and then sped back out to The Clement and had pulled into the same spot he'd been sitting six hours earlier. He still had no plan about how to approach the problem and hoped that someone would just see him and raise Georgette without him having to walk up there and knock on the door. He turned off the headlights and sat in the drive with the engine running. It was a frosty windless morning, and daylight was still an hour out. He had been staring at the light from the big porch that pointed out toward the riverbottom when he became aware of Fowler standing at his window.

He rolled the window down and could see there was alarm in the man's expression.

"Mike Wakefield's disappeared. I'm worried about him. I need to find out if Georgette knows what happened to him."

Fowler's face softened only slightly, as though in relief. He turned abruptly and strode toward the house.

It was almost an hour, and the sky was alive in a glorious winter dawn that cast gold and red and pink across the horizon. He had seen Fowler drive away up river into the darkness shortly after he'd entered the house. Finally, he saw Georgette step off the porch and pull a coat up tight around her neck and tighten a scarf. She was not happy to see him.

She walked out and opened the door and jumped inside the pickup and wiped her nose.

"I don't know where he is."

"What do you know?"

"I told him. You told me to tell him. I did."

Trace whistled through his teeth. "I'm sorry. I shouldn't have poked my nose in your business."

"You got no reason to be sorry. You was right. I should'na ever let it go as long as I did. Even so, he's better off."

"What's the last you saw of him?"

"I told him. He fixed dinner for me, and I went out there, and before we started eatin', I told him. He didn't say nothin' at all. He just walked out to his pickup and drove me home and never said nothin' at all."

She had a distant, damaged look, as though she had come back from a war and was having to go back again. He recalled what she'd said. "What if you're just blank?"

"I'm sorry. I know he's your friend and all. I did'n mean for all this to happen."

"I know you didn't."

"I gotta get back in there."

"What's it like?"

"You mean with Mrs. Clement?"

"Uh-huh."

"It's the worst thing in the world."

CHAPTER 20

June 1966

"Are you serious?"

"As lye soap."

Trace had tried to get out the door when Lloyd Craig had waved him over for a game of checkers. He had hauled hay all night long and wanted to get in bed. Lloyd had whipped him quickly, and Trace had hopped up to go when he leaned in over the checkerboard and whispered, "I seen that buddy of yours."

"Where?"

"On a rig. Out north of Fluvanna. He was workin' evenin' tower. That'us a week, maybe two weeks ago. They were pretty close to runnin' pipe on it and fixin' to just hop over and drill another one. Prob'ly still there."

"How would I find it?"

"You know where Fluvanna is?"

"Generally."

"You turn west off a 84 toward Fluvanna and go about three miles. There's a county road runs north up there a couple a miles. You head up in there about dark, you'll likely see the lights. It's the only rig runnin' in there right now."

"How was he? How'd he seem?"

"Oh, you know…had that old far away oilfield stare."

Trace went out and bought a couple of Dr Peppers and took one in for Lloyd. "Much appreciated."

*****

It was nearing sundown when he turned north up the county road. The rig was sitting on top of a bluff overlooking the highway. He had driven around a half-dozen oilfield roads that snaked around in different directions, and each one had taken him the wrong way. By the time he finally drove up on the rig, it was dark, and he could see the headlights of the traffic down below on the highway. He parked the pickup next to a couple of others below the derrick and walked up the gangway to the doghouse. It was empty, so he stepped through and stood in the doorway looking out on to the floor where three men were working around the drill pipe. One, the driller, was standing back operating the brakes and throttles, and the other two were operating the big tongs and appeared to be disconnecting the pipe that was being lifted out of the well. Only the driller noticed him, but he seemed busy, so Trace just watched.

The other two were completely covered with gray drilling mud. Each time they'd break a connection, they took a piece of corrugated tin and wrapped it around the pipe. When the driller lifted up on the disconnected pipe, the mud would fall out of the pipe and spray everywhere. One of the two working the floor was Mike, though it took him a while to tell. He was coated from top to bottom with that light-gray fluid, and the hard hat and goggles he had on pretty much disguised him. After a while, Mike had finally noticed him and yelled out to the driller to hold up. He stepped around through the equipment and mud and up to the door.

"What in the hell are you doin' up here?" He was yelling above the sound of the engines.

"Good question."

"Listen, there's a Airstream out yonder the geologist stays in. Go get in it and kick back. We're gonna be at this awhile, and I'm workin' a double through morning tower. I'll come out and roust you when we're done."

He made his way back down the gangway and could hear the work underway by the throttling up and down of the draw works. The rig was swarming with crickets, and rotting scum of the dead insects underneath the rig smelled like death. The Airstream was sitting out in the dark across the location, so he walked out across the graded caliche and knocked on the door. Mike hadn't said whether the geologist was in there. It was empty. He fiddled around in the dark and found the light switch and immediately felt uncomfortable. He hadn't seen a trailer that fancy before. It appeared to be brand-new, and other than the smell of it, which was not much different than the doghouse, and the odd microscope on the kitchen table, it looked like something a movie star would stay in. An air conditioner was humming in the ceiling and muffled the sound of the diesel engine throttling up and down on the rig. He sat down on the sofa in one end and flipped through a magazine. Finally, he turned out the light and stretched out and fell asleep.

*****

"Wake up, you knothead."

He sat up and wiped the corruption out of his eyes. Mike was standing outside the door of the trailer. He looked his old self, clean as a whistle.

"Foller me into town. We'll grab a bite."

The sun was well up, and there was activity all around the rig with an assortment of service company trucks positioned all around the derrick. He jumped out of the trailer and followed Mike off the location and down into town. A half hour later, they were ordering breakfast.

"Not so much as a word."

Trace could see his earlier impression was wrong. He didn't look like his old self. He looked harder. Even a touch of meanness in his expression. His eyes were darker, withdrawn, bloodshot.

"Didn't have anything to say, and if I had, I would'na felt like sayin' it."

"Here's somethin' you mighta said. 'I'm leavin'. I didn't commit suicide'."

"How'd you track me down? Never mind. Lloyd Craig, wadn't it?"

"Well, I gotta get back. I'm getting ready to cut silage, and I gotta get things squared away."

"That's it. You come all the way out here, and that's it?"

"What? Oh, you think now we oughta just pick up and shoot the shit and all like nothin' ever happened, after six months without so much as a kiss my ass. Naw, I got all I need. I'll tell Lydia and Wmearle and Blas and Tito and everbody else you didn't go drown yourself or whatever. You're alive. Everbody can put their minds at ease, and we can all just go on about our business knowin' you're safe and sound and a perfect absolute asshole."

"I figured there was more to come."

Trace stuck a piece of bacon in his mouth and chomped on it, emphatically chomped on it.

"Lemme guess what's next. Some variation on I-told-you-so, I reckon."

Silence.

"Oh, I see. You been savin' up for this, hadn't you? Sorry, I keep talkin'. You go ahead. I expect you got the whole sermon all memorized."

"I went out there and washed the dishes, just so the house wouldn't smell like somethin' died in there."

"What that house needs is a good fire. But I appreciate it all the same. Whenever I get back out there and strike a match to it, it'll be good to know the dishes was all washed."

"You look rough."

"Doin' doubles'll do that."

"So you decided you would'n drown yourself or hang yourself like any normal suicide, you'd spread it out as long as you could to maximize the misery."

"It's a wonder how I been able to make it this long without you bein' there to lift my spirits."

"Well, that's kinda the point, ain't it? It wad'n me that wadn't around. I's right where I always been. You're the one disappeared."

"Listen, hoss." He paused and looked out the truck stop window. "There ain't nothing there for me. Momma's moved off. Daddy's dead. Bank took everthing but the house. I thought I had somethin' worked out that made sense. One thing that I figured mattered. But you was right. I'll give ya that. I was a damned idiot. I didn't even have that."

"So what now? You just gonna grind yourself into the ground? I expect you're rollin' in the dough with all that overtime. Can I have it when you finally get killed?"

"I'll speak to my lawyer."

"So for real. You ain't comin' back?"

"You're givin' me way too much credit. As if I got a plan. I had a plan. I spent all my time thinkin' about it. Lookie where it got me. So now, I ain't got a plan and don't intend to have one. I get up in the morning. I go out and work, and I keep at it as long as they let me so if I'm not out on the rig, I'm at least too tired to do anything but sleep. That don't give me any time to think about nothin', which is just the way I wont it. If I wake up some day and think I need to start plannin' and thinkin', then I might just do it. You never can tell. I ain't foreclosin' on nothin'."

"Dang, that's inspirin'. I'll call a meetin' for Sunday night and let the other guys know how you got yourself a lobotomy."

That seemed to get Mike's attention. He perked up a bit.

"Y'all still doin' that?"

Trace pulled out the little pocket spiral notebook from his shirt pocket. Mike cocked his head to the side and smiled.

"Well, that's good. I'm glad to hear it."

"Listen dumbass. Get this outta your system. You ain't the first person that ever got done wrong by a woman. I admit it'd be embarrasin' if she wadn't so dang good-lookin'. There ain't nobody faults you for that. Hell, they're all sayin' there but for the grace of God, ya know."

"What about Wmearle? I bet he's pissed."

"He don't get pissed. Not really. Tell ya the truth, he seen it comin'. He had a new guy in there inside of a week after you cut out. I'm thinkin' he's just gonna sell out and move off to where his daughter is."

"Where's that gonna leave you?"

"Don't know. I'm bettin' he don't make a move until I graduate. Wouldn't be like him."

"After that?"

"Maybe college. I got my cattle to look after. If I don't get drafted."

"Who's callin' who a dumbass."

"Come again?"

"You honestly think Fowler Clement is gonna let you get drafted?"

"Why do people keep bringin' that up? What does he got to do with anything?"

"Son, you can be dense. You don't even know what's comin', do you?"

"Well, I guess I don't, even though a lotta other people seem to think they do. So tell me swami, what's a comin'?"

"All right. You wanna know, I'll tell ya. Here's how it'll happen. That old lady's gonna die. When she does, everthing is gonna change. He'll come after you. That old man is richer'n Solomon's banker. He ain't got nobody. No kinfolks. No children…nobody to give it all to. Are you seriously sittin' there tellin' me that had'n ever occurred to you? Everbody knows it. That ranch and all that oil and money, and I've heard tell there's a hell of a lot more'n that goin' on with that family down in Mexico. What's he gonna do with it other'n give it to the only person left that's family?"

"When did you start on the dope?"

"Hey now, you're the dopehead. Speakin' of, you ever remember any more a that?"

"I don't know. I kinda remember it. I just can't remember what was real and what I was dreamin'. It's hard to describe. I'm a recovered dopehead. Let's just leave it at that. I did hear they sent all of 'em to the pen. Shorty and Herbert told me they did'n know nothin' about it."

"Well, I ain't kiddin' about Clement. And you can act ignorant about all that all you wont to, but it ain't changing what's comin'. And Shorty and Herbert are fulla shit. Somethin' scary about those two."

"Yep. They're either two harmless old country farts or absolute double-naught spies."

"I gotta go. Wmearle's gonna be worried about me."

"I'm glad you come out here, you pest. Tell everbody I'm sorry."

"Tell 'em yourself."

CHAPTER 21

The drive home had been miserable. Mike seemed irretrievably despondent. Trace had seen the roughnecks lined up in the morning when Lydia would open up, headed out to daylight tour, and again around eight or nine when they'd come filtering in after morning tour. There weren't that many old ones, and a lot of them were missing parts, mainly fingers and toes. He had wanted to sign on to a crew, but Wmearle had said no. One of the few times he had ever straight out told him no. "That oilfield will chew you up and spit you out." Trace could see it, the way the men would wear their bodies out long before their time. He hated seeing Mike doing it, and the wear was already evident after only six months.

What Mike had said about Fowler bothered him too. He had refused to admit that there was any kind of reckoning to be had with the old man. The judge had said some odd things to him a couple of times, and Weaver had also. But he had always dismissed that as wishful thinking by people who didn't understand how clean the break had been. To him, that had all happened in a bare instant when Fowler had walked by the pickup that night, with him and Mike and the two little ones sitting there, and in that one moment, Fowler had stopped and saw them and passed them by. He had always been conscious of the fact that almost everyone he came in contact with knew the story, and that there was some kind of unspoken arrangement whereby they all swept the whole thing under the rug. It hadn't occurred to him that there was another part they all knew about that he didn't. That the story wasn't played out yet. Mike had seemed sure of himself, and that was unsettling and left him wondering first, if it was true, and second, whether he had any interest in having any part of it. He knew how to think about a thing methodically, to consider the pros and cons of a thing, but this was different. He had no real idea how to imagine such a thing happening.

When he pulled into the station, Lydia was glaring at him.

"Wmearle is just about ready to call the law."

"I told him where I was goin'."

"You did'n tell him you weren't comin' back. Did you find him?"

"Yeah. He was there all right. Livin' and breathin', at least."

"Give him a good cussin'?"

"Some. He's kinda beat down. I wadn't too mean."

"Law, I'm gonna ring his neck. Numbskull."

"I better go see Wmearle."

"Yes, you better. He's thinkin' you mighta fell in the same hole Mike did, and now there's two of you dead in the bottom of the same well or such."

*****

He needed time to think. When he got out to the Hearndon place, he walked out into the sudan patch. It wouldn't be ready to cut for another week, but it was starting to burn. By the time he had finished walking down one row, he'd decided not to wait. He would start cutting tomorrow.

He walked through the pasture and up to a set of tank batteries. A cow had gotten through the fence and was out in the sudan somewhere, but the grass was too tall. He thought if he could get up high, he might be able to see down in there and run her out, but she was well-hidden in the tall grass. He would have to be careful with his cutting. Just as he was crawling down off the top of the tank, he saw the sun reflecting off something in the mesquite thicket on the hill overlooking the sudan patch, so he set off on foot to check it out.

The Plymouth Fury was parked at the edge of the hill. Trace hadn't been up to this spot before, and he was surprised how much country you could see. It seemed odd for somebody to be out in the late afternoon necking or carrying on. He remembered Georgette sitting out in the middle of the cotton field. Maybe people just drove out to sit and think. There was a man sitting in the driver's seat, and Trace called out when he got up close to the car. The man motioned him around to the passenger side.

"Howdy. You in a bind of some sort?"

"Get in outta the hot sun."

Trace hesitated. The man reached over and pulled a leather wallet out of his left shirt pocket to show him a badge.

"I interuptin' something?"

"I wish. Clarence Kohl." He stuck his hand out, and Trace shook.

"Trace Clement."

"Oh, I know. You're a busy man."

"Do we know each other?"

"No. We've not met. I've been watchin' you for a couple a weeks now."

"Why?"

"Oh, I don't mean that way. I mean I been sittin' up here on this hill, and I see you over there ever day."

He had a big set of binoculars sitting in his lap.

"You ever heard of mercury?"

"You mean like in a thermometer?"

"Yeah. Same stuff. We got a gang of thieves that's operatin' around here. They're hittin' these gas wells and bustin' the bellows meters apart to get the mercury out of 'em. Price a mercury's gone way up for some reason. They're hittin' these wells in broad daylight."

"You a deputy?"

"Ranger."

That impressed Trace.

"I never heard a such."

"Me neither, until this come up. The mercury's not that big a deal in and of itself, but the destruction is costing people a lot of money on these wells."

He had never paid much attention to the oil wells. From their vantage point, he could see at least twenty off in the distance.

"Bet it's like findin' a needle in a haystack catchin' 'em."

"Bein' patient narrows the odds. We been trackin' where they hit for three months now. This area is due. You're the boy got tangled up with that gang a bikers, aren't ya?"

"Yessir. Not a good day."

"From what I hear, they didn't have a very good day either."

"Yessir. I'm not clear on what happened exactly. They slipped me some dope of some kind, and I was in a state."

"Bad business. Somebody got western with 'em, though. I'd like to get to know whoever that was. Give 'em a medal or something."

"Well, if I see anything, I'll...how would I get a holt of you if I did see something?"

Kohl got a card out of a leather portfolio and wrote a number on the back.

"Number on the front is the office in Abilene. Number on the back is my house. Good meetin' ya."

"Same here."

*****

Trace walked back down the hill and across the pasture to the barn, fueled up Hearndon's tractor, and hooked up the cutter and the silage buggy. Now that he knew where the man was, he seemed obvious up there on the hill. Somehow, though, he had never noticed him before.

Night was falling, and he walked over to the stock tank and sat down on an old wire spool under a giant mesquite tree. The black inner tubes he'd thrown in there during the cold spell were still floating. Barn swallows were circling the tank and dipping down one at a time to get a drink. He first noticed them when he lay back against an old tractor tire and looked up at the darkening blue sky. A single star was visible in the twilight. When he first glimpsed the little swallows, he had thought it was just a floater in his eye, ephemeral, insubstantial. But as he continued to focus, he could see them, maybe a hundred or so, flying in a high circle above the tank. Slowly, the circle descended until the swallows were now circling just above the

173

willow trees around the border of the pond. One by one, they would fall out of formation and dip down and skim the water for a drink. Finally, they began to ascend again, and the circle rose and rose until he could only catch a glimpse, as though they were again just floaters in his eyes, coming and going. And then there was nothing.

He thought about Mike already back at work on the evening tour, and Iladio somewhere down in Mexico now, and Nicholas off in Vietnam doing God knows what, and his grandmother sitting alone in her house in east Texas with that picture of Nathan Bedford Forrest and the stillness and quiet that would be both her friend and her torture. He felt like all his attachments were moving apart from him in some kind of slow motion explosion with him at the center. That explosion had started nine years ago now when they first began to fly away. And it was continuing, one after another, and next it would be Wmearle or Lydia, and he wondered whether he had been wrong all this time, and maybe the old man hadn't flown away at all, that maybe he was in the middle of the explosion too, and Junior and Leticia and Stella and the little ones had been part of that same explosion with him, and Fowler left in the middle of it, and above and behind it all, Quanah Parker was sitting astride that wild mustang with that solemn and undefeated gaze that said, "I told you it was all going to change."

CHAPTER 22

September 1966

The drums coming from the gymnasium were booming across the school grounds as he walked into the little group of rooms next to the superintendent's office. Miss Bledsoe had asked him to come by before leaving school. The pep rally would be occupying everyone in the school before the team headed out for a Friday-night game. The superintendent's office had a window unit in it, and the cool air felt wonderful compared to the blazing heat outside. Miss Bledsoe waved him inside.

"Come in and sit down. Would you like a sodi pop?"

"Yes, ma'am. That'd be nice." He laid his hat on the desk and sat down.

She stepped into a small break room and got a couple of Cokes out of the fridge and popped the tops.

"So have you ever been to any of the pep rallies?"

"Once. Not my cup a tea."

"I gathered that. Outside of your classwork, you don't seem to have ever been involved in much of anything around here." She opened a manila folder with his name typed on the colored tab.

"Just always seemed to be too busy, I suppose."

"We have a sit-down with all of the seniors when the year starts. The first one should have been back in your sophomore year. As I recall, your momma had just passed, and the counselor at the time didn't think it would be a good time to sit down and talk about your plans. To tell you the truth, I think a lot of the teachers were wary about talking to you. Anyway, they never got around to it. This is my first year being the counselor, so I get the privilege."

"Why wary? I don't bite."

She laughed. "I know. Let me ask you this. Why don't you go to the football games and pep rallies and such things?"

"Like I said, just not my cup a tea. Plus, I got things to do."

"Ever feel like you don't have much in common with everbody else?"

"I suppose."

"Well, almost all high school kids feel like that, when in fact, there's almost nothing they don't have in common with everbody else. It's like they're rolling off the end of an assembly line. But sometimes, a person feels like that because that's the way it is. I think you don't have much in common with these other kids. It's pretty easy to counsel kids when every conversation is pretty much the same. You're not the same. That'd be why they were wary."

"We ain't gonna get into another talk about my family and everthing, are we?"

"No, I know about all that. That doesn't interest me, at least not right now. I expect you've got plenty of people poking around in your mind about that. So no, not unless you want to."

"What then?"

She sat back and sipped on her Coke. She was wearing a white sun dress with gigantic yellow sunflowers all over it, and her hair was wrapped up into a high swirl on top of her head. Miss Bledsoe must have been in her late twenties. Trace didn't engage in the gossip among the boys, but everyone knew there had been a big row in the school board about her the previous spring. Some of them had wanted her fired because of some of the racy literature she assigned in her classes, but the superintendent had not only persuaded them to keep her, but he had added the senior counseling to her responsibilities as well.

"I've been a teacher for eight years now, in three schools. I read a *lot* of papers. I read a lot of essays and book reports and term papers. You'd be amazed at how much they all seem to be the same: the same grammatical habits, the same perspectives. Every now and then, somebody sticks out. You stick out."

"How so?"

"Hmmm. Now you're putting me on the spot."

She thought for a minute, sipping her Coke. "It's hard to explain. Something about the way you write from a peculiar angle. Here. Do something for me."

She hopped out of her chair and started moving some cardboard boxes out of the corner of the office. She disappeared out the door and returned with a chair and put it in the corner. "Stand on top of that."

"Pardon?"

"Stand on top of that. Right up in the corner. Come on. Do it now."

Trace stepped up on the chair, his head very nearly at the ceiling and turned around.

"Now look around. Weird, isn't it? Probably nobody ever looked at this room from that angle before. You're the only one. Even whoever built this place and painted it and everything, they were looking at the wall, not the room. You'd be the first to *see* it from there. Now hop down. That's the way you write. Seems to come natural. It sticks out."

"Innerstin'. But I ain't sure what difference it makes."

"I'll get to the point. The question is: what are you planning to do with yourself once you graduate?"

"Yeah. That. Wmearle's been after me about that, several times now."

She didn't push; rather, she sipped her Coke and waited for him to go on.

"Listen, if I were bein' honest, I'd say I'm gonna work. I'm gonna look after my own rat-killin' like I always have."

"Voltaire would appreciate that."

"Voltaire."

"From a book he..."

"Yeah, I know. *Candide*."

"I forgot. You read everything. Right. Cultivate your own garden. So, yes, there's honor and dignity in keeping to yourself and doing good honest work, presumably in the service of others. Lookin' after your own rat-killin', so to speak."

"So what's wrong with that?"

"Who says there's anything wrong with it? It's always an option. It's what most people do. But there are other options. There are a lot of different roads to take. That's what we're talking about here. How do you choose? Because it's getting time, and if you don't start choosing, time is going to choose for you. I'm sitting here listening to all that racket coming out of the gym right now. You know what it makes me think about?"

He shook his head and swigged his Coke.

"There's more than a few of those kids that will be on the other side of the world within a year, fighting in a war they have not the first notion about. Today, they're thinking about football and girls and their pickup trucks. They may be just like you, thinking they'll hide out in this little quiet corner of the world and get married and have kids and rosebushes, and on and on and on, as though they don't have any interest in what the world is up to. But before they know it, they're going to find out the world has something to say about all that."

"Yeah, I got a friend, Nicholas, that already had to go. So you think I oughta go to college even if I got no idea what I'd want to do it for?"

"What I think you should do is not what matters. You need to decide. My part is to tell you that you have the grades, and I'll tell you for sure you have the capability to succeed academically. So if there's any doubt in your mind that you're suitable, we can put that to bed. Secondly, we need to look at whether you want to explore. Because the whole idea of university is to open up the world to you in ways you'll never get out here, doing what you're doing. Standing up high in the corner of the world. Choosing a profession is important, but I don't think you need to get in a hurry on that. The main thing is, do you want to educate yourself? Decide that, and decide it soon. We need to get that underway right now."

"Some crazy stuff going on at colleges lately."

"I know. That was awful what happened down there. All those people going about their business…you wonder what they were thinking about, and then just like that, everything in their whole world changed because of one crazy man up on that tower."

She looked out the window, and they both sat listening to the booming of the drums from the gymnasium.

"You know any hippies?"

She giggled. "Yes. I suppose I do. That was not a question I expected to come out of your mouth. But, yeah. I have known some people you might call hippies."

"I run into some of 'em. Didn't like 'em much."

"I think I know what you're talking about. Not sure those people were exactly what you'd call hippies, more like thugs, but I heard about it."

"Seems like all you see on TV is hippies doin' this or that. Everbody mad about something. People gettin' assassinated. You married?"

"I was. Didn't work out."

"Sorry, that'us kinda personal."

"No harm done."

"We cain't stop any of it, can we?"

She paused for a long while and said simply, "No."

*****

By the time he shut the tractor down, he had decided. He'd had almost four hours of plowing to think it through. Cattle were up almost four dollars, and he had worked through how he would sell, let the leases go, and how much he would have left over after he paid Compton off. He had no information on how much it cost to go to college, but he figured he would have almost ten thousand dollars once he settled up with everybody, and surely that was enough. It was dark when he quit, and he stopped short when he realized he was getting ready to plant wheat he would never graze. But then Hearndon had turned over the place with the pits full of winter feed, and the wheat in good shape, so it seemed fair enough that he do the same.

179

Lydia had surprised him when he stopped by the station after seeing Miss Bledsoe.

"Mike's home."

"Home. When did you see him?"

"He's been home a week. I been tryin' to catch you all week, but you hadn't slowed down enough for me to grab you. He only come by here the onest though."

And so it was dark when he passed the place where he had lived up until he was seven years old. There was no house there now, Fowler having long ago bulldozed it and buried every indication that it had ever existed. The place where the house had stood would be going into wheat now. Fowler didn't grow cotton, and now the only evidence that it had ever been there was the gravel drive over a caved-in tinhorn that led across the ditch to a barbed-wire fence where there was no gate. Still, he never passed it without looking down, as the ditch rolled by to see the culvert and the remnants of the old drive.

The Wakefield place was pathetic. The little yard outside the front porch was still bordered by the dilapidated picket fence, but inside, the weeds were as tall as the fence, and the little concrete sidewalk was barely visible through the grass runners that stretched across it. The only light was the blue glow of the television in the front room. When he mounted the steps, he stopped at the sight of hundreds of empty beer cans that were piled level with the front window and sloped off into the tall grass below. He opened the screen door and stepped into the front room.

"Come in and grab ya a cold one."

Mike was laid out in the old recliner that was covered in a quilt, likely on account of the fabric having long since deteriorated.

"Don't get up."

"Oh, I ain't."

"Whatya watchin'?"

"Show called *The Cat*. Turn it down, I ain't innersted anyhow. I like to watch that Laredo show though. It's comin' on after."

"Lydia told me you been home a week. Looks like some more'n that to me."

Mike was pretty far gone. He had always been wiry, but now he was gaunt. The house had a putrid sweet smell that he figured was probably coming from the beer cans outside the window, if not from Mike himself.

"I lose track."

"That'll happen when you stay sloshed for a week or two straight."

"Señor, you ain't been here two minutes, and you start in. Why're you just standin' up there like that? Sit down. Take your hat off. Lighten the hell up."

Trace tossed his hat on the divan and sat down facing Mike.

"So you crapped out workin' yourself to death, so now you're gonna try drinkin' yourself into the ground."

"Ease up, willya? They stacked the rig. I'm just takin' a breather."

"Why'd they stack the rig?"

"Sub had a crack in it. I guess they weren't in a hurry to get it fixed. Lucky the whole thing didn't fall in."

"So what's up with the beer? Looks like you've been through about a hunnerd cases."

"Some people got a drinkin' problem. I got a drinkin' opportunity. Turn that up. Laredo's comin' on."

"Well, get your shit together. It's just been me and Blas and Tito now forever. Time for you to get flanged up and help out. Sunday night."

He paused on the front porch and looked to his left and remembered the three of them in that same bed with Mike in the kitchen, and his mother in there on the divan that he'd just gotten up off of. No one had slept that night but the two little ones.

*****

It looked like rain. The smell was in the air, and he could feel the damp on his skin. It had been dry, but it was September, and it always rained in September. Blas and Tito drove in right behind him. He had worried for two days whether Mike would show. If he didn't, Trace figured he was through. But he was there, and he was sober, though he looked like death warmed over.

"Que pasa fellas?"

Tito and Blas nodded and tipped their taco shell straw hats. Trace was smiling, even though his inclination was to grieve Mike some more.

"How's ol' Maximo, Blas?"

"Fine. Big."

"Good to see you again, Tito." Tito nodded. He wasn't much of a talker, but he had turned out to be a handy fellow.

"Okay, I got two jobs. First is kinda nasty. Mike, you know Horace Belknap passed away a while back. Nelda went out to put some flowers on the grave, and it had fallen in, and it was evidently smelling pretty bad. She got upset. It was just a pine box, and it didn't last long. We gotta load up some dirt and go cover it up."

"I can do that. Where's it at?"

"Weaver told me it was right along the north fence of the cemetery. There's a stone. Lydia told me Mr. Burk got a sack of bluebonnet seeds from the highway department. She wanted me to put some out around there and see if they'll come up in the spring."

"I'll go see him on the way out."

"Okay, I got several sacks of clothes here for Luciano's kids. Blas, can you and Tito take 'em by to Irena?"

"What's the deal?"

"She ain't doin' too good since Lucy died. Miss Bledsoe told me the kids started school with a bunch of wore out clothes. She give me some money that the teachers took up, and I added some. I hope I got the right sizes. Anyhow, she might like it better if Blas and Tito took 'em by instead of me. Blas, she don't need to know where it come from. What'sa matter Mike, no refreshments?"

"Fresh out. Don't give me that look. You don't even like it anyhow."

Blas and Tito hopped in their truck and rolled off the side of the hill. Trace jumped back onto the tailgate and opened a cooler and tossed a Coke to Mike.

"I got some news."

"Tell it."

"I decided I'm gonna chuck it in and go to college."

"That, I didn't see comin'."

"Why?"

"I don't know. I guess I just figured you for a fixture. Where'd you get this wild hair?"

"Wmearle has been pester'n me about it. Miss Bledsoe too. She said I can if I want to."

"Well, a course you *can*. I just never figured you would."

"Whaddaya think?"

Mike leaned back against the bed of the pickup and looked off across the river bottom toward the lights of the town.

"I think that's fine. Bud, it ain't often these days I have a straight thought. But here it is. You go and do that. You go and don't turn around and look back until you're good and ready, and if that's never, then that'll be soon enough. Damn, son. You surprised me. I thought you were too hardheaded to launch off and do something like that. I'm proud of you. I shoulda brought whiskey!"

*****

Trace sat bolt upright in his bed. It was still dark, and there was no sound coming from the station. Still, he had the sense that the night had passed, and it was near dawn. He felt as though he'd had his hand on an electric fence and could feel all the nerves in his body burning. He'd had the nightmare before. He stood at the base of a dark stairway with massive wooden finials on both sides. A tapestry of fine soft carpet was anchored at each step with a brass rod. He was compelled forward, up the stairs, and was powerless to either stop or retreat. And so he stepped slowly up the stairs in a strange dim blue-gray light filtering through the drapes of a tall window at the top of the landing. When he reached the head of the stairs, he turned toward large oak double doors with massive brass handles. He could not remember reaching outward to open the doors. It was as though they were subject to the same motive force that propelled him forward and through to a large bedroom. In the soundless and even dimmer light of the room, he could smell a rich scent of cigar and whiskey and leather. The figure of a man lay motionless behind the large oak corner posts of the bed, under blankets carefully made and long undisturbed by movement. And here he stopped, frozen against all effort by the same force that had propelled him. The figure of the man was partially hidden by the corner post, and in the dim light, he strained to see the face of the man and could not, but some things he knew. The man was dying. He could see no motion of the man's breathing, but he knew he was not dead. He was impossibly thin, as though his body were being subsumed by the bed itself. And still he stood, unable to move closer or even to his side, and he began to struggle against whatever it was that bound him. When he saw the boots placed beside the bed, he knew that they were his own, familiar, even though they looked nothing like the pair he wore every day. And so the terror set in, and he began to struggle violently against the thing that held him motionless. And then he would wake up.

Wmearle bumped around in his room for a bit and emerged into the little kitchen and wheeled up to the table, his hair typical haywire.

"You're up mighty early. What time is it?"

"Almost five. Poured you a cup."

"*Gracias*. Have a hard time sleepin'?"

"Yeah. Had a bad dream."

"Wanna tell it?"

"No. I don't think I do."

"Sometimes helps. Have a nightmare, and it seems horrible when you have it, but if you talk it out afterwards, most times they seem silly."

"I'm okay."

"Suit yourself. Wont me to cook you a breakfast?"

"Naw. Go about your readin'. I'll get it."

Trace popped open a can of biscuits and put the pan in the oven, then put the bacon in the frying pan. He had been sitting at the table in a stupor for some time, and when the bacon grease spit and landed on his belly, he suddenly noticed that he was wearing his hat and underwear and nothing else, so he popped into his room and quickly threw on his clothes and boots. He could hear Lydia's broom sweeping outside.

CHAPTER 23

October 1966

Ford Compton was genuinely surprised. He sat forward in his chair and pulled a fresh cigar out of a leather bowl made out of a preserved bull scrotum.

"You're gonna have you a sweet deal here. They're up almost four dollars since you bought 'em, and I expect you've got about what, twenty or thirty more you've accumulated? You got a buyer?"

"I'm gonna see whether Alvin has any prospects of movin' back. If he don't, I know a man over in Stonewall County that might be interested. If he ain't, he'll know some people. I ain't planning on goin' to the sale barn with 'em, though."

"You told Alvin yet?"

"Yeah. But he wasn't ready to commit to anything. I should hear back this week. I wanted to come over and tell you what the plan is."

"Appreciate that. Why are you bailin' out, if you don't mind my askin'?"

"Like you said, they're up four bucks. I don't want to carry 'em over till spring when I'd just be sell'n 'em then anyhow. Price might go back down."

"I mean, why are you sell'n at all? I thought you were in this for the long haul."

"Oh. Well, I thought I was too. But I decided I'm gonna go to college, and I don't think I could look after everthing from afar the way I'd want to."

"You thinkin' about that ole draft, arn't ya?"

"No. That hadn't played into it."

"Really? A lot of 'em *are* worried about that. I was thinkin' about it myself on your account."

"Well, to tell you the truth, I hadn't thought that much about that angle. I was more thinkin' about whether I wanted to spend all that money on school or not. I got a teacher seems to think I ought to."

"You got a smart teacher."

"Well, I ain't decided where I'm goin' yet. She seems to think I can go pretty much about anywhere."

"Yale bein' one of those?"

"Yessir. She mentioned that one. Not sure I want to get that far from home though. How'd you know about that one?"

He ignored the last part. "You do. They send you a letter, you go there. You don't blink an eye on that."

"I'm not even sure what I want to study yet."

"Son, I'll shoot straight with you here 'cause you sound like you're ignorant as…well, I'll be nice here. You don't get to go to Yale from here. I know this is sensitive territory here, but you don't get to go to Yale unless somebody with some stroke gets you in there. If nobody ever told you this before, I'll tell you. Your granddaddy went there, and his daddy before him went there. So you got a shot at going. That kind of thing plays into it. Everybody knows you don't trade on your name. You've made that clear as a bell. I appreciate the hell out of that. This here is the exact place where you put that aside. My advice is if they send you a letter, you go there."

Trace was stunned. Compton had heretofore kept any mention of Fowler out of their dealings.

"I didn't know that. Are you tellin' me Fowler's got involved in this?"

"No idea about that. Son, I could lay a lot on you about how there's lots of kids around here that don't have the advantages you've got. And by advantages, I mean talents. How they'll be off in Vietnam getting their ass shot off for no good reason. How you have some kind of obligation to own up to those advantages. I expect that would piss you off. You'd be right 'cause you've earned all of this for yourself, where they've been out playin' games and chasin' girls. That's not what I'm sayin' here. I'm sayin' if you got a shot at this, you take it because you can. It's as simple as that."

*****

Trace had the same feeling on the way back to town as he had that first time he had felt Ford Compton's boot on his neck, as though he was being pushed into a place he didn't want to be. He pulled off the highway and down toward the school building. He had an appointment with Miss Bledsoe to fill out applications, and he was sorting through how he would confront her about what he thought was some kind of complicity with Fowler about him going to Yale. When he turned into the school parking lot, there were two sheriff's cars and a couple of highway patrol cars parked in front of the gymnasium. The two sheriff's deputies were walking Sammy to the car in handcuffs.

Trace skidded to a stop and flew out of the truck toward Sammy. "What are you doing?"

"Son, step back." The officer holding Sammy by the arm gave him a stern look. Sammy smiled blankly at him.

The superintendent pulled Trace away, and the deputies slammed the door and began pulling away from the gymnasium.

"What are they doing with Sammy?"

Miss Bledsoe was on the sidewalk in front of the superintendent's office, and she hurried over.

"Edith Blackwell says Sammy molested Sadie. They were arresting him, Trace."

"Oh, good lord. Y'all know better than that!" They both just looked at him.

"They have to do their jobs, Trace."

He started to argue, but he could see the two of them looking at him as though he were a child. He turned and walked back to the pickup and sped off.

*****

Clarence Kohl's wife had answered the phone, and Trace had left the number for the station and instructions for Lydia to come and get him if Kohl were to call back.

"What's this about?"

"I appreciate you comin' out here. I needed to talk to you."

Kohl had agreed to meet him at the same place, on the hill overlooking the field on the Hearndon place.

"Okay."

"I got a friend got arrested today. They're sayin' he molested a girl at the school."

"Who arrested him?"

"County sheriff. Couple of highway patrols were there."

"What's that got to do with me?"

"He didn't do it. He's gonna get railroaded unless somebody does something."

"What makes you think he didn't do it? Can't imagine they arrested him for no good reason."

"Listen, I know you don't know me hardly at all since we only met the once, but I didn't know who else to talk to. Everbody seemed like it was a done deal that he did it, apparently just because that woman said so, but I know the man. I've known him for years. He's harmless. That woman is nuts. There ain't no way he did it."

"I don't know what I can do for you. They'll have to sort through the evidence and see how it shakes out."

"You don't understand. This is gonna kill him. He didn't do it."

"What makes you so sure a this?"

Trace still had one foot out the door of the Plymouth. He hadn't wanted to tell Kohl more, but it was pretty clear he was going to have to.

"Listen. Sammy was in the war. World War II. He got tore up real bad. He's got scars all over, and he got brain damage. He showed all us boys his scars before at one time or another. He don't know any different between one and another. He's simple, you know."

"I'm not follerin'."

"He got his...balls shot off. Everthing really. His private parts. Listen, if he's a pervert, I'd know about it. He ain't. He ain't got a thought in his head about anything like that. The man is a hero. He lost everthing, and the only thing he's got left in the world is that job at the school, and the only thing anybody has to be afraid of is if somebody were to get after one of those kids 'cause then he might actually go berserk on 'em and kill somebody. But he ain't no pervert, and that lady is the one who's nuts."

"Does anybody else know about these injuries you're talkin' about?"

"I doubt it. Like I said, he's like a child. When he showed us, it was like he didn't even know the difference between that and a scar on his elbow. But there's a couple of us seen it. I know even him showin' us would look bad if people found out. Somethin' like that gets in the wind, everbody goes crazy, but I'm tellin' ya, the man ain't got a...there ain't no sexual thoughts in him. It just ain't that way. Edith Blackwell is the lady's name, and she's the one with the screw loose. I could tell by the way everbody was actin', they already got him tried and convicted on the say-so of a damned busybody."

"Whew."

"Is there anything you can do about this? Somebody's gotta get her to back off."

"Hard to uncook an egg. Lemme get into it, and I'll see."

"Much obliged."

CHAPTER 24

November 1966

Trace sat alone in the pew. He was flipping through the worn pages of the little spiral pocket notebook while one of the deacons proceeded with the announcements.

"...and we need to remember some people in our prayers: Nicholas Nieto and Billy Doan and all those serving in Vietnam, Leticia Clement, the Lara family...anybody else need mention'n? Yeah, Lucas Blankenship is in the hospital in Abilene for his gallbladder."

Wmearle had wheeled himself up to the front of the aisle and waited for the announcements to finish. When the man sat down, Wmearle pushed forward and wheeled around to face the congregation.

"Let's bow our heads. Lord, we thank you for another day that we can come and worship you. We thank you for the rain we've had and the changin' of the season and the cool weather. We thank you for this great country we live in, and for the food we have to eat. We thank you for the hope that we have in Jesus to spend eternity with you in heaven and for sending him to die on the cross for our sins. We ask you to be with Nick and Billy and all the soldiers fightin' in Vietnam. Please watch after them and bring them home safely. Please look after Irena and the family. And help us to remember to look after them too. We pray for Fowler and Leticia and ask your comfort for them in their suffering, and for Lucas and Shellie while he's havin' his procedure. And Lord, please be with Sammy while they're getting that sorted out. We pray he'll be released soon and be back where he belongs. Be with us now as we settle in to worship you and help our hearts and minds to be how you'd want 'em to be and forgive us of our sins. In Jesus' name, amen."

Sandy Long was doing the songleading, and he slowly made his way up the aisle past Wmearle. Sandy would be pushing eighty years old, and he moved like it. But he still had a strong pure voice. Plus, he tended to have perfect pitch, and Trace always liked his song selections. But Sandy was rickety, and everyone held their breath when he ascended and descended the steps leading up to the pulpit.

> *When I survey the wondrous cross*
> *On which the Prince of glory died,*
> *My richest gain I count but loss,*
> *And pour contempt on all my pride.*
> *Forbid it, Lord, that I should boast,*
> *Save in the death of Christ my God.*
> *All the vain things that charm me most,*
> *I sacrifice them to His blood.*
> *See from His head, His hands, His feet,*
> *Sorrow and love flow mingled down.*
> *Did e'er such love and sorrow meet,*
> *Or thorns compose so rich a crown?*
> *Were the whole realm of nature mine,*
> *That were a present far too small;*
> *Love so amazing, so divine,*
> *Demands my soul, my life, my all.*

Weaver went long. He had spent most of the spring and summer in the book of Hebrews, and it was to be the final sermon on the topic before the annual holiday sermons on thankfulness and the gospels would begin. He was usually reliable about finishing up on time, but not today.

"And so we see in Hebrews the grand design. That Jesus was there, in the beginning, and it was through him that the universe itself was created. We see the story of God's work with mankind, from the patriarchs and the law of Moses to the kings and the prophets, all of it leading to the cross and Jesus' rule over all things, for all time, at the right hand of God. That it is through his perfect sacrifice, his glorious high priesthood, that grace has been extended to us. That because of that perfect sacrifice, we can transcend that barrier that separates us from our God. He calls us now to draw near to him, to allow his presence in our souls to perfect us."

A couple of the old men couldn't wait for the invitation song to be over before they quietly slipped out the side door and headed toward the bathroom. Wmearle was anxious to get out and back to the trailer to watch the Cowboys play Philadelphia. It was a glorious fall day as they wheeled across the parking lot to the truck.

"I betcha they get beat."

"How do you reckon? They beat 'em fifty points last time."

"Exactly. But this'll be in Phily, and I bet they're gonna get ambushed."

"I don't think Weaver wanted to turn loose a the book of Hebrews."

"I know it. I hope that roast ain't burnt."

"I thought a somethin' I never thought of before this mornin'. Did you ever think of how the Bible is like a human?"

Trace slammed Wmearle's door and put the wheelchair in the back of the truck.

"When it starts, people were innocents, like babies, they didn't know anything. Later, when they learned about sin and death, they had the patriarchs, Noah and Abraham and so on, that had all the authority, just like a child has a daddy or his parents. When a kid grows up, they leave their parents, and they don't live under their law anymore. They live under the *law law*, like the Israelites and Moses. When they get to be a Christian, they don't live under the *law law* anymore. They live under Jesus, and when they die, they go to heaven, just like Jesus does. So it tracks all along the way."

"Bud, that's an innerstin' observation. I'm a little embarrassed."

"How so?"

"I gotta confess I mainly had my mind on three things this morning: the Cowboys, that roast, and gettin' home to pee. That's some pretty deep thinkin' on your part."

Wmearle leaned against the door and watched him turn out onto the pavement toward the trailer. The boy had been acting like a grownup for years, but he hadn't noticed till that very moment that he was now, in fact, grown-up. Those steel-colored gray eyes and the set of his face were unmistakably Fowler now. Even the boy's posture and the gait of his walk were beginning to look like the old man. He was even stooped over a bit on account of his hat rubbing the roof of the cab.

Trace got the roast out of the oven and set it down on the table on top of a couple of potholders. He poured them both a glass of iced tea and sat down to wait for Wmearle to finish up in the bathroom. He felt bad for Wmearle. He could hear him banging around in the little room trying to lift himself over and onto the wheelchair using the trapeze bar. He never complained about losing the use of his legs.

When he wheeled himself up to the table, Trace didn't wait but said a quick prayer, and they began filling their plates out of the roaster pan.

"I reckon you're right. I'm not sure how all that works. Man was created in God's image. If all the things in the Bible were imagined by God, I expect he's got his fingerprints all over everthing in creation in one way or another, so it would stand to reason that those patterns would be recognizable. I'm takin' my plate and getting in my chair. It's kickoff time."

*****

Trace sat with Wmearle through the whole game, which he couldn't remember ever having done before. Wmearle had been right. The Cowboys lost. He had spent the game stretched out on the couch with his long legs hanging over the end. Patterns. He could see patterns emerging in all things, societies in upheaval and settling back into quiet again, over and over. He wondered where Quanah Parker and his contemporaries fit in the tapestry of patterns, but couldn't make any sense of it. Wmearle kept interrupting his thoughts, yelling at, or for, Don Meredith; it was sometimes hard to tell which.

His thinking about going off to college had been a way of circumventing pattern. Before it entered his mind, he had felt himself being propelled through time, the absolute of his circumstance forming the stream in which he floated along, and which he had unconsciously considered irrevocable. And so he had decided suddenly, so as to step out of that stream unnoticed, to watch the eddy from which he had emerged close behind him and continue absently forward. He had felt euphoric the moment he had decided, and that euphoria had not diminished until the morning when he once again began to think of the pattern of all things.

Wmearle stretched out the recliner to get a nap. Lydia had brought them a blackberry cobbler before church, and Trace filled another bowl before slipping out to get in the truck and check on the cows. Mike came skidding up and ran over to the trailer.

"You need to get over to the school. They brought Sammy back. Something is wrong."

*****

When he pulled into the gymnasium parking lot, the superintendent and old Claude Hardwicke and another man were on the steps outside.

"What's happened?"

"Trace, you know Sheriff Hardwicke. This is Dan McMillan. He's the district attorney. Sammy's in a state. He just got upset about something, and he's all excited and not bein' coherent."

"What did you do to him?"

Sheriff Hardwicke turned to him with a stern look. "We didn't do anything to him, son. We released him from the jail this afternoon and brought him back over here. He was fine until he got down there in his room, and he just kinda went haywire."

"I don't understand. Why'd he get released?"

The district attorney stepped forward. "Because he didn't do it. Sheriff Hardwicke got to the bottom of it and…he just didn't do it. So we dropped the charges and brought him back."

"Mind if I go see him? He knows me."

"I know he does. I'll walk in there with you and stand right outside."

They walked through the darkness of the concession area and past the trophy cases into the gym. The pigeons were flapping in the high windows, as they always did. When he stepped down into the dank stairwell to Sammy's room, he could hear Sammy mumbling. He was pacing back and forth quickly across the room, and his nose was running to the point the snot was down his face and had wet the front of his dark green work shirt.

"Whatsa matter, Sammy? Comeer and sit down. Tell me what's wrong."

Trace put his arm around him and could feel him trembling and hot. Sammy was still stout and muscular, and his shirt was beginning to sweat through.

"They gone. They took 'em away. They don't won't 'em to be around me no more. They all gone."

"Who's gone? You mean the kids?"

"They gone. They all gone on accounta me."

"Sammy, look at me now. Look at me. I ain't gone, am I? They ain't gone at all. It's Sunday. You know they don't come on Sunday. You know that. They come tomorrow like they always do. You know how it is. You count five days, then there's two days where they don't come, then they come again for five days. They come tomorrow."

"They come tomorrow?"

"They come tomorrow, just like always."

Sammy slumped down a bit and slowly slipped into that state of quiet that Trace had seen a million times, staring blankly at the boilers on the opposite side of the little room.

"I'm gonna run upstairs and get you some snuff. I'll be right back. You okay? Sammy, you okay?" He stopped and pulled out a handkerchief and wiped Sammy's nose and chin.

"Yessir, Mr. Trace. Need some Copenhagen."

"I'll be right back."

*****

Hardwicke walked him out to the parking lot. Before they stepped out of the dark concession room, he stopped short.

"That was good information you gave to Kohl. He got in there and interviewed Sadie and that mother a hers. He was gentle on Sadie, but boy howdy, he lowered the boom on that Blackwell woman. It was a sight to see."

"I'm not following."

"Well, he's a pro at that interrogation business. Once he interviewed Sadie and knowin' what he knew about Sammy, he knew pretty quick they were lyin' and that Sadie'd been coached on what to say. Little girl don't know come here from sic'em about such things, but her momma told her what to say. Only, they didn't know about Sammy's condition, so what momma told her to say didn't hold up. Kohl laid out the whole thing and got her in a corner just cool as a cucumber. Then he made her give a deposition about exactly how she lied. Had a stenographer and everthing. He had her thinkin' she was going to the pen for the rest of her life. Fella never so much as raised his voice. Just good questions in the right order."

"Why would she do a thing like that? It's just evil."

"Ha. Evil. I suppose. She was gonna sue the school and try to get a pile of money outta their insurance. That was her grand plan. Get a lotta attention in the process. Never gave two thoughts to Sammy."

"What about Sadie? How's she gonna fare in all this?"

"Momma's got the shit scared out of her. We won't hear nothing more outta her. Sammy ain't gonna remember nothing. I expect the teachers'll look after Sadie pretty close. Can't help she's got a bad momma. I think everthing is gonna be okay. I wish you'da called me."

"I tried talkin' to the deputies and the highway patrolmen. They didn't seem to be innersted."

"Anyhow. I appreciate you getting involved. Saved his skin. I bet he settles down pretty quick now. I don't know if he ever slept a wink while he'us in the jail."

*****

"Mike, I'm gonna sit up with Sammy tonight. Can you go tell Wmearle I won't be home tonight?"

"Sure."

Trace pulled the little spiral notebook out of his pocket and handed it to Mike.

"This used to be yours. I wrote a couple of things on the last page need handled. Say hi to Tito and Blas."

He reached into the pickup and got a roll of Copenhagen out of the glove compartment and pried a can out of the plastic. When he returned, Sammy was indeed asleep on the edge of his little cot. Trace laid him back on his pillow and took off his shoes and socks, then pulled a sheet up over him. The windows along the top of the room were glowing a deep orange, and he stood up on a chair and looked out to see the whole of the western sky illuminated by the fall sunset.

CHAPTER 25

Summer, 1955

Junior Clement had tried to go easy on the beer, but they were an hour north of Del Rio now, and he was getting sleepy. Trace was lying across the seat of the pickup with his head in his lap. Tarantulas were crossing the highway in his headlights as they snaked through the limestone cuts in the hills. He rolled the window down and held his head out into the breeze to wake up. Trace sat up and looked over the dashboard.

"Where are we?"

"Between Del Rio and Sonora. We had'n gone far."

"There's lots of 'em."

"Creepy, ain't they."

"Yessir. I wouldn't wanna be on foot out there in the dark."

They were passing deer and javelina and varmints of every kind.

"Everthing is out tonight."

"You have a good time?"

"You bet."

"I'm glad I brought you along. You make for good company."

"I met Mr. Ramos before."

"You did? Where? Grampa's house?"

"Yeah."

Junior had a hollow feeling in his stomach. He had made promises, and he had been occupying his mind with the excuses he would give and the lies he would tell to get more time. David had made an elaborate effort in throwing the barbecue and getting all the hands in for the charreada at his house. He had acted as though he was receiving some foreign ambassador or potentate with effusive introductions and speeches. But it had all been a charade. When the evening closed and they retreated into his private library, he gave his answer while he was pouring each of them a Scotch.

"My answer must be no."

He gave no reason or excuse. No beating around the bush or apologies offered. He handed Junior the crystal glass and waved toward the chair in front of the fireplace.

"Your boy is the spitting image of somebody else we both know."

"So I've been told."

"You don't see it?"

"Maybe I'm not looking."

"Ha! I see your point. The world would be a fearful place if there were two of them. Still, he's a fine boy. I know you're very proud. How old is he now?"

"Fixin' to turn seven."

"I'm scheduled to be in Mexico City tomorrow, so I have an early morning. Iladio will be here for breakfast, and I asked him to show you around. You should let him take you up into the mountains. Can you stay for a time? I will be back here in two days, and you are welcome to stay as my guests."

"I'll be needin' to get back."

"Very well. Thank you for coming to visit. You're welcome any time. Give my regards to the old cowboy when you get home."

"I will."

*****

"How'd you like the charreada?"

"It was pretty good. How come they don't break their legs?"

"I expect they do sometimes."

"Then why do they do it?"

"It's a old tradition. That comes from some old-time cowboyin' where they sometimes didn't have any better way of catchin' a wild

199

horse. Some situations, you need to know how to do that sort of thing, and ya don't have the luxury a bein' gentle about it."

"I need to pee."

"It's still another half hour to Sonora. I can pull over."

"Yeah, I better."

Junior slowed to a stop, and Trace looked over the dashboard. He could see two tarantulas on the road in the headlights.

"Just hop out and run around there in front of the headlights where you can see. They ain't gonna mess with you."

He opened the pickup door and looked the ground over good, then hopped out and ran around into the lights in front and unzipped his britches.

"That'us about as fast a pee as I ever saw anybody pull off. Stay put. I need to do the same now that you conquered all the giant spiders."

When they were back on the road, Junior turned on the radio. Trace knew the song by heart, and Junior told him to sing it.

"So did you like Iladio?"

"Yessir. He's real nice. He took me out to the cookout at the rodeo while you were visitin'. They had goats and pigs. You just go up there, and they cut a big chunk off and put it on your plate."

"He's comin' to live with us."

"At our house?"

"No. On the ranch. His daddy wants him to work in America so he can learn about things."

"That'll be all right. How come we don't live on the ranch?"

"That's a complicated question."

"Fowler don't wont us to?"

"How come you call him Fowler, stead of Grandpa or Grandaddy or somethin'?"

"Everbody else calls him Fowler. You do too."

"No. Him and me don't seem to agree with each other mostly. It ain't all his fault either, so don't hold it against him."

"I'd like to live on the ranch. There ain't nothin' to do in a cotton patch."

"Maybe you will one of these days. It ain't goin' nowhere."

*****

Trace didn't remember Junior carrying him into the house and putting him to bed. He heard the sound of Fowler's pickup pull up to the house before his eyes had opened. When he rubbed the sand out of his eyes and rolled over to look out the window, he saw Fowler emerge from the pickup and put his hat on. Junior met him at the front steps.

"You went."

"I told you I was."

"And he turned you down."

"I figure you'd know all about that, wouldn't you?"

"Not the way you think."

"You're tellin' me you didn't get word down there and wave him off?"

"I did not. I never needed to."

"But he knew better than to cross you."

"That would have never entered his mind."

"Well, clue me in, Papa. What did enter his mind?"

Fowler stared at him with that grim, clinched expression, his steel gray eyes boring through him.

"It would have been a careful calculation. One in which your prospects or the thought of money or repayment, and least of all, profit, never entered in. Only honor was in play. You forced him to sacrifice some of it just by going down there and asking."

"You're gonna have to explain how in the world it dishonored him for me to just ask."

"It wasn't his honor I'm talking about."

"So this is you. He didn't want to take a chance it would make you look bad."

"Son, I don't know how I can get through to you on this. It wasn't about me or him. It was you. He would not allow himself to be involved in you dishonoring yourself. It was simply never possible for him."

The two stood, staring at each other for what seemed like an hour to Trace. Suddenly, Fowler's eyes caught his movement in the window, and the intensity drained from his face. He lowered his head and shook it once, then turned abruptly toward the pickup to leave.

"You know I'm not gonna stop. You know that, don't' you?"

Fowler turned for only the briefest moment and met his eyes again.

"Yes. Son, I suppose I do know that."

CHAPTER 26

March 1967

"Mr. Clement, she ain't takin' her food like she ought to. I cain't tell if she cain't swallow, or if she just don't wont to."

"All right. You go on. I'll sit with her a minute and come down, and we can visit."

Georgette had grown accustomed to things that had horrified her at first. The blank stare, the cleaning of the woman and of the soiled sheets, the slow and soulless movement of her taking the soft food. She gathered up the tray and fluffed the pillow behind her head and stepped around Fowler standing at the foot of the bed. As he did every morning, Fowler eased into the chair beside her and began speaking to her in the soft, conversational way of an old couple, as though they were sitting at the table downstairs reading the paper over coffee. He did not stay long. Georgette had cleaned the dishes and moved the soiled linens out into the washroom and was busy wiping the kitchen down with a washrag.

"Sit down with me for a minute here."

She was no longer intimidated by Fowler as she had been at first. But she had no basis or experience with which to comprehend him. They did not converse other than the exchange of basic pleasantries and practical facts. She had been living in his home for over a year now, taking care of Leticia and cleaning and cooking for him, and she had watched him, sitting by her bedside, reading to her from a book or a newspaper, his steady ritual of starting each day and ending each night leaning close in to her and speaking softly, not to her ear, but moving himself over her into the focal point of her lost stare, and speaking softly some gentle *good morning* or *good night* and then kissing her on the parched and medicated lips.

"I need to…" He stopped, leaning forward in his chair with his elbow on the table and his other hand on his knee as though he were about to lift some terrible weight.

"I need to talk to you about Mrs. Clement's condition. Some time ago, you probably remember, I had Dr. Kemp out here to check on her. Routine thing. Georgette, this is pretty hard here now. I need to prepare you…for what's coming. You need to know, and if you don't think you can handle it, I understand. I can get some extra help, and you can keep on doing as much as you want to, as long as you want to. You've done a wonderful job with her. I'm so grateful for how sweet you've been. I think she knows too, somehow. Anyway, remember a couple of weeks back you mentioned the sore, how it was smelling bad and all, and I just told you not to worry about it?"

"Yessir."

"That was hard. I was probably a little short with you. It didn't sit well with me. I suppose I hadn't digested it yet myself. I chewed the doctor up pretty good about that. I wanted to get her into the hospital to get some treatment, and he wouldn't do it. Here's the thing. I know this is tough. He told me it doesn't matter. I still have a hard time even saying that out loud, but I trust him. We just have to trust him."

"I don't understand. That's a horrible thing to say. He don't even wonna treat her?"

"No. The thing is, it's that it won't matter. It won't heal. It's never going to heal. The way he explained it, her body is shutting down. Her brain and her, well, everything, is beginning to fail. He assured me that she's not in any pain because of it, that the things the body does to fight an infection aren't working right anymore, but he promised me she can't feel it. If she could, there would be signs, and there aren't. So that's why I said not to worry about it. I'm sorry. I suppose I wasn't exactly past my own worrying about it then. But I think now he's right. She doesn't need to get yanked out of here and be in a hospital for something that won't help."

She felt a wave of despair pass through her and wilted slightly. She had not observed death before.

"I wanted to tell you this because the time is coming soon. He told me how it would be. What to watch for. He said one day soon, she'd stop taking her food. Whatever part of that place in her mind that kept wanting it would stop. I know this is unsettling, and you're awfully young to be in the middle of something like this. If you decide it's too much, you just say so, promise?"

"Yessir. I'm gonna be okay."

"So I need to tell you the rest. I'm sorry. It's mighty unpleasant. But I don't want you to be surprised when it comes. She may take her food again. So keep trying. At least, for a while yet. He said she may stop and start again, and then one day, she won't ever start again, and it will begin to go faster and even without having food, she'll still be needing cleaning up after, and then sometime, even that will stop. When that happens, I'll stay with her by myself until it's done, and I'll need you to do some things for me. There'll be some people for you to call. I'll give you a list. There will be a lot of people out to the house. You won't need to cook anything. The church will take care of that, but there'll be a time where there are just a lot of people coming around to visit, and you may not have a lot of help in the kitchen."

He sat back in the chair and stared out the back door where the bird sounds were echoing across the bottom lands. She hadn't noticed the hair was thinning, and his face was drawn and thinner than it had been, the red, ruddy texture of his face ending abruptly at the line where the old Stetson would sit, and above it, the pale, unblemished skin of his forehead.

"I'll be fine, Mr. Clement."

"That makes one of us."

*****

"Why don't you buy yourself a decent pickup?"

"Ain't nothin' wrong with this one."

205

"Other'n bein' twenty years old and half of the windshield busted and generally looking like Jed Clampett. Son, you're so tight, you squeak. You only replace half the damn windshield, why?"

"Only one I look out of mainly."

Mike tilted his head. His face expressionless.

There's a planet somewhere where that makes sense, but it ain't this one.

"It gets me where I'm goin'."

"How do you expect to ever get a woman to go anywhere with you? Big ol' hole in the floorboard. When's the last time it had a functioning muffler?"

"Can't recall. Disintegrated a few years back. Anyhow, I don't think we need to talk about the glories of women."

"You ain't queer or nothin', are you?"

"I ain't exactly even sure what that means, to tell you the truth, and if you are, keep it to yourself. You know dang well what I mean."

"Well, you need to get over all that."

"Pot. Black."

"I reckon."

Blas and Tito bounced up over the brink of the hill and pulled alongside Trace and Mike.

"*Mio camarada.* How are ya, Tito?"

Tito simply nodded and flashed a big smile.

"When are you gonna bring that hoss out here with you, Blas? I still ain't even seen him yet."

"*No. Marina no me dejara.*"

"Tell her we would'n corrupt him until he's at least seven or eight. Anybody heard anything outta Nicholas?"

"We got a letter. He got shot. It was nothing. He's okay."

"Dang. He say where he is?"

"*Si, pero no se.*"

"What you up to this week, Jed?"

"Not much. Me and Shorty and Herbert are tearing down a old barn for Mr. Holloway…and no, I ain't seen her."

Mike wasn't looking good. He seemed energetic, but Trace could tell he was still drinking hard. The beer gut was getting obvious, and he had a dissipated sag in his face and had evidently decided to give up on haircuts. He let the comment about Georgette pass.

"Well, somebody, probably some a your buddies up at the school, decided to take out ever'body's mailbox out on the cemetery road. Looks like they took a baseball bat to 'em. There's about six of 'em that we need to go fix. Trace, if you'll bring the posthole diggers, I'll get the posts, and it shouldn't take too much. You might wanna pass the word at school. Mailboxes is one thing. If they were to graduate up to knockin' over tombstones, somebody is gonna regret it. Let's do it tomorrow evenin'. Charlie's well is out again. I don't remember what happened last time, do you?"

"It was just rats or squirrels chewed up the wire. Prob'ly the same thing again. I'll run out there."

"Blas, I heard Irena is packing up the family and moving off. Y'all heard anything?"

"*Si. Cuando termine la escuela. Familia en San Angelo.*"

"Sorry to hear that. Check with her. See if she's gonna need any help with anything. Sure would be nice if somebody had a truck we would'n be embarrassed to use."

"Mike, I ain't buyin' no pickup. It ain't like I'm gonna need one where I'm goin'."

"Well, I'll grant you don't need to show up there drivin' that thing. They don't have streets at Yale?"

Trace ignored him.

"That's it. I'll see y'all tomorrow evenin'. Y'all'll be on your own for a while. I'm hookin' up with a rig in a few days, so I'll be out of pocket for a while."

*****

Trace turned up the river road instead of toward town on his way out. There was no light at the river cabin, and the spring weeds were up to the porch. He felt around the wall outside the door and flipped the breaker lever, and light spilled out of the window across the porch. The old house smell was thick inside, and the coffee cups were sitting beside the sink as he and Mike had left them. He thought to himself, that had been over two years ago.

The cabin had once been a lively place. Fowler would bring in people from Mexico and Dallas and entertain college friends with David Ramos and quail hunts and barbecues. There had been a shooting range off one side of the porch where they would shoot skeet, and Fowler would position Trace behind a pile of hay bales to operate the clay pigeon machine. There had been kennels for the dogs, and riders would appear at dawn to flank the hunters. Trace would follow with Fowler in a tremendous old Dodge Power Wagon to swap dogs periodically. And in the late fall, they would all be there with their rifles to hunt deer and turkey and pigs in the frost-covered mornings, and he would sit with Fowler or Junior and some visitor he had never known in a blind, until the man would get his deer, and then he could talk again if he wanted to. Then later, the springtime fishing trips when Wmearle and his friends would come out, and they would chop the poles from a paradise grove and tie the lines and stab them in the soft mud along the banks and bait them with perch and Redhorse minnows they would seine from the river and run the lines from a flat-bottomed boat in the darkness for yellow cat. And Wmearle would take them into the river to the holes where the men would reach with their hands into voids under rocks and in the soft mudbanks, and grab the tremendous fish barehanded and heave them into the boat, their hands and arms bleeding.

And now there had been no one in over ten years. He pulled down the Bugler can and rolled himself a cigarette and stepped out onto the porch in the cool spring night air, the river silent and dark before him. He closed his eyes and imagined he could hear the clatter of hooves in the ledge rock across the river and Iladio rising up out of the river in the firelight, his horse glistening. In the quiet still of the night, he could imagine them all, Junior shooting silhouettes from the porch, and Fowler sitting under the pecans with some old men discussing who knows what, and the firepit glowing in the dark with the Mexicans tending the dinner, and whiskey and cigars and Fowler having none of it and Junior having all of it, and Wmearle, bare-chested and wet and his wire-wheel hair standing out, laughing about the tremendous fish and showing the scrapes where the fish had taken the hide off, and up on the bluff above the ledge rock, the wild mustang, rolling its eyes still at him, and Quanah looking down, penetrating down with that steady determined curiosity.

"What are you going to do?"

CHAPTER 27

May 1967

The Lowake Steakhouse sat in an open plain of cotton fields east of San Angelo. The gravel parking lot was full of pickups lit by the small neon sign out by the highway. Mike had left a message with Lydia for Trace to drive down and meet him. He figured Mike would treat him to a steak to celebrate his graduation the following evening. He walked through the glass front door and past a refrigerated meat counter displaying steaks. The room was lit with neon beer signs, and every table had a pitcher and large glass mugs spread about. Mike was sitting at a table with a pretty young brunette he had not seen before. He popped up out of his chair and slapped him on the back.

"Comere. I got somebody I wont you to meet."

"Trace, this is Belle."

She got up and walked around the table and hugged him. "I heard a lot about you." Trace was looking over her shoulder at Mike. She smelled like suntan lotion.

"Belle's short for Annabelle. Otherwise known as Mrs. Michael Wakefield."

He was stunned. Mike pulled out his chair and sat down. "Sit down before you get flies in your mouth."

Belle took him by the hand and stepped back to look him up and down.

"You're right. He is handsome."

Trace hadn't moved. His eyes going back and forth from Belle to Mike.

"Come on. Sit down, and I'll tell ya all about it."

"When did all this happen?" He plopped down and sat his hat in the empty chair.

"Yesterdy afternoon. Went to the JP in San Angelo. You look like you seen a ghost."

"Sorry. I mean. Congratulations. Belle, I'm sorry. Nice to meet you. Congratulations." He looked at Mike.

"Señor, you caught me by surprise."

He was discombobulated. He had thought he had Mike diagnosed. Either he was making one of those knee-jerk mistakes that would wind up in disaster, or he'd been wrong all along about how hung up he had been over Georgette.

"We been datin' for a couple of months. I popped the question last weekend, and we didn't wanna wait."

"How'd y'all meet up?"

Belle spoke up. "I was out at the rig with daddy, sittin' out in the sun in the car. Mike come out and brought me a Coke." She smiled, looking at Mike.

Trace was in true form, trying not to stare at Belle. She was a beautiful young lady. He found it frustrating to not be able to look a pretty girl in the eye without feeling embarrassed.

"Where are you from, Belle?"

"Abilene. Daddy's a oil operator. Mike was working on one of his wells."

"What's he think about all this?"

Mike cut a glance at Belle. "He don't know about it yet. We're headin' to Abilene once we get done here to go see them."

Trace looked over at Belle. First impressions could be tricky, but the way she was looking at Mike was reassuring. He could see none of the reticence that he'd seen in Georgette. Mike was lit up.

"You ever even met him before?"

"No. Seen him out on the location a couple of times. Name's Chance Wortham. Don't go worryin'. Belle says he ain't one to go around killin' a new son-in-law."

"Good to know. Belle, what possessed you to hook up with this piece a work?"

She answered without taking her eyes off Mike. "I don't know. Maybe he looked like he needed savin'."

"Well, civilizing is more like it."

"Mike said you were a turk."

"He says a lot of things. Pay close attention. Once ever year or so, he'll say somethin' that makes sense. You don't wanna miss it."

The steaks came, along with a pile of onion rings and a pitcher of iced tea. Trace was surprised there had been no beer on the table, but he figured Mike was wanting to put his best foot forward when he met the old man. They seemed easy together, and the longer they talked, the more he was satisfied that this was going to work out fine.

When they walked out onto the gravel parking lot, Mike and Belle both hugged him, got into a little white Mustang, and drove away. Trace walked out to his truck and reached in and got his makings, and in the red light of the neon steakhouse sign, he rolled himself a cigarette. It was a hot still night, and there was lightning across the northwestern sky. He pulled out onto the highway and headed toward home.

*****

He could see Mike's taillights far up ahead on the straight blacktop. The car came up behind him and passed. Whoever it was was punching a hole in the wind, probably going 120. He saw Mike's brake lights tap right before they dropped over a hill that led down to a stop sign where the blacktop intersected with the main highway. When the speeding car reached the same spot, he noticed its brake lights had never come on. There was a brief flash of light from beyond the hill, and he wondered whether it had been a lightning flash.

When he topped the hill, his heart got in his throat. The fast mover was accordioned just beyond the stop sign with steam spilling out of the front. A semi was jackknifed a hundred yards down the highway. When he plowed into the ditch and around the jackknifed trailer, he could see the mangled wreckage of the Mustang comingled with the undercarriage of the tractor. He jumped out of the pickup with it still rolling and ran toward it.

Suddenly, there was a large black man, his white shirt covered in blood, in front of him. "Son, hold on."

When he moved to go around him, the man stepped in his way. "Son, hold on." Powerful hands grabbed Trace by the shoulders and held him. "You don't wonna go over there."

"They're my friends." He struggled to move, but the man was strong, and his hands held his shoulders tight.

"You don't wonna see. Look at me, son! You don't wonna see. They gone, son. They gone."

*****

He had stumbled across the ditch into the tall grass and sat, in shock. For a while, the black man had walked around as well, not knowing what to do. He had left to walk back up the highway to look into the fast mover but had come back shortly and sat down beside Trace.

"They dead too. Wadn't nothin' I could do. He just run up behind that car and never even slowed down. Knocked 'em right out in fronta me."

The man's face was covered in blood, and a large gash had opened above his eye.

"He didn't never even slow down."

It was an hour before the highway began to fill up with highway patrolmen and ambulances and tow trucks. The cloud had overtaken them, and the rain was driven by a ferocious wind. He sat and watched them going about their business. In time, a patrolman walked over and leaned down and yelled over the wind and rain.

"The driver says you know the victims."

"Michael Wakefield."

"No. No family. Mother somewhere. I don't know where."

"Belle. No. Annabelle. Wortham. Chance Wortham. Abilene."

"No. He wad'n drinkin'."

"No. Me neither."

"Donis Weaver."

"Just Jones County."

The officer had left. The squall had lasted only a few minutes. He sat, drenched in the steaming grass and watched the lightning flashes recede to the east. In another hour, the ambulances were beginning to pull away when a black Lincoln pulled to a stop on the other side of the highway. He knew who he would be and watched him out of some unearthly detachment as the man walked with uncertainty toward the patrolman, and he knew what would come next, the moment when the man found out, and he watched in the flashing blue and red lights as the man diminished suddenly as though a giant weight had settled down on him, and he thought of Fowler and how he had seemed undiminished, his determination seemingly immune to the sight of Junior lying on the dinner table. But this man was not undiminished. He was watching him being crushed in the steaming wet of the springtime storm and the thunder booming in the distance, and he watched him as though he were among them, among the dead, because he felt nothing.

"Son." The man was shaking him gently on the shoulder. "Son, I'm gonna have somebody pull your truck off the pavement and leave it here. You come go with me. You probably don't need to be driving."

The inside of the Lincoln was cool, and the cigar smell had saturated the interior. He was moving down the highway with the stripes disappearing into the grill, and the images of Belle and Mike kept entering his mind, and he would not allow them. It would be impossible to permit them as only a memory, and so he would not allow it. Still they came, and pictures of Mike in the light of a moon on top of the gravel hill overlooking the river flats and sitting in the café in Snyder with his hair slicked back, and in the stark light of the filthy jail cell in Acuna and in the cabin smiling over the diamond ring and out on the porch with the snow falling and the ducks landing in the dark waters of the Clear Fork. And each one he swatted away and refused to admit them into the past.

The man stopped his car in a broad circle drive on a street lined with ancient live oaks. Trace stepped out of the cool cigar smell and into the steaming darkness and looked up and down the street at the darkened mansions with the manicured lawns and the utter quiet, and it seemed as though it was all a remnant. There had been life there, with families and meals and parties and children and arguments and laughter, and now that had all passed into oblivion with only the silent, sentient live oaks remaining over it, and the mansions yet to diminish as they would surely diminish with time. And the man opened the massive door and led him into a library and poured liquor into two glasses and handed him one.

"I shouldn't offer you a drink, but here, just sip on that."

Trace sat down in a large wingback chair. He smelled of wet grass, and his beaver hat was soaked. He took it off and sat it on the floor beside the chair.

"Who are you?"

"Trace Clement."

"Clement? You related to Fowler Clement?"

"Yes."

"I'm Chance Wortham. I'm Annabelle's daddy. How do you know Annabelle?"

"Mike Wakefield was my friend. I just met her for the first time tonight."

"I don't know him. I don't know what she was doing out there. She was supposed to be in school. Now I gotta go upstairs and tell her momma she's gone." He slumped into the sofa and took a drink.

"Sir, her and Mike got married yesterday. They were married."

"Married?"

"Yessir. They were on their way here to come tell you."

He watched the man. He had a confused, defeated expression. "Married. Who was he? I never even heard of him."

"Mr. Wortham, I can tell you just what I know. Him and her seemed like they were happy. Like they loved each other. He was my friend. She married one of the best men I ever knew. You ain't ever gonna know him, but if you had, you'd a been proud a both of 'em."

Wortham drank again, draining the liquor, and before he could swallow, he was finally overcome and burst out crying, the whisky spilling out of his mouth. He dropped the glass onto the carpet and cried into his hands until he finally gathered himself again and raised his head up, the snot smeared across his face.

"Is there somebody I can call for you, son?"

"No sir. There ain't nobody."

CHAPTER 28

He sat down on the porch, exhausted. He had spent most of the day cleaning up Mike's house on the assumption that there would be people. There were always people, bearing covered dishes and pies and asking if there would be anything they could do.

But there had been none this time. He had hauled off the beer cans and taken a yo-yo to the weeds in the yard and washed the porch with a water hose to rid it of the stench of the stale beer smell. The inside had not been so bad, as Mike had apparently taken to sleeping in the recliner full-time. There were no groceries in the house and the refrigerator was bare.

He had attempted to box up the few personal items—toothbrushes, razors, and such. But it had affected him, and he went back outside in favor of more physical labors.

Wortham had made calls during the night, and before morning, a man had appeared and driven him back to the site of the wreck to get his pickup. He had spent the night in the chair listening to the wailing of the woman upstairs. Among the calls he had heard bits of was one, apparently to Fowler: "No, he seems to be okay…wasn't involved…yes, dead…"

Lydia had been with Wmearle when he got home, and he saw the look on their faces when he pulled up outside the trailer. He had hugged them both, but he had been robbed of any words to say. He simply couldn't speak. So he had quickly changed into his work clothes and headed to the Wakefield place.

He turned the tap and held the water hose over his head and let the cool water run down his back. When he finished and looked up, Donis Weaver was standing in the sidewalk.

"You've got things looking downright presentable."

"Figured there might be some folks come around. Guess I was wrong."

"No, I don't expect anybody will be out here. No family to look after."

"What brings you out this way?"

"You."

"I'm okay."

"Of course you're not okay. None of us is okay today." He sat down on the concrete porch. The heat was stifling, and he took off his floppy straw hat and wiped the sweat from his forehead. Trace sat down beside him.

"I made arrangements today. Afterward, I thought I should have consulted you first. If you want, we can do whatever you think would be best. It'll be tomorrow afternoon."

"Who's the pallbearers?"

"You, Blas, Tito, Iladio, Iladio's oldest boy, and Frank Murchison from the feedstore."

"Iladio?"

"He's coming in with Juanita and the kids and his sister."

"Hadn't heard that. That's good. Awful nice for all them to do that."

"Son, he doesn't know about Mike yet."

"I ain't follerin'. What're they doin' here then?"

"I spoke to him this morning to tell him that Leticia Clement passed away during the night."

*****

He had thought to skip the graduation, but when he got to the trailer, Wmearle had his tie on, sitting outside the trailer.

"I didn't know whether you'd decided to pass or not, so I got ready just in case. If you don't wanna go, nobody'd fault you."

Truth was, he had no interest in it whatsoever, or in anybody who would be there, save Wmearle and Lydia, and Miss Bledsoe, maybe. But it was a proud moment for Wmearle, and he wouldn't deprive him of it.

"No, I reckon I'll do it. Won't get another chance."

"Son, I cain't imagine how bad you're feelin'. Ain't any of us gonna be the same without that knothead around. He'd be proud a you goin' ahead with it, I think."

"I guess you heard about Mrs. Clement."

"I did." Wmearle had no intention of trying to guess what that meant to him.

"Hell of a thing."

"Get in there and get your duds on. You're already late."

Lydia made a freezer of ice cream for after, and the three of them sat outside in the summer night and told stories about Mike Wakefield until the wee hours. When she finally got up to go, she put her hand on his shoulder. "There'll be a surprise for you at Mike's funeral. I think you're gonna like it."

*****

The church building was full when he and the other pallbearers walked into the auditorium. He had expected only a few, there being no family.

Donis Weaver spoke for only a short while, reading at first from the first chapter of James: "Pure religion and undefiled before God and the Father is this, To visit the fatherless and widows in their affliction."

"Oftentimes, we preachers are called upon to preach people into heaven. Today, that won't be necessary. I'm going to sit down and let some others speak, instead, about this good man."

And so began the long procession of common people, speaking haltingly, uncomfortably, about some act of kindness, a leaky faucet, a pet or a horse that needed to be put down when the owner couldn't manage to do it, a rattlesnake in the cellar. The foul chores and simple tasks related by a hundred obscure and simple people. The stories went on for almost an hour, the significance of each adding to what had been told before.

When the last of them had told their story, Weaver resumed the pulpit.

"We usually read the fifteenth chapter of John to mean there is no greater love than to die for your friends. But perhaps we lay down our lives for our friends by laying down the living part as much as we ever could the dying part. Michael Wakefield laid down his life for his friends every day by giving them the living part."

The six of them stood to the side of the grave. Weaver had told the funeral home not to bring the tent and the chairs, as there would be no family members to sit in them. Afterward, Trace shook hands and smiled for the familiar people that he remembered. Iladio looked odd in a sharply tailored suit that seemed an odd contrast to the taco-shell straw hat. He had introduced Trace to Maria Louisa, whom he remembered vaguely from long past times at the hacienda in Musquiz. She was far from the same person, though, having grown into a beautiful woman now, but she regarded him formally and carefully, and he remembered how rude she had been when he knew her as a child.

Trace gathered the four of them up before they dispersed.

"Tomorrow night. Regular time. On the hilltop."

Suddenly, the man standing behind them caught his eye. He had seen him in the crowd, but somehow hadn't recognized him.

"Mr. Wortham."

"Son."

They shook. He had hardly noticed the man before. He could tell he had had a rough life, his face creased and brown, and his hands the hands of a working man. He had evidently hit it big somewhere along the way.

"I'm sorry. I was kinda in shock the other night. I appreciate you takin' me home with you. I don't know if I was thinkin' exactly right."

"Me neither, to tell you the truth."

"I'm surprised you come."

"Ever since you told me they got married, I been thinking about it. Kids kinda run off without runnin off, if ya know what I mean. Belle found this guy and fell in love and married him, and I never even heard of him. I guess I just wanted to come and find out what sort of person he was. I'm mighty glad I did. You was right, I guess. If I had known him, I'd a been proud of them both."

When he turned to leave, he could see Lydia pushing Wmearle toward the gate near the highway. Alone, outside the remaining circle of people, stood Georgette.

"Georgette. I'm glad you decided to come."

"Me too. Surprised to hear you say that, though."

"Why's that?"

"I figured you'd still be sore at me over how it went with me and him."

"No. There ain't no reason to think that way. Everthing ain't a fairy tale, and everthing ain't any one person's fault either."

"It felt like it at the time."

"He found somebody you know."

"I heard. They got married, just before."

"He was happy. They were happy. I think."

"I'm glad a that. There's somethin' else I need to say to you."

"About what?"

"I told you somethin' wrong. When you was out at the Clement that mornin'. You asked me what it was like in there."

"I remember."

"I told you it was the worst thing in the world."

"I expect it was rough."

"But I was wrong."

"How so?"

"It's hard to describe. It was bad. Hard for me at first. I hadn't ever done nothin' like that before. Cleanin' a person, you know. And her just starin' and couldn't talk or nothin'. It affected me. I had to get outta there sometimes."

"Well, I know that'd be hard on anybody."

"But I was wrong. It wadn't the worst thing in the world. I'm not sure but what it ended up bein' the most beautiful thing I'll ever see in my lifetime."

He still had the confused expression on his face.

"As bad as all that was, I ain't ever seen anything like what it was like with them. That old man was so tender, and even with her in the shape she was in, he was so sweet, like if she needed cleanin' he'd leave, so she wouldn't be embarrassed, like just on the outside chance she could still know what was happenin', and Lord, I know it was killin' him, but he didn't ever quit, even till the very last. At the end, he spent two days in that room by her bedside and never come out even once except to talk to that man the other night that called about the wreck, and then right back in there.

Anyhow, I was wrong to say somethin' like that. I expect two people lovin' each other the way they did, anybody would be lucky if it ever happened to 'em. I never seen anybody love another human bein' as much as I seen out there. I thought I oughta tell you that."

*****

The service that morning had been much different. There had been only a graveside service and a much smaller crowd. Judge Reynolds was there, Lydia and Wmearle, and a carload of bankers from Fort Worth. Congressman Burleson was there with his wife, and a group of lawyers from Mexico City were there with Iladio and his family. Fowler sat there alone in a row of chairs next to the casket, his pale skin shining in the morning sun, and when Weaver had finished his thoughts, only he approached him to say a few quiet words. The rest simply passed by behind him touching him softly on the shoulder. Weaver stood to the side for the longest while until only Fowler was left with Leticia, standing removed, watching, while Fowler sat there, utterly alone.

*****

Trace was waiting on the hilltop when the rest pulled up and parked. Iladio had shed the suit, but still had on his starched white shirt. He passed around some solo cups and poured a shot of whiskey into each, then reached behind him and pulled out the little spiral notebook he had found next to the recliner in the Wakefield house. He plopped it on the tailgate of the pickup and raised the cup.

"Happy trails, knothead."

"Vaya con dios."

CHAPTER 29

June 1967

Fowler skidded to a stop in front of the trailer and flung the door open. Wmearle was sitting in the wheelchair on the porch. Fowler had fire in his eyes.

"What the hell happened?"

"Like I told you on the phone, he's gone."

"Enlisted?"

"Yessir. Marines."

"And you had no idea about it?"

"Not till he walked in at breakfast this morning and told me. I never seen it comin', Mr. Clement. I promise."

Fowler looked at him with rage and pleading and defeat. "What the hell is he thinking?"

"He's been real quiet all week. I expected that. He seemed okay through the funeral and everthing. I shoulda known he was puttin' on."

"Marines!"

"That's what he said. Kept it to hisself until his bag was packed."

Fowler took his hat and slapped it down against his thigh. "My Lord."

"I'm sorry. I couldn't budge him. I told him we could get him out of it, but he was determined. He done it this way so we wouldn't have no way to stop it."

"Did he give you a reason?"

"He just said it was somethin' he had to do. He wouldn't say much."

Fowler slumped down and sat on the porch steps beside the ramp.

"Wmearle, don't be apologizing to me for anything. This is my doing. Nobody else's. In a million years, I couldn't repay you for everything you've done. I have no business questioning you that way. I'm sorry."

"What are we gonna do?"

He sat for a long time staring down at the caliche and the red ants darting back and forth across the gravel. Finally, he stood and put his hat on.

"It's done. It's all done."

*****

Trace squatted in the elephant grass beside the faint trail leading up the valley at the base of a steep jungle-covered hillside. He had not seen any signal. The point man had simply squatted and become still, and suddenly, the sound of the men behind him moving through the tall grass had stopped instantly. They sat motionless, listening, alert. After a while, the point man rose and continued up the trail. He had lost track of how many times this had happened. So far, his unit had not engaged in a fight.

They had been a week in the bush. The CH-46 had dropped them into an elephant grass patch in the bottom of a narrow valley that, for all he knew, was the same one he was in now. Oleys, as they called them, boarded, or were carried into the back of the chopper, and the six of them had been ordered to clear the rotors and squat.

When the giant chopper lifted into the air and thundered down the valley, the platoon sergeant waved them in behind him and trotted up a narrow path toward the throat of a steep gorge. The others were there, on overwatch for the LZ.

"Names."

"Bose, Carlyle, Clement, Ramirez, Teaque, Garrett."

Like everyone he had seen so far, the man looked awful, tattered and filthy, and in a bad mood. The men who had boarded the chopper were virtually naked.

"Clement. You checked out on this?" He pointed at an M-60 and a couple of ammo boxes on the ground.

"Yessir."

"It's yours. Fall in with Carson, second squad. Do anything he tells you to do and don't do anything *unless* he tells you." He pointed to a small fierce-looking black man glaring at him.

"Yessir."

The platoon sergeant directed each of the replacements. "Lulu, on point. Carson, get him squared away. Jerome, set up here and hang out for a bit. Give it a half hour to see if we attracted any attention, then catch up."

Carson took Trace's M16 and put it aside, then lifted the two straps over his shoulders, suspending the weapon across his belly, then grabbed the ammo box straps and looped one over his head on both sides. Minus his M16 and cartridge straps, he figured he had gained another fifty pounds.

"Luck of the draw, huh."

"How so?"

"Comin' in with five little guys. This guy's a bitch, but you'll get used to it." He laid the ammunition belt across the feed tray and slapped it down. "You sure you checked out on this thing."

"Yessir."

"Drop the yessir business. You stay right on my ass until I tell you otherwise. That's on F, but I don't wanna see your finger on that trigger. We get in the shit, I'll tell you what to do."

He was glad to be out of the camp and in the open. The constant whining and vulgarity and noise had grown old quick. But the landscape was a mystery to him, the density of the vegetation, the smell of rot, and the humid sickly heat of the place.

It was past sundown when the column held up, and Carson had turned to tell him to stay put. The platoon sergeant huddled with the lieutenant and the squad leaders, and shortly Carson returned and motioned to the squad to move up into the hillside jungle and dig in. The clouds had dropped down the mountainsides, and a slow steady drizzle had begun. They spread their ponchos across the top of their hole, and Trace flopped the end of the M-60 over the lip facing out across the narrow valley. The wall of green that faced him was motionless and quickly faded in the mist to total darkness.

"I'll give you this, you don't talk much. Good habit to get into," he whispered.

"What happened to the guy had this before me?"

"Jungle rot. Got out of hand. I told him to lose the underwear, but he never would. Be lucky if he don't lose the family jewels. Tell you the same, lose the drawers and don't forget to take your Dapsone. Where you from?"

"North a Abilene, Texas."

"Sounds right. I'm from Texarkana. I got family in Dallas. Name's Laverelle. Lieutenant taken to callin' me Kit. Thinks it's cute to call a black boy Kit Carson. May be a compliment. Who knows? Everybody be callin' me that now."

Carson spent most of the night telling him whatever came to mind about how to cope with the leeches and jungle rot and trench foot and a hundred other plagues. Sometime before dawn, Trace asked his first stupid question, "How do you ever sleep in this place?"

"I think we're gonna call you Rawhide. How 'bout that? Be like Matt Dillon on the 60. I tell you how. In another couple a days, you ain't never gonna be worryin' about sleepin' ever again. You be worryin' about how to stay awake. Them gooks are always right out there."

"You hadn't seemed too worried about it."

"Peabody got our six. He about fifteen feet up the hill behind us. I told him we'd be jabberin'."

It was an almost tangible darkness, yet he could see Carson's eyes somehow, his dark skin a part of the pervasive blackness all around him. Somewhere in that darkness, a deep and distant rumble began that reverberated through the mist. Trace looked at Carson.

"Arc Light. B-52s. No tellin' where. Somebody whole day just got ruined, though."

"How come he give me the 60?"

"Just 'cause you big. Them other'ns wouldna made it this far. You seemed to handle it okay. Sergeant Vinson be watchin' you though. Gotta have a good man on the 60. Howerton, guy you replaced, one big-ass man. Took down by a little microbe."

"It ain't that bad."

"We'll see. Maybe you carry it, maybe you don't. We get in the shit, that baby gotta ring out. Everbody lookin' to it. You just graduate?"

"Mmm, hmm."

"Snatched you up quick, did'n they?"

"I did'n get drafted."

"Bullshit. You tellin' me you enlisted?"

"Mmm, hmm. Was headed to college and decided not to."

"Listen to me, boy. You keep yo mouth shut about that. Peabody, you hearin' me? You too."

"Why?"

"Cause everbody think you a psycho, that's why. You ain't a psycho, are ya? It's a serious question."

"Not as far as I know."

"We'll see."

Then there was a time when he could see it. The motionless green wall in the same thin drizzle. Carson opened a can of peaches and handed them to Trace, then lit a small chunk of C-4 plastic explosive and began making coffee in an empty C-ration can.

"We see how you feel about yo baby there once you hump it over that mountain over yonder."

*****

No sooner had Carson stood to move than he hit the ground flat on his belly. Again, Trace eased a step to his right and squatted and heard the cessation of movement in the grass behind him. Carson cocked his head as though straining to listen. After another ten minutes or so, Sergeant Vinson eased up behind Trace and slowly dropped low next to Carson.

"What's buggin' ya, Kit?"

"Twice. Twice I heard gooks talkin'. Then it was gone. I'm sure of it though. Couldn't get a bead."

The sergeant craned his head backward. "How about you?"

Trace simply nodded no.

"Let's get off this trail. Take a line just inside the bush on the edge of the hill. Put him on point." He crawled backward on his hands and knees until Trace couldn't hear the brushing in the grass. Trace eased up and passed Carson to his right and only stopped briefly for Carson to whisper at him. "Eyes ever'where. Stinger out. They here."

There was just too much to watch: the elephant grass flats to his left, the bamboo thickets and jungle ahead and to his right, the ground and the space right in front of him for wires and dap loi or mosquito mines, which Carson had told him wouldn't kill you, but you might lose a toe. His back was aching, not from the weight of the pack and the M-60, but from the strain of moving so slowly and deliberately. He longed to be able to step out and stretch his body. Suddenly, Carson yelled behind him, "Tubes!"

Trace had turned to see what was happening, only to see nothing but jungle behind him. It took him too long to register that the whole column had hit the deck. The mortar round blew him sideways and into the face of the hill, shrapnel lacing through his face from side to side just beneath his cheekbones. The blast had knocked the wind out of him, and he lay in the rotting vegetation unable to breathe or center his vision. There were more explosions, and Carson was suddenly on him, turning him and looking around his body for blood and yelling out for the corpsman. Suddenly, a large slug of blood passed through the back of his sinus into his throat. He coughed and gagged, spewing the blood across Carson's chest, and turned on his side gasping for breath. Carson was yelling again, but the ringing in his ears made it difficult to understand.

Then the corpsman, Taylor, was over him. "Whatta we got?"

"I don't know. I think he got it in the face, he's spittin' up blood, but I cain't find no holes in his chest. He got six or seven bleeds on his side, but I looked at 'em and ain't none of 'em arterial."

He heaved out another gout of blood and gagged and then threw up into the weeds.

"Sit him up. He's gonna be okay."

"The hell?"

"Went right through. His momma ain't gonna like it much, but it ain't gonna kill him. Rawhide, can you see me?"

Trace nodded.

"Can you move?"

He wheeled over on all fours and faced up the hill, the M-60 flopping down under him.

"I'm movin' back to see if anybody else needs me."

"Taylor, dammit."

"Listen, I'll check in with the lieutenant. If we don't need him, I'll be back, and we can give him the syrette, but we're gonna need him, messed up or not."

The green wall on the other side of the flats erupted in explosions from artillery that walked upward through the valley into the saddle ahead of them. The lieutenant was hurrying up the line with his RO at his elbow.

"Unknown strength. One Oley. Non-priority. Over."

"Sixty-ones. Three of three. Over."

"Damn right," Carson said as he watched the hillside rock with explosions.

Trace continued to bleed into the back of his throat, but holding his head down had slowed it somewhat. He could see the blood, already congealing in lumps in front of him and fresh drips from both sides of his face spattering his arms. He could hear Carson shouting orders and the radio cackling and the lieutenant.

Then Carson was in front of him. "Arright, Cowboy. You there? You still with us? Get it together. We gotta dig in."

He pulled himself slowly up the side of a tree and turned facing back along the slope. Men were furiously digging with their E-Tools. Peabody and Earls and Carson next to him. The jungle was spinning, and his stomach was retching. A powerful, dull pain was growing in his head, as though it were being inflated, and his eyes began to swell shut.

Carson was tugging on him, and suddenly he felt the weight of the M-60 and his packs and the ammo boxes.

"Damn, man. You a sight. Taylor says you gone' be okay, but damn."

He looked down for the first time. The fatigues along his side and chest were plastered to his body, the blood drying quickly and matting it to his skin.

"Okay, hoss. Git down in here. They prob'ly comin'. Look at me now."

He turned, looking. Suddenly angry. Angry at everything.

"Yep, lights is on. We fixin' to be in it. Toss me that can."

The cloud ceiling had begun to drop again, and the fine drizzle had started. He felt a torpor settling into him that contradicted the rage that seemingly had no focus and no face or reason. He was simply angry.

"You keep yo' wits about you, it gone' be okay. Remember, bursts. Don't go meltin' that barrel. Taylor'll be back in here sometime and check you out. They'll git you outta here sometime, but right now, we gotta rock and roll."

*****

He lost all sense of time in the night. Looking out of the hole, he wondered if he was seeing darkness or whether his eyes had finally swollen completely shut. He could tell his face had swollen horribly, but he felt no fresh blood. There was a constant urge to suck the blood out of his sinus to relieve the pressure he felt in his head, but doing so would produce another kind of pain into his head that was sharper, and he wondered how much blood he had lost.

Sometimes, he would sense movement and look to his right to find Carson gone.

Peabody must have seen him somehow. "He's makin' the rounds. Checkin' holes. Keepin' everbody on their toes. Lucky if he don't get shot."

He hadn't spoken and was not sure he could. The slightest movement of his jaws would spike the pain in his head. Suddenly, Peabody had his hand on Trace's elbow. "I..."

The flash of muzzle blasts roared out of the elephant grass, and an answering roar unleashed from the line to his left and above him. Tracers were coming up at them in bright streaks that left bright lines all across his vision, and he felt the sting of dirt hitting his face. He pressed the trigger and held for a couple of seconds remembering Carson's instructions. "Bursts." It felt like pressing the throttle on some outrageous machine, and he followed the tracers that now flowed away from him into the flats. The pain in his head was withering. With each press of the throttle, the burp of sound would amplify the pressure behind his eyes, and with each grenade flash, he felt the anger amplify also, and a metallic taste was in his mouth. At some point, he saw figures moving inside the grenade flash to his left and stood and swung the M-60 across the space where he had seen the shadows. He heard screams and a muffled thud. The light flashing in his eyes between the stars he was seeing and the explosive flashes and the tracer fire and muzzle flashes caused him to lose all definition of the miasma of light in his head. A great concussive blast erupted down the line and in front of him, and still he fired, following the incoming tracers and counting to three each time, and now the ringing in his ears comingled with the cacophony of sound of the blasts and the rifle fire, and he could no longer distinguish sound or direction.

And then there was blackness again, and Peabody's hand was on his elbow, and Peabody was close and talking in his ear, but he couldn't hear, or understand, the blood dripping out of his nose again. Peabody had the feed tray open on the gun and was flopping another ammunition belt in. He slapped it down and patted him on the shoulder, and now there was no light, and the stars in his eyes subsided back to the tangible wet darkness all around him.

*****

With light, there was silence. Carson returned and whistled when he saw Trace's face, which was now solid blue, and the sharp features were now rounded, as though an inner tube was being inflated to near popping.

"Sip some coffee, hoss. You need to get somethin' in yo' belly."

He wretched and spewed black vomit across the front of the hole.

"Swallered a bunch of blood's what you did. That'll curdle your innerds. Sip some more. I'll heat up some grub."

He produced another lump of C-4 and poked his K-bar through the lip of the can to make a handle and held it over the flame.

"You done okay, hoss. Smoked a bunch of 'em. Cain't talk?"

He tried, but the movement of his jaw sent a streak of white light into his vision, and so he stopped.

"S'all good man."

He stood up, and a wave of nausea swept across him, and he fought the darkness that began to constrict his field of vision. It passed. The narrow strip of jungle between the hole and the elephant grass looked as though it had been cleared. There were bodies in the black soil, some in pieces. He stood looking at the horror of a battlefield for the first time, his anger growing, and now he had that metallic taste in his mouth again.

"Sit yo' ass down, hoss. Get yo head shot off."

He watched him wave the pork and beans over the flame. The smell was nauseating.

"Claymores got a bunch of 'em, but you got yo' share, no doubt. Dickey 'bout to be overrun when you stood up and mowed 'em down. He said to tell you thanks. Here, try to open yo' mouth."

The white light again. He struggled to dislodge his jaw and finally put his hand over his chin to pull down. He felt an unfamiliar shape as even the skin around his chin had swollen into some foreign dimension. The pain almost made him faint. Carson put some beans on the end of his K-bar and gently slid it into his mouth.

"Just suck on those for a bit. We ain't in no hurry. First platoon comin' up the valley behind us, third'll be comin' over the hill before noon. My guess is the gooks de deed. Smart sumbitches."

He tried sucking on the beans. Whatever he did hurt. He sipped on the coffee and thought about the Thermos he kept with him in his pickup. The clouds had not risen, and the rain had turned from mist to a downpour. Then he could hear Carson talking behind him. Lieutenant Jennings was lying prone behind the hole.

"Hell no, he ain't okay. I ain't sure what he is. Cain't talk. He gotta get out. He messed up. Corpsman ain't been by since it happened. He needs to come check him out."

"Damn." Carson lowered his head then looked back up. "Lieutenant. He a machine in the shit."

Jennings dropped an extra ammunition box in the hole and was gone.

"We buggin' out. Taylor dead. Saunders in third too. You gone have to hump it. They thinkin' we get up to that saddle, it'll be clear, and they can get the birds in and you outta here. 'Bout two clicks."

He nodded. He was finding it hard to process what the words meant. He could hear them now, the ringing had subsided, but the words he heard were unintelligible.

And then there was a time when they were moving. Carson had told him again to stay right on his ass, and they climbed, at first through the elephant grass, and then through bamboo thickets where Peabody and Earls went ahead with machetes and then through a rocky gorge with the mist from the falling water comingling with the downpouring rain. Near the end of the day, they emerged into a rice paddy that sat in the saddle between two hills. The vegetation on both had been leveled with artillery during the day. Third's platoon was in place on one hill and were busy digging in. The clouds were settling in, and soon they were in a deep, drizzly fog.

Trace was in a stupor. For hours, he had tried to focus on a single belt loop on the back of Carson's pants, thinking of nothing more than that belt loop to guide him and keep his mind off the pressure in his head. With each step, the matted blood in the fabric along his side would pull the hairs in his legs. As the day had progressed, the shrapnel wounds had reopened, and the fresh blood would release the fabric from his skin. He felt dizzy, and occasionally, the peripheral vision would begin to constrict to a small hole, and he would focus on the little bobbing belt loop as though the surrounding jungle and grass and mountains had been negated from existence.

The belt loop stopped. He dropped to one knee, and Carson was in the little hole in his vision.

"You be out in a bit. Let's git that gun off you. Third's in the clear up on the hill. They'll get the birds down in here. You there, hoss?"

Trace nodded. Somehow, he didn't want to turn loose of the gun. Carson carefully lifted ammunition belts over his head, then gently pried the gun out of his hands and lifted the straps off his shoulders.

"Damn, man. You a mess. They gone get you fixed up, though. You be okay. Now get outta them britches. They new. Somebody else can use 'em."

He heard the thundering flap of the choppers somewhere outside of the little hole in the center of his vision, each thump of the rotors causing a pressure wave that he felt course through his head. Carson began undressing him. By the time they grabbed his arm to lead him into the chopper, he was wearing a helmet, a flak jacket and somebody else's boots, otherwise stark naked from the waist down. The thunderous vibration of the CH-46 caused him to see stars again from the pressure, and his peripheral vision again began to constrict until, finally, the little hole vanished altogether.

CHAPTER 30

NSA Hospital, Da Nang
Vietnam
November 16, 1967

Dear Wmearle,

I guess you knew this, but it turns out I'm not very smart. I had not been here a week and got myself wounded. I'm all right. No missing parts. I expect I'll be here in the hospital another week or so and then back out again. I am sorry about how I left. I know you and Lydia are worrying, but I'll try to be careful. The hospital here is first-rate. Some of the nurses are pretty also. I was out of it for several days. I guess they had me doped up, but I'm feeling ok now. I knew about you closing down. I'm happy for you that you'll get to be with Sylvia and the kiddoes. Just pile all my stuff in the pickup and see if Lydia will mind parking it over at her house till I get back.

I don't have much of an impression of Vietnam yet, except it's green and soggy and rains all the time, and it doesn't smell very good, or at least it didn't. They say the Marines are big on getting the mail out in the bush, so write me a letter and tell me how you're doing. Tell Lydia to be nice to everybody. I forgot to pay out at the station before I left. If you could pay her, I'd appreciate it, or she'll be mad at me. I'll pay you back when I get home. It's not much.

T

PS. If you could do me one favor. I usually take Sammy a can of Copenhagen once a week. If you could, get Lydia to take a roll up to the coach at the school and let him dole them out. Tell her I'm good for it.

*****

He licked the envelope and addressed it and laid it on the tray in front of him. The hospital was, indeed, first-rate, but he felt he was about to explode from the confinement. He could breathe again now through his nose, although it felt like the inside was still raw. The first week had been a horror with two separate surgeries to remove bone fragments. Now a third would be done by a plastic surgeon. A doctor walked into the quonset hut and approached his bed.

"Still no smell?"

"Nope."

"Okay, may be gone. There's a lot going on with the ganglia in there behind the nose. You may have issues with mucous production or taste. You may have a diminished response to allergic stimuli. How about the feeling in your chin and face?"

"Feels weird. Kind of dead. It itches."

"It's hard to say how it's going to be. We've removed most of the bone fragments. You may get some of it back, but only time will tell. The surgeon is mainly going to be concerned with appearance. The swelling is almost gone, so we're looking to do a little work on the scarring. Otherwise, what's done is done. How's the leg?"

"Itches like crazy, but it's not hot like it was. When can I get up and move around?"

"A lot of bugs out there in the bush. Some of them are wicked. I want you to stay put for another couple of days to let things stabilize in there. We want everything inside to heal over before you go to bouncing again. The remaining fragments will encase themselves pretty fast. We don't want them migrating around. Lots of nerves in there you want to keep. They'll be in here in an hour or so unless the ER gets backed up again. Unless something new comes up, you're done with me."

"Thanks, Doc."

"Duck faster."

"Will do."

The ward was quiet but for the whirring of the air conditioners. The injuries among the rest of the men were horrific. There was no conversation in the ward. He held the stainless steel tray up to his face and looked at the reflection. The blue bruising had turned into a greenish-yellow over most of his face. Dark areas remained under his eyes and around his nose, but the swelling had almost gone, and his features were returning to their normal shape. The scar from the shrapnel was now prominent on both sides of his face, sitting just under each cheekbone, about an inch wide on the left and fully two inches wide on the right. The one on the right leaving a deep crease that looped downward and under the cheekbone. The doctor had explained that the fragment had entered on his left and had tumbled once inside his head. The exit area on the right side of his face had been much worse. A quarter inch higher and he would have lost the entire orbit of his right eye.

He looked around the ward. He had been the only one with all of his appendages remaining. He remembered Georgette. "It's the worst thing in the world." He wondered, is that the worst thing in the world? To be blown apart and still be alive, without arms and legs? He wondered if he had misjudged her: the attitude she'd had about Mike and the rudeness he had seen when he stopped by her car out in the cotton field that day. Turns out she had a pretty good reason to be out of sorts. She had been sensitive about Mike, and probably under a lot of pressure to put up or shut up, right when she was in the middle of everything with Mrs. Clement. It had happened several times now, that he would think of them, the people at home, and for a moment, he would be overwhelmed with the desire to undo it all, to be among them again.

He had known for a month before he enlisted that he would not go to Yale. Miss Bledsoe had planted that seed, the idea that the others at the school were dumb saps who had no higher purpose than to be sacrificed, whereas she had somehow deemed him special and worthy of some higher calling, worthy to be saved, when she knew and he knew that he had no idea why or what he should go to study. He had felt again the latent privilege that had dogged him everywhere, none of it of his own making, unspoken, unmentioned, except by Mike, who had seemed so sure of himself that day in the café in Snyder. Somewhere, somehow that had to stop. His only reluctance had been Wmearle, and he still flinched at the pain that it had caused him that morning in the trailer. Wmearle had been sure that Mike getting killed had sent him into some kind of tailspin, that his decision had been rash, and he was pretty sure he had failed to convince him otherwise. Wmearle had seen war, and the horror that came across his face had devastated him. But by then, the die was cast, and Wmearle had finally stopped his protestations and lowered his head and dallied with the syrup on his plate, finally gathering his thoughts.

"I cain't describe what it's like. You'll see it soon enough. There ain't no magic advice about war. There ain't but one thing matters when you're in it. It's the man next to you. You keep that man alive."

He thought about what it meant to lose his smell. What did Georgette smell like? Not that he would ever have known anyway, but now it hit him that he had lost something, the smell of rain on the hot grass in the summer, the smell of the trailer and the bacon frying in the morning and the fermenting silage in the pits that he fed to the cattle, the smell of men working, the smell of the river on the rise. He'd never placed much of a value on that before, but now it seemed to settle on him that something important was gone.

The quiet of the ward was unnerving. The whopping sound of the incoming choppers were frequent, and at night there were mortar blasts, the streaming sound usually high overhead and aimed at the Marine compound across from the hospital. Occasionally, he could hear the surf, a half-mile distant, booming against the shore in the night. In the dark, he would think of Quanah perched on the hill across from the river cabin or riding into the blinking yellow light of a summer night. What would he think of all this? How would he adapt? And Weaver, what about that business of laying down your life for your friends? Not your death, but your life? Had he abandoned them for his own selfish reasons? Somewhere among them all was Fowler. The thought of him lurked in the background of his mind, no matter how much he tried to deny it, even to himself. Would even this release him?

A gurney appeared in the doorway with a number of corpsmen. He closed his eyes to say a quick prayer. Mostly, it was just thinking of each of them, one by one. He did this until the mask was on his face, and the man told him to count backward from one hundred.

*****

"Sheriff Rawhide! Look at you brother! Lemme look at that face. Peabody, I think he look meaner'n ever. Whatchu think?"

Carson twisted his chin left and right. The bright red slashes across his face had faded and receded, leaving deep creases.

"I see you got that sixty in yo genes now. Where'd you come by that?"

"Already on the chopper when I got on. Somebody lose theirs?"

"Kinda did. We short one. Got blowed up. Long with the man carryin' it."

"Who?"

"You did'n know him. Wheeler. Came in on the ride you took out. Bought it two days ago. You see Howerton while you in there?"

"No. But I asked about him." Trace didn't like spoiling the moment with bad news.

"What gives?"

240

"He's out. Shipped home. It wadn't just the jungle rot. Turned out he had leukemia. I got no idea if the jungle rot was related."

"I did'n know you could catch leukemia."

"Pretty sure you cain't. They musta just missed it when he was comin' in. What's on the agenda?"

"Jennings is out. Moved up to battalion. Got a new lieutenant. Runnin' around talkin' to everbody, tryin' to figure out how to be. All of 'em do it. Vinson straighten him out, I reckon. Boys is beat. Humped it all week long. NVA we bumped up against when you got here dartin' in and outta Laos. We bumped into 'em again two days ago. Pretty nasty day. Weather cleared up just when we needed, and somebody got the artillery fired up. They de deed. They'll let us rest up a day, then we back in it. Grab a beer. They dropped it on us for Thanksgiving."

"Not my cup a tea."

Carson looked at him like he was an idiot. "You get over that. Throw you up a hooch and sack out. Somebody get you when it's time to go on watch."

He sloshed through the mud toward the edge of a small finger of elevated dirt that ran down across the saddle and tossed his pack. He sat in the bright sun and looked around what had become the company fire support base. He felt weak. The four weeks, most of it bedridden in Da Nang, had sapped his strength. The short trudge from the LZ to the sandbagged bunker where he found Carson had winded him. The M-60 had seemed manageable before, but he figured it must have just been adrenaline. Now it seemed heavy and cumbersome. He needed to eat, so he fished out a can of fruit cocktail and sucked it down.

The clouds were seeping up the valley below, and soon the saddle was engulfed in fog. Above, he could barely make out the tops of the two hills still shining in the sunlight, bristling with barbed wire strung crudely below the crest on posts chopped out of bamboo. He thought how odd it was that such a thing appeared beautiful with the clouds swirling up the valley.

Water began to form on everything, condensing out of the fog. It had been sticky and hot only moments before, but now the mist blowing up the valley was chilling him. He popped open the rubberized canvas poncho and draped it over his head.

That first week, he had caught on to the routine everyone seemed to be preoccupied with. How many more days in country? He'd told himself then he wouldn't play the game, but now he couldn't help it, eleven months, six days, and one wake up. He squatted in the grass with the water dripping off his hooch and found himself thinking about Georgette again. It would be the last time he felt good for another year.

CHAPTER 31

January 1969

The light inside the station was still burning when he walked into the light. He stopped and watched the blinking orange light. The block behind the station had been cleared of all the rubbish and equipment, and a tall chain-link fence surrounded a white crushed limestone yard. The remnants of the ramp they'd built for Wmearle were piled in a heap behind the station. The temperature was dropping fast with the sundown.

"You owe me for eight rolls of Copenhagen."

She had hardly looked up from the ticket box.

"Sorry, lady. I'm dead broke." He dropped his duffel bag in front of the desk.

She jumped out of the chair and hurried around the desk, looking at him with that same old amazed intensity. She put her hands on both of his arms and stared up at him, looking over his face. She had water in her eyes, but her face didn't tremble, her lips pressed hard together, and her chin jutting out.

"Well..." she paused for a long time. "Sit down. I'll pour you a cup."

"What happened out back?"

"Fella Wmearle sold to. Deal was, he'd leave the trailer, so you'd have a place to light when you got back. Wmearle made him promise. He wasn't gone two weeks, and the knothead towed it off. Been trying to get me to sell out too. Don't like me right in the middle of his little empire."

"It's all right."

"I guess you're just gonna lay down right there then tonight."

"Hadn't planned that far ahead."

She handed him the coffee. It was awful, but it was so much better than the instant stuff that came in the little C ration packets he was used to. He smiled and sipped it, missing the various flavors of pork and beans or beef stew that were always left in whatever you heated the bush coffee in.

"Time'll get away from ya."

"Heard from Wmearle?"

"Oh yeah. He called ever time he got a letter from you. Kept me updated. They're livin' at Granbury. It's over between Fort Worth and Stephenville. Sylvia and her husband moved out there. Wmearle's got himself a place out on the river outside a town. She checks in on him all the time. He ain't doin' real good, Trace."

"He never said nothin' in his letters. What's the matter with him?"

"Bad circulation. On account of the accident. Toes are black and blue. He's worried they're gonna take 'em off."

"What about Nicholas? He oughta be back by now."

"He's back. Out on the Clement. He got hurt a little worse'n what he let on writin' home. Liketa died, I heard. Anyhow, he comes in ever week and seems to be doin' okay. What's your plan?"

"I'm gonna sleep for a while. Then I'm gonna make a plan. How's that for a plan?"

"Sounds pretty good."

"You got my pickup?"

"I do. Went out and started it up ever now and then just to keep the battery hot. Rat moved in last winter and ate all the wires outta the firewall. I got Snub at the gin to come wire it back up, so you oughta be able to drive it to wherever you go to trade it in on somethin' decent."

"May just do that. Whatta ya hear outta Georgette?"

Lydia frowned, not with any disapproval. It meant the question was unexpected.

"She's out at Fowler's still. Looks after the house, cleanin' and cookin' and whatnot. Right now, I expect she's in Abilene. Mrs. Holloway is in the hospital havin' a operation. Female sort of kind." She sipped her coffee, thinking.

"You're bigger. You grown. Put on a bunch a muscles anyhow. What's that all over your neck?"

"Oh, it's goin' away. It's a rash you get bein' in the jungle and bein' wet all the time. It's a lot better now."

"Sounds miser'ble."

"That it is."

"You're welcome to come stretch out on my couch."

"I know it. I think I'll head down to the old river place. I'll walk ya to the house though. Oh, one other thing."

He got another can of Copenhagen, and she turned out the lights and locked the front door, and they walked through the cold stillness of the evening down the caliche street to the little house.

"You home for good? I mean, they ain't gonna call ya back or nothing?"

"No, I'm done with the Marines. They can call me back, but they won't. Who knows, though, about the other part."

"I'm glad you're back in one piece."

She hugged him around the waist and disappeared into the house. The pickup was under a shed in the backyard, the inside almost full of clothes that would no longer fit him, his hat sitting on top, slightly chewed. He sat and smiled. The pickup had never seemed so pathetic before, but the spider-webbed half of the windshield and the hole in the floorboard and the rat smell were sufficient to make him agree with Lydia about a new truck. But he would never trade this one.

*****

The dim light was on in the back of the gymnasium. He stopped in front and stepped out onto the gravel parking lot and listened. He could hear coyotes yapping out on the edge of town and the distant sound of trucks out on the highway that you only seemed to hear in the wintertime.

He walked through the darkness of the gym and down the stairwell to the boiler room and knocked. Sammy was sitting on the cot, as he always seemed to. A little radio was playing quietly. Sammy looked up and squinted and smiled.

"Mr. Trace."

"Hi Sammy, 'member me?"

"Oh yeah."

"How ya been?"

"Always good."

Trace handed him the snuff can. "You been takin' care a things while I been gone?"

"Yessir."

He had always felt tender about Sammy. The scars had made a big impression on him as a child, and so he had always known in more than an abstract sense that there was a horrible cost to war. Now he looked at Sammy, and a deep sadness swept over him, and he sat and stared at the boilers along with Sammy while Loretta Lynn sang on the radio.

Sammy turned and stared at him, and Trace tried to figure if he was looking at the scars in his face and if they had any meaning to him, but Sammy finally just smiled, and Trace could see that he had lost some more teeth, and then he'd turned back to wherever his thoughts stayed, and Trace took the can of Copenhagen from him and put it in his pocket and slipped out again into the cold night.

*****

There were no lights when he flipped the breaker. The dead grass almost completely obscured the two ruts of the lane leading down off the hill. He flicked his zippo and found a coal oil lamp in the closet. The cabin was slowly decomposing in its disuse. A portion of the porch had collapsed under a giant pecan branch that had fallen. Rat pills littered the floor.

It was a bright night with a clear sky and a full moon. The ground was damp. He stood listening to the owls hooting up and down the river bottom. The moonlight was on the water, and he could hear the quiet sound of it going over the shoals below the horseshoe curve of the river. He breathed in the crisp cold air and felt the shallow, dull pain in his lung. The surgeon had said it was a deflected 'round, not moving at velocity, but it had had enough energy to penetrate the flak jacket and imbed itself in his lung. That had made three stars on his purple heart, and he was out, first for two weeks in the hospital in Da Nang, then a month at Subic Bay twittling his thumbs. The second had been a joke. A deep gash across his back from falling down a steep ravine during an attack. The battalion commander had gotten exercised about something during what turned out to be an important fight, and for a brief moment, handed out purple hearts to everybody in the company with so much as a mosquito bite. That had been a fluke, as the Corps was known for being rigorously deliberate with medals.

He gathered wood from what remained of the pile beside the porch. Some varmint scurried out from under it and into the darkness under the cabin. He made coffee over the fire and rolled a cigarette, then tossed it into the fire after one drag. Nothing smelled right anymore.

He pulled the top off a can of Vienna sausages and stabbed at them with his K Bar, thinking how ridiculous it was that he was still eating out of a can, then stretched out on the dusty couch in front of the fireplace and slept.

It was late in the night when he heard the snap of the twig. He lay completely still, orienting its direction, listening for the next sound. His hand moved carefully to the place across his belly where the trigger of the M60 should have been, and his heart jumped when his hand closed around empty air. Then he felt the warmth from the fireplace and began to resolve himself back to reality, still listening for the next footfall out in the damp leaves and grass. Then he heard the breath and knew it was a hog, and he calmed himself, having never opened his eyes.

The next morning, he began to burn the clothes from his pickup. He had, against all reasoning, gained weight in the jungle. It seemed he had been hungry for a year. He went through the pockets of each pair of Levis and saved the belts and socks and underwear, but the shirts wouldn't fit around him, particularly his arms. He sat on the cabin porch and drank coffee and watched the squirrels in the pecan trees.

He had lied to Lydia. He knew they could pull him back in. The pickup was sitting in the lane next to the cabin. He knew he needed to get a new one, but the prospect of presenting a draft to the dealership would surely alert Compton to the fact he was home and could set off a chain of events he didn't want to think about yet.

Later that morning, he left the department store with an armful of new Levis and shirts and a denim jacket and headed toward Abilene. The civilian clothes they'd given him in San Diego he left in the trash.

*****

The woman at the volunteer desk at the hospital directed him to the OR waiting room where he found Georgette sitting with her father. He had felt purpose from the moment he had boarded the DC-8 at Subic Bay, but suddenly, clumsiness gripped him, and he found he had no ready excuse for why he was there. She didn't recognize him at first, then rose and walked across the room. He'd grown accustomed now to the look, the rapid darting of eyes across his face and then away and then back. She had a puzzlement in her expression.

"I heard your mother was up here, and I thought I'd stop by."

She didn't respond, just looking at him with the puzzlement in her face.

"Sorry, it's a bad time. I'll catch up with you…"

"No, she's gonna be in there for a couple of hours."

Georgette turned and said something to her father and walked back.

"We can go outside and talk."

"Come go with me. I know a good place."

He headed toward the elevator and tried to remember where the stairwell had been. Soon, they were stepping out onto the roof where the little park bench sat.

"How'd you know about this place?"

"Come up here once when Wmearle was in the hospital."

She sat down and surveyed the view. "Pretty up here. I didn't even recognize you." Then she was embarrassed. What happened to his face wasn't what she had meant.

"I mean you're bigger."

"S'all right. I'm gettin' used to it."

"Turn around here. Look at me."

She held his chin between her thumb and her knuckle and turned his head back and forth, giving him a close examination. She traced her finger along the deep crease under his cheekbone.

"It's not as bad as you prob'ly think. You still look the same mainly. I bet that hurt like hell."

He laughed. She was straightforward.

"It was a while back. But yeah. Like the guy in *Romeo and Juliet*, 'tis not as deep as a well nor as wide as a church door, but 'tis enough, 'twill do."

"I don't know what that means."

"Means it was bad enough."

She looked at him a long time, thinking he would go on.

"Why'd you run off?"

"I'm not sure I know how to say."

"I know how that is. I almost never know how to say why I do stuff."

"You're wonderin' why I come up here. To the hospital, I mean."

"A little bit. Yeah."

"I had a lotta time to figure out how to say it, but it's kinda left me."

"You mean you had a speech figured out?"

"No, not like that. It's just things are hard to describe."

"Well, I ain't gonna bite you. So just plow into it."

"There was a lotta times when I thought about you. I don't know why. It'd be dark, and I'm sittin' in the rain, black as pitch, and I'm just sittin' there waitin' for whatever was gonna be next, and I's just by myself with my thoughts. Then I'd think about you, for some reason."

"Well, I suppose that's nice, I guess."

"Here's the thing. I needed to tell you. It was good. When I thought about you, it was a good feelin'. Maybe it ain't reasonable. Like I ought not make a thing out of it, but back there, it was dark. In all the evil and corruption and filth and the killin' and everthing, I'd just focus on the thing that I could that was good, and it was usually you. It was a comfort. So I needed to tell you that."

She crossed her legs and leaned forward, pulling the wool jacket up around her, squinting into the sun. A cool north breeze was lifting golden strands of hair up and across her face.

"Cain't imagine. Maybe it ain't unreasonable. A person can get lost, I know that for sure. I thought a you sometimes. Maybe not like that. I'd wonder what became of you, though. God knows the old man worried over it."

"How is he?"

"He's changed. He'll go off and just be all day out on the ranch by hisself. He ain't the same since she died. Maria comes sometimes, and he'll brighten up and dote on her, but she don't ever stay long and…you know Maria?"

"I knew her when I was little, or met her anyway."

"Tough cookie that one."

"Hah."

"Anyhow, I worry about him. He seems kinda helpless."

"Hard to feature that."

"I know. It's a contradiction."

He smiled. It seemed an odd formulation for Georgette. He watched the long strands of hair lifting into the brilliant sunshine. The dry cool air and the clarity of the wintertime blue sky and the warmth of the sun on his face, all of it was peaceful and satisfying.

"What's next for you?"

"I gotta go see Wmearle. After that, I don't know. What if I was to call and take you out to a show or go eat or somethin' when I get back? Would you want to?"

"A course. But you don't need to do all that. It's nice just to talk. It's awful quiet out on the ranch."

He walked her downstairs, and they took the elevator back down to the lobby, and she hustled off to the waiting room. He called and got Sylvia's number from Lydia and walked out to his truck to head toward Fort Worth. Once inside, he changed his mind. It was a piece of junk. The hell with Ford Compton.

CHAPTER 32

"And so the syndicate is prepared to waive the default and extend the forbearance related to the covenant breach for a period of six months. Mr. Clement, I know you probably regard this issue as a formality, given that everything else is in excellent order. We know we're well-collateralized on this deal. But we do have regulators, and they do have a say. I regret to say that the issue of your succession plan is material because the Grupo Elsinore facility is material to each of the members. I know it's a sensitive matter, but when we meet next time, we'll be prepared to terminate the facility if you're unable to reach resolution on the matter."

Fowler remained expressionless, and after a few moments, the banker began gathering his reports and straightening his tie, hoping that one of the other consortium members would jump in with some support.

"You've expressed your position. Can we move on?"

"I think that's about it. Again, Mr. Clement, Miss Ramos, we wish to express our appreciation for your continued business, and we look forward to our meeting in August."

The three men and their lawyer hastily gathered up their things and left. Louisa's attorney from Mexico City walked them out of the conference room and closed the double doors behind him.

"You look tired, Fowler."

"I am tired. It makes me tired listening to a weasel like that. You think they'll pull out?"

"Why don't we leave it for the moment and go up to our rooms and rest for a little bit. We can eat dinner here at the hotel tonight and talk about it."

He lifted his hat off the chair next to him. "You handled yourself well today, Louisa. David, would've enjoyed watching."

"Maybe he was."

"May be."

They took the elevator up and went to their separate rooms. Fowler had been impressed with Louisa and relieved that she was so clearly ready to run things. He walked into the room and stretched out on the bed and closed his eyes and began to remember distant deals and meetings and fights, with David always in the game, always a force.

Grupo Elsinore had been David's idea. He had always thought of it as a joke, that he and Fowler were the masters of the castle, and would pronounce it *Elsinor 'aye*, so that it would sound like a Spanish word, just to mess with people. Fowler had often reminded him, "You do know, everybody died. It was a tragedy."

The partnership itself had been Fowler's idea. It had been clear by the time he graduated that the remaining royalties from the Monahans property would be throwing off significant cash. Bill Reynold's purchase of the river ranch had taken most of the cash from the sale of the minerals, but even with the collapse of the oil prices, he was accumulating a substantial sum. He had proposed that he and David form a partnership and begin investing their wealth together. What followed had been months of late-night talks in the bar of the Taft Hotel in New Haven.

David's family wealth had been centered in Madrid, an empire begun by his great-grandfather in the shipping business. His grandfather had purchased the land in Mexico and had somehow held onto it through each of the revolutions that had come and gone, and it had passed down to David as the sole heir. David would receive the proceeds of his trust upon graduation, which included the direct distributions from the shipping conglomerate.

And so he had proposed Grupo Elsinore as the name of the corporation, and it had been organized in Bermuda with the help of David's family attorneys. In the forty years they spent together, the two had never removed money from the partnership, each year agreeing to plow the returns back into the company to be invested almost exclusively in commercial real estate at first, then later diversifying into timber and mining assets. The Depression had challenged them at first, but they had begun purchasing carefully and steadily at rock-bottom prices with the sole criteria that the revenues would cover operating costs. After the war, they had begun the same process in Europe. By the mid-fifties, the value of Grupo Elsinore had exploded, dwarfing the wealth either had outside the partnership, and to both of them; the great satisfaction was that their participation was largely anonymous.

Louisa was nothing like David. Serious. Direct. He wondered whether the partnership, being Patrón over the house and the ranch and the estate, would burden her life beyond the hope of simple happiness. She had obviously done her homework and had ripped into the investment manager when he had delivered a property manager's report on investments in the UK.

"Dismiss him."

"Ma'am? It's a simple typo on the report. I'm sure he can iron it out."

"I know it's a typo. I backed into the number myself. Had the typo not been there, the correct number would have still been unacceptable."

"Yes, but the environment there has been extremely challenging with all the developments in tenant rights, and the courts getting bogged down, among other things. I think the results are understandable."

"How do you know about those issues?"

"I'm just familiar with the market, and I stay in touch with each of the managers. I've been there myself."

"Precisely."

"Ma'am?"

"You did not mention that you read about them in the report. You didn't mention it because there is nothing in the report about any of that. It's not in the report because the report is sloppy and incomplete, up to, and including, the typo that would have been fixed if the man had simply taken the time to read it before sending it in. You don't dismiss a secretary for a typing mistake. You dismiss the author of the report who doesn't take the time to so much as read it before submitting it."

"Yes, ma'am. It shall be done."

Fowler had enjoyed the display, although it bothered him that his own lack of interest might be obvious and hypocritical. He hadn't even glanced at the numbers. But he was happy to let Louisa take the reins.

He worried for her. How would a girl like that marry? What kind of man could bind himself with a woman worth a hundred million dollars, one who would be Patrón, husband or not. How could she trust anyone that way?

*****

He opened his eyes, waking to the sound of downtown traffic far below. He had been in the Adolphus many times over the years. It was Let's favorite place, and she had loved to stay in the fancy old hotel and go next door to Niemans shopping. He swung his feet off the bed and gritted his teeth. He was determined not to fall into the moribund gloom that had dogged him ever since she had passed. He thought of the boy again. He always thought of the boy. Was he still alive? How bad had the injury been? He stomped his foot on the floor and stood, stretching against the pain running down his leg. He splashed some water on his face in the lavatory and headed down to the lobby to wait on Louisa.

Instead, she was waiting on him, dressed in an elegant black dress. There had been a time when he might have worried whether it appeared improper for him to dine alone with a beautiful young lady. Now it was as though they were all alone, walking through the grand lobby toward the restaurant, the anonymity of their partnership, a shield against the world.

She ordered a gin and tonic. He only wanted ice water. When the drinks came, she leaned forward.

"I wanted to think a little bit before I answered you."

"About the bank?"

"About the bank."

He frowned. He didn't want to rehash the business of the day.

"It's important we get this out of the way."

"Okay."

"Grandfather was very emphatic that this time would come. He lectured me for hours about it. Over and over." She smiled.

"About what?"

"He said, people would make assumptions about my motivations. Because they expect everyone to have the same motivations they do. That the professors at Stanford, and the lawyers in Madrid and New York would have the same ones, and therefore the same assumptions about me. And it would be important for me to be educated about the way they viewed the world because it would inform me about the way they would view me. But he told me to always remember that they know nothing about me, or you, or our partnership. Only you and me know that. They think our motivation is profit, and maybe risk, how much our piece is worth, and maybe tomorrow or some other day it might be that, but the important thing is this. Our motivations are whatever me and you decide they are at any given moment, and nobody else is privileged to know what that is, ever. Only you and me decide."

"David. I can hear him saying that. Damn the world!"

"Exactly. Damn the world!"

"But I'm not following you. How does that relate to the forbearance?"

"Damn them. We never, ever, let them decide what our motivations are. If you have a problem deciding this thing with your grandson? That is our problem together. You, we, will answer that in the time of our choosing, not theirs. If that is never, then so be it. But they will not choose or force you to choose. If we have to sell a third of the portfolio to repay the debt, and we lose a lot of money in the process, and you, we, would rather do that than make a hasty decision about something much more important, then we do that. We do what we choose. To hell with them."

Fowler simply stared in admiration. It was like he could see David's spirit flickering in her eyes, as though they were back in the Taft Hotel bar at two in the morning plotting strategy. His emotions welled up in him, and he wondered how he had been so fortunate to find such a partner.

"Thank you, Louisa. It takes a burden away."

"He said when the time came, if I said that, I would feel good. I do."

"Me too."

"To be of one mind with another is a precious gift, he would say. He was talking about my grandmother, of course. But sometimes when he said it, he was talking about you. He loved you very much."

"Maybe the one thing I ever got right."

"He weighs on your mind. Your grandson?"

"I don't even know where he is. Somewhere in Vietnam."

"And you think that's your fault?"

"In this case. I'm almost certain it is."

"What can I do?"

"I don't know. I'm afraid to do much of anything anymore. Pray, I suppose."

CHAPTER 33

Wmearle didn't have the control Lydia had shown. Trace was embarrassed to see him quivering his lips and choking on his own breath. He leaned down over the chair and hugged him and caught his hat falling off the back side.

"Come on around back. I'll show you the fishin' hole."

Wmearle had somehow fashioned a platform elevator out of a boat hoist. He wheeled out onto the deck and grabbed the electrical control cable and pushed the button. The deck dropped down about six feet to the level of a floating dock sitting out over the water.

"You build this?"

"Had it built. I ain't good for nuthin' no more."

"Snazzy."

"Pull ya up a chair. Lemme look at ya."

Wmearle lifted the lid on an old water-cooled Coke box and handed Trace a Dr Pepper.

"You gonna act like Lydia didn't fill me in on your troubles?"

"I figured you had plenty on your plate. It ain't like there's anything can be done. 'Sides, Sylvia already hovers over me enough for everbody."

"Lemme se 'em."

Wmearle scooted his feet out of the slippers. The toes were black. The feet were a dark bluish color up above his ankles.

"Damn. When's the last time you been in to see the doctor?"

"This mornin'. He gimme the choice. Whittle away or do the deed all at onest. I opted for the whole shebang. They'll take 'em off at the knees next Monday."

Trace was stunned. He had seen a lot of things, but this was Wmearle.

"Don't get all sideways. I been knowin' this was comin' for a year now. Honestly, I'll be glad to get it over with. It ain't like I'm usin' 'em anyhow."

"Does it hurt?"

"Pretty much constant."

"I wish I'd a known."

"A lotta that goin' around."

"You know how it is. Comes a point you can't describe what's goin' on, even if you wanted to, and I didn't feel much like wont'n to anyhow."

"So I knew about this." He made a slash across his face. "What else didn't you write about?"

"Nothin' that matters. I'm fine. Mostly."

"Mostly."

"All right, but you'll laugh. I got a strange affliction. When I got hurt, the doctor told me I prob'ly wouldn't ever be able to smell anything anymore on account a the shrapnel mighta cut through a nerve ganglion behind my nose. One night, I was sittin' out in the bush on watch, and all of a sudden, it was like somebody was baking bread, smellin' it like I just walked into the kitchen. I tried to ask the fella in the hole with me if he smelled it, but he shushed me. We had to be real quiet. Didn't go away, just goin' around smellin' bread bakin' everywhere for a week or two, right out in the bush. Nobody else could smell it. One mornin' I woke up, and the bread bakin' smell was gone. Ever'thing smelled like butane, like when the gas is leakin'. Stayed that way for a week. I could smell, but I only had one smell at a time, and everthing smelled like that one smell. Time went by, and I rotated through lots a different smells, like food and BO and everthing else. Some of 'em good and some of 'em horrible, but only one at a time. You could let a skunk spray on my face, and it'd be just as likely to smell like after shave lotion. Ever'body thought I was crazy."

"Is it still that way?"

"Pretty much, sometimes a thing will smell like it's supposed to."

"What are ya smellin' right now?"

"Horseshit, wall-to-wall." Wmearle belly laughed at that one. "Seriously?"

"No, not really. I cain't smell much of anything right this minute, but when I do, I smell kitchen grease all the time. It ain't real pleasant. There was one time where all I actually could smell was horseshit. Not a good week."

"Is it always gonna be that way?"

"I don't know. I asked the surgeon in Da Nang about it a couple a months ago. He said it was called dysosmia. He said the shrapnel prob'ly didn't get all the nerve, but just damaged it, so my brain is trying to sort through learnin' how to smell again. He said there might come a time it would sort of start gettin' back to normal, but it probably would always be out of kilter."

"At least it used to."

"Pardon?"

"Somethin' you said in your letter seemed odd. I remember it. You's talkin' about how it smelled, and you said, 'At least it used to'."

Traced had messed up. He hadn't written Wmearle about the bullet. But he hadn't seemed to notice him mentioning the second trip to the hospital.

"Strangest thing I ever heard of."

"You oughta be on this side of it. You visit the latrine, and it smells like a flower shop, and it might be vice versa."

"So you seen Lydia, she doin' all right?"

"Seemed same ole. Things looked different."

"Son of a bitch. She told me what he done. Wadn't nothin' I could do. Took his word on it. He won't be around long, though. People like that get a reputation."

"No harm. I'll find a spot."

"Drive me into town. Let's go eat a bite."

Wmearle grabbed the control wire and hit the hoist. Soon they were on their way into town.

"I'm surprised this thing is still runnin'. You've about run the wheels off it."

"'Bout decided to spring for a new one. I did some shoppin' in Abilene. But I'm gonna keep thisun. I just gotta find a place to park it first."

Wmearle was quiet. Trace could tell he was thinking something. Over dinner, Wmearle told stories about work from the days when he first took over the shop. He had never talked about it when they lived together in the trailer. Trace figured he was missing it.

"You goin' to church with Sylvia?"

"Yeah, it's okay. They got a young kid for a preacher. Scared of his own shadow. But he's okay. People are fine. I still cain't remember ever'body's name, though."

Afterward, they returned to the dock. It had warmed up for a bit during the day, but with the setting sun, it soon became too cold for Wmearle, and they went back inside the little house.

"Plop down on the couch there. I'll make us a pot."

Trace tossed his hat on the couch and looked around the room at the meager possessions. A few photographs were placed around the room of Wmearle and Jeannie and Sylvia when she was little. Trace had seen them all before. Wmearle had not kept much from their home, saying that everything in there reminded him of Jeannie. He didn't like the idea of Wmearle alone. He remembered the smell of the trailer. Now, all he could smell was kitchen grease.

After a while, Wmearle wheeled himself out of the kitchen with the coffeepot in one hand and two coffee cups in his lap.

"You're gettin' handy with the chair."

"No other option."

"How do you occupy yourself?"

"I sit around and stare out across the river mostly." He smiled. "This ain't workin'. Sylvia thought it would, but I cain't do this. I been talkin' to a man in town runs a big gunsmithing business. I think I'm gonna throw in with him and maybe build me a workshop. Gimme somethin' to do, fabricatin' parts and whatnot."

"I'm sorry. I know it's rough."

"Them's the breaks. It ain't all bad. The kids come over and we fish. Sylvia's over here ever day with them, so I have fun with that. Can I ask ya something?"

"Course."

"How come you up and enlisted? Without even talkin' to me about it? I thought back then, it was 'cause Mike gettin' killed rattled ya, but now I ain't so sure."

"No. It wadn't that." He leaned back on the sofa and stretched his legs out across the rug. The new clothes hadn't been washed yet, and the new boots were hurting his feet. Nothing felt comfortable.

"I's stupid is why. It's hard to explain. It seemed like it wadn't my life. I's runnin' around doin' ever'thing, cowboyin' and wheelin' and dealin' and actin' like I was runnin' my own show, but ever'where I turned around, it seemed like I was gettin' pointed in some direction, and I's just floatin' along with it."

"It seemed to me like you *was* runnin' your own show."

"It was a lotta things. Things people said. Miss Bledsoe outta all the colleges in the world just happened to fix me up with the one Fowler and his daddy went to. Ford Compton makin' me a loan on them cattle like he was so impressed with me. Even Mike seemed to think what I was gonna do was already a done deal. I just needed to break it all up."

"You think it was all a big conspiracy? You think I was in on it?"

"Like I said. I's stupid. Maybe a little bit."

"So your idea to fix all that was to jump right in the middle of a war?"

"It wadn't like that exactly. Somethin' Miss Bledsoe said when she was talkin' me into Yale stuck in my craw. About all them others that'd be goin' over there that didn't have a choice. That I had some kind of obligation since I had these amazin' gifts. It seemed like ever'thing was just unfoldin' according to some plan I didn't make, and it didn't seem right."

"I always thought you'd a come and told me about all that."

"I shoulda. I know."

"Bad, wadn't it?"

"You know how it was. You done it."

"Yeah."

"You's right about one thing. About the man next to ya. I never did forget that. Got real quick to where that was the only thing. That, and one other."

"What's that?"

"I think I'm in love."

Wmearle's eyes bugged out. Then he started to laugh, and before long, he laughed so hard he farted, and then the two of them were laughing hysterically. Finally, Wmearle got control over himself.

"This ain't somebody over there?"

"Nope."

"Well?"

"This I ain't sayin' no more about."

"Well, all righty. I reckon."

CHAPTER 34

He slept on the couch, and he did not wake in the night. He heard Wmearle wheel himself into the kitchen and knew it was five o'clock. He listened to the coffee percolating and heard every now and then the soft sound of the pages turning. When he smelled the bacon frying, he got up and pulled on the boots and poured himself some coffee.

"Now where you at?"

"Book a Mark."

"I lost that Bible you give me. It was in my pants when they stripped everthing off of me before I got evacked."

"Why'd they strip you down?"

"I didn't get it at the time. It was for my clothes. I had brand-new fatigues. They wear out pretty quick in the rain and whatnot, so they took 'em for somebody else, even if they did have some holes in 'em. When they put me in that chopper, I was pretty much buck naked except for my boots and a flak jacket and a helmet. Tell me what you're studyin'."

"Ponderin' is more like it. 'And he said, Abba, Father, all things are possible unto thee; take away this cup from me: nevertheless not what I will, but what thou wilt.'"

"He knew they were comin'."

"I cain't get it clear. He was of two minds. Prayed for two things that were opposite. He did'n wanna die, so he prayed that. Then in the next breath, he prays for what God wills, even though he knew what God was willing to happen, so it was the opposite. How do ya do that?"

"I'll tell ya this, there were a lotta times I left the second part off."

"I expect so. But see what I mean? He had a conflict in his mind. He mighta been the only one that could ever really say that prayer and mean it, I mean both, at the same time."

"How so?"

"Because he was both man and God at the same time. He was both weak and strong at the same time. Weak enough to not want to suffer and strong enough to submit to what was required. I don't know if people can ever really be like that."

He got up and took the biscuits out of the oven and set the plates out. It was over a year and a half since he had eaten a real biscuit, and sitting in the warm kitchen with it dark outside and smearing the cane syrup on it caught him by surprise. His mind had gone back in time to all those mornings in the trailer, and it was as though the year and a half had not happened, and they were not in the little lake house, but in the trailer, and he imagined hearing the sound of Lydia sweeping the pavement outside, and the loss of it all, the loss of his ignorance, and his smell and Mike and the boys, and it fell down over him like a shadow.

Wmearle sopped his biscuit in the syrup and watched the sadness in Trace's face.

"What's next for you?"

"I don't know. I figure I'll hang out here with you until you get your operation done."

"No."

"Whattaya mean no?"

"I mean no. I gotta go through this myself. I'm gonna be in the hospital for a while. Sylvia's all geared up to look after me. There ain't all that much to it, anyhow, just be layin' there till I get healed up enough to come back here."

"Still, I wanna be there."

Wmearle swallowed the last of the biscuit and brushed his hands on his pajamas.

"Here's what I wont. I wont you to get on with it."

"Get on with what?"

"Get on with livin'!" Wmearle was suddenly passionate. "I mean you gotta square up and deal with it!"

"Deal with what?"

"You know damned well what!"

Trace shook his head and looked at his plate. "I ain't even sure what *it* is."

"Son, it's *who* you are. Who are you gonna be." He leaned back in the wheelchair and winced.

"Listen to me. I's lazy and scared and did'n know how to talk to you about everthing. I knew that when you split. That hit me pretty hard. I asked you if you thought I's in on the big conspiracy, and you said maybe a little bit. I knew right when you said that, that you couldn't even trust me. I laid there in bed last night, and I just kept gettin' madder and madder. At you, at me, at him, hell, mad at everbody. 'Cause you was right, and it wadn't just a little bit. I thought just 'cause I took you in and loved you, and you loved me, and we was fast friends and all that, that it was good enough. That I done right by ya. But I's wrong. And you got ever reason in the world to not trust a solitary soul in this world. It is facin' up to all that. Put it to bed and move on and go love on that girl and be whoever you're gonna be, but put all this corruption behind you."

"I don't think I know how."

"Lemme ask you somethin'. Are you angry? Are you mad?"

Trace remembered the night he got hit. The rage that had come over him, directed at everything and nothing, with no source or origin, but drawing it out of himself still, until the gun had gone silent. And the rage and the pain and the maelstrom of light flashing in his head had been like a relief. He had thought later in the hospital that if he could have killed every person on the planet at that moment, he would have.

"I don't know. Maybe so."

"I never thought it. You never once acted like it. But I think you are, and I think you got ever reason to be. At everbody. Includin' me."

"I ain't angry at you, Wmearle."

"Maybe you oughta be."

"Well, I ain't."

"You up and went to Vietnam rather'n sit down and talk to me about what was eatin' you."

"I told you. I's stupid."

"Stupid's got nothin' to do with it. You didn't come talk to me 'cause you couldn't trust me not to go trottin' out to see Fowler Clement and chain you down or something. And you's right 'cause we likely woulda done it."

"I ain't blamin' you for nothing, Wmearle. You been nothin' but good to me."

"You ain't listenin'. Listen to me now. Good wadn't good enough. I went along with it. Ever bit of it. It was wrong."

"It wadn't you. It was him. It was them. You cain't take that on yourself."

"What did he do?"

"Everthing."

"Say it out loud. What did he do?"

"I'll tell ya what he did. His own grankids, sittin' right there where their daddy just got killed, and he walked right by. He looked right at me square in the face, dammit, and kept on walkin', that's what he did."

"Then that's what you gotta go deal with. You gotta go ask him why he did that. If a human bein' has a right to anything in this world, it's that he's got a right to be loved when he's a child. You had ever right to demand that, from all of us, and we let you down. Even me."

"But it's done. It cain't be undone."

"That ain't the way it works son."

"How? I don't see it. How you gonna go back and redo it?"

"That ain't what I mean. You oughta know that by now. Everthing that ever happened to all of us is part of us. Ever horrible thing I ever said to Jeannie, ever one of those German bastards I killed, ever time I talked to Fowler about how you were doin' in school, and what the doctor said about you when I took you in, and never once did I stand up on my hind legs and tell him it was all wrong. But here I am. I ain't dead. The man sittin' across the table from you ain't perfect. I'm sorry,

I didn't have the guts to do what'as right. You ain't perfect. He ain't either, but we ain't any of us dead yet."

"But I cain't change him."

"How do you know? How do you even know what he thinks about anything? You think he hadn't had it bad?"

"I know. Georgette told me some of it. But that's a different thing."

"Son, you can be hard. There ain't no different thing in the soul of a man. We're all of us just one thing, and everthing bleeds into everthing else. You cain't take a man and divide him in two and put the good part over here and the bad part over there. All of this is part of you, and it always will be. Nothin's ever gonna bring your momma or your daddy back and make everthing happy and nice, and nothin's ever gonna change what Fowler and Leticia Clement did."

"Then what's the point of any of it?"

"It's what's out in front of you. You can spend the rest a your life draggin' that sack a rocks around, and it won't get any better. Or you can live, you can hope, you can change what happens even if you cain't change what did happen. So fix it. And if you try, and you cain't fix it, then leave it behind forever and live!"

The light was beginning to come, and he could tell it would be a gray, cold winter day. He got up and threw the dregs of his coffee in the sink and turned and leaned against the counter, not knowing what to do next.

Wmearle wheeled around to face him. "You know better'n to think I don't wont you around, don't you?"

CHAPTER 35

Trace stopped in the gravel drive in front of Shorty's house. The gray winter clouds had moved out, and a warm south wind had come up, and now the sun was drifting down toward the horizon. He had passed on going to church with Wmearle. He had no place to go, and no one to go home to. Still, his pickup had pointed back in the same old direction.

Shorty was sitting in a rocking chair on the front porch in his underwear smoking a fat cigar. His face and forearms were dark brown, as were his legs from the thigh down. The rest was a pasty white.

"The prodigal!"

"Make yourself comfortable, Shorty."

A half-empty bottle of tequila sat on an upside-down paint bucket. Shorty hopped up and went inside, returning with a coffee cup.

"Pull up a chair and have a sip. Want a cigar?"

"No thanks. Where's your partner?"

"Herbert? Herbert's gone."

"Where to?"

Shorty poured some tequila in the coffee cup and extended it, then sat back and puffed on his cigar.

"So you been in it, looks like."

Trace sipped from the cup. The tequila had a chemical taste he couldn't place. He figured his nose was lying to him again, but it wasn't so disagreeable that he would risk offending Shorty.

"So I wonta know something. Was it you and Herbert got me out of that jam with the biker gang?"

"It was."

"Mike guessed at it. I don't remember much."

"Sorry we dumped you out and run off. We had somewhere to be. Couldn't afford to get tangled up. Sad thing about him too, by the way."

"Where's Herbert?"

"Big Spring. Veteran's hospital."

"He get sick?"

"In a manner of speaking."

"What's that mean?"

"We had a problem in Cienfuegos. Herbert had a girl." Shorty stopped talking and drained the rest of his cup.

"Herbert had a girl problem?" Trace was smiling.

"It wasn't romantic. Wasn't like that. He was workin' her. Got attached. He knew better. I guess he just got tired of the game. Anyway. Cute young thing. She slipped up somehow. Got picked up by the DGI. Tortured her, put a bullet in her head, and dumped her in the road. Brutal sons a bitches."

"DGI?"

"*Direccion General de Inteligencia.* Secret police. Herbert, he just shorted out. He was gonna start a damned war."

Trace was astonished. Every time the jokes had come up about Shorty and Herbert being spies, he had laughed it off.

"What happened?"

"I popped him over the head with a fish club and got him on a boat. He ain't doin' right though. Like I said, he just shorted out on me."

"I am sorry to hear that."

"Now, as they say, I gotta kill you."

Shorty was looking at him without so much as a hint of expression. Trace smiled, but quickly felt a cold chill sweep over him. He met Shorty's eyes and stared right back at him, and after a few seconds, Shorty's face softened.

"That's the way of it, isn't it?"

"What?"

"The veneer of civilization is so very thin. One second you're human, and the next, it's mayhem, base atavistic mayhem. It alters a man. I can see it's altered you."

"Maybe. Sometimes, I feel like I'm the same."

"Two years ago, you'da wet your pants when I looked at you that way. Now I see you starin' back at me, and I can see you've seen some death, maybe a lot of it. Prob'ly over and over again and apparently not particularly scared of it anymore. You can't cover that up. Your eyes tell on you."

"It's different bein' back in the world. I can't figure it out. There's just too much goes through your mind to sort out."

"But it is just the one world. The one you were in over there is the same one you're in now. It's all just one place. Herbert spent a lifetime in and out of those same jackpots. Crawled in and out of the absolute sewage of the world over and over, and then, just like that, he couldn't reckon with it anymore."

"How did you and Herbert take out that whole bunch down on the river?"

"Oh, it wasn't as big a deal as you'd think. They were high as a kite. You take a blackjack and a little dark, and it...you know the biggest part of it is, you just wade right into it. You get the right attitude about you, you can walk right up to 'em, and before they know what's happening, the world goes dark on 'em. Prob'ly couldn't a done it if they hadn't all been wasted, but they were. We had that roll a wire in the pickup, and we worked pretty quick. You were the one we were worried about."

"I'm not rememberin'."

"I was standin' in the brush watchin' everthing. Herbert was ready to plug somebody if things had gone the other way. All of a sudden, you just jumped up and ran off like a rattlesnake bit you. When you hit that tree, it sounded like a major leaguer hittin' a baseball."

"I still got a kind of a knot there."

"You got a bit more than that looks like to me."

"Mortar round. First week in the bush."

271

Shorty crossed his legs, the white tops of his socks showing over the top of his boots. He flicked the ashes off the end of the cigar and poured more tequila in his glass.

"There'll be a choice. There'll be a time when you have to choose."

"Choose?"

"Whether to live in this world, the real one, or one you make up for yourself so you don't have to reckon with it."

"Make one up?"

"People do it all the time. Me and Herbert both missed it. We thought it was either this world or that one. Either you go home and play like the world ain't what it is and have your life and marry up and move on, or you get out there and mix it up with all the corruption and evil in the world. Most people pull the blanket up over their head and go about their lives. Me and Herbert went the other way. Turns out there's a big market for old farts who don't look like much who happen to know how to deal death."

"So you think it's either one or the other?"

"No, I'm sayin' that was a false choice. We both thought it was one or the other. I'm sittin' here lookin' at that empty house over yonder, and I got no regrets, but if you get confused and think you gotta choose between this world and that other world, you'll miss the point."

"Which is?"

"Like I said, it's just one world, and we're all in it. But that don't mean the choice is between stickin' your head in the sand or turnin' into a monster. The choice is between having your eyes open or closed. A man can live a life with his eyes open without becoming the thing he hates."

"It don't seem that clear to me. Seems like you gotta pick a side."

"A lot a people struggle over that. We did. A lot of 'em don't make it. They come home all right, but they don't ever come out of it. What's that feel like, where you got hit?"

"It's mostly healed up. It's been over a year now. My face don't work exactly right, like some of it feels dead. My smeller is fouled up. It ain't like it's botherin' me too much."

"Point is, it'll remind you. It'll always remind you that world is out there, the way it is."

The sun was setting, and the wind was dying. The mesquite pasture was bathed in the soft gold of the winter sunset, and he could hear quail calling in the dusk.

"I'm not sure I know what you mean, Shorty. I cain't hardly imagine how this place and the place I been can be in the same world."

"Grow up! You take some gook in the bush or one a those commie bastards in Cuba or the guy changing tires down at the fillin' station, they're all made outta the same lumber, and it's all crooked. What you gotta figure out is that all a that, and I mean all a the worst of it, is part a the same world where there's the best of it. It ain't the whole part of the world. You've seen the worst of what it can be, whether it's that mayhem that's right under the surface of all things, or the absolute horror of it like you seen over there. What you gotta know. What you gotta do, is to see the other side of it all, and see'n it all, you gotta know that the good of it prevails."

"How do you know it does?"

"How do I know it, or how do I prove it?" Trace just looked at him.

"All those times we's out fartin' around, build'n fence or whatever, carryin' on, you were with us sometimes. Thing is, we both knew that was not for long, that we were gonna be back at work somewhere, in that other world, soon enough. We both lost our families. There wadn't nothin' left for either of us, except each other. Just plain old friendship. But that was enough, ya see. You wouldn't think it would be enough, but it was. The good prevails. It just does. You gotta find a way to see it. Everthing else is the abyss."

"You ain't got any place to go to, do you?"

"Not especially."

"Sack out over at Herbert's. He ain't comin' back."

CHAPTER 36

Fowler was awake before he opened his eyes. His first thought was that it was late, and he needed to check on Let. It would be almost two years now; yet, each morning, his heart would race for those few moments before he remembered, and in that brief moment sitting before the fire with his eyes closed and the blanket draped across his legs, there was hope, for her, for him, for it all. Then he opened his eyes.

A fresh chunk of wood was sitting on the coals, just now beginning to flame. Georgette would have quietly passed, as she did every morning and worried that the room had grown too cold. He could hear her in the back kitchen now, and the voices. The men were coming in. His steel gray eyes watched the flames lapping up across the log, and the hope began to recede from his mind as though it belonged to a different time in a different place, and now it was leaving, almost with apology.

He rose and advanced up the stairs to their rooms. He would not sleep there. Each morning, he passed the immense oaken bed to perform his ablutions, its undisturbed quilting having established itself as a monument to all he had lost. He began to think about the men. The idea had been growing in his mind. What if he didn't come back? What if he wouldn't? What would happen to them? To the land?

When he eased himself down from the bottom step of the staircase and stretched his legs to lean into the pain, he noticed that it had grown quiet in the kitchen. By now, the men should be eating and talking among themselves. He looked at the clock on the buffet across the dining room, again, suddenly feeling the sense of being late. Perhaps they had already eaten and left to begin their work. But the clock said six o'clock. He passed the long formal dining table and walked into the back of the house where the kitchen stood between it and another long table, the one for the men, topped with stainless steel and lined with benches on each side. The table was mostly empty, though the food was laid out on the kitchen counter. Georgette and a game warden sat at the far end of the table drinking coffee and chatting. The Clement cookroom was known to be open to anyone who happened to be nearby.

When Fowler entered into the room, both looked up and ceased their talking. When he raised his eyebrow in a question, both simply moved their eyes toward the back door. He opened the door and stepped out on the porch. The men were gathered in a circle in the darkness, only the dim light from the kitchen spilling out across them, and again the talk ceased, and he saw the hats turn toward him, still standing in silhouette in the doorway.

Trace stood at the back of the circle where he had been talking to Blas and Tito and Nicholas. Then Trace saw him, standing now, backlit in the doorway, the same old sweat-stained Stetson sitting low across his eyes, the same erect attitude and bearing. The now-familiar rage began to rise in him, not with any hate, but dread and frustration, as though he was once again huddled in the old pickup truck next to Mike and the two little ones, watching him there, hard and implacable, and once again ready to see him, and simply pass by.

He could not see his face. The silent clouds of smoke from the men breathing into the frosty winter cold hanging suspended in the light between them. Then Fowler moved, moved with determination down the steps and through the circle of men and embraced him, trembling in his arms in that fear and rage and frustration. The men watched in silence, and still Fowler held him. Then he was released, and Fowler stepped back, still in silhouette from the kitchen lights, and Trace could see only the slightest glint of light in his eyes.

"Go in. Eat. Warm up. I'll be back in a half hour." He stepped around him to the side, then stopped, and laid a hand on his shoulder.

"A half hour. No more. Then I'll be back here."

He disappeared into the darkness, away from the men and the house and out into the flat pasture of the river bottom, walking at first, then moving fast, stumbling through the prickly pear and mesquite in the darkness. Upward, into the bluffs that lined the river valley, slipping in the loose gravel and clawing his way up and onto the ledge rock at the top where below him, and now half a mile away, the light still spilled out of the house, and the smoke curling upward from the chimneys, and the first hint of dawn stretching across the eastern horizon, and he fell to his knees and wept, his voice heaving in great gasping spasms, and he fell forward onto his elbows, his head now resting on the rough limestone ledge rock, and he began praying.

*****

The men ate quickly then began drifting out of the kitchen, each knowing there would be no talk of work on the ranch this day. Nicholas had held his chin up to the light, much like Georgette had, looking at the deep scars across his cheeks.

"*Es todo cuesta abajo desde aqui.*"

"How do you figure?"

"What's going to happen? Somebody gonna shave your head and send you to Vietnam?"

They talked for a bit and compared where they'd been and what they'd done. Then Nicholas grabbed his hat and walked out with the game warden. They'd found a couple of gut piles out on the ranch where someone had been poaching deer. Georgette was cleaning the table and banging around in the kitchen.

"Want a refill?"

"Please."

She poured him a cup and sat down across the table.

"What's goin' on?"

"I'm not sure I know."

"So why did you come out here?"

"I promised Wmearle I would."

"I suppose you think that's an answer."

"Well, other'n that, I don't know."

"I'ma let you think about it."

She hopped up and left him alone with the fire crackling in the great stone fireplace at the end of the room. His mind was swirling. The moment when Fowler had wrapped his arms around him had confused everything he thought he knew in the world, and for a moment, he had even clinched his fist as though to defend himself. There, with Fowler's arms around him, his mind had replayed that first firefight after he had been hit, the light flashing inside his swollen head, and then there had been the sound of the crickets in the cottonfield as he sat between the desolate rows with the little ones, and finally the last set of headlights appearing up on the road and him knowing whose they'd be. He thought about Herbert, finally lost to some miserable distillation of the insanity of the world. He had stayed only a brief time in his house. Herbert's rooms were sterile. Bereft of any trace of identity. There were no pictures in the house. No mementos of experience or family or tradition. No indication whatsoever of the life of its inhabitant, as though whatever there was of meaning or fidelity or experience existed only in his person, and that, too, now was lost. He couldn't stay there.

So he had driven away, back toward town, not knowing where he would sleep. When he had neared the river bridge, he saw them. A brief flicker of headlights casting out into the darkness from the bluff. It was that time; and in that brief moment, he had hoped that he would find them there, continuing, meeting still and carrying it on.

When he topped out on the gravel hilltop and pulled the pickup into the circle of vehicles, he had been hopeful. What he found had been a half-dozen high school boys smoking dope. They had recognized him and soon began prodding him for stories about Vietnam. How many had he killed? Had he been wounded? He quickly turned around to get back in the pickup to leave.

"Hey, why're you runnin' off?"

"You boys need to find a new place to party."

"Why?"

"Because I said so." He glared at them in the moonlight, and they made no argument.

He heard the door open, and Fowler stepped into the kitchen. He removed his hat and laid it on the steel tabletop and sat down, wincing from the pain. Trace had not seen him up close for many years, and now, across the table, he seemed reduced. His gray hair was thinning, and despite the handsome structure of his face, the sadness of it was overwhelming. He was confused. In the moments before Fowler spoke, he frantically tried to grasp what it was that had propelled him to be in this spot.

"I gave up hope I'd ever see you again."

Trace couldn't speak. He felt as though he were paralyzed, frozen in place. Fowler diverted his eyes to the fire, and they sat in silence, both struggling to gain a foothold. After a while, Trace blurted out.

"I never held it against you. Not really. I always knew it was her." Fowler's eyes darted back at him.

"You're wrong about that. It was me. It wasn't her, or you, or your daddy or your momma. It was just me."

"Why then?"

Fowler seemed to settle into himself, his hands clasped in front; he lowered his head, the shame weighing down on him.

"Somewhere along the line, I must have been just a teenager, I got it in my head I could fix a thing. It was in the oil fields. I was out there trying to get a start, and it seemed like whatever needed fixing, I had this thought I could do it. And I did. Whatever I did seemed like it worked out. One thing led to another, and every time, I always seemed to come out ahead. I was a damned fool. When the time came…I guess everybody has those times, I thought I could fix it. I thought I could put it all back together. I remember how certain I felt. All I needed was some time, and we could make it right. Such a fool.

It wasn't her. I don't want you to ever think that. A person can't help being broken. She wouldn't have been able to look at you without seeing him, at least not at first. So all I thought we needed was some time. I just needed enough time to keep everything from blowing apart. But there was not one minute that I didn't think I could fix it all. Now I can't imagine how I could have ever thought that. How can you do everything, every little decision, thinking you're right, and wake up one day and find out what it all added up to was monstrous?"

"But you left us. You walked right by and looked at us and just kept walkin'. How could you do that?"

"That's what I mean. I never gave it two thoughts. I never gave it two thoughts because I didn't think that's what I was doing. I thought I was fixing it...from that first minute when I saw your father dead, I thought I was fixing it, as though that, of all things, was something that *could be* fixed instead of...just mourned. Where the absolute arrogance of such a thought came from, I just don't know. What's worse is, I never had the slightest inkling of it until Let had the stroke, because she was part of it, just like you were, and the little ones. Until that very moment, I still thought I could see it through, see it fixed. I saw it plain enough, though, when Wmearle told me you enlisted."

"What makes you think that was about any a this?"

"Doesn't matter. It was how I knew time ran out. It's how I saw it, finally, the utter folly of it all."

"Well, it wadn't all about you."

Fowler was looking up now. He was looking at the scars, thinking of David and the many fights they'd had about this very moment, his eyes intense now, almost desperate with sadness.

"I need to know."

"Know what?"

"I need to know if you can ever forgive me. I need to know if you could ever believe I love you. That I always did."

CHAPTER 37

Fall, 1875

Quanah sat on a rock on the eastern flank of the Double Mountain. Five of the seven had made it in during the night. Two more were still out. They had time. A long dark roll cloud stretching across the sky had passed overhead, moving southeast, and the first rays of the rising sun illuminated its belly in pink and crimson. Underneath it, far to the south, the smoke from the fires they had set was being turned back on itself. The whole of the southern horizon was alive with light from the billowing prairie fire and its wall of white smoke and the refraction of the dawn. They wouldn't be coming. Not this far, just for horses. They had taken no people in the raid. In any case, they were too far ahead, and the fire would slow them up. They had time.

He could see the horses hobbled in the bottom of a grassy flat in a draw at the base of the mountain. They had started with eight, stolen forty, and three had died on the ride north. They would finish eating another before leaving for the Yellow House. Nobody had been killed, but they had not killed anyone either. So the others would be grumpy.

The roll cloud had brought a cool north wind down off the caprock, and the others were sleeping now, having been horseback for most of four days since the raid. In the night, they had eaten and then laid down in their tracks to sleep. He had moved up near the top of the mountain to sit and think. In the darkness, he could see parts of the line of fire they had set. What focused his attention, though, were the fires dotting the prairie to the east. Buffalo hunters. Descending on the plains in the thousands, the extermination was well underway and would soon be over. They had killed many, and he himself had almost been killed by them, and of all the whites, for those he felt true contempt.

They had watched a small settlement near San Antonio from hiding places in the hills for a couple of days before descending late in the night to take the horses. There had been a half-moon, and they had seen no lanterns lit as they had slipped away. They had split up at the Pashahono and set the grass ablaze to cover their trail. Quanah rose and walked down into the small gully where the fire was smoldering. He took a small leather pouch from the thong on his horse and approached the slaughtered horse lying beside the fire. He reached up into the open cavity where the liver and guts had been taken and grabbed a large handful of the kidney fat near the horse's spine and threw it on the coals, then took his knife and sliced off a piece of horsehide. The fat began to spit and bubble in the fire. He kneeled and pulled his leather pants down and held the tip of his knife in a small flame for a few moments. The mesquite thorn in his thigh was beginning to swell. He took the hot knife and parted the skin with its point to root out the thorn, then took the horsehide patch and used it as a glove to pick up the bubbling glob of fat. Holding the wound open with the tip of the knife, he squeezed the boiling fat out of the glob in his hand and let it run into the wound hole, curling his lip from the sting. He tossed the horsefat aside and opened the leather pouch and spilled its contents out on a flat rock. Coneflower and willow bark and sage and prickly pear pulp and a tin full of grease he had taken from the surface of a pond in Oklahoma. He mashed them together into a pulp with the butt of his knife and smeared the poultice over the wound and wrapped it tight with a section of tanned deer hide.

The others would sleep for a while, so he pulled up his pants and walked down the hill and across the pasture to the horses. They were matted in dirt from having rolled around in it with the sweat lather covering their bodies. They were tired, near to the point of death. But he figured with a couple of hours of rest they'd be fine to make it to the Yellow House.

He held his hand out and brushed the seed heads of the grass swaying in the breeze. Fall was here, and it would be cold soon. His plan was to move the band up from the Yellow House onto the Llano and head west, in case McKenzie and his soldiers decided to come after them again. They would head west, then south, and winter in the southern canyons. The defeat at Palo Duro weighed on him. McKenzie had killed fifteen hundred Quahadi horses, and with them the lifeblood of the band. The waste of it. The cold determination of the man. Quanah had walked among the carcasses rotting in the grass at the top of the canyon, the smell of death heavy on the wind. He had been close enough to see him with his own eyes several times and had decided the man was inhabited by a demon. But he had outwitted him and wondered now if the rout at Palo Duro would quench the man's thirst.

The whites were a mystery. He could see their genius and, in some of them, the determination, even savagery. Their tools and clothing, how they built things and organized themselves. But they could also seem so stupid, so ignorant of the land, apparently unable to consider using it to their advantage rather than huddling inside their little houses like some prairie animal. They were so easy to kill and rob, but still they came. He thought about Medicine Lodge. The humiliation of watching Ten Bears submit to the soldiers. He had added to the humiliation by berating them for the capitulation, but his heart had not been in it. He knew then that they were inevitable.

The breeze whispered in the tall grass. The horses caked in sweat-mud stood watching him with their heads down, and above him, sandhills squawked in the sky. The band was tired. The chase McKenzie had given, up and down and over the caprock and out onto the Llano and back again, so many times. It had worn them down, and they looked to him now with doubt in their faces. The warriors seemed to want to die. They did not share his curiosity about the whites or his willingness to simply rob them rather than killing and taking scalps. But when they killed, the whites came harder and kept coming longer, and there was a cost to that. He remembered past raids, where they had killed, the warriors yelling and holding the scalps in the air. There was one, he always remembered it, where he had walked through the frame house with the sound of the killing coming in through the windows from outside. The things they had were strange and interesting. A piano, which he had never seen before, the sound it made when he touched it. The steel firebox and the images of people on paper hanging from the walls. He had wanted to stay and study those things, but someone had put fire to the house, and he'd left, watching the house and barns go up in flames behind him. The waste.

He didn't mourn the murdered or grieve about them. Since his earliest memory, the murder of the whites, and the murder of his people by the whites, had simply been a fact. So there was no revenge in his heart. The struggle for power over other people was simply a fact of existence. But these whites were not like the Apache or the Kiowa and the eternal conflict on the plains. They were coming.

He heard the riders in the distance to the south coming up from the river. He cocked his head to listen. It would be the other two coming in. He sprinted up the hill and met them at the mouth of the little gully where the others were rousing from their sleep. They had not been followed. There was no hurry. He squatted near the fire and told them it had been a good raid. That they had been smart and had outwitted the whites who were also smart. He knew they felt empty to have not taken scalps, so he insulted the whites and said they would be too lazy to come this far. So they had some time to eat and sleep. He mounted his horse and told them he would go on ahead to the Yellow House and tell the band of their success. That he should go ahead and prepare to celebrate them when they arrived.

In truth, he wanted to be alone. Sensing that of all the things he had considered, the one thing he hadn't considered was what it might be like to lose the ability to be alone, to point your horse into the wind with no boundary in the world. He had always had that, and having always had it, had never considered a world of limits.

He eased the horse over the flank of the mountain, taking care to appear to be in no hurry and headed west. His instinct was to fly, to feel the air in his hair, to command the horizon, to ride until the horse would die and then mount another and then another and cover the whole of the country because he could.

It would take him two days to cover the eighty miles. He didn't intend to push it now. The others would take their time as well. And so he would have time.

He dropped into a shallow draw and followed the sand bottom for a couple of miles, then mounted the cut bank and drifted into a vast grassy flat. He spooked a great bull bison out of its bed. It was alone in the flat, and when it jerked to its feet and stumbled on its front legs, he could see that it was gutshot. He wondered how much the bull had left in him and watched it closely without moving forward. It fell and thrashed in the grass, and once again stumbled up on its feet, its stomach contents spilling out of the wound in its flank. He watched it, dying, wasted for any purpose, slobbering in fury at nothing. It went down again, and he could hear it heaving in the deep grass. He moved on across the flat and up the steep bluffs to the north, and he could hear from time to time the bellowing of the bull in the flats behind him.

As he rode, he began to slowly gain elevation, and he could see to the east the land descending in a great basin. The sky was clearing behind the cloud front. To the west, he could now see the caprock shining in the distance, which to his instinct meant safety, for few would pursue a man into the Llano above. Twice, he heard the thundering booms of the .50 cal buffalo guns far to the east. He was thinking about the Wichita country. He had known it for most of his life. Now he considered it differently and wondered what it would seem like to have a boundary beyond which the land would be owned, circumscribed by the whites' ideas about property and dominion. His senses were acute, being instinctively directed toward threat and opportunity and food and escape. Now he felt his senses turn to the sounds and the smells and the crunch of the hooves in the tall grass. Was this passing away from his sight forever? Would it pass from the sight of his people forever?

And then he knew it. He knew that he would lead them down into the southern canyons to winter, and then he would prepare them for the last move, the one to Fort Sill. He pulled up on the pony and turned to look out upon the great theater of his life. The hunts, the moonlight raids, great feasts of celebration with the drums beating in the darkness through a summer night, then stretched backward and spread his arms in the glow of the clear morning sun and closed his eyes to listen to the wind in the grass.

CHAPTER 38

May 1976

Trace opened the door to the pickup and let William crawl up into the cab. William bounded over to the other side and opened the opposite door to let the dog in.

"I told you, he needs to ride in the back."

"What if he falls out?"

"Then he falls out. Won't happen but once. He's gettin' too big to ride up here. 'Sides, I expect he stinks."

He reached over and took the dog and tossed him into the bed and got back in the cab.

"Why's he stink so bad?"

"He rolled around in something dead."

"Why do they do that?"

"Don't know. It's just somethin' dogs like to do. You tired?"

"Nope."

"Well, you oughta be. You made a hand today. Hungry?" The boy smiled.

"Mama's prob'ly got it on the table. I'll drop you off. You get those chaps off and leave your boots on the screened-in porch before you go in, or she'll throw a fit."

"You're not hungry?"

"I'm hungry. I just gotta go to a meetin', then I'll be back home."

William was up in the seat next to him sitting on his knees. Trace would push in the clutch, and William would reach down and pull the stick shift into gear. The straw hat and chaps and spurs had become his standard outfit. Trace dropped down off the hill to the river cabin and eased up to the porch. He was dreading the meeting with Maria. When he came to a stop and opened the door, William climbed down behind him and waited for Trace to let the dog out the back.

"You get in there and wash up. The dog stays outside. Hear me?"

He was already gone. Trace got back in the truck and began backing out. He could see Georgette watching him through the kitchen window. She had little use for Maria and had come back to the cabin early rather than stay at the big house to wait on her. He drove slowly down the ranch road. He was in no hurry to get there. The ranch was a sea of grass. The cattle they had worked during the day were fat. The road passed away from the river, and up onto the high ground mesquite pastures, and as the sun set, the yellow light of dusk had begun its daily amplification of the colors of the landscape. He emerged from the mesquite to see the big house sitting in the little bend of the river below. Somehow, it had circumvented the fate he had observed in other houses where the occupant had passed. They seemed to wither instantly, having lost the motive force that compelled them to exist. The big house seemed still alive without them, without Fowler and Leticia. He thought to himself, maybe it knows. Maybe it's waiting on us. That would be for Georgette to decide. They were happy where they'd been the last seven years and were in no hurry to alter their course. He could see Maria's car parked outside, the driver in his black suit standing beside it.

When he walked into the dining room, Reynolds was there, smoking a cigar. Maria sat across from him sipping on a cup of tea. The judge was long retired now and had been helping Fowler before he had passed. He was frail, and no longer wore the bow tie that had been his signature for decades. The judge smiled when he came in, but Trace could tell there was tension radiating from the other side of the table.

"Maria, welcome. Judge, good to see you. You're looking well."

Judge Reynolds stood and shook his hand. "And here I was just telling Maria what an honest man you are."

"I'm gonna step in the kitchen and get me a sodi pop. You wont one, Judge?"

"I believe I will."

When he sat down, Maria hadn't moved or spoken. He had never grown to like her and had a pretty good idea that she didn't like him either. But Fowler had helped him with that. They had returned to the ranch one night after a meeting in Dallas. Maria had been her typical self. Imperious, arrogant, and dismissive, even toward Fowler. Fowler could tell Trace was angry on the ride home. When he stopped to drop him off at the cabin, he killed the engine.

"She sits at the end of centuries of tradition. Her position, her role, is not of her choosing. That's not to say she didn't agree to it. Nobody forced it on her, unless you want to call five centuries of tradition a kind of force. It was supposed to be her father's job, but he disavowed it, dishonored it. I remember how David told me. He didn't add on to it, or for that matter, even say it, but I got it. Esteban dishonored the family. I don't even know how, and it's not even important how, and Iladio just wasn't able, so it fell to Maria Louisa. And she acceded to it, probably even knowing what it meant. She will never marry. She'll never have her own family, not that she can't exactly. But she won't. She's carrying it, holding everything together until there'll be somebody to step up, one of Iladio's. She's carrying a kind of honor that doesn't leave much room for weakness or even failure. There's a trust that has existed between David and me and between Maria and me that is precious to all of us. She's looking across the table at you, or rather, not looking across the table at you, in this case. But she's sizing you up, and right now, she doesn't know."

"I'm not sure I'm gonna be able to make much of a dent in that armor of hers."

"This isn't a normal case. I'm not telling you to be sweet. She'll decide on her own what kind of character she's dealing with. I'm just telling you there's something there you should respect. The only compliment you can pay her, is to take that seriously."

*****

"Maria, I'm sorry to keep you waiting so long."

Maria sipped her tea and didn't respond. She had an air of serene contempt he had come to expect. Trace had often marveled at Maria's appearance. She seemed perfect, with not a stray hair out of place, a complexion that might have been chiseled out of Carrera marble. That mask of perfection was also devoid of any expression. For that, she let her words do the work, and they could be lethal.

"I didn't keep you waiting because I had cattle to work. I apologize, but I'm late because I felt like I hadn't made up my mind how I wanted to proceed, and I didn't want to come in here and confuse the situation on account of my own indecision. So please forgive me."

He had her attention. She gently set the teacup on the saucer and moved it out of the way. "And so now, you know how you want to proceed?"

"The judge has been with the lawyers in Dallas. We know how much money we'll need. The estate has to be settled, and there's a tax to be paid, and the money will come from Grupo Elsinore. You know that I'm not competent to determine how that is to be accomplished. As I understand it, there are three options. The first is that the Clement estate simply withdraws from the partnership, the second is that the partnership liquidates sufficient assets to make the distribution, and the third is that Grupo Elsinore levers up to make the distribution. When I say I needed to make up my mind how I want to proceed, I didn't mean choosing one of those three options. I meant I needed to decide how to come in here and be your partner in this. I hope you can forgive me if I have difficulty in comprehending your interests. But I know the history of the partnership, and I know it is a precious legacy of our grandfathers. But there is simply not enough time for me to learn the intricacies of the business and the impact those choices will have on that legacy."

"These are things I know. What I don't know is what you mean by being my partner."

"I mean you have my complete trust. We have this problem. We'll work through it, together. Whatever way it goes, I'll rely on you, and I know I can trust you."

"Do you? And how did you come to that conclusion?"

"I think you love your grandfather. I think you'd cut your own throat before you did anything out of self-interest or that would dishonor his memory."

She regarded him for an uncomfortably long time, the judge sitting at the end of the table puffing on his cigar. Finally, she raised her eyebrows and breathed a long sigh. "Perhaps."

The three of them sat with only the sound of the clock ticking on the buffet, echoing through the big house. Finally, Maria closed the little leather portfolio and leaned toward the table.

"Perhaps I need to be a partner too. I have never invited you and Georgette to my home. You must come, and bring William. She will not want to come. Convince her. We will try."

*****

Trace and the judge watched the taillights move up the road toward the hills. Spring had been brief, as it often seemed to be, and the fresh cut grass around the big house smelled like summertime. It was one of a few smells that had returned, and Trace was thankful for it. They turned and walked around the house toward the porch facing the river.

"I'm gonna go inside and see if Fowler had any Scotch stashed somewhere."

"Good luck with that."

After a few minutes, Reynolds appeared on the porch with a bottle and two glasses.

"Boy. Learn somethin' new ever' day."

"Oh, it wasn't for him. I was here once when Ramos came up to see him. He kept a bottle just for him. I don't think I ever saw Fowler take a drink. Let me pour you one."

"No thanks."

"Still not tasting right?"

"Tastes like turpentine to me."

"Not to me."

"You seem in good spirits."

"I am. I came out here planning on mediating a divorce. You handled that about as smooth as I ever coulda expected. Why the change of heart?"

"I'm not sure. I didn't want her to see I wasn't sure. I always had the idea she didn't have any use for me. I prob'ly misread that all along."

"In what way?"

"I think its frustration more than she doesn't like me. I think she needs me in the thing."

"Oh, I doubt that. She's not likely to be in any kind of bind over this deal."

"I don't mean financially. I mean the nature of it. How it came to be. What the thing means. She needs a partner. Like a counter-weight. She needs somebody that can be her equal, and she ain't got anybody alive like that. She's frustrated because she's tired of waiting on me. I ain't sure yet whether that'll ever be me, but I'm gonna give it a chance. I feel like I owe her that, at least."

"Georgette on board with it?"

"Time'll tell. I'll give her this. She's held her tongue with Maria ever single time, and I could see it was all she could do to keep from moppin' the floor up with her."

"Good for her. Self-control isn't what it used to be in this world. Strange seeing this place empty."

"We still meet up here every morning for breakfast. Me and Georgette come over and cook early. The hands keep it up."

"You gonna move in here?"

"Like I said, time'll tell. We like the cabin. William's in the river all the time. I always liked the spot."

"Too much a Fowler and Let here, I expect."

"There's some a that. This is their place. The cabin seems like our place."

"A woman'll change that. They have a way of putting their brand on a home. I always thought it was remarkable how they do that."

"Well, she sure flanged up that cabin."

"Have you heard from Wmearle?"

"Yeah, well, that's the thing. I did. He's miserable. Sylvia's kids are growin' up and don't come around much anymore, and he's stir crazy. I had a thought about us movin' over here and lettin' him have the cabin. I hadn't mentioned it to Georgette yet, though. We could take care of him okay, I think."

"You oughta do that. I wouldn't worry about bein' in here. Once she gets a hold of the place, it'll be hers. You'll probably be remodeling for the next ten years. I better head home."

*****

When Reynolds left, Trace went into the house to turn out the lights. He took up the teacup and saucer that Maria had left behind, assuming some servant would naturally come along to do that. He put them in the dishwasher and turned out all but the one light in the back cookhouse, then returned to the study to put away the half-empty bottle of Scotch. The house was silent now, and in the remaining light, he could suddenly feel them. The bookshelves lined with the books Fowler had read staring down at him: Plutarch's *Lives*, Twain, Blackstone, Dante, and Fitzgerald. All of those thoughts had passed through him, passed into his mind, and had become some part of who he had been. The painted china sitting in the display cradles; she had seen them and thought them beautiful and wished to somehow share the beauty of what she had seen with whoever came to her home. To her, they had been precious. They had built this home, and thus, every detail of it had been born of their imagining and their creation—the placement of the rock in the hearth, the lamps and shades and trinkets, the furniture and the rugs—and it all bore the marks of—them—the steady and inexorable pressure of their humanity. He stared at Fowler's chair, the leather creased and cracked, and the bone-handle knife he'd used to open letters still sitting ready on the table beside it. And the hearth, the seat of warmth in the room, swept of ashes and the grate bare, and the blackened rock, the sole remnant of a thousand fires.

When he walked out on the porch overlooking the river, the night sounds from the bottoms were rising, and the deep bellow of a bullfrog boomed across the waters. There was still some hint of light on the ledge rock on the hills opposite the house still glowing with the remnants of the sunset. Fowler was dead now two months. It had only been four months since they had learned how soon it would be. But they had been in no hurry with each other by then. They had had time, and Fowler had long ago come to a peace, probably for the first time. It had been difficult at first, after that morning, knowing how to talk to each other. That had come slowly, cautiously. He had been frozen that morning, as though the very muscles in his throat were paralyzed. He saw Fowler sitting before him, the pain of it all written on his face, in his voice. His mind catapulted from one outrageous memory to the next with such speed that he could scarcely focus, the latent hatred and frustration and fear intermingling randomly with those early memories, the good ones, of hunting and dogs and trips to the drugstore and driving the ranch in the pickup with him and him bigger than all imagination, and loving him completely, and then back again to the sound of that gunshot in the night, and the silent nod of his head across the space of the hospital waiting room and him leaving, always leaving, and him looming silent out of the predawn cold outside the house that morning, leaving even then from the house in the darkness, and still, he could not free his voice to speak, even if he had known the words. And somewhere out of the chaos of his thoughts, there had emerged a choice, and once he saw it, he knew. And so he had simply nodded his head, and Fowler had seen it, and he had seen the light of hope come back into Fowler's face, and then Fowler had nodded too, and he felt suddenly the brilliant freedom of it, from the forgiving, and they spoke no more about the past forever.

*****

When Trace shut the door behind him and stepped through the door of the kitchen, Georgette had a towel over her shoulder and was studying a cookbook, apparently working on a new recipe.

"I put him to bed. He won't be asleep though." He opened the door to William's little room in the back.

"Bud, you asleep?"

"Nossir."

"You said your prayers?"

"Nossir, I's waitin' on you."

"You know how to do it. You don't have to wait on me."

"I like doin' it better with you."

"Okay." He twisted himself out from under the covers and kneeled beside the bed.

"Pop, can Grandpa hear me when I'm prayin'?"

"I don't know."

"You said he's in heaven and God's in heaven. If God can hear me, maybe Grandpa can."

"I don't know about that. Maybe he can and maybe he can't. For sure, though, if you just tell it to God, he would get the message. I know that would work."

"Okay. God, thank you for Momma and Pop and Grandpa and Tito and Blas and Nick and Danger, and thank you for the cows and the babies, and please tell Grandpa hi, Amen."

"Get your hiney in bed now, it's late." He pulled the sheet up over him.

"What was that about Danger in your prayer?"

"I named my dog Danger."

"Innerstin' name. I thought you named him somethin' else yesterday."

"I did. I changed it."

"Well, that's a good name. I'm sure he's dangerous. But stick with it, or he won't know who he is. Now go to sleep. Love you."

When he got back to the kitchen, he could hear the whimpering outside the door. He walked out and sat down on the porch, and the little dog followed him, nipping at his hand. Then he could smell the perfume on the dog, and he began laughing, the happiness of suddenly smelling, and then the almost-simultaneous understanding of how the dog came to smell like perfume hitting him all at once, and Georgette opened the door and saw him laughing in the darkness and looked at him like he might be drunk, and he reached out and pulled her up to him, laughing still.

"What's the matter with you?"

"Cain't a person just be happy?"

ABOUT THE AUTHOR

Leslie K. Hammond is a retired financial executive and now works as a volunteer chaplain for the Texas Department of Criminal Justice. He lives in Abilene, Texas.